# ON THE NIGHT OF A BLOOD MOON

A Peter Michaels Thriller

by

# Peter Karl

**TELEMACHUS PRESS**

Cover designed by DiDonato and Associates

Published by Telemachus Press, LLC
7652 Sawmill Road
Suite 304
Dublin, Ohio 43016
http://www.telemachuspress.com

Visit the author website: www.BloodMoonTheBook.com

ISBN: 978-1-948046-52-7 (eBook)
ISBN: 978-1-948046-53-4 (Paperback)
ISBN: 978-1-948046-54-1 (Hardcover)
Also available as an audiobook

Library of Congress Control Number: 2019902812

Category: FIC050000 FICTION/Crime or FICTION/Historical/Thrillers

Version 2019.03.15

*On the Night of a Blood Moon* is a work of fiction based on actual events. More than 5,000 pages of documents have been reviewed including: courtroom testimony, actual audio taped confessions, videotaped confessions, transcripts of court approved conventional overhears, police reports, laboratory analysis reports, hundreds of newspaper and magazine articles and numerous face-to-face interviews with those involved in the actual event. Although much of this manuscript was developed from that research, except for a few public figures and actual locales central to the story, actual events, names, characters, businesses, places, events and incidents are either products of the author's imagination or used in a fictitious manner. Any resemblance to actual persons, living or dead, or actual events is purely coincidental.

This book contains language that is strong, rough and abrasive. Some may find the language offensive. Please note that this language was chosen by the author solely to faithfully reflect the way the persons depicted in this story would actually have spoken. It is the typical language spoken in the streets by common criminals and of those who arrest, prosecute and defend them in court and of those whose lives are touched—and permanently stained—by them.

# ON THE NIGHT OF
# A BLOOD MOON

# PART ONE

# CHAPTER 1

A Blood Moon is rare. Any Chicagoan who looked skyward on the night of October 17,1986 gaped at the spectacular red moon. It was an exceptionally vivid total lunar eclipse. Its reddish glare only occurs when the earth and the moon's orbits perfectly align with the sun and tilt at an exact 5.5 degree angle, blocking out most of the sun's direct light especially from its blue spectrum.

This particular Blood Moon would not be remembered as a unique astronomical phenomenon but instead it would serve as an ugly reminder of the violence that has haunted Chicago for years.

~~~~

Two drug addicted career criminals roaming the streets of Chicago's near Westside, looking for another score never noticed this cosmological wonder that brightened the night.

The short one, with long, shiny, greasy black hair was weaving and dancing to an imaginary song. The tall one, with a closely cropped Afro, zigzagged and stumbled along the sidewalk, muttering incoherent things running through his mind. The "crack" they just smoked left them euphoric.

"Give me a hit on that motherfucker, man it cold out here."

"This shit be good. You got any more a' dat?"

"No! I got some happy stick but ain't much left."

"We needs to find some 'Merch' (merchandise)."

~~~~

The short one had a happy life until he became a teenager and was recruited into a gang at thirteen. The Gangster Disciples welcomed their newest "shooter" two days after his family moved into their new neighborhood on Chicago's Westside. Gangs love kids. They are young, fearless and willing to go to jail to make an impression on the gang's hierarchy. The short one and the Gangster Disciples were a perfect fit.

By the time he was16, he was on his way to the penitentiary. His first conviction was for rape. He believed, *those women owed me, if they didn't have no money, I gots to get something.*

He didn't mind prison; at least in Chicago's Juvenile Detention Center he had better food than he did at home. The only thing on his mother's menu was the heroin she cooked up and shot into her veins daily. His father was never home. He was without supervision since he was ten years old. Being a Gangster Disciple in Juvie made him a big fish in a small pond; and when he was transferred to Joliet State Prison a year and a half later, the boy became a man and his criminal education began.

Two years later, he was grinning from ear to ear when he first walked out after his mandatory release. It took just five months for him to have another run-in with the law, this time for theft. Three weeks later, he was arrested again for armed robbery. His rap sheet was growing as fast as his reputation with the Gangster Disciples.

Before he was 21 years old, he was on his way back to prison for attempted rape and indecent liberties with a child. His education of the system would continue for four and a half more years before he was paroled.

He liked drugs; they made him feel carefree, euphoric and lethal. He really didn't care how many crimes he committed to feed his habit. All he cared about was staying under the police radar. He did for three and a half more years but violence marked his behavior like a prison tattoo. Every day that he was on the streets and not in a prison cell, crime was just second nature to him; it was survival.

~~~~

The tall one met his new buddy by chance just two months earlier in August. They became instant friends. They worked as muscle on newspaper delivery trucks, hired by drivers to do the heavy work, lifting paper bundles from the trucks to newsstands and coin boxes on their routes.

The tall one was not a Chicago native. He came to the Second City by way of Queens, New York during his high school days. He bounced back and forth between the two cities as a teenager. He left school in the eleventh grade.

At 22 years of age, he and his new friend started living a life of crime and drug abuse immediately. On this crack-induced night of October 17, they started early.

The new Jewel supermarket, located at Racine and Harrison Streets, not only provided nearby neighbors with more quality food than they would ever need but it also provided criminals with plenty of opportunities to break into cars and take anything of value in exchange for fast cash and easy-to-purchase drugs.

The city was gentrifying on the near Westside, especially at the "Medical Village" as it was called. The area was not only undergoing massive expansion and neighborhood development but it also enjoyed institutional growth including the University of Illinois, Chicago, Rush-Presbyterian-St. Luke's Hospital and The University of Illinois Hospital. This new environment provided plenty of not-so-streetwise students who left their cars filled with valuable property, inviting criminals to take it away from them.

As their "crack" high wore off, the tall one and the short one were getting desperate to get more money for more drugs, so they left familiar territory and started roaming the nearby neighborhood streets seeking some new opportunities to steal.

~~~~

"You guys aren't pooping out on me are you?" Ruth Lezkowski said with a giant smile as she entered the study hall. She radiated joy and happiness and self-confidence. Ruth Lezkowski came from a totally different world. She had a family filled with love, understanding and support. They went to mass every Sunday followed by family dinners in the afternoon. Prayers were common in her house along with open communication between brothers and sister, mother and father.

Ruth was a sweetheart; everyone loved her, especially her mother. Violet Lezkowski called her only daughter her "bonus child." She was the last of six children born to the Lezkowski's in Springfield, Illinois. She lived in the same ranch-style house all her of life before she left for college.

Ruth was always very goal-oriented. Quiet, studious and determined, she dreamed of being a doctor from the time she entered the eighth grade. She wanted to be the first one in her family to go beyond four years of college. She worked a number of jobs starting in high school to help finance her advanced education. She was a driven woman. The lowest grade she ever received was a B+ in high school calculus. She was valedictorian of her graduating class and represented Northeast High School in all academic events the school participated in. She was in the top of her class academically in medical school. She was an enthusiastic small town girl anxious to go to the big city to fulfill her destiny: Dr. Ruth Lezkowski.

She was attractive at five feet six inches and 117 pounds of muscle. She sported blue eyes and blonde hair. Ruth was never the brunt of blonde jokes because she was way too smart for that. She loved to run and stay in-shape. Even when she was away at school, she went to mass at Notre Dame Church every Sunday. The church was 1200 steps from the front door of her apartment. Ruth's cheerful smile lit up a room. She dated but was so immersed in her studies that she didn't want a permanent relationship although many men tried to capture her heart.

Mothers would want their sons to marry Ruth Lezkowski. She was the perfect woman.

~~~~

October 17,1986 was a typical study day for Ruth, a second-year student at Rush-Presbyterian-St. Luke's Medical School. Exams were just around the corner, she studied for long hours in pursuit of her dream. Ruth wanted to make her brothers and mother and father so very proud of her. So on this morning, dressed in a light blue running suit to be comfortable for the long tedious hours of study, she left her near Westside apartment, a few blocks from the hospital, to begin what would be the longest, most horrific day of her life.

~~~~

Ruth stretched; her eyes were tired from hours of study. Yawning she glanced at one of her study mates, Edward Radney, who looked as tired as she felt.

"Should we call it a night?" she asked stifling another yawn.

He and a few others in the group nodded. It was nearly one o'clock.

Reaching for the ceiling, Radney felt his spine decompress. He opened and closed his fingers into fists. "Want me to walk you to your car?"

Nodding "yes," Ruth remembered a series of car burglaries recently. She felt better having an escort and was grateful for Edward's company.

Ruth gathered her books, tucked them into her backpack and with Edward by her side walked to her car.

"Oh, my God! Look at that brilliant moon. I've never seen a red moon before."

"Yeah, it's called a Blood Moon. They're rare and this one is extremely bright." Radney said. "I've seen one in California when I was a kid."

Ruth was still smiling and looking skyward when she said, "Get in and I'll give you a ride home." She fumbled with her keys, opened the door and slid into the driver's seat.

"Thanks." he said. "Lock your doors."

"Oops, I forgot. Thanks. You know I always lock my doors." She pressed the fob, heard the click and drove away.

~~~~

It was approximately one o'clock in the morning. It was crisp, the temperature hovering at 49 degrees. Ruth could see her breath in the morning air. It was refreshing after being cooped up in the warm study areas all day. It brought a smile to her lovely face. She was living her dream.

Minutes later Ruth turned into her cobblestone alley looking for the closest parking spot behind her apartment building. She had no idea what was lurking in the shadows.

Her brothers back in Springfield warned her constantly to always be aware of her surroundings and to be vigilant in the big city. They even gave her a stick sharpened at one end for protection to keep in her car between the seats. It was bigger than a broom handle, smaller than a baseball bat about the size of a police baton. She was very safety-conscious, but she would not be ready for what awaited her on this chilly morning as she exited her car.

~~~~

The headlights from Ruth's four-door beige Subaru coming down the alley offered the two criminals the opportunity they had been waiting for all night. As Ruth parked her car several doors away from her apartment, they slithered into the shadows of her building, blending into the unsuspecting darkness. Ruth got out of the car, grabbed her purse and keys and started walking towards her apartment door. She was thinking of her warm bed and some much-needed sleep. She was tired. It truly was a long, trying day. She was worried about her final pathology exam. For some reason that subject bothered her more than anything else this semester.

She also missed her secret lover. The man she met in Germany that summer. Her military man. Her brother's Army buddy. The man no one knew about had her distracted. She smiled, thinking about the last time she saw him, when he pulled her into his arms for a kiss that she felt in her toes.

It was then that the short one with the long, shiny, greasy black hair emerged from the shadows and stepped in front of her, startling her as she stopped and froze in disbelief. Two feet separated them when he snatched the keys from her hand. The tall one grabbed her from behind with a knife to her throat, hand over her mouth, whispering in her ear with his foul breath from cigarettes, reefer and crack, "We don't want to hurt you, just be quiet."

The short one got into the car and drove back up the alley. The tall one with his knife pricking Ruth's neck dragged her into the car and forced her into the back seat. It all took less than 30 seconds, but to Ruth Lezkowski it felt like hours. She was hidden from view and unable to reach for the door handle to escape. Frightened and shaking, she whimpered, "Please don't hurt me. I'll give you whatever you want."

Ignoring Ruth's pleas, he drove the car out of the alley onto Racine Avenue towards Roosevelt Road, where a University of Illinois campus police car was patrolling.

"Get down" He yelled at his partner as the police car approached. The tall one fiercely grabbed Ruth around the waist, wrestled her down and out-of-sight, saying, "I promise, we ain't gonna hurt you, we gonna let you go."

Ruth's eyes darted back and forth in fear. The knife that pressed into her neck made her heart pump faster. Blood rushed to her head, her temples ached. Hope appeared in the depth of her soul, as the possibility of being rescued seemed so close but that hope vanished as she heard them say, "the police just turned away. That motherfucker be gone."

Ruth's body went limp with disappointment as her captors laughed. She sensed their relief and that made her feel helpless as her chance of freedom just drove away. *Oh my God they're going to kill me,* she thought.

~~~~

With money taken from Ruth's purse, the tall one got out of the car and the short one exchanged places in the back seat to keep her quiet.

"Where's he going?" Ruth quivered, trying to see where they were noticing a glimmer of the Blood Moon.

The short one pushed her head down roughly, "Shut up. He's just gettin' some liquor and beer and shit."

After leaving the liquor store with a 40-ounce bottle of Budweiser and a half pint of dark whiskey, he went to a little all-night restaurant next door and grabbed a hot dog and an order of fries. Then he ran across the street to one of the project's high-rise buildings and got a bag of reefer. This little shopping spree took less than five minutes.

All this time, Ruth was in the back seat of her car, crying and pleading with her kidnapper to let her go. When the tall one got back into the back seat, he noticed that she was even more frightened and nervous.

The short one then drove south on Racine, past the ALBA Homes, a low income Chicago Housing Authority Project, to an isolated spot up a narrow road by a railroad track service area. The road was hidden from street view by dense trees and bushes. Railroad cars that were to be moved and unloaded were parked to the South.

Ruth's eyes moved rapidly back and forth frightfully as she noticed a drastic change in the scenery. The urban setting of streetlights, houses and the sounds of traffic disappeared as they drove up a hill into the darkness then isolation. Stillness and quiet enveloped them. Ruth was shivering with the realization that something terrible was about to happen.

"Everything'll be alright. We ain't gonna hurt you," the tall one reassured.

Terrified beyond comprehension, Ruth continued to beg her captors not to hurt her and told them she'd do whatever they wanted.

They tried to comfort her, but that didn't last long as they parked the car in oblivion, nowhere to be seen or heard. They wanted to party. They passed the half-pint of dark whiskey, ate the hot dog and fries and then they drank the 40-ounce bottle of Budweiser. For dessert, they rolled a joint and said to Ruth, "Let's fuck."

Ruth was filled with pure terror, *oh; my God this isn't happening* she thought *this can't be happening.* "No," she pled, "No, please, no." Cold, shivering and scared, she cried out, "Don't hurt me."

"Take your pants off bitch," the tall one commanded.

She couldn't move, frozen in time. All she could think was: *God why is this happening to me.*

The slap to her face stung. The tall one reached with both hands and pulled down her jogging pants. She felt the cold air on her skin. She was trembling as he raped her. She was facing him, his breath was foul, and her eyes were shut and watering. Her prayer was silent. "Please God help me." Shivering and crying out in pain the entire time, she just wanted it to end but the more she cried the wilder he got.

When he finished, he grabbed ahold of his shirt and hers and wiped himself off. He then shoved her over to the side and got out of the car on the right-hand passenger side.

The short one was next and got into the backseat with her. She was still terrified and crying, "Don't hurt me."

"Shut up, bitch."

He pushed her down and forced her legs up in the air touching the ceiling of the car then he sodomized her. "You gonna like this baby."

"You're hurting me, you're hurting me. Stop. Stop."

He was violent. Smiling. Drooling.

She never stopped crying from the pain, and screaming "You're hurting me, you're hurting me, stop, stop." He didn't stop and she kept hollering, "My God please, please." When he finished, he got dressed and he moved to the front seat and said, "Now that wasn't so bad, was it?"

Ruth, exhausted and in excruciating pain begged, "I did my part now let me go."

Ruth's agony, her screams of horror and her calls for help dissolved into the nothingness of the early morning air from that lonely desolate area.

When a police officer found her body, it made the 30-year veteran sick to his stomach. So much so that he would retire within a year.

The Medical Examiner's report concluded that any one of three major injuries she sustained could have caused her death. Ruth's skull was crushed by a chunk of concrete the size of a softball. She suffered numerous fractures and lacerations, and a bloody shoeprint was on her body indicating that she could have been stomped to death. She had nine broken ribs.

The dark rage that took Ruth Lezkowski's life lasted three-hours and 40 minutes. Her savage murder would consume the Chicago Police Department's undivided attention for more than three months, and ultimately for years, until the case was finally closed.

Ruth Lezkowski was 23 years old when she died on the night of a Blood Moon.

# CHAPTER 2

"News ... Michaels."

Peter Michaels always answered the phone immediately. His mentors ingrained that into him years ago in his native Detroit. The WJJ-TV newsroom had an eight by five-foot sign with red letters above the assignment desk. It boldly proclaimed, "ANSWER THE PHONE." It paid dividends every day of his career.

Michaels was born and raised on the lower Eastside of Detroit in a blue-collar neighborhood. He was the only boy with three sisters. He was the youngest and he was pampered. He credits his sisters for his ability to communicate so well with women. He knew from the time he was in sixth grade that he wanted to be a reporter. He graduated from Wayne State University in Detroit with a degree in Journalism and Mass Communications. He had just gotten out of the Army, married his wife Katie and had his first baby girl Clare. He was anxious to start his career.

Michaels was the 12th person to interview for a writer's position. He won the job on sure cockiness and true grit. As he sat in news director Dave Kelly's office, he looked him directly in the eyes and said, "Call me immediately when you decide to hire me. I can start anytime!"

Kelly said, "Hey, I am not saying you got the job!"

Michaels, stood up, shook Kelly's hand, and said, "I'm your guy. I just had my first child. I'll work my ass off for you. You'll never regret it."

The call came two days later and Michaels was at the WJJ-TV Studio's front door before the janitor left the building the following Monday morning.

~~~~

Michaels started off as a scriptwriter for the early newscasts under the watchful eyes of Lou Prato and Jim Clark. Prato, who was never without a cigar in his hand or mouth, challenged him to get better and Clark, a former Detroit News Editor, was forever criticizing and correcting his copy to make him a true professional.

Michaels made a good first impression. He was confident, self-assured but not imposing. He was six feet tall, 185 pounds, with stylish brown hair parted on the left side and combed over his ears. He had the look of a tennis player not muscular not thin, but trim. His father was a tailor and all of his suits fit like a hand in a glove. Michaels was easy going, the kind of guy everyone liked to have a beer with. He talked freely about sports or politics and he laughed hard.

~~~~

Jim Clark just looked like a newsman, shirtsleeves rolled up, tie loose and a dominating presence. He was one of the first newspaper editors to make the transition to television. A Pulitzer Prize winning pro that just commanded respect. "Show me what you got Michaels. I need this car/train accident script for the noon show," he demanded.

Michaels took the copy for the re-write. His stomach was churning, his hands were trembling, his mind was racing and Clark was smiling. He knew his rookie writer was one nervous son of a bitch.

After reading the copy, Clark howled, "What the fuck is this *War and Peace*. I wanted a 15 second reader. Look Michaels, the best way to write copy is to think about how you would tell this story to your wife or buddy sitting at the kitchen table. Get to the point and make it simple to understand."

From that point forward, Michaels developed a "Mickey Spillane" style of writing that won him literally more than a 100 Journalism Awards during his career.

~~~~

After six months, he was promoted to produce the weekend newscast with Jerry Blocker, who was believed to be the first black anchorman in television. Blocker was a former English teacher who took a chance at reporting and anchoring the news when there weren't that many African-Americans in the television business. He had an engaging smile and liked to laugh. Michaels liked him the very first time they shook hands. It was a friendship that would last a lifetime.

~~~~

Michaels paid his way through college by working at Hazel Park Racetrack parking cars and he's loved horse racing ever since. After his first day on the job, he was made the head cashier for the valets. He was quick on his feet and could disarm any potentially bad situation. He had a knack with strangers. He said it was the best education he'd ever received. It made him very streetwise.

His bosses, Armando Gazillo and Gino Cantillano were the alleged leaders of the Detroit Mafia. Michaels set up the only interview Armando Gazillo ever gave to the media for his station. Michaels set up the interview with one condition; he had to be there. It was a no brainer.

After that interview, Michaels told Blocker, "You know I could have done a better job with Gazillo than Conrad did. Shit, I think he was actually afraid to ask him tough questions. I'm not intimidated by any of that bullshit. I live by my mother's mantra."

"What's that?" Blocker asked.

"My ma always told me, 'Don't forget the people who clean the typewriters, remember where you came from and when we sit on the toilet, we all look the same.'"

"You have one wise mamma," Blocker said with a smile.

~~~~

Within a year, Michaels was promoted again, to produce all the early newscasts. Michaels had a personality that charmed the on-air talent, who can be very egotistical.

A show producer is the main person behind the scenes of the newscast. He or she is the architect so to speak, making all the main content and timing decisions. The producer decides the lead story, and subsequent story order, how much time each story will last, which stories will feature a taped reporter "package" and which will be read by the anchor. The producer determines the length of the weather and sports segments. They set the pace of the broadcast, placing shorter stories strategically throughout the show. They try to retain the audience with a "teaser" going into commercial breaks, in order to optimize ratings. And if anything goes wrong of course they take the blame.

Before long, he was once again promoted to produce the highly rated eleven o'clock news but Michaels' life was about to change dramatically.

Michaels and his wife just found out she was pregnant with their second child. If it was a boy he'd be named Gustav and if it was girl she would be Iris. His dream to be an on-the-air reporter came in 1972 when he went to work at WXRJ-TV in Flint, Michigan.

For five years, Michaels worked as a weekend anchorman and daily reporter. He was a nervous wreck doing live newscasts. He hated it. It was reporting that he loved and it didn't take him long to look where other reporters dared to go. He reported on corruption, malfeasance in county government and the stealing of federal funds for fake drug investigations. But the story he was most proud of was the PBB disaster that hit Michigan dairy farmers.

Doing a routine story at Michigan State University's School of Veterinarian Medicine he learned of the PBB Scandal.

"Why are all those cows dead?" Michaels asked the vet while looking at some pictures posted on the wall.

"They're contaminated with PBB."

"What's that?"

"Polybrominated biphenyl (PBB) a fire retardant material called Firemaster, BP-6 that was accidently mixed into livestock feed. It had devastating effects on Michigan's dairy cattle and other farm animals."

"Do you know how or where this stuff got in the feed?"

"We're not sure but we suspect Bay City."

"How bad will it be?"

"It killed: 1.5 million chickens, 30,000 dairy cattle, 5,900 pigs and 1,500 sheep."

"What do you do with them?"

"Their carcasses are being buried in landfill sites across the state" the vet said.

~~~~

WLR-TV, Channel 8 Eyewitness News, the number one rated television station in Chicago hired Michaels in 1977. His investigative reports were catching the attention of many news directors around the country. Johnny Wiseman was the first to offer him a job after meeting with him for only 20 minutes. He didn't hesitate a second, it was his dream come true. Wiseman liked the fact that Michaels was a "deems and dose" kind of guy. "Pugnacious" was the word he used.

After his first week Michaels started breaking stories with an edge causing seasoned Chicago reporters to ask, "Who is this new guy?"

Michaels' motto was simple, "Every time you reached into one of Chicago's sewers you could pull out a great story." He was never disappointed.

~~~~

"News ... Michaels"

"Is this Geraldo Rivera?" the woman asked.

"No. This is Peter Michaels. I'm the next best thing in Chicago. Who is this?"

"My name is Darlene and I'm in the hospital dying."

"Dying, dying from what?"

"From Blue Light. You know T's and Blues. It's a poor man's substitute for heroin. It's killing lots of my peoples. The shit's like poison."

Michaels was now totally engrossed. He reached for his reporter's notebook and bit off the cap of his ballpoint pen and asked, "What makes it so dangerous and lethal?"

"Blue Light, it's two different pills we gets from the doctors at the clinics all round town. You break em' down and cook em' just like smack and inject em' in your veins. The problem is your veins crystalize where you inject it. Your veins ... they just dry up."

"Where are these clinics?"

"The biggest one be at Madison Street by the produce market. You can't miss it. They be open at 7 am. You'll see all the peoples waiting to get in. You know what I'm saying. You gotta do something about this shit man. It's killing people."

"What do you say to get the drugs?"

"You go in and tells the doctor that you got a backache and runny nose. Then they give you the T's for the backache and the Blues for the runny nose. Just like dat, you know what I mean.

Everyday, I'd go to a different clinic and do the same thing; backache and runny nose.

An hour and a half later, Michaels leaned back in his chair and looked at his watch and knew he was in trouble. Late again, disappointing the girls and picturing the wrath of Katie but he smiled. He knew he had the outline of a major drug scandal that was costing the taxpayers of Illinois tens of millions of dollars in Medicaid fraud and it was killing dozens of addicts.

Talwin and Pyribenzamine were legal drugs that were illegally dispensed from six shady health clinics in black neighborhoods around Chicago. Talwin was for a backache and Pyribenzamine for a runny nose.

Addicts would heat the drugs in a spoon, suck the combo into a syringe, and inject the drug into any vein that would accept the mixture. The combination could cause dizziness, chest pains and vomiting. It was proving to be deadly in many cases, but it also provided a heroin-like high that was basically free, paid for by the taxpayers.

Michaels and his producer Doug Longhini went to work the next day. Michaels started surveillance from a van in front of the medical clinic and Longhini started poring through public records.

Longhini worked for a government watchdog organization "The Better Government Group." He was an investigator when Michaels first met him. The BGG was started by concerned people as an organization that would watch over political corruption, government waste and malfeasance in office. It was totally funded by private money. The not-for profit group wanted no connection to political money, no strings attached to any political party. They were a major influence in the City of Chicago.

Michaels thought Longhini was the best researcher that he had ever met. It was a joint investigative project between his station and the BGG. Michaels was so impressed by Longhini, he convinced his news director to hire him the next day.

Longhini's competitive nature developed when he was an all-state high school football running back for Joliet Catholic High School. He set many statewide records with his abilities on the field. Longhini was five feet, nine inches tall. He was muscular but with a more natural look not like a body builder. He was well disciplined and maintained his physical condition by running at least four times a week.

Very few people ever knew that Michaels and Longhini formed the very first "Investigative Team" in the history of Chicago television. The two of them were committed to giving a voice to the voiceless.

In 1982, Wiseman moved to Los Angeles. Michaels and his team won the prestigious George Foster Peabody Award but his contract with WLR wasn't renewed. Driven by revenge, he moved across the street to WMAC-TV, the NBC, Owned and Operated station in Chicago.

Michaels new home and his new attitude were about to skyrocket his career.

# CHAPTER 3

" News ... Michaels."

"Hey Michaels, Kennedy here."

Michaels put his coffee cup down, leaned back in his chair, interlaced his fingers behind his head and smiled.

Sergeant Robert Kennedy was a 20-year veteran of the Chicago Police Department. He had an overbearing personality. He was tall, handsome and confident. Kennedy was the Director of News Affairs and he was one of the first sources of information Michaels developed when he arrived in Chicago. After being introduced and sharing a couple of beers at Kitty O'Shea's in the lobby of Hilton Hotel on South Michigan Avenue, the two of them hit it off even though they had some philosophical differences.

Michaels won his confidence when he told Kennedy, "You know, you are in control of what every police beat reporter wants."

Kennedy asked, "What's that?"

"Information."

Kennedy wore that mantra proudly and with bravado.

"Hey, Sarge, what's up?"

"Have you been listening to the citywide police scanners, man? There was a brutal homicide overnight of a second-year medical student from Rush. Every available detective from Area Four is working it. It's the biggest heater case we've had in a long time" Kennedy said.

A heater is a case that is going to draw a lot of attention to the city hall and negative publicity was the last thing that newly elected mayor, Harold Washington, wanted or needed. These types of cases usually generate political pressure on the police department. It's one of those cases they wanted solved yesterday.

Kennedy ran his fingers through his hair, closed his eyes and took a deep breath, "God, it's horrible. She was beaten savagely. Blood everywhere. A Chicago and Northwestern Railroad copper discovered the body at about 4:30 this morning."

"Can you get me that report?" Michaels asked.

"Give me two hours and then go to Manny's and see Grace, the cashier where they sell the lottery tickets."

~~~~

Manny's Coffee Shop and Deli is a Chicago landmark.

Michaels loved the place because it touched the essence of Chicago. It's located on Jefferson Street, a half-block north of Roosevelt Road. The menu offered mouth-watering homemade recipes and its corned beef is to die for. Its interior looks the same as it did in 1964 when Manny's moved to its new location.

Peter Michaels and Doug Longhini walked in the door and right into the food line. It was packed as usual and on any given day at lunchtime it was filled with the city's top attorneys, politicians and movie stars.

"This place just exudes energy," Longhini said.

"I know. Hey, order me a corned beef and pastrami on rye. I am going to see Gracie."

~~~~

OCTOBER 18, 1986

"Tonight, the brutal murder of a second year student from Rush-Presbyterian-St. Luke's Medical School. Her body was discovered early this morning on Chicago's near Westside" said Ron Magers, the WMAC anchorman, live from the studio on the six o'clock newscast. "Dozens of detectives are on the street at this hour looking for the killer or killers. Our Peter Michaels is at the scene and we must warn you, some of the information is very graphic and disturbing. Peter?"

Michaels had his head down and his eyes closed as Magers introduced him. He not only got the visceral police report of the brutal murder but he also saw some of the crime scene photos. It made him sick to his stomach. The pictures were so explicit and gruesome. It was a crime of dark rage. He took a deep breath, looked into the camera and began his report.

"Ron, this brutal murder occurred on the night of a Blood Moon and it has led to the largest police manhunt in recent Chicago history. This horrific crime has shaken this city and its police department."

Michaels could hear the producer's verbal cues in his earpiece telling him that his pre-recorded package was ready to air. Once he was cleared, he then took a deep breath and checked with his cameraman to make sure everything was fine with the picture and lighting.

The taped report began: "The battered body of 23-year-old, Ruth Lezkowski, was found this morning at 4:40 by a Chicago and Northwestern policeman near the 1500 block of South Loomis in a very isolated area.

"Officer Daniel Starks saw the body on the ground alongside her car. His police report states, the victim was face up and appeared to be beaten and choked. Her head was covered in blood and she had what appeared to be rope or similar type abrasions on her neck. The victim also had an imprint of a shoe across her stomach. She was wearing a light blue-colored jogging outfit.

"Her 1983 tan Subaru sedan appeared to be ransacked. Tools that were stored in an ammunition box in the trunk were scattered around the area near her face. A sticker on the windshield identified her as a medical student at Rush-Presbyterian-St. Luke's Medical Center.

"One of the weapons that was apparently used to kill her was a softball-size piece of concrete. When crime scene investigators put it in an evidence bag, it was covered with blood, but it's coarse surface made it impossible to capture any fingerprints. It was found under the victim's car near the right rear wheel.

"The report went on to say that the front driver's seat was stained with blood but the passenger seat was a pool of blood. When officer Starks exited his car he reported, 'Blood was still dripping from the front door.'

"Chief Medical Examiner, Doctor Robert Crine, pronounced Ruth Lezkowski dead at the scene at 5:40 AM."

News footage of the crime scene activity dissolved to a headshot of Dr. Crine telling Michaels "I've seen my share of brutal crimes in my life but I have to tell you, I've never ever seen anything this gruesome. It is going to take us some time to determine an exact cause of death, but from what I saw up there she could have died from at least three major injuries, each one worse than the last."

Michaels heard the standby queue in his earpiece, looked down at the monitor in front of him and when he heard "go" he looked up at the camera and with a smooth transition said, "Police spent hours at the scene gathering all types of physical evidence," using his hand held microphone he made a subtle gesture for emphasis, as he continued, "but Unit-6 has learned <u>exclusively</u> that Officer Starks also reported seeing a black male about 19 or 20 years of age, five feet, ten inches tall. He was dressed in a black leather coat, black jeans and he was wearing what appeared to be a shower cap on his head. He was walking away from the scene as Officer Starks turned onto the road where he made the grisly discovery of the beaten body of Ruth Lezkowski. Ron back to you in the studio."

The red tally light on the camera went black and his cameraman took the camera off its tripod and with a concerned look on his face asked, "Peter, are you alright?"

"No, I'm not." Tears welled in his eyes, as he was thinking about his two teenage daughters, Clare now 16 and Iris who turned 13 this summer. "I just can't image what it would be like to have something this horrific happen to one of my girls." Then he said to himself. "Oh, my dear sweet Jesus, protect them."

# CHAPTER 4

I
n 1986, the Chicago Police Department was broken down into six separate area headquarters and each of them included four distinct police districts. The area headquarters handled the major crime investigations for all of the districts but each individual district responded to all routine police calls. Each Area also had a Gang Crimes Unit and a Tactical Team assigned to it. There was also a Cook County Circuit Courthouse attached to the Area Headquarters that handled all the hearings for those arrested in the four districts.

~~~~

Michaels hung up the phone, took his feet off his desk, stood up and looked over at his partner, shaking his head.

"God, that community where Lezkowski was killed is one tough ass neighborhood." Longhini said.

"Yeah, people are afraid to sit on their porches for fear of getting shot," Michaels said. "The residents are proud people. I did a few stories there but once they start trying to improve the quality of life in their neighborhoods the fucking gangs just take everything over."

"The Vice Lords, the Gangster Disciples and the Black Disciples are in constant conflict and drug turf wars are leaving a lot of dead bodies on the streets. It's got to be the busiest police area in Chicago."

"It is. I just talked to Commander Maurer and he told me Area Four alone recorded more homicides than 37 different states this year and last. It was so busy, as a matter of fact, that property crime detectives were forced to work homicide cases," Michaels said.

~~~~

James Maurer was the Commander of Area Four Violent Crimes. He was in charge of all the detectives assigned to both violent crimes and property crimes. Maurer, who looked like, and modeled himself after General George Patton, was a no-nonsense type of person who was well known in the Chicago media for his off the cuff remarks. Often times Maurer went to police events in the wintertime dressed in his long camelhair overcoat accompanied by his two bull terriers named Margaret and Marmaduke. The street cops loved him. He was the ultimate cop's, cop.

Never too shy to speak his mind, Maurer's quotes often made headlines. He called the Lezkowski homicide the most violent and savage crime he had ever seen. It was a murder that hit close to home because his wife was a medical student. She was outraged by the brutality of the it.

Detectives theorized that the killers were adult males from the nearby ALBA homes. The ALBA Homes were a very densely populated housing project where police officers responded to dozens of calls every day. Known on the streets as "The Village" or more commonly to residents as "The Vill." The ALBA Homes was one of the largest public housing project in the city. Only the Robert Taylor Homes on the Southside and Cabrini-Green on the near North side were more populated.

In total there were 3,600 units in the complex of high-rise and low-rise buildings. Seventeen thousand people lived in the ALBA Homes. However, there were only 8,500 listed residents on the signed leases in the development.

The ALBA Homes, for all its crime, misfortunes and blight, made for very good backdrops for Hollywood movies and television shows. Just two blocks east of the ALBA Homes, the very successful television drama *Hill Street Blues* was filmed at the retired Maxwell Street Police Station. Its bright blue garage doors flying upwards was the show's signature opening title scene. Many story lines were developed from the surrounding ghetto areas. Television shows like *ER* and *Chicago Hope* also filmed many scenes in and around the ALBA Homes.

The 1989 film *Next of Kin* starring Patrick Swayze had many scenes filmed in the ALBA Homes. In one major dramatic scene in particular, Swayze hid from some thugs chasing him inside the Robert Brooks section and he bribed a young boy to misdirect his pursuers.

Television viewers and moviegoers outside the city limits of Chicago had no real idea how truly violent and vicious this area really was.

~~~~

"Isn't the Lezkowski homicide scene near the ALBA Homes projects?" Longhini asked.

"A stone's throw away. Man, that poor woman had to be so scared. I can't even imagine. That area is so desolate and hidden. You drive up this single lane road with trees, tall weeds and thick bushes smothering the driveway. If you weren't careful, you could scrape the sides of your car when you drove up there. It like consumes you."

"Aren't there all kinds of trains there?"

"That property is owned by the Chicago and Northwestern Railroad. Hundreds of railroad cars are parked there on the tracks, which run parallel to the vacant lot where Lezkowski's body was discovered. It's like a Wal-Mart on wheels for the criminals that make a habit out of stealing from them on any given night. Most of those thieves come from the projects. That's the reason the Railroad Police constantly patrol the area numerous times each day and night," Michaels said.

~~~~

Rush-Presbyterian-St. Luke's Hospital was immediately put under the microscope and criticized for its security protocols by the media.

Doug Longhini walked back from the Associated Press wire machine with a piece of paper that he handed to Michaels. "Did you see this? It just came over the wires, it's a $25,000 reward for the arrest and conviction of the killer or killers issued by the hospital."

"That was quick."

"Shit. They had to do something quick to mitigate the pressure. I hear City Hall is going crazy."

"Yah think? With the brutal murder of a white female medical student tensions gotta be high in the Medical Village and nearby Little Italy, not to mention all the suburban people who come to work there every day."

"Yeah, I heard Harold was shouting mad. He used all the material from our police brutality series and campaigned on an anti-crime platform. It was helpful in getting the first African American elected mayor in the history of Chicago politics."

"Tell me about it, Janie (Mayor Jane Byrne) chewed my ass off after we did that *Beating Justice* piece. Remember? She was pissed." Michaels said with a smile, shaking his head.

~~~~

If you have ever seen the police reality television show *48 Hours*, you know that the first two days after a homicide occurs are the most crucial hours to solve the case.

Commander Maurer quickly assembled dozens of detectives and patrol officers, to form his team that would launch this massive manhunt for the killer or killers of Ruth Lezkowski. He appointed Jack Evans and Lee Scholl as the lead detectives on the case.

Evans, the more experienced of the two, received dozens of police commendations since he graduated from the Police Academy in 1970. Evans had prematurely gray hair that made him look older than his 42 years. He was five-foot, nine inches tall with a skinny frame. When he walked in a room he just looked like a cop. He had a reputation for being tenacious as a bulldog and he was never afraid to work around the clock.

That tenacity however caused problems at home. He had five kids, all in private schools. So he worked a lot of overtime and a side security job to make extra money. He was not home very much and his wife was getting madder and madder. Evans had an incredible knack of reading whether or not the people he was interviewing were being truthful.

Lee Scholl was an up and coming detective, a quick learner who was never afraid to take on the worst assignments. Scholl had only been out of the academy for seven years before he got his first break as a Property Crimes detective in Area One, another crime-ridden area on Chicago's far Southside. Scholl was five feet, ten inches tall with a muscular build. His closely trimmed black hair was combed straight back. He had blue eyes and he walked erect, head high.

Scholl had two teenage girls. One was getting ready for college and the other was a junior in high school. His wife was a hot-tempered Italian who often raised her voice in everyday conversation. They were madly in love.

Scholl jumped at the opportunity when Maurer had him reassigned to Area Four two years ago. He and Evans worked several cases before and Scholl was chomping at the bit to be part of this brutal homicide investigation.

In 1986, many of the crime fighting tools that are used today did not exist back then. For example, DNA and the high-tech forensic analyzing equipment were not available.

~~~~

Evans and Scholl walked the crime scene. Yellow police tape still surrounded the area where Lezkowski's body was found. The collars of their overcoats were pulled up. Evans had a Blackhawks knit cap pulled over his ears. Scholl never wore a hat. He hated to get his hair matted. He'd rather be cold. He was. They could see their breath when they talked.

"I want to visualize everything that happened up here," Evans said.

"My God, that poor woman," said Scholl as he looked at the crime scene photos, trying to imagine how this brutal murder went down.

"This happened on the night of that Blood Moon thing. Are you superstitious about any of that crap?" Evans asked.

"No! Never thought about it but it sure is eerie."

Evans was brought back to reality when he saw that Lezkowski's car was still at the scene. "Take those seats out and get them over to the lab. There may be hair samples and the killer's blood may be mixed in the pool of blood that was coagulating on the seat."

"So what do we have?" asked Scholl.

"We have lots of blood samples, hair samples, sperm samples and one palm print on the windshield. We got a softball size concrete block that we believe is the murder weapon covered in blood but no prints. There was an imprint of a size 12 or 13 shoe on her chest from one of the killers. We have a possible suspect. Black male about 16 to 20 years of age who was seen by the driveway wearing a blue or green shower cap," Evans said.

"I'll try to compile a list of known sex offenders from the area."

"I'll put together a list of people we need to talk to right away."

~~~~

The Chicago Police Department had a database with the names of sex offenders and other known predators, but in 1986 they weren't computerized. Criminal mug shots were the actual pictures that had to be searched one at a time, shuffling them like a deck of cards. All incident reports were written with typewriters by police officers that often used two fingers to strike the keys. Investigative reports, supplemental reports, rap sheets showing a criminal's arrest record were filed in drawers no-where near a detective's desk. These names could not be recalled with the click of button. It was the Dark Ages compared to the investigative techniques of today.

~~~~

As in any homicide investigation, the last person known to see the victim alive was the first person the police wanted to talk to.

"Let's go see what these guys, Radney and Bauer have to say. They were the last two to see her alive," Evans said.

Medical student housing was close to the hospital. The Center Court Gardens apartments were a series of three-story brick structures on Harrison Street. There were three different types of units from a studio to a two bedroom. They were about ten minutes from Area Four Violent Crimes. Edward Radney lived in a one bedroom and Anthony Bauer lived in a studio.

Scholl pressed the buzzer for unit 203.

"Can I help you?" Radney asked.

"Chicago Police. We need to talk to you," Evans announced.

"Come up to two and turn right. I'm three doors down on the left."

The elevator was slow. The metallic doors sounded like they needed lubrication. The walls were painted a beige color; the rug was a little darker and worn. The building was well maintained but lived in. Radney opened the door just as they approached and were ready to knock.

His apartment was clean but sloppy. Books and papers were scattered over the kitchen table. A stethoscope hung over one of the chairs. Radney looked tired.

"I've known—knew—Ruth for two years. We attended many classes together. I got to know her better this year because we shared lab assignments. Ruth was smart, witty and very security conscious."

"How do you know that?"

"She told me 'her brothers drove that into her psyche.' She was very conscious about locking her car door. Anyway, we finished studying around 12:50 and we were gathering our things and she asked me to walk her to her car, which was parked in spot A-7 on the seventh floor of the parking garage.

"She said she was very tired and needed some sleep and that she would see me in a few hours. We were getting ready for our final lab exam in pathology. She drove me home and said good night. I told her to lock your doors. She said don't worry, I always do. I said good night and she drove away down Loomis."

"Where are you from?"

"The Los Angeles area."

"You plan on leaving anytime soon?"

"No. I don't think so."

Handing him his card, Evans said, "If you leave town let us know. Where does Bauer live?"

"Downstairs in 108 but he's not here now, I think he is over at the hospital meeting with his advisor."

"Here give him this card and tell him we want to talk to him."

As they were walking back to their car, Evans said, "I'm thinking if she was so security conscious, she had to be out of her car when they grabbed her."

"I was thinking the same thing."

~~~~

OCTOBER 18, 1986

Ron Magers led off the ten o'clock newscast with an update on the murder investigation. He began, "Tonight at ten, a massive police manhunt is underway as Chicago Police homicide detectives converge on the Medical Village area looking for the killer or killers of a second-year medical student.

"Peter Michaels is at Area Four Violent Crimes with the latest. Peter."

Michaels heard his cue, looked up from the monitor and began his report. "At least two-dozen homicide detectives hit the streets shortly before noon today trying to find those responsible for the brutal death of Ruth Lezkowski."

Michaels was cued that he was no longer on camera but was reading voiceover video footage of detectives at their desks.

"Commander James Maurer assembled the team of Area Four Violent Crimes investigators within minutes after they returned from the crime scene. It will take some time to process all the evidence that was gathered. This is the largest manhunt in recent Chicago history. The I-Team has learned that scores of detectives interviewed 25 people from Lezkowski's neighborhood and at Rush's Medical School as they try to piece together the time line of this savage murder.

"We have also learned that the bloody car seats from Lezkowski's 1983 Subaru were shipped to the Crime Lab for further analysis.

"An autopsy is currently underway. Police know that the victim died from severe blunt force trauma.

"Area Four Violent Crimes Commander, James Maurer, met with reporters just a short time ago." The director then faded into the interview of the commander.

"At this point, we believe the perpetrators of this crime are adult males. We have begun a massive effort to identify all known sex offenders and predators within a three-mile radius of this horrible crime. No matter how long it takes we will find the killer or killers of Ruth Lezkowski."

As soon as he heard the words "Ruth Lezkowski" Michaels knew he was live on camera and he began:

"There is a lot of evidence from the scene that has to be analyzed, blood samples, sperm samples, pubic hair samples and fingerprints that were left on the car's window. Unlike crime shows on television, all of this analysis takes time. Valuable time, Ron, as you know the most critical time in a homicide investigation like this is the first 48 hours. That precious time is ticking away, quickly."

Michaels signed off and his shoulders slumped. He was tired and troubled. He and Katie had another spat before he left for work. The fights were starting to be more frequent and the topic was the same.

"You work too much and never spend time with the girls," she scolded.

Maybe she's right, he thought, I can't remember the last time I saw Clare play tennis.

# CHAPTER 5

D octor Robert Crine sat at his desk, leaned back in his chair, closed his eyes, squeezed the bridge of his nose and then shook his head. He was tired, sweaty and unnerved. Dr. Crine worked for the Cook County Medical Examiner's Office for 11 years. He graduated from the New Jersey Medical School. He had been in private practice for three years, but he felt his real calling was in forensic medicine. He loved being a medical examiner. He had autopsied thousands of crime victims but this was the first time that he could remember anything this savage and vicious in his entire career.

It was three o'clock in the morning when he reached for his eighth cup of coffee. It was hot, black and strong, just the way he liked it. He hoped the caffeine would jolt him back to feeling anything but drained.

When he closed his eyes, he wasn't worried about falling asleep. He was reminiscing about his second year of medical school and what Ruth Lezkowski must have been like. His thoughts brought him back to his childhood and his dysfunctional family. About how his alcoholic parents worried more about having a bottle of Southern Comfort in the liquor cabinet than having a bottle of milk or juice in the refrigerator. He shrugged thinking about how this woman, whom he had just spent hours with, was beaten to death. She reminded him of his baby sister, same height, same hair color, same blue eyes and how he protected her. He remembered the day when he was 12 years old that he made up his mind that he would become a doctor. The day his drunken mother kept hitting him with the wooden leg of a chair that she kept around for such occasions. She broke a rib and caused bloody welts and bruises under his left breast with this beating. He was determined to make the best of his life and try to help people understand things that were actually unexplainable.

He wanted the homicide detectives investigating the death of Ruth Lezkowski to know exactly what they were dealing with. What a horrible, vicious, sadistic bastard or bastards, her killer or killers, were. He needed to talk with Commander James Maurer to warn him. He knew some detectives particularly those who had daughters might become enraged by this autopsy report he was about to file. In his past experience, he had seen some cases jeopardized because some of the investigators had become furious with those arrested for a horrendous violent crime. He wanted none of those problems to interfere with this case.

He would give Maurer at least another hour to sleep; that's how long it would take him to finish dictating the results of his autopsy. His secretary would be in at six o'clock to begin typing the report. It would take her awhile; it was fairly lengthy by anyone's standards. He was now feeling nauseous; a combination of adrenaline, caffeine and disgust.

~~~~

At 8:30 a.m., Peter Michaels was having a cup of coffee looking at Katie's ass wishing they were in bed when his phone rang. He got that "I just messed up" look on his face as he picked it up on the third ring. It was Kennedy. "Hey man, what's up?"

"Man, we just got the Lezkowski autopsy report, I have never, ever read anything this grotesque in my life. It's brutal. My God, that woman must have suffered," said Sergeant Bob Kennedy.

"Any chance I can get my hands on it?"

"Give me some time, you can get it at Manny's. I'll have it there in an hour," Kennedy said.

"Thanks, I owe you," said Michaels.

"Yeah, sure." Kennedy hung up.

Michaels' thoughts of *make-up sex* disappeared fast after that phone call. He got up from the kitchen table, kissed Katie on the nape of her neck and went upstairs to take a shower.

~~~~

Commander Maurer had the biggest office in Area Four. The sun filled the room on this morning and revealed all the dirty water stains on the glass windows that occupied the upper portion of the east wall. Three people could sit in front of his old military style gray metal desk and a few more could stand around comfortably.

At nine o'clock, Maurer was at his desk talking to Lieutenant David Copelin, who was sitting in one of the chairs and Sergeant Tom Swartz was leaning against his favorite wall next to the door. His lower back ached.

Copelin and Swartz were responsible for coordinating everyone's work on the Lezkowski homicide. All information had to flow through them to keep everything consistent and to make sure all information was correct.

Copelin was short and muscular with prematurely graying hair. He was more of the silent type. When he spoke, everyone listened; he was the "E.F. Hutton" of Area Four Violent Crimes. He drank iced tea constantly and he was seldom without a cigarette nearby. He was very disciplined until it came to smoking Camels, no filter. It was a habit he tried to break every other week because his wife and three kids never stopped nagging him about it but nicotine stained the blood that flowed through his system. He was addicted.

Swartz was 41-years-old, about six feet and weighed 190 pounds. He had blonde hair and red eyes. He worked long hours, didn't sleep a lot and he liked his Pinot Noir. Swartz was a talker; the troops gave him a nickname behind his back "Sir Talks A lot." He always had a smile on his face, but he was smart and sharp as a tack. When it came time to be serious he could focus on the situation like a laser.

"How we doing?" asked Maurer. "What have we got, anything?"

"We talked to dozens of people already. No one saw a thing," said Swartz who was just beginning his watch. His file already contained 15 pages of supplementary reports from the night before. Investigators file daily reports on any progress during any investigation; they're called supplementary reports.

"The only really good lead we have is the black male that was noted in the Railroad police report," said Copelin. "We have canvassed the area where she lived, 24 people, nobody saw anything."

"I want these posters of Lezkowski put up everywhere in the ALBA Homes project, on every light pole, every telephone pole, on every bulletin board in the hallways, in every room where people gather over there," Maurer said. "I'm going to talk to the boss, meaning the Superintendent of Police, and see if he can get City Hall involved and get Streets and Sanitation workers to put these posters on every pole within a two-mile radius of the ALBA Homes. We've got to keep shaking the bushes."

"Call all the guys into the squad room, I need to talk to them. I got a call from Dr. Crine this morning. That fucker woke me up at 4:30. I haven't been able to sleep since. This autopsy report is ugly," Maurer said.

~~~~

Twenty minutes later, Maurer had everyone assembled in the squad room. "Listen up" Maurer began his lecture to put the fear of God into his detectives. He wanted nothing to go wrong with this investigation. "For those of you who were at the scene, you know how brutal it was and for those who weren't, I have the autopsy report right here. I want everyone to read it. I want all of you to see what we're dealing with and I want all of you to contain any anger you may have. Listen to me very carefully, because your careers may depend on what I'm about to tell you. Whenever you bring any Person of Interest in for questioning, I want Polaroid pictures taken. Front and back, up and down in his shorts. I want no marks, no bruises, and no hostility. I don't give a shit what it takes. I do not want any one of you to lose your temper. I want to make sure we do this by the book. Do I make myself clear?"

Maurer paused for effect and looked out at his detectives. Some rubbed the sleep from their eyes. Some pinched the bridges of their noses. Some scratched their heads. All nodded affirmatively.

"I don't want anything to come back to bite us in the ass on this thing. I don't want to give these dirty rotten bastards any opportunity to hurt this investigation in any way. You all know how hard it is to get the State's Attorney from Felony Review to approve charges."

Everyone in the room was paying attention. They never saw Maurer this worked up before. He was intense. He wanted results.

Time was ticking away.

~~~~

Michaels and Longhini were sitting at their desks on the 19th floor of the Merchandise Mart in the WMAC-TV newsroom. It was an open roomy area filled with the activity of people coming and going, stopping and talking, organized confusion. Longhini was pulling his hair as he had just finished reading the autopsy report. "We've got to give this to Phil. This stuff is just so gruesome. We can't put this on TV like this," Longhini said.

"I agree. I'll make some calls and see what's going on today," said Michaels. "I know this just started but it looks like these guys don't have much to go on. Your idea of a Lezkowski profile is great."

"Yeah, I have a few ideas," said Longhini.

~~~~

Even though the working theory on this homicide was that the killer or killers were adults and were probably from the ALBA Homes, Detectives Jack Evans and Lee Scholl had another thought. More often than not, someone who knew the victim commits a crime of rage. This was a crime of dark rage. Evans and Scholl were locked into a theory that maybe the doctors were somehow involved. They returned to Rush-Presbyterian-St. Luke's Medical Center to re-interview Doctors Edward Radney and Anthony Bauer and get their fingerprints. Radney had no hesitation but Bauer asked, "Are we suspects or something?"

"Not at all," Scholl lied. "We just want to eliminate everyone so we don't waste our time."

After that they went back to Lezkowski's apartment where they discovered a footprint in the alley near a parking area, two doors down from where Ruth generally parked. The alley was like cobblestone. Tiny weeds were still sprouting between the concrete and the bricks, reaching for the late fall rays of sunshine. There were a few garages. Gravel formed the pavement that became the makeshift parking areas behind the three flats that lined Flournoy and Lexington Streets.

The same Crime Scene Investigator who was at the murder scene the morning before got out of his car and walked up to Evans and Scholl.

"What do you got?" asked Officer Gary Landis as he reached into his squad car's trunk to pull out his camera. Landis walked slow and hunched over. He was tall, six-three. Lanky, the hair shortly cropped on his head was thick and dark brown. His glasses slid down his nose. He had a master's degree in criminology. He loved being a Crime Scene Investigator. Even though he was a national champion shooter with both shotguns and pistols, he dreaded the thought of ever pulling his weapon to shoot someone in the line of duty.

"Look at this footprint," said Scholl. "It looks very similar to the one on Lezkowski's chest, doesn't it?"

"Looks like same size, same sole pattern but you know we don't have enough to make out any particular brand. You know like Nike, Converse or New Balance, nothing," said Landis.

"Yeah, I know," said Evans. "But it sure does suggest that whoever grabbed her, grabbed her right here. At least we have something to work with. Let's go re-interview the people who live in this building."

~~~~

Most of the reporters gathered in Magers' office at one time or another everyday. Not only was he a true professional and the best anchorman in the city, he was a good friend and a great person to be around. Always smiling, always laughing, always ready to help someone out.

His office had a glass wall so he could look out over the entire newsroom. He was a very organized and a driven person. He was passionate about what he did.

"Hey what's new?" Magers asked as Michaels walked into the room.

"Look at this autopsy report. I have never seen anything this gruesome in all the years I have been doing this. Look at these graphics," he said as he handed Magers the report. "Man that poor woman was tortured, beaten, stomped, kicked, punctured, you name it, and I saw some of the autopsy pictures. Turned my stomach."

"Did you see these. News Affairs just dropped them off to the newsroom." Magers said as he handed Michaels a copy of the flier that was being posted all over the area of the murder.

"Yeah, I saw this earlier. Pretty girl."

City crews from the Department of Streets and Sanitation and police officers posted the fliers with a picture of Ruth Lezkowski everywhere in Area Four.

"Apparently they are working, Maurer told me earlier they have received about a hundred calls already that they're following up on."

"I think of my daughters when something like this occurs. It has to be the most frightening thing that can ever happen to a family," Magers said.

"Believe me Mage, I have not stopped thinking about Clare and Iris."

"How's everything with you and Katie?"

"I don't know. We are starting to have some rough times."

# CHAPTER 6

T he dawning of the third morning of the Lezkowski homicide investigation was getting underway, as bleary-eyed detectives gathered in the Area Four Violent Crime squad room, mugs of hot coffee in their hands. There was a sense of urgency building; things were already starting to look bleak. The first 48 hours of the crime had expired. There were already 37 pages of supplementary reports in the growing file, and not a single solid real lead. Evidence was being analyzed at various crime labs across the city. The death certificate that was issued this morning officially listed the cause of death: blunt force trauma injuries.

Lt. David Copelin was sitting at his desk, a Camel burning in the ashtray, smoke drifting up in the air which was filled with dust spots floating through space like tiny snowflakes reflecting in the morning sun seeping through the shade less windows, the ice in his tea melting away just like the Lezkowski case in front of him. He was becoming very concerned that it was going cold, quickly.

Copelin organized a group of detectives to look through every rape and/or sexual assault case, every robbery in and around the ALBA Homes area, and every home invasion case in the 12$^{th}$ District. It was a herculean undertaking but he wanted no stone unturned. He was counting on good old-fashioned detective work that could lead them to the killers.

He also wanted to strengthen their liaisons with the University of Illinois, Chicago Campus Police and the Chicago Northwestern Railroad Police, so he put a team together to open more lines of communication. Within a short time, a few calls started coming in. The first was from the C-NW railroad police; they had just pinched a thief, who robbed one of their boxcars a short distance from the Lezkowski crime scene.

In Chicago, police use the term "pinch" when they make an arrest. Most other police departments use the term "collar." The terminology, however, is basically the same from years' past; when you arrested someone, you grabbed by the collar.

Detectives Aldo Palombo and Thomas Britten were assigned to question the suspect. Palombo was half Italian and half Irish. However, his dark olive skin betrayed his Irish blood. He looked 100 percent Italian. He was five feet, eight inches tall, his full head of jet-black hair was combed straight back. He was a few pounds overweight and he walked with a slight limp. He was contemplating a hip replacement after he slipped down some stairs at Police Headquarters a few months ago. His family was in the pharmaceutical business but he wanted nothing to do with it. Ever since he was a kid playing cops and robbers, he wanted to be the cop.

Britten on the other hand, looked totally Irish. With his red hair and mustache twisted ever-so-slightly at its ends, he could be cast as a leprechaun in Broadway plays. A little shorter than Palombo, Britten walked with a sense of purpose and he liked to dress in expensive suits and Ferragamo shoes. His wife was a highly respected physician and surgeon who was the Head of Surgery at the University of Chicago Hospital. He, like Palombo, always wanted to be the police. He loved being a detective and he, like Commander Maurer, had a personal interest in solving this case.

Palombo and Britten got to the C-NW Police station on Canal Street within ten minutes and immediately started to question the suspect, Leroy Banks. He looked like he just came down from a reefer high. His eyes were sagging, his white tee shirt was turning gray and his washed out jeans were hanging down his skinny hips, slightly showing the crack in his ass. When Britten brought up the Lezkowski murder, Leroy freaked and said, "Hey look a here, man, I did the train shit, but fuck man, I don't know nuttin' bout no fucking murder."

The detectives looked at each other and said, "Well then I guess you don't mind us taking a swab from you and getting your fingerprints."

"Man, you can have any fuckin' thing you want but don't put no murder on my black ass," he said.

The detectives smiled, swabbed him, printed him and turned him over the Railroad police, who processed him for burglary. Leroy Banks was scared shitless and his record contained only one minor misdemeanor for a similar burglary. They felt confident he wasn't involved in the Lezkowski case, but at least they had a record of him and they knew where to find him. It was just one more supplementary report to fill out.

~~~~

Detective Jack Evans had just finished putting medical student Edward Radney's information into the Department's Alpha file. The Alpha file was an antiquated card filing system that recorded if a person was arrested or ever had contact with the police. It would list any contacts, victims, offenders, witnesses and description of the crime if one were committed. Evans thought Radney would not show up, but he put him in the Alpha file anyway, you just never know. He also ran Radney's name through the Los Angeles Police Department's criminal records database because he lived in California all of his life before he got accepted at Rush-Presbyterian-St. Luke's Medical School.

Detective Lee Scholl took a call from the University of Illinois Chicago Campus Police Department.

"They just arrested a suspect for threatening a woman with a stick, on campus. They think he's a nut but let's go talk to him," Scholl said.

Team members had spent endless hours looking for the stick that Ruth Lezkowski had in her car for protection. Anxiety and anticipation were building as they hustled out the door and over to the Campus Police Headquarters. They needed a break in the case.

They met the arresting officer, who told them the suspect was in a holding cell.

"Who is this prick?" Evans asked looking at the arrest report.

"Samuel Peppers. He's from Tinley Park Mental Health Center. He's a fucking fruit cake."

Samuel Peppers was tall, skinny and spaced-out.

"Hey, Sammy, why'd you threaten that student near her dormitory with that stick?" Evans asked.

Peppers was catatonic. There was no life behind his filmy eyes. He was mumbling some incoherent phrases under his breath.

"He ain't our guy" Evans said. "Look at this stick that the police confiscated when they pinched him. It's nothing like the one Lezkowski had in her car."

"Peppers is AWOL from Tinley Park. He went missing yesterday." Scholl said. "I just hung up with hospital security. He was at the Institution on the night of the murder."

Peppers was processed by University Police at the 12th District for a misdemeanor. He was then returned to the Tinley Park Mental Facility located in a far southern suburb an hour and a half drive from downtown.

~~~~

Crime Scene investigator, Gary Landis, called Lt. David Copelin with some news from the tool mark section of the Crime Lab about the shoe print that was found on the body of Ruth Lezkowski and in the alley where she may have been kidnapped.

"We've identified the gym shoe as Reebok, EX-O-Fit," Landis said. "It only comes in a high top style in either black or white."

"Thanks. I'm looking at a theft report. A boxcar near the scene of the Lezkowski homicide had three cartons of the shoes stolen about three weeks ago." Copelin said.

"I'll send the results to the FBI's Crime Lab at Quantico to see if they can come up with anything more. Oh, Yah, we also found some purple fibers, which could have come from a coat, both inside the car and in the trunk." Landis said.

"Good. Thanks. This information gives the dicks one more thing they can use when they interview anyone in the future."

~~~~

Evans was sitting at his typewriter filling out his new supplementary report on the suspect from the university that threatened a co-ed with a stick. He was fucking this and motherfucking that, as he was making typos on every other word as he poked his keyboard with his two index fingers.

Supplementary reports were time-consuming but necessary for the accurate and consistent flow of information in any police investigation.

Scholl was sitting at his desk, feet up, looking at the ceiling closing his eyes running his fingers through his thick hair, thinking what they could do next, when the phone rang. "Area Four Violent Crimes, this is detective Lee Scholl."

"Hello, I'm a friend of Ruth Lezkowski," said the woman on the other end, "I may have some information for you."

Scholl perked up, signaling Evans in a circular motion with his index finger, indicating urgency.

"Ruth told me if anything ever happened to her, I should call the police and give the name of Larry Jones."

"Who's Jones?" Scholl asked. "Does he date her, or are they just friends?"

"I think he took her to Giorgio's Disco Club on South Michigan Avenue." she replied. "He works at a collection agency on South Michigan, I think around the 200 block or something," she said and ended the call.

~~~~

The City of Chicago is laid out in a perfect grid starting at the intersection of State and Madison Streets. Madison separates all streets north and south in the entire city. The streets north have names and streets south have numbers. The Lezkowski crime scene was at 1500 South Loomis, which basically means it was 15 blocks south of Madison Street. State Street separates east and west streets. There are fewer neighborhoods and streets heading east because of Lake Michigan. This numbering system was set up in the early 1900s, because as the city started to grow, people started to complain about getting lost all the time.

~~~~

Scholl was off his chair and moving before the phone hit its cradle, motioning to Evans let's go. "What's up?" asked Evans.

"Anonymous call from a friend saying Ruth warned her about a boyfriend named Larry Jones and that if anything ever happened to her call the police."

This was the first significant lead they had in three days, a connection perhaps, someone who knew her. Normally in a homicide this is the best kind of suspect.

~~~~

Traffic was heavy on the Eisenhower. Even though it was ten o'clock in the morning, road construction on every street heading east towards downtown was backing up everywhere in the city. Getting to Giorgio's Disco Club on South Michigan Avenue seemed like it took hours. Scholl was thinking about turning on the lights and siren but that would just cause more confusion so he just kept hitting the steering wheel with his fists, mumbling, "Fuck, fuck, fuck." He was temperamental, he had another bout with his wife about not spending enough time at home earlier that morning.

"What's with you man?" asked Evans.

"I'm just getting all kinds of shit at home. She was screaming at me again this morning. 'All you fucking do is work.' She is really pissed."

"Hey, brother, I know what you mean. That's all we fight about. I work too much."

The Club was closed when they finally arrived, but the door was open. Walking in, they were immediately greeted by the manager with concern marking his face. With a look of utter determination on their faces, they immediately stood out as police detectives. "Can I help you?" Dennis Decker asked.

Evans introduced himself and Scholl and immediately asked if he knew of a man named Larry Jones. He didn't. Decker said, "Let me check the members' list on our new computer in the office." When he came back he was shaking his head negatively, "I looked up both Jones and Lezkowski, not in there," he said. "But you know this is a public club, I'll ask the night manager and get back to you."

~~~~

Worldwide Credit was just down the street. When they entered, Larry Jones was sitting in his office looking over some financial files on his desk. His shirtsleeves were rolled up and his gaudy tie was loose around his neck. "What can I do for you?" Jones managed to say, looking up at them suspiciously.

Scholl introduced himself and Evans. Handed him a picture of Ruth Lezkowski, he asked, "Do you know this woman?"

Jones looked at the black and white picture for a while and then handed it back. "I've never seen her before, why do you ask?"

"We were told that you and her go to Giorgio's Disco," said Scholl.

"Let me see that again." He took the photo once more, and this time took a longer look. "I may have seen her in the club several times with a group of girls. Yeah! I think, I saw her with several 'pimp-type' dudes talking to her."

Evans then asked, "You think you can identify these 'pimp-type' dudes if you looked at some photos?"

"Yeah, sure," he said. "I can do that after work around eight o'clock if you want. I want to fully cooperate with you guys. You know, I'm going out with a white girl so I'm not confused by white features," he said.

"Thanks, we'll see you later tonight. Do you know where Area Four is on Harrison?" asked Evans.

"I know where it is, I grew up on the other side of the "Ike" over on Madison," he said.

The "Ike" was the common nickname for the Eisenhower Expressway, Interstate 90, which ran east and west in and out of the City.

~~~~

As Evans and Scholl were walking back to their car, Evans said, "Man, that son of a bitch was nervous as hell, did you see him shaking when he was looking at that photo."

"Yeah, let's see if he shows up later. We should go back and talk to the roommate; maybe she can fill in some of the blanks. I'll call 'Sir Talks A Lot' and fill him in," said Scholl. While Scholl was on the phone with their sergeant, he was informed that Rush-Presbyterian-St. Luke's Medical School Security just called the office and said that the same woman who called us called them and told them, "Jones killed Ruth Lezkowski."

"I like this guy a little bit, but let's not get hasty here," said Evans. "We know where to find him."

~~~~

The detectives pulled up to Ruth's apartment building on Flournoy Street. The area was changing rapidly. Investors were buying up properties and spending fortunes refurbishing them. Three flats were the hottest real estate in the Medical Village and the Little Italy areas. Taylor Street was the main drag that defined Little Italy. It was best known for its Italian restaurants that attracted local residents and tourists from all over the world. Little storefronts selling Italian Ice and folklore about Chicago's notorious mafia also made Taylor Street one of the most popular areas in the city. Taylor Street is where the infamous Mobster Sam Giancana ran his organized crime syndicate.

~~~~

Evans rang the bell, they were admitted and walked up to the third floor rear apartment that Ruth Lezkowski shared with another medical student, Cathleen Germain. "Hi again, anything new?"

"Maybe," said Evans, "Did Ruth know a guy named Larry Jones, and did she frequently go to Giorgio's Disco Club?"

The surprise look on Cathleen's face changed to a quizzical expression "You're kidding, right?" Shaking her head, she continued, "Ruth would never go to a Disco Club downtown. No. Never happen. If she ever drank two beers or a glass of wine, that would be a lot for her. She doesn't like the stuff. Who is this Larry Jones?"

"We got an anonymous tip today that this black guy and she went to Giorgio's Disco Club on Michigan Avenue."

"No way. She was my roommate for two years. The only black guy I know of that she spent any time with is Charlie Berriman. Listen, Ruth didn't have a racist bone in her body, but I'll tell you she was a small town girl and she didn't date a black guy. She was too busy studying to date anyone, anyway. She didn't want to have anything to do with a guy in her life right now. She barely had enough time to jog and go to church on Sunday."

"What about this Charlie guy, tell us more about him," Scholl said.

Cathleen was sitting on the edge of the sofa, leaning forward, forearms on her knees and a yellow coffee mug with black letters that spelled **RUSH** held gently with both hands. She thought for a moment or two, "Charlie and Ruth knew each other for years. They both went to school in Springfield. I think Charlie would have loved to have more than a friendship but she just considered him a good friend, and from what she told me she wanted to keep it that way. He lives in Philadelphia now and works for some big medical company there. He comes here to visit her every so often and they'd go out to dinner, but that's about all. He stayed here a few times and slept on the couch, so that's how I know they weren't dating. He invited her to Philadelphia and even offered to pay her airfare, but she never went.

He wanted her to visit him last summer, but she went to Europe instead. He also wanted her to visit him this spring but she went to Phoenix." Cathleen straightened up with a surprised look on her face, "You know I just remembered something, Charlie gave her a negligee from Frederick's of Hollywood last Christmas. She was stunned and a little embarrassed."

Evans and Scholl looked at each other with raised eyebrows and both of them at the same time pushed their shoulders back and twisted their heads from right to left and then continued to take their notes.

"Charlie was here a few days ago. I think he had to go to court for a ticket or something like that on the 17th. It was strange he never called and he usually does when he comes to town."

Evans and Scholl stood up and Evans said, "Thank you for your time. We'll be in touch I am sure. If you think of anything else give us a call."

As they walked down the stairs and reached the front door, Evans looked Scholl in the eyes and said, "We have to find this motherfucker."

# CHAPTER 7

B y the end of the third day after the Lezkowski homicide at least 48 detectives, patrol officers, sergeants, lieutenants and upper-command personnel had been involved in the investigation and that didn't include the clerical staff. More than 50 people had been interviewed and 17 of them had been re-interviewed. It was a massive manhunt that was stalling before it had any real traction. The first 48 hours had passed and the case was going cold in high gear.

~~~~

Detectives Jack Evans and Lee Scholl were antsy. Although the working theory of the case was that the killers were adult black males from the projects, they had a theory of their own *it was someone who knew her.* They were in pursuit of Charlie Berriman, who appeared to really have something for Ruth. He was in town around the time of the murder but hadn't been seen since. Evans and Scholl wanted to know why.

~~~~

Larry Jones arrived at Area Four Violent Crimes at 9:30 p.m. He wasn't necessarily late, because no exact time for his voluntary visit was clearly established but Detectives Palombo and Britten, sitting in for Evans and Scholl, expected him an hour earlier. When the detectives met him in the vestibule, they were taken aback because he already lawyered up. They thought this a little odd because the supplementary report they read minutes before stated that he wanted to fully cooperate.

Jones introduced his attorney, Maurice Goldman, to the detectives whom he, himself, just met him a few hours earlier. Goldman was young, handsome and dressed in an expensive tailor made suit. He was an up and coming criminal defense attorney who would be a very busy man during his career in Chicago.

After the formal introductions, they went to an interview room across the hall from all the activity for a little privacy. Jones said, "Where are those other two guys I met this morning?"

"They're looking into another matter but don't worry we work very closely here at Area Four," Britten said.

They took their seats around a beat up metal table that looked like it had seen action in World War II. The chairs looked worse and they were not made for comfort, just the opposite. Jones and Goldman sat at one corner and Palombo and Britten at the other. Britten laid his file folder on the table but didn't open it. "So let's go over what you told the other detectives."

Jones reaffirmed that he thought he had met Ruth and a couple of her girlfriends at Giorgio's Disco Club about a month ago. "I may have sold her some cosmetics. I have this here new side business, I'm trying to develop with a line of female cosmetic products that are just being introduced into the Chicago market."

Britten then opened his folder and handed Jones three very clear color photos of Ruth Lezkowski. He looked at them for what seemed like a long period of time and started backtracking on his original statement, "Maybe it wasn't her."

Britten said, "I gotta tell ya Larry. We're liking ya' as a suspect here."

"A woman called us earlier today and stated, 'if anything happened to Ruth the police should look for Larry Jones.' That's you. Ain't it?" Palombo said.

"Hold it right there." Goldman interrupted with a surprised tone and immediately smoothed his Louis Vuitton tie with his hand as if it were an iron. He leaned forward and frowned, and his expression became more serious. "Mr. Jones came here on a voluntary basis to cooperate in the fullest with the police. Is this some sort of ploy that you're pulling here to trick him into making some kind of confession?"

"We're just trying to figure why some woman would try to implicate Mr. Jones here in a very serious crime that has this city on edge," Britten said. "He told us earlier that he knew her from the club and now he's saying he is not so sure. Where were you on the night of October 17th and the morning of October 18th?"

Before his attorney could stop him. Jones blurted out, "I told you I would cooperate and I will. I'll do whatever you want, man. I did nothing to that poor woman. I thought that maybe I met her. Now, I'm not so sure."

Before Jones' attorney could step in, Palombo immediately leaned forward, "Will you give us your fingerprints, a blood sample and take a polygraph test?"

"I'll take your damn lie box." Jones said, "I was with my new girlfriend, we went to Counselors Row, (a trendy restaurant on LaSalle Street) and we met Mack, my buddy. We had a few drinks and something to eat. We left at nine o'clock, took the El to 87th Street and me and Anna Marie walked to my momma's house. We got there around eleven and went to bed. Just ask them, my parents and Anna Marie."

Britten slid over a yellow legal pad, "Names, phone numbers and addresses."

Jones immediately starting writing when Palombo asked, "Do you have any idea why anyone would want to implicate you in this homicide?"

Jones stopped writing, leaned back in his chair, looked up at the ceiling, shook his head and smiled "I can't believe that she would do this to me." he said.

"Who, What?" Palombo asked.

"Natasha," Jones replied.

"Who's that?"

"Natasha Symington. We were engaged for two years; I broke it off a couple of months ago. She was really pissed; said I'd pay the price."

"Put her name down and how we can get in touch with her. If she made us waste all this time, we'll file charges against her," Palombo said, "for filing a false police report."

As Jones wiped the ink off his fingers and palms from being printed, he said, "Listen, man, I didn't do this. Check my alibi and you'll see."

"We'll check it all out, thanks for coming in. We appreciate your cooperation," Britten said.

They shook hands and Goldman followed his client out the door, shaking his head as they left.

Palombo looked at Britten, shaking his head as well, "This looks like we wasted a lot of valuable time."

"What do they say?" Britten said, "Hell hath no fury like a woman scorned."

"We'll see who has the last of 'hell hath no fury,'" said Palombo as he limped out of the squad room. His hip was aching and his mind was racing as he thought about surgery. "Let's get some sleep. It's been a long day. See you tomorrow, it'll be another long one, you can bet your sweet ass."

~~~~

As Palombo and Britten were walking out the door, Sergeant Tom Swartz grimaced with pain and reached for his lower back. He was shuffling the accumulated supplementary reports when he noticed that several different people made mention that a suspicious-looking man was driving up and down Flournoy in front of Lezkowski's place. He was driving in an off-white or light-tan van with no windows on the sides, asking the women if they were Ruth. He was described the same way by all those interviewed as "a large male, white or Hispanic, on the heavy side with wavy black hair" and he was wearing what they described as some kind of "blue uniform shirt."

Swartz picked up the phone and called 12th District Patrol and requested that a squad periodically patrol the area looking for the van. He had a follow up plan formulated for Palombo and Britten when they came back to work in the morning. He had a skeleton crew on this watch trying to follow up with people who were not available to be interviewed during the regular business day.

Detectives responded to 31 tips they had received since they discovered the body of Ruth Lezkowski. The only solid lead at this time was Charlie; Ruth's wannabe boyfriend.

~~~~

Doug Longhini had just gotten back from Springfield, the state capitol 200 miles from Chicago, or 178 miles as the crow flies. It took him about four hours to make the drive. Road construction had been clogging up roads and highways in the state for the last four years, making travel by car a tedious experience. Even though Springfield is the state's capitol, it only has about 120,000 residents. Six of them are the Lezkowski family. They lived on a tree-lined street of bungalows that describes most working class people throughout Illinois.

Ruth's funeral was that morning. Longhini hired a local crew to videotape the service. The Cathedral of the Assumption was at full capacity. Hundreds filled the dark-brown wood pews looking toward the front of the sanctuary where a tapestry of the Virgin Mary hung, taking up most of the wall behind the black marble altar. The Church itself was adorned with gold, symbolizing its sacredness. The sunlight streamed through the leaded windows depicting many of the Church's saints in mosaic-style colored glass. It also produced a halo effect over Ruth's casket that was breathtaking. The service took almost two hours. The homily delivered by the family priest was a tear-jerking description of this incredible woman who was robbed of life in such a brutal way. At the age of 23, Ruth Lezkowski had made a lasting mark on this community where she grew up.

~~~~

Peter Michaels had a meeting with his news director Phil Rivers, a few hours earlier. The Lezkowski story was slowing down and the fall ratings season was coming up. The I-Team was expected to produce a series that would have an impact on the city. The pressure to produce investigative packages was intense because the station had committed a substantial amount of money to finance the I-Team.

Rating seasons generally happen three times a year. Preliminary ratings for October actually set the stage for the November Sweeps. They are the most important of all of the rating seasons throughout the year. Every ratings point means money for the station. The prime viewers are considered those between the ages of 18 and 35. The higher the ratings the more money a station can charge for its commercials. The number of viewers recorded also determines the bragging rights for each station. Whether it is number one or number three makes a big difference in how a news department can advertise its credibility.

~~~~

"Newsroom ... Michaels."

"Hey, I am a copper in twelve," the voice said. "We don't have enough bodies to patrol the streets anymore. All our calls are getting backed up on every shift. It sucks and it's getting dangerous, and now they're talking about making us one-man cars."

"How can I get proof?" Michaels asked.

"Let me see what I can come up with," he said.

"What's your name?"

"Later," he responded.

"Wait a minute, let me give you my private number."

"Okay, I'll call you in a few days. I'll get you all the proof you need," the officer said.

~~~~

The Chicago Police Department was supposed to have 13,500 police officers, when in fact, there were probably less than 10,000 on the job. The workload in busy districts like the 12th was very demanding. Patrol officers couldn't answer calls in any sort of timely manner so two-man cars suddenly were about to become one-man cars, placing many officers in danger.

Michaels smiled at Longhini and said, "We might be onto a blockbuster story for the November Sweeps."

Magers looked up from the newspaper he was reading as Michaels and Longhini walked into his office. "How did the funeral go today?" he asked.

"Pretty sad day in Springfield. The place was packed."

"Where was the service held?"

"The Cathedral of the Assumption in downtown Springfield. Very ornate. Very Catholic. Very traditional."

"I just viewed the tape. That town is in shock. She was quite a woman. The priest called her a child of God who never spoke an ill word about anyone her entire life," Michaels said.

"Everyone I talked to said, 'this sort of thing isn't suppose to happen here.'" Longhini said.

"It's hard to believe that there are people in this world that could do such a thing. Man it was brutal. Only in Chicago, there are a lot of fucking crazies out there." Michaels said.

# CHAPTER 8

D etectives Jack Evans and Lee Scholl started their day at 7:15 with breakfast at Lou Mitchell's on West Jackson Boulevard, a half block from Chicago's Union Station. Lou's is a Chicago institution. Its outside marquee sign boasts that they serve "the world's best coffee." It is good, freshly ground and strong! Lou, himself, usually greets everyone at the door with a friendly smile as he gives them a doughnut hole or small box of Milk Duds candy. People from all over the world eat there. They're open only eight hours a day, serving breakfast and lunch, seven days a week. There's nothing bad on the menu. It's all homemade and delicious.

The seating consists of tightly packed booths that line each side of the restaurant with one long table running down the middle. You may be sitting next to someone from Sweden, South Dakota or the Chicago Stock Exchange. There are no strangers at Lou Mitchell's.

Evans and Scholl sat at the counter on red swivel stools right behind the cashier that took patrons money, cash only. Evans ordered a cottage cheese omelet, coffee and freshly squeezed orange juice, another favorite at Mitchell's. Scholl had fried eggs sunny side up, sausage, potatoes and coffee. It was going to be another long day.

~~~~

The drive to Traffic Court was less than a mile and a half, but it took nearly 20 minutes.

"Look at this fucking traffic. I hate driving around here with all this construction. Wacker fucking Drive is like a parking lot, everyday," Evans said.

"Man, who shit in your corn flakes this morning?" replied Scholl. "You are one grumpy bastard, today."

"I had a fight this morning before I left the house. She's tired of me working all the time. No time for the kids. No time for the family; all that bullshit."

Inside their unmarked car, things got quiet for the rest of the drive but the outside noise of the city waking up filtered through the closed windows. Streets and Sanitation crews were repairing potholes and curbs, horns were honking as cars weaved in and out of lanes, sirens were screaming, and drivers were giving each other the finger. It was a typical morning in downtown Chicago.

~~~~

They parked in the police lot and walked into Traffic Court on the LaSalle Street side. The building looked tired. The brick on its façade was dark red almost crimson. The two-story structure with its clock tower was sitting on prime real estate just north of the Chicago River paralleling Wacker Drive. It looked odd, like a pair of brown shoes with a black tuxedo, out of place with new buildings going up all around it.

The floors were worn, the walls painted a dingy yellowish color were in need of a fresh coat, and dust balls gathered in every corner of the building. Thousands of people passed through its doors, halls and courtrooms everyday. The six courtrooms on the first floor handled the major cases. Courtroom 106 handled the most serious of them all, like manslaughter with an auto or DUI's, drunk driving. Six upstairs courtrooms handled the minor violations like running a red light or a stop sign; this was where Charlie Berriman's case was heard.

Traffic Court attorneys generally dressed in wrinkly suits and pants with no creases. They wore shirts with loose ties around their necks and collars unbuttoned. Their shoes were scuffed and hadn't seen polish since the day they were purchased. They all gathered at the Clerk of the Courts counter near the LaSalle Street entrance and waited to meet their clients, usually for the first time. They would spend a few minutes discussing their clients' cases anything from parking tickets to DUI's. Having an attorney, however, had its advantages; defendants got preferential treatment, because no matter where your case was on the docket, you moved to the front of the line and your case was called first. Like fast food, in and out in less than five minutes.

It's amazing how efficient this archaic system worked day-in and day-out.

~~~~

Peter Michaels knew Traffic Court very well. He won the prestigious George Foster Peabody Award for a series of reports called: "Traffic Court: Justice or Joke." The report centered around fixing parking tickets and easy sentences on drunk drivers.

He also broke one of the biggest stories in Chicago Journalism history called "Operation Greylord," which was an investigation by the FBI into the scandalous behavior of judges, court clerks and police bagmen. His reporting brought about the indictment of the highest-ranking judge in Illinois history to be charged and convicted of corruption.

Judge Raymond Laverne would "SOL" parking tickets by the thousands for a fraction of the money owed to the county. "SOL" *means* "Stricken on leave to reinstate." It is a motion the state makes to dismiss a case but it allows them to reinstate the case with court approval or the state can indict the matter without court approval. It happened a lot in cases where the State decided to pass on a preliminary hearing and bring a direct indictment. In Traffic Court, however, it was a simple way to dismiss parking tickets without bringing a lot of attention to the court's action.

The judge's bagmen would identify scofflaws, people who don't pay their parking tickets, contact them and offer them a sweetheart deal to fix the tickets for cash under the table. They got so bold at fixing parking tickets that they would even take checks when the scofflaw didn't have the cash on hand. That's how Michaels caught them.

Michaels found out how the system worked and, with a cashed check in hand and signed "SOL" receipts with the judge's signature on the screen; he reported it on the ten o'clock news. Six hours later the FBI swarmed all over Traffic Court with subpoenas to collect all the evidence from the Clerk's Office, leading to numerous federal indictments and convictions for years.

Michaels filed 138 reports on the "Operation Greylord" scandal before it was over.

~~~~

Evans led the way to the basement where all the records of completed cases were on file. It looked like a dungeon; electric coffee pots that were brewing throughout the day appeared at various locations on the edge of someone's desk. The fluorescent fixtures hanging from the ceiling worked hard to light up the workspace. A third of the tubes were black and dead, waiting for a maintenance man to bring them back to life. The clerks moved from file cabinet to file cabinet, processing cases that came from unending stacks of lawsuits reaching to the ceiling, a never-ending supply of paper, systematically filed by their appearance dates. Clerks were days behind.

Evans approached the counter, showed his badge and asked, "Can you locate a ticket for running a red light issued to Charlie Berriman? It was adjudicated on October 17th."

Ten minutes later the clerk handed the file over to Evans. "Yep, he was on the early docket. Says here his ticket was dismissed in room 203." Evans mumbled, "He was on his way by 10:30."

Charlie Berriman was in Chicago the day before Ruth Lezkowski was brutally murdered.

~~~~

Palombo and Britten's day started very differently at the Area Four Violent Crimes squad room. The coffee from the nightshift that was thick, strong and stale and it seemed to exemplify everyone's downer mood. The faded light green walls, dark stained ceiling tiles, and depressing light from the overcast sky filtered in through the dirty windows and just added more gloom to the atmosphere in the squad room.

Palombo pulled out the Jones file from last night and slipped his parents' phone number to Britten to call. He called Anna Marie, the girlfriend. She answered on the second ring. He identified himself and stated the reason he was calling. She was expecting his call and confirmed that they were in fact together the night of the murder. She said she would be glad to come to the station. Palombo told her that would not be necessary at this time, but that he may be in touch with her in the future.

Britten had the same conversation with Jones' parents. They said he was definitely at their house on the night of the homicide arriving somewhere after ten o'clock, because they remembered watching the news with Ron Magers and it was over.

Palombo called the crime lab to ask if they had a chance to check Jones' prints to the ones found at the crime scene. They did and the prints didn't match. They put Jones on the bottom of the list of suspects. It was time to move back to square one.

Britten was still steaming and determined to charge Natasha for filing a false police report and wasting valuable time, but there were more urgent things pending, like finding the killer.

~~~~

Evans answered his phone. It was Cathleen Germain, Ruth Lezkowski's roommate. She had just talked to Charlie in Pennsylvania.

"What did he say?" asked Evans.

"He said he flew into Midway Airport on Thursday the 16th in order to appear in traffic court. He met with a couple of college buddies, David and Carl, from Carbondale, Illinois, for dinner in Greek Town on the 16th. He said he didn't know why he didn't call Ruth but he just didn't."

"Did he go to the funeral in Springfield?" asked Evans.

"No! I asked him why, and he stuttered when he said that he just didn't want to go but didn't give any specific reason. He asked me what the police thought happened to Ruth and who might have done it."

"You got his phone number?" asked Evans. She gave it to him and they hung up.

~~~~

Earlier Evans and Scholl checked police databanks from Chicago, Springfield, Bolingbrook, Illinois and Philadelphia. Charlie Berriman had no criminal record. He only had the one traffic ticket that was dismissed on the 16th. He didn't have an Illinois driver's license.

~~~~

Charlie Berriman picked up his phone on the fourth ring. He sounded relieved when Detective Lee Scholl identified himself.

"I thought I'd be hearing from you guys, sooner or later," he said.

"Why is that?"

"Well, I knew Ruth all of my life."

"Tell me your whereabouts when you came to Chicago."

"Okay. I flew to Midway on the 16th. I rented a car from Hertz. I planned to go to Southern Illinois University for the homecoming on Saturday. I also wanted to visit my dad; he has cancer and I try to see him whenever I can. I had dinner at the Parthenon restaurant with two of my buddies from Southern on the 16th in Greek Town. I went to traffic court for a ticket on the 17[th.] Then I returned my original car and got a bigger one because me, David, Carl and a girl named Jodie were going to drive to Carbondale Friday afternoon."

"What are their last names?"

"Carl Sherman, David Kurtzmen and Jodie Richards."

"Do you have their phone numbers?"

He gave them to him and continued, "We left for Southern a little before noon and checked into a Best Inn Motel at around six o'clock. After we checked in we went to a homecoming function at the student center and then we went to three campus bars. I got back to the hotel around two in the morning and went to sleep. Carl took the car because he was staying with his old college roommate. We hooked up at about eight the next morning. We had breakfast and then went to a tailgate party before the football game. After the game I called my dad, and that's when I found out about Ruth."

Scholl knew that Carbondale was about 330 miles from Chicago and his explanation of events seemed to be in the right time line.

"Why didn't you go the funeral?" asked Scholl.

"I called Mrs. Lezkowski and offered my condolences but I just couldn't bring myself to go. I felt bad about everything, the horrible way she died, you know. I was totally stunned. I just couldn't do it. I visited my dad, flew home, returned to work, and here I am sick to my stomach."

"Thanks for your help. If you come back to Chicago let us know. We may have some other questions for you."

"Okay, I will," he said and they hung up.

~~~~

Evans called the Carbondale police and asked them to check the Best Inn Motel registration for Charlie Berriman on the 17th.

Scholl call David Kurtzman and got him on the third ring. Kurtzman confirmed Berriman's story almost verbatim and said he would be glad to come to Area Four if necessary. Calls to Carl Sherman and Jodie Richards went unanswered.

Charlie Berriman's alibi was starting to look pretty solid.

~~~~

Another call to Area Four about the off white or tan van with a suspicious looking driver inspired Lt. Copelin to send Palombo and Britten over to the Rush-Presbyterian-St. Luke's Hospital Administration Office. The detectives talked to an assistant administrator and discovered that 8,000 people were employed at the hospital, 3,000 of them were nonmedical personnel, such as security, maintenance or housekeeping. They started by eliminating all the women and focused on anyone who owned a van. Britten requested a list of all vehicles that went in and out the parking garage on the 17th and 18th of October. Hundreds of vehicles had to be checked out, countless hours of gumshoe police work were accumulating, but no matter what paths the Lezkowski homicide investigation was leading them, they were motivated to find the killer or killers.

~~~~

Longhini was typing his bio on Ruth Lezkowski and Michaels was working the phones when the six o'clock news producer, David Beedy asked, "Where are you guys on the Lezkowski case?" Beedy was the station's top news producer. He was assigned all special events because he was a meticulous planner. You had to cross every T and dot every I with him. He was a great writer, organized and very time conscious.

"Doug's finishing Ruth's bio and I just got off the phone with some sources. They got nothing. The cops are running off in every direction. They're even examining every violent crime in the district that is remotely similar, like grasping at straws. The only possibility of a story is combining her bio with the fact that the two primary persons of interest aren't that interesting anymore," Michaels said.

"I need to know if we have enough to run with it in 20 minutes," Beedy said.

Michaels and Longhini sat across from one another, feet crossed and up on their desks. They both hated to wear suits unless it was necessary. Michaels always had a suit coat, white shirt and tie if he had to go on air. Being an Investigative Reporter gave him the freedom to work stories for months on end as long as the results boosted the station's ratings when they aired. It's part of the television business, a fact of life for Michaels and Longhini.

Michaels would wear jeans and a black Harley Davidson tee shirt to work every day if he could. He settled for nice looking shirts and pullover sweaters at this time of year. Longhini, also liked jeans but he was always stylish wearing a shirt and sometimes a tie with a casual sport jacket. It was his GQ look.

Whenever Longhini was in deep thought, he had this habit of pulling his hair one strand at time, slowly, gently, smoothly, like he was playing a fine instrument. Longhini had a full head of black hair parted on the side and combed back. His brown eyes had dark circles; he read a lot but didn't sleep a lot. He studied in Italy when he was in college and he could read newspapers in several different languages. He was keen, smart and determined. When he got on a story he was like a bulldog on the hunt.

~~~~

Sitting in Ron Magers office for their daily bull session, Magers asked, "This Lezkowski story is losing steam, isn't it?"

"Yep, the cops are all over the place but little information is surfacing right now. We are trying to keep the story alive. So tonight we put together a background piece on who she was and how she lived her life."

"Let's see how it plays but I don't think the producers will run it again on the Ten."

"I know. Once that first 48 hours passes it gets really tough. This case will be solved when someone is arrested down the road and says they know something. Mark my words." Michaels said.

~~~~

Michaels and Longhini, with no story on the ten o'clock news, walked over to the Billy Goat Tavern on lower Wacker Drive. The Billy Goat was the home of the curse against the Chicago Cubs Major League baseball team. Its owner, William Sianis, took a goat to Wrigley Field when he attended games. The goat smelled so foul that it offended other fans so Sianis and his goat were kicked out of the ballpark during the fourth game of the 1945 World Series against the Detroit Tigers. He was so incensed that he allegedly declared "them

Cubs, they ain't gonna win no more" and they lost the series to the Tigers that year. The walls of the Goat were covered with newspaper articles and memorabilia about the Cubs' curse, which was immortalized by Syndicated Columnist Mike Royko, who had his own red swivel stool at the end of the bar. He occupied it at least five nights a week.

As Michaels, an avid Detroit Tiger fan, walked up the four steps reaching for the bright red door, he could only grin because he knew the New York Mets had beaten the Boston Red Sox in the 1986 World Series. In the critical sixth game of that series, Red Sox First Baseman, Bill Buckner made the infamous error through his legs that allowed the Mets to advance to the final game. As Buckner walked off the field, he showed the national television audience that he had a Cubs batting glove under his mitt at the moment he committed the error. The Cubs have not won a World Series in 78 years.

As always, when you opened the red door of the Billy Goat Tavern you were greeted with the words "cheeeesee burger, cheeeesee burger," the phrase that was made famous by John Belushi on the hit television comedy show *Saturday Night Live*.

Michaels and Longhini didn't want to eat. They just wanted a beer. A long month lie ahead of them.

# CHAPTER 9

A s the Ruth Lezkowski homicide investigation entered
November, everything seemed to be moving in slow motion.
A lot of police work was getting done, but the investigation
was going off in a lot of different directions, and detectives were back
to square one.

All the subjects involved in the Charlie Berriman phase were re-
interviewed and their stories all matched. The Carbondale Police
Department verified that the group did indeed check into the Best Inn
Motel and attended school functions the entire Homecoming
weekend. Once a prime suspect, Charlie Berriman was moved off the
list.

The same was true of Larry Jones. His alibi checked out and his
prints did not match those found at the crime scene. After considering
charges against Natasha, his ex-girlfriend, with all that "Hell hath no
fury" anger, they decided to let it go. It would take too much valuable
time and time was of essence and it was running out.

Medical students Edward Radney and Anthony Bauer were re-
interviewed and re-interviewed again. Computerized time records
sought by detectives of when they left and entered their dorms
verified Radney's story but Bauer had been holding back. Radney's
fingerprints and saliva did not match anything at the crime scene so
he was ruled out as a suspect but they both agreed to take lie detector
tests in the future. Bauer however, was not as cooperative as Radney.
He wasn't interviewed as much either. Their names appeared on
dozens of supplementary reports in the Lezkowski file.

Hundreds of hospital parking records were thoroughly examined but it led to a dead end and the suspicious van driver in the victim's neighborhood seemed to be going nowhere. A patrol officer stopped an off white van on Flournoy, the driver somewhat matched the description of the suspect in the supplementary reports, but the guy worked for a garage door company. He was in the neighborhood repairing doors that were vandalized from burglaries in the area. He was thoroughly investigated and cleared, but that phase of the investigation took days and days of valuable time.

In the first two weeks alone, detectives looked into numerous complaints from girlfriends turning on their ex-boyfriends as possible offenders to thieves robbing railroad boxcars. It takes time to take the report and more time to find an offender on the street. Most of these guys with criminal histories turn and walk the other way when they see a squad car coming at them. It's not that they're guilty of something—its just instinct.

When detectives Britten and Palombo finally found Leroy Jameston, with the street name "Ugh," they discovered he had a record for sexual assault in the ALBA Homes area. Once Ugh/Jameston found out the police were looking at him for the Ruth Lezkowski murder he didn't hesitate to cooperate with them. The Leroy Jameston investigation took days of painstaking research, hours of time searching for his criminal records, getting him printed and swabbed. Eventually, he was cleared. Anything new brought fast and immediate attention from all the detectives at Area Four.

~~~~

"Area Four Violent Crimes, this is Evans. How can I help you?" Evans said, answering the phone.

"This is John Madison. I'm a substitute teacher and I heard something in my classroom the other day about the Lezkowski murder," he said.

Evans shot up from his well-worn office chair and reached for the ballpoint pen, he always carried in his left breast pocket. "What do you have?"

"I was assigned as a substitute at Crane High School to teach a law course, yesterday. Near the end of the day during sixth period, the class was discussing penalties of crimes and neighborhood unrest. A student brings up the subject of unrest around the hospital area and the Taylor Street area because of the killing of that medical student. I asked him, you mean the Ruth Lezkowski case? He says, 'Yeah that one.' At this point, another student, who was sitting in the second row from the window, stated that he had a run-in with the police and had spent some time in the Audy Home for vandalism. Then he says, 'I know how it happened, she was raped first,' he said. Then the bell rang as the student was mentioning something about the keys to her car. However, I couldn't hear the rest of it because of the noise, everyone was rushing to get to their next class."

The keys to Lezkowski's car were never found and police spent hours and hours trying to determine where they might be. This information was never released to the press. It caught Evans' attention like an electrical shock raising the hair on the back of his neck.

Crane High School is a four-year public school located on the near Westside on Jackson Boulevard. It opened in 1890, but it was renamed Richard T. Crane High School in 1903 when it moved to its present location on Jackson. It was all male until it went co-ed in 1954; that's when the school de-emphasized manual training. However, it continued to offer classes in mechanics and trade skills. For years it was one of the pride-and-joy schools of the Chicago Public School system. It shared space with Crane College, the first Junior College in Chicago, from 1911 to 1969, until the College moved out and became Malcolm X College. Scores of successful people are part of the school's notable alumni including: George Halas, the famous Chicago Bears player, coach and NFL pioneer and Berle Adams, the music executive and founder of Mercury Records.

Evans' interest was also piqued by the mere mention of the Audy Home. Detectives over the years have solved hundreds of cases from information that was developed from juveniles being held in the Audy Home.

~~~~

Chicago is the first City in the world to establish a Juvenile Court. In 1899, a movement was started to transform the maltreatment of children by abolishing child labor, establishing educational programs, creating playgrounds and strengthening family life for immigrants. The women of Hull House and the all-male Chicago Bar Association, successfully passed legislation to remove children from adult jails and adult poorhouses. The biggest dilemma was where to house these children while awaiting trial. At first, the boys were held in a cottage and stable, and the girls were held in an annex of the Harrison Street Police Station. By 1907, reformers built a new courthouse and established a facility that separated delinquent boys and girls and dependent children. The Audy Home officially housed 489 youngsters awaiting adjudication or trial in adult criminal court. For years the Audy Home has been plagued by overcrowding and economic distress as well as challenges of appropriate programming, punishment and safety concerns. Some things never seem to change in Chicago.

~~~~

Evans asked John Madison if they could meet at Crane High School this afternoon.

"What time?" asked Madison.

"When does sixth period begin?" asked Evans.

"12:30."

"How soon can you get there?"

"Twenty minutes."

"See you at the principal's office." Evans motioned to Scholl to get a move on and Scholl was two steps behind him as they ran out the door.

~~~~

Introductions were made and they proceeded to Room 111 where the sixth period law class met. However, when they got into the classroom, the student of interest was not there. The class was stopped and Madison asked the class if they remembered him from yesterday and they all acknowledged that they did. When asked if they remembered the conversation about the Lezkowski homicide several students raised their hands.

A female student, said she thought it was a student named Paul Barkley, another person said she knew Paul Barkley and it wasn't him. John Madison agreed saying, "That's not him."

As Evans and Scholl were leaving, a security guard, Ernie Waters, told them that there was a gang fight in the school earlier that day and there was a lot of confusion and most of the students were extremely afraid. Quite a few of them were cutting afternoon classes and leaving the building because of this fear. "Me and some of the other security guards have certain students we can talk to. We'll see if we can help you identify the student you're interested in."

Evans handed him his card, thanked him for his help and then they headed back to Area Four with a renewed glimmer of hope that something might come of this information.

~~~~

Detective Aldo Palombo looked up from his desk at Area Four Violent Crimes and watched as a woman walked in who seemed out place. "Can I help you?"

"Yes, I'm Dr. Mary Rider. I work at the H.M.O. Clinic on West Harrison. I was at Rush this morning and noticed this pinned to the bulletin board outside the medical library where Ruth Lezkowski used to study a lot. Actually, I noticed it right after the murder but it just occurred to me that it might have some value to your investigation."

"What is it?" asked Palombo.

"It's a poem that was written on this manila folder," she said, as she handed it over to Palombo.

He picked it up by pinching his thumb and forefinger of his right hand on its corner and placed it on the desk. He opened it with the tip of his pen. The handwriting read:

> "For her, Ruth Lezkowski.
> A memory forever.
> The sunsets we worship, the faces we love.
> She sleeps in beauty amongst the flowers;
> Sunlight and stars for a crown."

Puzzled, Palombo asked, "When did you find this?"

"On October 19th right after she was killed. I should have said something earlier but it didn't dawn on me. I got to thinking this may be something, so I brought it here," she said.

Palombo took out a pair latex gloves, picked up the folder, placed it in an evidence bag, tagged it and asked,

"Do have any idea who wrote this?"

Dr. Rider shook her head and said, "I have no idea. I hope it helps."

"Thanks, we'll process this for prints and I'll let you know if it leads to anything."

Dr. Rider left and Palombo looked down at his notes where he wrote the words from the poem for his supplementary report and shook his head and said "Strange ... fucking strange. Only in Chicago."

~~~~

Michaels was sitting at his desk turning his new mobile phone around in his hands as he was studying it. The Motorola DyanTAC, 8000X was referred to as the "brick." It weighed a little more than a pound. Phil Rivers gave it to him with a stern warning not to abuse it, because it cost more than a dollar a minute to talk. The phone had been on the market for a little more than a year and it cost $3,500.00. It took ten hours to charge the battery for 30 minutes of talk time. It could be programmed to hold 30 phone numbers and it had a screen that showed the number of anyone calling the phone. *Amazing*, Michaels thought, but he was old school, and he kept a small black leather-bound phonebook in his pocket. Every time he got a new source of information, he would not only put their phone number in the book but also the name of a husband or wife and children, if they had any. He had great sources and he worked hard to gain their confidence. When calling one, he would look at the book and ask how the kids were doing in school or how the wife was. It put people at ease and made them talk more freely.

Michaels was thinking this "brick" is going to change the way people communicate and it could change the world. That's when his desk phone rang.

"News ... Michaels."

"Hey, you dat guy who works for Ron Magers?" the voice asked.

Michaels smiled. "Yeah, dat be me."

"I know who kilt that white nurse up by the tracks."

Michaels straightened up. "What's your name?"

"I wants the money."

"We don't pay for information," Michaels said.

"I means the reward money, the $25,000."

"I can see what I can do about that. Let's talk, what's your name?"

"I'll meet you at the ALBA Homes Community Center. You know where dat be?" he asked.

"Yeah, I'll be driving a black, four door Ford. How do I recognize you?"

"You be there in an hour I'll finds you," he said as he hung up.

Longhini, looked concerned, "Who's that?"

Some guy said he talked to someone who said he killed Lezkowski. I'm going to meet him over at ALBA.

"Are you nuts? Remember what happened to you two weeks ago when you got shot at, in Cabrini-Green?"

Michaels had hooked up with two tactical officers, known as the "Ski Patrol" from the 18th District investigating a "T's and Blues" drug operation at the Green. A chase ensued and they were shot at.

The "Ski Patrol" consisted of two Polish Police Officers who partnered together for the last seven years. Duane Wantuck was six feet, four inches tall, muscular like a body builder, shoulders erect and straight. He walked with confidence. His blue eyes were engaging and his smile was trusting.

Steve Rakoczy was a little shorter, six feet, two inches tall. His military style haircut made his face look full. His brown eyes constantly searched his surroundings. He seemed to have nervous energy and he didn't like to sit still for long. They were both Catholic. They were both dedicated police officers that cared about the community they served.

Cabrini-Green was considered the worst of the Chicago Housing Authorities properties. It was located on prime real estate on the near North-side, a short walk from the fabled Rush Street area with all its fine restaurants, nightclubs and bars.

To the police Cabrini-Green's geographical boundaries seemed endless. It was bordered by Clybourne Avenue and Halsted Street on the north, Chicago Avenue on the south, North Larabee Street on the west and Hudson Street on the east. It was divided into ten sections with 3600 midsize and high-rise apartment buildings that were either red brick exteriors or poured white concrete exteriors. By 1962 Cabrini-Green housed 15,000 residents. Different violent street gangs ran competing drug operations throughout the entire complex. Crime and gang violence made it the hottest crime spot in the 18th District. Cabrini-Green became a worse slum than the one it was built to replace.

Mayor Jane Byrne moved into Cabrini Green in 1981. It was viewed as a publicity stunt to help downplay the violence of everyday life. She lived there officially for three weeks but in reality, she only spent three nights there.

"You know, Peter, we can't solve this murder. We can't fingerprint people and shit like that."

"Yeah, I know. I'm just going to go talk to this guy and I might be able to bargain some information at Area Four for some future exclusives," Michaels said.

"You're nuts!"

"Yeah, I know. See ya later."

~~~~

Michaels was waiting in his car in front of the ALBA Homes Community Center when someone rapped on his window. David Marteen slid onto the passenger seat. He was dressed in a brown wool coat, dirty blue jeans with a Chicago Bears woolen stocking cap on his head. He smelled like reefer and some other odor that Michaels couldn't decipher, but it triggered a gag reflex.

"Whatcha got?" Michaels asked.

"What about the 25 grand?"

"I'll see what I can do, maybe hook you up with one of the detectives and work something out for you. First I've got to know what you know. What's your name?"

"I be David Marteen. I was walking down Ashland with my buddy, Roberto Grimes, and we stopped to talk to this dude, called 'Big Dog.' As we was talking, these two other black dudes come walkin' outta the gangway next to the building. One of them was carrying this long cardboard box, you know. He asks me if any cars are coming. I look around and says, No. I don't know this motherfucker at all, man. He turns to his buddy and says, 'He mustn't know about me—that I'm the one who killed that girl on the tracks.' Swear to God man, I say to myself man, 'shit.' Then I notice he had a shotgun in that fuckin' box. He wanted to know if any cars were around cuz he was fittin' to rob a beer truck that was parked down the street. I just wanted to git my ass outta there," Marteen said.

"I don't blame you. Give me your phone number and Roberto's. I will be in touch or one of the detectives would love to hear about this, I'm sure. I'll ask about the reward money," Michaels told him.

They shook hands and David Marteen got out of the car, but the scent of his presence lingered like the smell of rotten eggs. Despite the chilly November temperature, Michaels rolled down his window as he headed toward Area Four. It was a little more than a mile away.

~~~~

As Michaels entered Area Four Violent Crimes, Detectives Evans and Scholl looked up and noticed him. Evans said, "Hey isn't that that prick Peter Michaels from Channel 6?"

"He isn't that bad, a lot of coppers like him. He does a lot of good stories about the police," Scholl said.

Some Chicago police officers hated Michaels' guts. They viewed him as the enemy because of a weeklong report he did on police brutality. Several years ago, Michaels and the Unit-6 Investigative Team did a scathing series of stories on officers who had at least three complaints of police brutality filed against them.

Karen Smothers was a fairly new hire into the Investigative Unit. She was young, petite and determined, a dynamo on wheels. She formed a group of college students to review every civil rights violation case that named Chicago Police Officers in the Northern District of Illinois' Federal Court. She was so organized, her notes so detailed and cross-referenced, that she had them color-coded. In the end, the team identified 147 officers with multiple charges.

The series shook the city and the Police Department. The new mayoral candidate, Harold Washington, used the stories as one of his three campaign platforms to defeat incumbent Mayor Jane Byrne.

To make matters worse, the reports won numerous local and national journalism awards, including the prestigious Robert F. Kennedy Grand Prize. When Ethel Kennedy presented Michaels with the hand-carved brass statue at her home in McLain, Virginia she told him it was the first time the Grand Prize was ever given to a television reporter.

The station was proud as a peacock and many police officers were pissed as hell.

"Is Commander Maurer in?" Michaels asked.

Pimping him, Evans asked, "Who's asking?"

"Peter Michaels, Channel 6."

"I'll check," said Evans.

A few minutes later, Michaels walked into Commander Maurer's office and told him about his meeting with David Marteen.

# CHAPTER 10

"I told you he wasn't a prick," said Scholl as he and Evans were exiting Maurer's office with the information that Peter Michaels had just provided the Commander.

"The jury is still out on that," said Evans as he reached for the phone to call the sergeant in charge of the 12th District "Tact Team." Tact (stands for Tactical) teams respond to violent crimes or drug-related offenses committed in their districts. They worked closely with other specialized units like Gang Crimes and Narcotics. The officers were generally young, aggressive and pretty smart. They always dressed in plain clothes, like leather jackets, baseball caps, blue jeans and guns.

When the sergeant answered the phone, Evans asked him to check around to see if any of his teams knew anything about a person on the street called "Big Dog."

~~~~

Evans was at his desk, re-reading his notes on the Crane High School student who had mentioned something about knowing the victim's car keys were missing and that she had been raped. It was one of the few hopeful leads they were looking into.

He answered his phone on the third ring and the 12th District Tact Sergeant said one of his guys think "Big Dog" may be Billy Hearns, who lives in the ALBA projects; and he's got a record. He gave Evans the last known address and they hung up.

Evans and Scholl wasted no time driving over to ALBA Homes. They walked up to the eighth floor of the 114th Street building. The elevator didn't work, no big surprise. Nothing seemed to work in these buildings. When they got to 808, Evans knocked on the door, hard "Chicago Police."

Billy Hearns answered the door and invited them in.

The apartment was in disrepair and dirty. The off white walls looked gray, not like a battleship, lighter, and there was black mold in the corners and on the ceiling above. Not a piece of furniture matched, it looked typical of many of the apartments in the projects. CHA residents seemed to struggle. He offered them a seat but they declined. This wouldn't take long.

"You, 'Big Dog?'" Evans asked.

"Yeah, I'm the oldest of four, so I guess that name just got stuck on me," he responded.

"David Marteen said you may know something about that woman who got murdered up by the tracks," Evans stated this instead of asking it as a question.

Big Dog/Hearns said he heard the same thing that Marteen was talking about it. "I don't believe any of it," he said.

"Why not?"

"It be bullshit, some dude just talking shit, man." Hearns said.

"You know the guy with the shotgun, the one who was ready to rob that Budweiser truck driver?" Evans asked.

"I think the dude with the shotgun is somebody named Jamaal Murray. I don't know him. Don't know where he stays and I ain't never met him before," he said.

Evans handed Big Dog/Hearns his card and said, "If you remember anything or find something else out, give me a call."

~~~~

When Evans and Scholl got back to Area Four Violent Crimes, he immediately entered Jamaal Murray's name into the "Alpha" file, but nothing came up, not even his name. He also tried the Youth Division Records, but once again nothing popped up.

Evans and Scholl agreed that they should run down this Marteen character and Roberto Grimes the next day and re-interview them. It was the end of another long, back to square one, frustrating day.

~~~~

Michaels was working the phones when the patrol officer called and told him about the lack of police officers available to respond to calls all over the City but in particular, in the11th and 12th Districts.

"You got the documents?" Michaels asked.

"Yeah, I got about 12 RAPs right now. I've got guys gathering others."

"What's a RAP?"

"They're called Radio Assignments Pending reports. Every page on every report states 'No Police Available,'" said the unnamed caller.

Michaels just heard the name of his new series, *No Police Available.* "We could make this a very big story in a couple of weeks," he said.

"You should bring a cameraman around as the third watch moves out tonight on the street. You'll see what I am talking about. Man they are all one-man cars on every shift, I'm not shitting you."

"I'll go tonight and start shooting. I'm trusting you. I dropped a couple of other things we're working on because this sounds like it could really be good."

"Get the pictures, you'll see and I'll call you tomorrow."

Michaels gave him his new "brick" phone number in case he was out of the office and promised he would get video, starting with the third watch tonight.

~~~~

Michaels requested Paul Nagaro for his "shooter"—a common television term for a cameraman. Nagaro is an Emmy-winning photojournalist. He was Japanese, about five feet, eleven inches tall, smooth black hair combed back, cut slightly over his ears, stylish. He was a very sharp dresser, designer jeans and every pair of tennis shoes he wore looked like they just came out of the box brand new, never scuffed. More importantly, he had a keen eye; he sensed action developing before it actually happened. He never seemed to miss the "money" shot. He's good—very good.

~~~~

The Area Four Headquarters building was a two-story black cinder-block facility. The five foot by eight foot second floor windows faced Harrison Street looking out over the Eisenhower Expressway. Up the stairs to the left took you to the Detectives offices on the second floor. Violent Crimes takes the area on the right and Property Crimes Detectives have the middle open area that is filled with old metal desks and broken down office chairs. No matter where you sat if you were at a desk, the view was the person sitting right across from you and sometimes that's not a pretty sight. It wasn't an aesthetically pleasant working environment but it was a remarkably busy place.

When you walk into the building through the revolving front doors you go straight to the 11th District Desk Sergeant. The District Commander's office was directly to the left and all the administrative staffs' offices are housed right behind his office. Behind the front desk was the Patrol Officers' squad room, where all watch roll calls were held. All the officers' lockers and showers were in the basement, along with a gun range and holding-cells for those arrested.

The blue and white patrol cars are decorated with the Chicago star on the front doors and the mantra "We Serve and Protect" on the rear fenders. They're parked in an adjacent lot that only exits onto Harrison Street.

As the third watch blue and white patrol cars were pulling out, Michaels and Nagaro were walking west toward the main entrance of the 11th District on Harrison Street. Nagaro, with the camera on his shoulder, was rolling video as the cars exited the lot. One car stopped and the driver started messing with the computer mounted on the dash and then shuffled some paperwork. Nagaro was shooting away until the driver finally stopped his busy-work and turned right on Harrison Street.

In a few short minutes Michaels had enough video to support a three-part investigative series. Though he would shoot more video and interviews in the next few days, he knew the most important part of this story would be the official police documents and the RAP reports that he was hoping to get his hands on by tomorrow afternoon.

# CHAPTER 11

D etective Aldo Palombo walked through the revolving door of Area Four Violent Crimes. It was cold for early November. His nose was running, his ears were cold and his hands were numb. Palombo shook the rain off his trench coat and hung it on the coat-rack with an old bent wire hanger. Walking to his battle scarred dented gray metal desk, he could feel the pain in his arthritic right hip flare up. He needed a hot cup of coffee.

"Hey Palombo, what the fuck are you going to do when it really gets cold? It's not even winter yet!" Tom Britten, his partner, joked as he put a quarter into the coffee kitty.

Sergeant Swartz walked over to their desks and handed them an incident report of a robbery with violent behavior, saying, "This was red-flagged this morning. It was one of the cases that occurred in the area of the Lezkowski homicide on October 17th and 18th."

"What is it?" asked Britten.

"Some 19-year-old kid said three black guys hijacked his car and beat him up, near 18th Street and Canal," responded Sergeant Swartz, "Around the time Lezkowski was murdered."

Britten grabbed the file, read the incident report and glanced at Palombo, "Let's go talk to this kid. He lives on South Carpenter in 'Little Italy.' This looks really good."

~~~~

Mary Dilotti answered the door and invited detectives Palombo and Britten in after they told her they were here to investigate the hijacking of her car on the night of 17th/18th of October. She called her son, Dante. He was about six feet tall, blue eyes, black hair, olive complexion and fairly muscular. Any signs of facial injuries from three weeks ago had disappeared.

"Tell us what happened when you were attacked," Palombo said.

He began by telling the detectives that, "I was at a party around the corner at a friend's house on Taylor Street on October 17th. I got there around midnight and then me and my buddy Anthony left the party around two and we walked around the neighborhood. I came home and took my ma's car without her permission. Me and Anthony wanted something to eat so we thought we would drive over to Lawrence's."

Lawrence's Fish and Shrimp was open 24 hours a day, seven days a week. It had been in business for more than 25 years and was a favorite to Chicagoans all around the city. Its dining area was small and worn, but it's an atmosphere that somehow seems special. Most people got their fish and shrimp to go in a bag with fries. The greasy combination was quickly absorbed staining the paper bag a rich ebony color. Most patrons grabbed plenty of napkins and took their food outside and ate in their cars in the parking lot that offered a great view of downtown. It was a Chicago thing. It was located on the 2400 block of Canal Street, not that far from the Lezkowski homicide scene.

But Dante said they never got to Lawrence's because they were attacked at a stoplight at 18th and Canal.

"This one guy reaches in the car and hits me in the back of the head so hard I hit my face on the steering wheel," Dante Dilotti said.

"Can you describe them?" asked Palombo.

"Not really. It was dark and it happened fast. I get outta my car and we start fighting. My car disappeared and I'm bleeding, so I walk home to tell my mom. She called the police and then she took me to Cabrini hospital."

"Do you mind coming over to Area Four to look at photos of some people known to frequent that area?" Palombo asked. "What's your buddy's name?"

"An-tin-nee. He lives around the corner on Taylor," he said.

"How do you spell that?"

"You know, An-tin-nee, A-N-T-H-O-N-Y," Dilotti responded.

Palombo shook his head "Got his phone number?"

"Yeah." He gave it to them from memory.

They called Benetti, identified themselves and asked him to come down to Area Four and look at some photos. He agreed, and they told him, they would be by shortly to collect him.

"Mrs. Dilotti we'll bring your son back when we're finished." The three of them left to get Anthony and headed over to Area Four Violent Crimes.

~~~~

Anthony Benetti was a year older than Dilotti and looked like he could be his brother. Same build, same dark hair, same olive complexion but brown eyes.

They put Dante Dilotti in a typical drab interview room, in need of fresh paint. It had a metal desk and straight back chairs. Britten gave him a stack of the mug shot books that were filled with page after page of known gang members in Area Four to look over.

They placed Anthony Benetti in another room. If you didn't know they were in different rooms, you could picture them with the same drab walls, the same beat up metal table and three old straight back chairs. The main thing was to keep the two separated and see if their stories differed. They did.

Benetti said, "I was at the same party off Taylor Street, but I don't know what time Dante left to get his mom's car. I can't remember what time he got back. I think we left the party around 5:30 to get something to eat." Anthony leaned back and looked up at the ceiling, thinking with a strained look on his face. "We was at a stoplight and tree black dudes come up and they hit Dante in the head. He gets out of the car and they start fighting. So I took the car while they was going at it and parked it on Halsted Street and I goes home."

Palombo looked at Britten and they got up and left the room. They went to Sergeant Swartz's office and told him there were too many inconsistencies in Dilotti's statement.

"Guess what he was wearing? Reebok gym shoes, the same brand of shoe that made the footprint found on Ruth Lezkowski's chest."

"Go back at the kid."

~~~~

Dilotti looked up from the mug shot book he was examining when Palombo and Britten re-entered the room.

"When you were walking around the neighborhood at 2:30 did you notice anyone or anything unusual?" Britten asked.

"Yeah, I saw some squad cars and a woman told me that a nurse had been raped and murdered in the neighborhood," he said.

"We are also investigating the Ruth Lezkowski homicide," Britten told Dilotti. "And what you just told us makes you a suspect. You have the right to remain silent. Anything you say may and can be used against you in a court of law. You have the right to an attorney. If you can't afford an attorney, one will be appointed for you. Do you understand your rights?"

Dilotti started shaking and was on the verge of tears. They left him in utter shock when they exited the room.

~~~~

"I'm going to remind you of your Constitutional rights again, Dante," said Palombo when they re-entered the room. After he Mirandized him again, Palombo sat back in his chair. "There are too many inconsistencies in your story for the night of October 18th. Your description of the robbery sounds way too improbable. It's not believable. So tell me what really happened."

I swear to God, I had nothing to do with that murder. I lied. I was scared to death. I took my ma's car without her permission and I totaled it," Dilotti said.

"So what happened?'

"I was at the party like I said. I met this cute girl, Maria Soratini. She was leaving at about 2:30 and I asked her if I could come over to her house. She said yes but she lived in Berwyn. She left, so I went and took my ma's car outta the garage and drove out to Berwyn."

Berwyn is a city about 11 miles west of Chicago. It's in the news often because of political corruption and shady police scandals. Democrats totally controlled the city. In its last election there were only four Republican votes cast.

"I got into this accident at 18th and Ridgeland, Dilotti said. "I hit this car. I wasn't wearing my seatbelt and went through my windshield. That's how I got injured. The car was totaled. I was really scared. There were some people in the other car; I told them I was going for help but I ran from the scene. That's the truth," he said.

"How'd you get home?"

"I went by a friend's house and woke him up and he drove me home," he said. "When I got home I made up this robbery story because I was afraid to tell my mom what really happened. She called the police. I went to the hospital and now I am dealing with this crap."

"What in the world were you thinking? You can't leave the scene of an accident, especially if there were injuries involved. You can go to jail for that." Palombo said.

"I know. I was scared man."

"I have a son your age. If he did something like that I'd kick his ass."

"I know. It was stupid but it's just me and my ma. I knew she'd be disappointed in me."

Palombo shook his head, thinking he needed to talk to his son about doing stupid things. "Okay. Then what happened?"

"On Sunday morning on the 19th, the Berwyn Police called my mother and told her the car was totaled. That's when I confessed to her and told her I was really scared and I was afraid of going to jail for making a false police report. She went along with my story then we recovered the car."

~~~~

Detective Britten confirmed with the Berwyn Police that the accident occurred that morning. They issued Dilotti three citations, one for speeding, one for running a red light and one for leaving the scene of an accident. They also said they were surprised the car could be driven because it had been so badly damaged, but the mother came and picked it up Sunday afternoon. His court date was scheduled for November 19th.

They also indicated that he went through the windshield and was badly injured.

"What kind of injuries did he have?" Britten asked the Berwyn desk sergeant.

"There was blood on the dashboard and some on the window where he hit it. That little bastard must have a hard head. But we don't really know because he left the scene. We are going to throw the book at him for that."

"Yeah, that wasn't very smart. The kid is scared shitless."

"Yeah, he told the people in the other car he would be right back but he never came back."

"Well he may be in trouble with you guys but it looks like he wasn't involved in our homicide," Britten said.

~~~~

Palombo winched in pain. His hip was killing him. He limped back to Dilotti's room and asked him if he would agree to take a polygraph test. He said he would do anything he could to help in the Lezkowski homicide investigation. Palombo made the arrangements for the polygraph that was administered an hour later. In the opinion of the test administrator Dilotti "was truthful and had no knowledge of and did not participate in the Lezkowski homicide." Dilotti was fingerprinted in the district lockup and his prints were hand-carried to the Identification Section. Palombo asked him if they could take his Reeboks and he voluntarily took them off and gave them to Palombo. The shoes were put in an evidence bag, inventoried and sent to the Crime Lab.

It took Detectives Palombo and Britten several hours to verify Dilotti's story. They found Maria Soratini and she told them that she did invite Dante to her house but he never showed. She didn't know why.

A patrol car took the relieved boys home and they were told not to leave town, that if detectives Palombo and Britten needed anything else they would be in touch.

~~~~

"News ... Michaels."

"I saw you at the 11th last night. That was me who stopped and fiddled with my computer and ticket book," the whistleblower cop said.

"Yeah, that gave us some interesting video. I thought that may have been you," Michaels replied.

"I hope you didn't shoot my face."

"Don't worry they'll never see your face. What you got for me?"

"I've got about two dozen more RAP reports. Is that enough?"

The newsroom was buzzing with activity as show producers were making last minute checks with talent and their scripts.

Michaels was trying to eliminate any background noise because he didn't want to spook his new source.

"In situations like this you can never have enough but this makes for a really good story. So are you going to tell me what your name is and how I can get in touch with you? We've got to get moving on this."

"I'm Officer Rick McDonnell. Here's my home number, but I'm hardly ever there. I'll keep calling you and I'll drop these reports off at your front lobby security desk."

"Thanks."

Michaels looked over at Longhini and said, "'No Police Available' sounds like a very good title to a very bad situation. I wouldn't want to be in a one-man car patrolling in Lawndale. That's some dangerous shit. Let's go talk to the boss. This is going to be a great one."

# CHAPTER 12

L t. David Copelin motioned for Sergeant Swartz to follow him into his office. Swartz had just hung up the phone with the Commander of the Training Academy. Copelin set his glass of iced tea on his desk, emptied the ashtray, and reached for his cigarettes. "What do we have? Is this getting away from us."

"These guys are wearing out their shoes and everything seems to come apart, but we still have the Crane High School student who talked about the rape and the car keys. Oh! And I got a new lead from the hospital this morning. I just got off the phone with Commander Milton at the Academy. I requested 20 cadets for another grid-search of the homicide scene. I want them to go inch-by-inch through the area again looking for her car keys. We may have missed something," said Swartz.

"We had three more homicides reported last night," Copelin said. "We're busier than one-armed paperhangers. Shit, that's seven shootings in the 11th and 12th Districts alone in the last 11 days. What's the new thing from the hospital?"

"A supervisor called and said some weirdo who works there always disappears after he signs in and he hangs out where the medical students study," said Swartz. "I'll give that to Evans and Scholl."

"You know how we are going to solve this thing don't you?" asked Copelin.

"Yep! We're going to pinch someone, somewhere, sometime and he's going to lead us to these killers," responded Swartz.

"Let's just hope it happens sooner rather than later. It's already November 11$^{th}$ and we are no closer to solving this thing than we were a month ago," replied Copelin.

"Tell me about it."

~~~~

Evans was shaking his head and thinking about the blowout he had with his wife before he left for work. He was stirring two spoons of sugar into his black coffee when Swartz walked up to him.

"Where's Scholl?"

"He'll be here in a few. He had to drop his daughter off at school today. What's up?"

"Got some weirdo at Rush, who caught the attention of his supervisor. It's worth a visit."

~~~~

Evans and Scholl walked into the Housekeeping Department of Rush-Presbyterian-St. Luke's Hospital and located Supervisor Kenneth Chandler and introduced themselves.

Chandler was old fashioned. On the wall in front of his desk next to the door, he had two white writing boards. One had the current month's work schedule and the other had next month's. He scribbled his notes with red, green and black felt pens. He was the only one who could decipher his logs.

"We have this guy working in housekeeping, Rashad Bishop. He's bad news, a real discipline problem. He's employed as a specialist and he used to be a security guard. We can never find him. He clocks in and then disappears. His shift is 1600-0030 hours. Bishop attends Martin Luther King University studying to be a legal assistant. He normally brings a backpack with books to work with him. Once he gets here, his supervisors can never find him. We don't know if he studies in the library that the medical students use or not. Our time clock is just ten feet from the Canteen where they get their coffee. Bishop drives a black van and parks either at the ground level lot just east of Ashland or he parks where Ruth Lezkowski parked in the multi-story garage.

"He came under investigation last year when one of the nurses started receiving obscene phone calls. The nurse told security that she recognized Bishop's voice. She said that Bishop told her he wanted her "to walk on his dick with high heels."

Detective Scholl's eyes popped open in total surprise and he shook his head, "He said what? This guy sounds like a real piece of work."

"We think he's on drugs," Chandler said. "On October 16th, I saw him walking out of the Cancer Research Center at 1710 West Harrison. I thought that was very unusual because he didn't work that day. We can't find him when he's scheduled to work and he's out there walking around by the hospital when he's off. It doesn't make sense. Then he calls in on the 18th and says he'll be late for work. Since he missed several days the week before he was terminated when he reported for work. He always wore white gym shoes."

"Do you know the brand?" asked Evans.

"Yes, I think they were Rebooks, white high tops," Chandler said.

"What's Bishop look like?" asked Evans.

"He's male, black, six feet, one inch tall, black hair in curls. He has a full beard and he's light complected. The reason we think he's on drugs is because some days he acts really weird and other days he seems normal," Chandler said.

Geraldine Tyson, the other supervisor said, "Bishop bothers nurses in the hospital all the time. He's always been a discipline problem and I think he's on drugs or something."

"If you guys think of anything else, give us a call," said Evans.

They turned and walked out of the office and Scholl looked at Evans and said, "This guy has to be a total jag-off."

~~~~

Evans got a hit immediately after he put Bishop's name in the Alpha file. He had an I.R. number and his record showed he had an UUW (Unlawful Use of a Weapon) arrest in 1982. He was pinched for Possession of Marijuana in 1985.

Every time someone is arrested, they are assigned an I.R. number that is an identification number. It is used as a point of reference in a criminal history. A new I.R. is assigned with every new arrest.

Evans made a note to recheck where Bishop's van was parked on the night of the Lezkowski homicide, because he did park near her in the multi-level garage.

Evans said to Palombo, "Did you see those booklets laying around the study areas at the hospital? They list every medical student's name, phone number, address and apartment number. That's not too safe."

"I also saw them in some hallways. Anyone working or walking around the hospital can have access to that information."

Sergeant Swartz walked up to Evans' desk and handed him a report of a woman living near the hospital complaining of being harassed numerous times.

"Why don't you guys go re-interview her and see if this Bishop is the one bothering her?"

~~~~

Kathleen Broderick let them into her new apartment. She was very nervous, scared really. She used to live in a gated community, but that apparently did not stop thieves from trying to break into apartments. Her complex at 1111 South Laffin had one-story apartments attached to townhouses. On the north end of the complex, there was a guard station that was normally manned by one guard. A wrought iron seven-foot fence wrapped around the entire complex.

Broderick told them, "I received a couple of phone calls on November 6th and each time I answered, the caller hung up. I thought that was strange. A short time later, I hear a knock on the door. I look out the peephole I see this black guy standing there asking for Craig."

"Can you describe him?" asked Evans.

"He was black, about 20 to 25 years old, he had long hair. It looked like it was pulled back in a ponytail. I can't remember if he had on sunglasses or not. He asked for Craig several times, and I said there's nobody here by that name, and he just turned around and walked away."

"Any thing else?"

"Yeah, so the next day when I got home, my roommate discovered that the front door had been pried open so I call the police. They come by and report the crime as a damage to property. I'm guessing the only reason they came by was because we are so close to the hospital." She was twisting her hands nervously and put her right hand to her chin. "The patrol officers talked to the carpenter who was repairing the door and he told them that he had repaired five other doors in the complex in the last five days. I said, 'Oh shit!'"

The apartment was protected with a ringer type alarm but the alarm was not connected to the security station. When you entered the code of the apartment, a buzzer sounded.

"I moved the next day. You would think with all the security in that place it would be safe, but after I found out six places were broken into in six days. I said, 'fuck this' and found a new place. I called the number of that last detective I talked to. I wanted to let you guys know that I moved."

Evans showed Broderick the mug shots of Bishop, but she could not positively identify him, "I'm sorry; looking through the peephole gave me a distorted look."

~~~~

The Unit-6 Investigative office was down the hall from the main newsroom at WMAC. The News Department took up the entire east portion of the 19th floor of the Merchandise Mart. NBC has been there from the time the Merchandise Mart opened its doors in 1930.

Often called the MART, it had 4,000,000 square feet of floor space. It was the single largest building in the United States until the Pentagon was built in Washington, D.C. in 1949.

Joseph Kennedy bought the Mart in 1945. It soon became the cornerstone of national conventions held in Chicago.

On January 7,1949, NBC started broadcasting live from their studios with two hours of programming a day. It now produces four hours a day of just news. Chicago is a very, very competitive news market.

~~~~

Longhini was slowly and methodically pulling on a strand of hair in deep thought reading a RAP report (Radio Assignment Pending) when Michaels walked into the office. He looked up. "How do you get these guys to give you this stuff? They are all still pissed at us for all the stories we do on the police department."

"It's my experience that the good coppers don't like to be around bad guys," Michaels said. "When we did the brutality thing, some of those guys just hated me but the command guys loved it. They don't want to be answering for those few officers who abuse their power.

I've never been anti-police. I'm all for the police. I'm just not for the few assholes that ruin it for everybody else."

"We should meet with Rivers and tell him we can have this ready by next week. Man, this shit is going to piss them off again. In the 37 RAPs we have, these guys are not able to respond to almost 425 calls; and this is just two districts," Longhini said.

"I think we got enough for a three-part series, 'No Police Available.' What a great title. It writes itself. Rivers may want to do some advertising on this and we need to make a list of whom we can talk to. We should tell him we can have it together within a week," Michaels said.

# CHAPTER 13

S ergeant Swartz was on the phone with Lt. Bruce Wayne from the Cook County Jail Work-Release Program. Lt. Wayne took a lot of abuse because of his name. Everyone at the Jail called him "Batman" but he looked nothing like the Marvel comic book hero. He was short, bald and almost blind. He wore thick black-rimmed glasses that magnified his eyes. "Batman" he was not.

Swartz was setting up a tedious assignment for detectives Palombo and Britten to examine the records of all 1,800 prisoners in the Work Release Program. He would then do the same with the Salvation Army's prison program. It would take days of time-consuming research, but Swartz was convinced that it was going to take this kind of old-fashioned police work to solve this case.

~~~~

The Cook County Jail is the largest single jail site in the United States. Its concrete 20-foot high walls with concertina wire spans 96 acres. It houses 10,000 prisoners, employs 3,900 law enforcement officials and 7,000 civilian employees. The jail is located at 2700 South California Avenue. It sits behind the George N. Leighton Criminal Court Building; commonly known as 26th Street and the 14-story Cook County's State's Attorney's Offices, which employs 800 assistant state's attorneys. The jail has held notorious criminals like: Tony Accardo, the one-time head of the Chicago Mafia, Frank Nitti from the days of Al Capone, infamous Gang Leaders Jeff Forte and Larry Hoover, nurse killer Richard Speck and mass-murderer, John Wayne Gacy. It was one of three sites in Illinois where 67 prisoners were executed by the electric chair up until 1962. The jail had been investigated for failing to adequately protect its inmates from harm, failure to provide adequate suicide prevention, failure to provide sanitary environmental conditions and failure to provide adequate medical and mental health care. The Cook County Jail was not a fun place to be.

~~~~

If they were smokers, it would be a four-pack assignment. Palombo and Britten knew this was going to take a lot of painstaking work, but it was a good idea and it could lead to something, so they begrudgingly got in their car and drove the 15 minutes to the Cook County Jail.

Lt. Wayne was in charge of those sentenced to work release in Cook County. Palombo and Britten's mission was to determine if anyone on work release failed to return to the jail at their scheduled time, and those who were not in the jail on the night of October 17th and early morning hours of October 18th. They also wanted to know the persons in the program who lived near Ruth Lezkowski, near the murder scene, and if they had any listed relatives in these areas. Wayne gave them the names of 1,800 inmates in the Work- Release Program and Palombo and Britten started making their lists.

"Do any of these inmates have jobs in the area?" Britten asked.

They added to their workload by determining another list of anyone who worked in the area that Ruth Lezkowski was known to frequent, with special attention to anyone who worked near the hospital. Five hours later, they left for the Salvation Army's offices where they were going to do a similar search of the corrections program.

~~~~

Cook County, Illinois is second only in population to Los Angeles County. Los Angeles County is three times larger in square miles than Cook County. In 1986, more the 5,200,000 people lived in Cook County's 23 cities, 111 villages and one town. Cook County was more populated than 31 other states.

~~~~

The Salvation Army operates a Corrections Program for the state and the Federal Government. Catherine Ruthledge is the Program's

Director. The Salvation Army's program was different than Cook County's. Inmates in their program have already been released from the penitentiary. However, they have not yet completed their full sentences. The inmates are released into the Army's program to acclimate them back into society. An inmate is not allowed a liberty pass or to leave the facility for the first three months unless they are going to their place of employment. If an inmate has been there for longer than three months, they may visit relatives, but home sites must be approved by the Department of Corrections. "We do call the relative's home to make sure the inmate is there." Ruthledge said.

Palombo and Britten got a list of 45 more names of people who had passes or who worked on the night of October 17$^{th}$ and the morning of the 18$^{th}$.

~~~~

They then went to Metro Corrections Center at Lake and Clark Streets that offered a similar program as the Salvation Army's. The director was out and his secretary said she would get them a list of inmates who were out on the evening of the 17$^{th}$ and morning of the 18$^{th}$.

Palombo and Britten already had the names of 145 people they had to contact, and the names would be distributed to other detectives on other watches to help investigate their whereabouts.

~~~~

Detective William "Billy" Rogers was one of those detectives that liked to work the midnight watch because it gave him time during the day to golf whenever the weather permitted. Rodgers was five feet, eight inches tall, thin but with a little paunch. He had a full beard prematurely turning gray. He had happy lines on his forehead that made him look like he was always ready to smile. Rogers had three addictions: cigarettes, golf and solving puzzles or riddles.

Before leaving for home, Rogers was sitting in Sergeant Swartz's office, smoking the last cigarette he had in his pack. "Something's puzzling me about this Bauer guy" he said. He had spent a long time re-reading all of the supplementary reports from the Lezkowski homicide. He found some inconsistencies in Dr. Anthony Bauer's statements, compared to the computerized logs of his comings and goings on the night Ruth Lezkowski was killed.

"I gotta gut feeling that they may have been more than just friends. They're both from Springfield and knew each other a long time."

~~~~

Evans and Scholl went back to Rush-Presbyterian-St. Luke's Medical School and the home of Anthony Bauer. "Sorry to bother you again but we need to ask you some more questions."

Bauer shrugged. "Sure."

"Tell us again what happened on the 17th?"

"I talked with her two times that day. I don't recollect if I called her or she called me. She wanted to come over to my place and use the microwave to cook her dinner, which she generally brought from home. I told her that the dorm was being painted and it smelled, and that it wouldn't be a good idea. I didn't see or hear from her again until about 10 o'clock that night, when she came into Schweppe Study Hall. She left and came back a few minutes later and asked me to walk her to her car later, but I told her I was leaving shortly to go home. I left at 10:30, walked through the tunnel after being at school since five."

"Did you ever leave prior to that?" asked Evans.

"I don't think so. To the best of my recollection I never left the study hall."

The computerized access tapes that monitor and print out times of entering and leaving his dorm indicated that he entered the dorm twice: once at 10:00 o'clock and again at 10:27.

"Did you ever lend your identification card to anyone who might have used it to come and go into your dormitory? Did you ever give it to Ruth?"

"Nope. Lending your ID card around here is no - no. Ruth was a frequent visitor but I don't give my ID card to anyone."

"What was your relationship with Ruth, have you known her a long time?" asked Evans.

"I knew Ruth in high school. We had a slight rift a few years ago when we were trying to get into medical school," Bauer said. "Ruth and I received these booklets to study for the medical school's entrance exam and one time I didn't have mine with me and so I asked Ruth to borrow hers but she said 'no.' I was a little pissed at the time but it was no big deal. I didn't see much of her after that and I didn't even know she got into medical school until I saw her in class."

"Would you submit to a polygraph test?" asked Evans.

"Sure. When? I'd like to do it sooner rather than later," Bauer said.

"Let me see if we can set it up today."

~~~~

Detective Evans could not schedule it immediately but he told Bauer that they could do it tomorrow which was Sunday. Evans told Bauer to be ready at 8:30 in the morning and they would pick him up at the hospital.

Two hours later, Bauer called Evans and cancelled the lie detector test scheduled for Sunday morning. "I have this big pathology exam on Monday morning and I have to study for it."

"This guy is pissing me off. He has been avoiding us now for a week. He may be hiding something," Evans said to Scholl.

"He did say he had a relationship with her back when."

"Yeah. I don't like the way this feels."

"I don't know. Hey, what's going on at home?"

"Man, she's pissed I haven't taken a day off since Ruth was murdered. She's hot."

~~~~

Evans and Scholl went back to Rush Medical School and found Edward Radney at his dormitory.

"You passed your polygraph test with flying colors," Scholl said.

"Never thought I wouldn't, but interestingly, I just left Anthony about an hour ago, and he asked me about it," Radney said.

"Like what did he say?"

"He asked me the type of questions I was asked."

"Did he seem nervous?"

"Fidgety, maybe. I told him it was very up front and that it's right to the point."

"Anything else?"

"Yeah, he said, 'did they ask you if you killed Ruth?'"

"Did he appear nervous?"

"He said he didn't want to know any more questions and said that he was going to consult with a friend about whether or not to take the test."

~~~~

Scholl was sitting at his desk staring out into space, thinking about how Detective Billy Rogers' theory may turn into something with Anthony Bauer. He had not cooperated very much. No blood samples, no saliva samples, and now backing out of the lie detector test. His thoughts were interrupted by Evans' scream.

"I told you that Peter-fucking-Michaels is a prick! Look at this!" He thrust the Chicago Bugle on Scholl's desk.

The newspaper was open to an advertisement of Michaels' upcoming investigative report on "No Police Available."

"That son of a bitch never stops with this police department," Evans complained.

~~~~

Ron Magers was sitting at his desk reading Peter Michaels' script on "NO POLICE AVAILABLE" when Michaels and Longhini walked in. "Hey, this is good stuff. You are going to piss them off again Peter."

"I know. The coppers are coming out of the woodwork. Hundreds of police calls all across the city went unanswered today because the CPD does not have enough police officers on the street to respond to routine calls."

"How do you get these guys to give you these reports?"

"I don't know. You know these guys get frustrated. They hate working in one-man cars particularly at night in these high crime areas. They never know how far back up is. I've got dozens of these RAP reports."

"What does RAP mean?"

"Radio Assignment Report. They have to be filled out after every watch. My sources have been grabbing them on different watches. They're just pissed and I think nervous. These guys feel like they're in 'Harms Way' every watch. They're so shorthanded."

"How many coppers are in the department?"

"They're budgeted for 13,500 officers but I don't think they have 10,000 on the job. And once you consider officers on sick leave, officers on furlough and officers who are deskbound, it gets even worse on the streets."

"What are they saying to you?"

"I talked to John Ives. He's the District Commander in 12. He's a great guy and has to take the company line. He told me, 'All calls are prioritized in the order of importance' and all that crap. 'No emergency call is going unanswered' in his district. He sidestepped the issue of one-man cars saying, 'the department makes changes all the time but officers are doing a great job.' It's all bullshit." Michaels said.

"This is a great November Sweeps piece, Peter. The phones will be ringing off the hook after the ten tonight" Magers said.

"Yeah and the next time I go into Area Four I am going to catch a ration of shit."

"Oh well. It's not the first time for you."

# CHAPTER 14

On November 20th, Peter Michaels was delivering the last of his three-part series, "NO POLICE AVAILABLE" on the six o'clock news. It was an updated version of the ten o'clock report from the night before. Cops on patrol were ecstatic. They were as happy as could be that their story finally got out to the public. But the man waiting to take Michaels' head off in the Green Room, getting powdered-up, was steaming.

The Superintendent of the Chicago Police Department, Frank Wheatley, was sitting in the WMAC-TV News Studio waiting to do a live interview with Michaels. He was trembling. He was so angry. If he could, he would strangle Michaels with his bare hands on live television.

Wheatley was appointed superintendent less than a year ago. He was a light skinned Afro-American, with a thick bull neck that was developed years ago when he was an all-state high school football player. His five feet, nine inches of height, framed what was once a muscular body. He now had graying hair on the sides of his head but none on top. The four gold stars adorning his dress blue uniform glistened from the studio's key lights. He looked impressive and very angry.

Michaels was dressed in a dark blue Hart Schaffner Marx suit patterned with very fine thin vertical red lines, a white starched shirt, a red necktie and highly polished black Franco Vanucci oxford shoes. His favorite suit fit like a glove and gave him total confidence. He learned years ago that you can dress down when you do research and grunt work out in the field but when it came time to do the target interview, you had to look sharp to be sharp.

As Michaels' taped package with more incidents of "NO POLICE AVAILABLE" in the 11th District was coming to an end, he got off his seat next to Anchorman Ron Magers and walked over to the interview set that was designed for two people to sit face to face on comfortable chairs. They were separated by a dark mahogany coffee table while the interview was in progress. Michaels approached the set and stretched out his hand to shake with the Superintendent but he would have no part of that. *This is going to be good* Michaels thought, as his taped story ended, the floor manager cued Michaels to roving camera three.

"With us tonight is Superintendent of Police Frank Wheatley," Michaels said into the camera. "Superintendent, what is your reaction?"

Before the word "reaction" got out of Michaels' mouth, the Superintendent lashed out at him "You and this television station should be ashamed of airing these stories, scaring the citizens of this great city half to death. Your reporting is opening doors to criminals all over Chicago."

"Are the stories of 'NO POLICE AVAILABLE' untrue?"

"You have no right to report the strength of the Chicago Police Department."

"Is the department up to strength? Do you have enough manpower to cover the city properly?"

With this question, Wheatley clenched his fist. He was livid. His carotid arteries seemed like they were about to explode. His blood pressure was flaring and he blurted out, "We are answering every emergency call that comes into 911."

Michaels kept pressing, "What about the calls of a home invasion? Are you answering them?"

"We are doing the best that we can."

"Why has the department assigned so many one-man cars in high crime areas?"

"How the department determines the deployment of officers around the city is an internal and strategic plan that I can't discuss in public. Let me tell you something, Peter Michaels, if I catch anyone in my Department leaking information to you, in the future, I will personally take disciplinary action against them."

With that, the Superintendent got up and stormed off the set, almost ripping his tie with his microphone that was still attached to it.

~~~~

Michaels and Longhini walked backed to the newsroom with giant smiles slapping each other on the back.

"The ratings for this spot are off the charts. Phil is ecstatic," Longhini said.

"The documents are so simple but so dependable. They can't be denied; signed, sealed and delivered. They made the piece," Michaels said as he sat down at his desk and his phone rang

"News ... Michaels."

"Man did you ever piss off the boss. No one here in News Affairs has ever seen him so mad," said Sergeant Bob Kennedy.

"You sure you want to talk to me? You heard his warning."

"He'll settle down. Hey, we may have a break in the Lezkowski case."

"What is it?"

"Some Gang Crimes guys may have gotten a hit. I'll let you know more when I see the supplementary report."

He hung up.

*Wow*, Michaels thought, with a grin a mile wide on his face. "That was one angry man!"

"Fuck 'em. Those RAPs said it all. I don't think the cops are going to be upset with us. They wanted this out in the open." Longhini said.

"I like Ives. I hope he's not pissed. He did not want to do that interview."

"He'll get over it. Let's go to the Goat for a beer."

"You're reading my mind. But I can't stay long. Katie is upset with all my time away from home."

~~~~

Detective Lee Scholl was sitting at his desk, feet up, no more steam rising from his cooling coffee. His mind was floating somewhere in space wondering if all the particles of dust or whatever he was seeing falling from the ceiling overhead would one day cause cancer in his lungs from breathing so much of that shit in all the years he worked here. His trance was broken by the sound of the "Bugle" being dropped on the desk across from him.

"You know I was at the Union meeting last night?" Evans said. "The leaders are happy as hell about that Peter Michaels' story. They were laughing at how pissed off Wheatley was. Did you see it?"

"No, I heard about it, though. I told you that Michaels guy isn't so bad. That's a really good story for all those guys in patrol."

"Yeah, that's what they were saying last night."

"You know how short we are. We haven't been this low, ever. Those guys hardly get a chance to eat."

Sergeant Swartz walked up to them and said; "Lou wants us in his office, now."

Lou is the given nickname of a lieutenant. Lt. David Copelin beckoned them with his hand that had a Camel burning between his index finger and his middle finger. He motioned them to sit down, Swartz stood behind them, with his back leaning against the wall.

"What's up, boss?" Evans asked.

Copelin, reached for his glass of iced tea that was weakening from its melting ice. "I just got off the phone with Lt. Bob Smith from the 10$^{th}$ District Tactical Unit. His Gang Team is working on some Mexican drug connection at Cook County Jail. They had an inmate set up to call this Mexican drug dealer for some heroin, but instead he called some dealer from the ALBA Homes named Ezekiel Hyde."

Area Four Violent Crimes detectives theorized that Ruth Lezkowski killers were black adult males, lived in the projects and were probably involved in drugs somehow.

"Lt. Smith overheard part of the conversation between the inmate, Delvin Blount, who was trying to score two ounces of heroin from this drug dealer, Ezekiel Hyde, and hears, 'what white girl?' When the conversation was over, Smith asked him, 'what about this white girl?'"

Blount said, "I was trying to make arrangements to buy two ounces of heroin from Hyde and he tells me he can't do it because he's down since that 'white girl got killed.' He said he knew who did it and there was a lot of heat around the projects regarding the case."

Copelin told Evans and Scholl to go pick this guy up and bring him in for questioning.

~~~~

Evans and Scholl walked up the four flights of stairs at 1410 West 14$^{th}$ Place and knocked on door 404, "Chicago Police—Open up."

Ezekiel Hyde opened the door and invited them in. Hyde was six feet, one, thin and wiry. His lifetime of drug abuse made him look a lot older than his 31 years. His teeth were yellow and decayed. His blue jeans were soiled and stained from rubbing his hands on his thighs. He was barefooted and his toenails were long and filthy.

The living room's air was stale and foul. It smelled like tobacco, either from cigarettes or reefer, and cooking grease, bacon or pork. The walls were stained. The couch's maroon material was worn, and the cushions were faded and ripped. The once white stuffing contained inside the middle cushion was bulging out through a 12-inch tear. It looked dirty gray.

His brother, Steven Polton, was in the room when Evans and Scholl entered and they recognized him immediately, cuffed him, Mirandized him and placed him under arrest for an outstanding warrant for armed robbery.

Evans asked Hyde if he would agree to come over to Area Four to talk about him having any information about the death of the white girl up by the tracks.

"I don't know nuttin' about that, but I'll come talk to ya'll," Hyde said.

~~~~

Evans put Ezekiel Hyde in Interrogation Room One and Scholl put Polton in Interrogation Room Three. Evans read Hyde, his Constitutional rights.

Hey man, I don't know nuttin' about no fucking murder of that white girl. I came here to cooperate wit you's guys" Hyde said.

"We were told you have information about this murder and that your drug operation was feeling the pressure from it," Evans pushed.

"I don't know nuttin' about no fucking murder and I didn't kill nobody."

"Would you voluntarily submit to a polygraph?" Evans asked.

"I'll do anything you want. I didn't kill nobody and I don't know nuttin' about that white girl getting killed."

~~~~

Sergeant Swartz handed Scholl several previous supplementary reports that named Steven Polton and another man known as "Raymond." They were with an unidentified white woman at the 1510 West 14th Place building on the night Ruth Lezkowski was murdered. "Read these before you question him," Swartz said. "I'll set up the polygraph tests while you guys are interviewing him."

Steven Polton was sitting hunched in his chair, quivering like he was going through withdrawal when Scholl walked in. Polton was thin, five feet, ten inches tall. He had an unkempt goatee and a wild Afro hair do. He was dressed in a faded plaid shirt, stained khaki pants and gym shoes, not Reeboks.

Scholl showed him the reports "We got witnesses that placed you with a white girl in the projects at 14th Place on the night Ruth Lezkowski was murdered." Scholl then Mirandized him with his Constitutional rights.

"I don't know nuttin' about no murder. I was not with any white woman in the projects in October." Polton stared at Scholl, his eyes begging to believe him. Polton was scared, that much Scholl knew.

Scholl was a tough interrogator and saw a time to strike. "That's bullshit and you know it. We've got people that put you there with a white girl. Who was it?"

"Man, please, I don't know shit man. Man, if I knew somethin' I be telling you."

"You gonna take a polygraph examination?"

"Man, I'll do whatever you's want. I didn't kill no white girl. I don't know what dis is all about," Polton cried in desperation.

~~~~

Evans and Scholl took two separate cars with Hyde and Polton to the Crime Lab for their polygraph tests. Each one had a different examiner.

Ezekiel Hyde was specifically asked if he had a telephone conversation with anyone where he indicated that he knew who killed Ruth Lezkowski. They were both asked if they had knowledge of and/or participated in the murder of Ruth Lezkowski.

The examiners said they both had failed the test as to knowledge and participation in the Lezkowski homicide. Evans and Scholl Mirandized them again, placed them under arrest and brought them back to Area Four.

Things were starting to brighten up.

~~~~

Hyde and Polton were put in separate interrogation rooms again. They both vehemently denied being part of the Lezkowski homicide.

Scholl this time went into Hyde's room and asked if he would voluntarily give saliva samples and hair samples.

He agreed to whatever was necessary denying with every proclamation that he had "no part in the murder."

It was the same for Polton as he agreed to give samples to Evans. They both signed permission forms and the mobile Crime Lab was notified.

An hour later, Crime Lab Specialist Gary Landis took their saliva and hair samples and put it all in separate evidence bags and tagged them. They also agreed to be palm printed which Landis did next. He hand-carried the prints to the Identification Section for analysis. It was quickly determined that the prints did not match those taken from the crime scene.

~~~~

Lt. Smith called and said his Gang Team identified the person named "Raymond" in the supplementary reports as Raymond Milton, who lived in the 1510 West 14th Place building in apartment 203 at one time.

Evans and Scholl went to the ALBA Homes while the rest of the evidence taken from Hyde and Polton was being analyzed. The second floor apartment was abandoned. It had no door handle or locking mechanism on the door so Evans and Scholl walked in. They searched the apartment and found a stainless steel hemostat with an unknown substance (possibly human flesh) located in the clamping portion of the instrument. A hemostat is a surgical tool used to clamp blood vessels during surgical procedures. Evans remembered from the autopsy report that one of Ruth Lezkowski's ears appeared to have been cut or severed. Evans put the hemostat in an evidence bag and tagged it.

~~~~

Sergeant Swartz made the line up arrangements for the robbery charge against Polton. He had detective Palombo contact the witness that identified him from a photo line-up for the robbery of the Amoco Station on South Racine the month before the Lezkowski murder. The witness agreed to come to Area Four and identified Polton in a line-up without hesitation. Polton was charged with armed robbery but he continued to deny that he had anything to do with the Lezkowski homicide, as he was put into a holding cell at the 12th District Lockup.

~~~~

Evans went after Ezekiel Hyde again and he continued to deny any involvement in the Lezkowski homicide. Evans said, "Delvin Blount told us he had a telephone conversation with you about buying heroin. Did you have a conversation with him?"

"Yes I did," Hyde admitted. "Delvin called me too score some drugs but I told him I couldn't sell him anything because there was to much heat around the projects. I did not tell him I knew anything about how that white girl got killed, but I did tell him the heat around the projects was because the white girl got killed. Man, I swear to you, I don't know who killed that girl."

Despite the fact that Ezekiel Hyde failed the polygraph examination, when all the other evidence came back, it did not put him at the scene, so he was released without being charged. He was told not to leave town and that even though they were releasing him their investigation is still not over. They wanted to find out who the white woman was with the guy named Raymond, the night Ruth Lezkowski was killed.

~~~~

"News … Michaels, Yeah! Yeah!" Michaels slammed down the phone. "Shit."

"Who's that?" Longhini asked.

"Kennedy. Those two Persons of Interest failed the lie box but none of the other evidence puts them at the scene. One was let go and other was charged with some armed robbery. No Lezkowski story tonight."

# CHAPTER 15

B y the time November came to an end, Chicago's weather was getting colder and so was the Lezkowski investigation. Now six weeks old, detectives had interviewed and re-interviewed 250 people, fingerprinted two-dozen suspects, administered 12 polygraph examinations and looked into approximately 150 phone tips. Crime scene evidence was analyzed and re-analyzed, a number of "Persons of Interest" had been identified, most of them cleared but one still stood out: medical student Anthony Bauer. He had not been very cooperative and now detectives believed, he had lawyered up.

Evans and Scholl discovered he had a roommate before he moved back to the dormitory. They went to pay him a visit.

~~~~

Sergeant Tom Swartz put together a team of property crimes detectives to pull all the parking citations that were issued within a mile radius of the murder scene and Lezkowski's apartment. A mammoth undertaking!

He also had a team of detectives pulling all similar violent assaults in the area that may have had vicious beatings of their victims with a brick or a similar object.

~~~~

Evans stopped by Central Warrants to check if Bauer had any sort of warrant against him. He also ran him again through the Alpha file. Everything came up negative.

Thomas Thompson moved next door to Lezkowski's apartment in September. Evans knocked on his door, number 301 on the third floor. Thompson invited them in and offered them coffee, which they refused. Thompson was 23-years-old, six foot, curly red hair, and not muscular, not thin, not fat, average. He looked blurry-eyed, tired, like he had been studying all day. He and Bauer shared a one-bedroom apartment for about a year but Bauer wanted more privacy and moved out in August. That's when Thompson moved to Flournoy.

Evans asked him about the long telephone conversations Bauer and Lezkowski often had according to her phone records. This is something Bauer never brought up during his interviews with detectives.

"It was not uncommon for them to talk for long periods of time, and normally it was Lezkowski who called him," Thompson said. "It was not unusual for her to call him back an hour or two later. I had the feeling she was checking up on him." He reached for a cup of coffee, took a sip and grimaced. "Ugh! That shit's cold. Anyway, after one conversation, Bauer asked me if I thought Ruth was good looking. I said, 'yeah, I thought she was sort of attractive.' Then he said, 'She thinks she's good-looking, but he said he didn't think she was that good-looking.' I thought that was odd because they had known each other for so long and they were such good friends."

"Were they romantically involved?" Scholl asked.

"Oh, I don't know but I don't think so, I can tell you she never spent the night here."

They thanked Thompson and Scholl gave him his card "If you think of something else, give us a call."

~~~~

They decided to go see Lezkowski's former roommate, Cathleen Germain again. They called ahead of time to let her know they were on the way. They walked up the stairs and knocked on her door. She turned the locks one at a time, there were three, and one of them was a dead bolt. It made a loud click. Her eyes looked tired like she hadn't slept much. She waved them in with a limp hand motion and she shuffled to her couch.

"Sorry to bother you but can you tell us again how you found out Ruth was killed?" Evans asked.

She snuggled into her couch, pulled her knees up to her chin and wrapped her arms around her legs and wondered *why are they asking me about this again.* "The police contacted me about six that morning and they came by to take me to the Medical Examiner's Office. I identified the body by pictures; I think they didn't want me to see her like that. I got back home around 8:30 and I called Edward Radney and woke him up. He was in total shock with the news." Suddenly she got an enlightened expression and sat up. "I then called Anthony. He was awake and alert when I told him about Ruth. In my opinion, he started to hyperventilate."

"Did he say anything?"

"Yeah, he said Edward was the last person to see her alive. He walked her to her car."

"Anything else you can think of?"

"Yeah, some friends told me that Anthony came to my apartment on the 18th but when he saw all the news crews and police hanging around, he turned around and left."

"Interesting," said Evans, "very interesting."

~~~~

Peter Michaels was already looking for their next investigation. Typical of the television industry's motto, "you are only as good as your last story," there is constant pressure to find stories that grab the attention of the viewer. Chicago is considered the most competitive television market in the Country for local news.

The station was very pleased with the success and ratings from the "NO POLICE AVAILABLE" investigation. People were still talking about how the Superintendent of Police went after Michaels in his live studio interview. Every time a Peter Michaels investigative story aired, the ratings shot up at least one rating point and that means a lot of money in advertising rates. Funding an investigative unit is a costly venture, with no guarantees of success.

Michaels and Longhini had numerous potential story ideas lined up at any given time. They were constantly looking for new stories. That is why Michaels was sitting in the office of the Cook County Public Guardian, John McMurry.

McMurry was the perfect person for the guardianship job. An ex-priest, now married with three children, he was totally dedicated to helping under-privileged kids. His five feet, nine inch frame was sculpted like a runner's body, thin, muscular, fit. He had piercing blue eyes; balding reddish-gray hair and he wore horn-rimmed glasses that made him look scholarly.

McMurry kept a foot-high stack of files on his desk. He was explaining how his office handles cases of "Throwaway Children." These were kids in the system that were sexually, physically and mentally abused by their foster parents. They are generally older teenagers and have been bounced around from one foster home to another. Some of them have moved more than a dozen times. Some of them have slipped through the cracks of the system and have disappeared. Some have gotten in trouble with the law. Some just run away, trying to leave their past behind them. There were boys and girls, white kids, black kids, and Hispanic kids. "Throwaway Children" had no boundaries.

"How many cases do you have?" Michaels asked.

"We have dozens, but I have isolated six that are of particular interest, from the amount of abuse these kids have gone through."

"Let me take a look at those and I will get back to you."

~~~~

Two detectives from the Area Four Violent Crimes Sex Team were in Lt. David Copelin's office discussing a recent sexual assault case that happened by the railroad tracks near the Lezkowski homicide scene. It involved a shooting, sexual assault and attacking railroad police officers. It captured Copelin's attention immediately.

Detective David Decker had been a member of the Violent Crimes Sex Team for six years. He had a sister who was raped as a teenager and to him his job was more of a vocation or a calling than it was work. He was extremely focused and driven. Decker summarized the case for Copelin.

"On November 16, A CNW Railroad Police Lieutenant and two other officers, while on patrol noticed a white-over-yellow van illegally parked on Railroad property at the 2600 block of West Taylor Street next to the main line of the tracks."

Copelin was listening intently. His fingers interlaced resting on his chin, "I'm sorry to interrupt but is that location like the secluded area where Ruth Lezkowski was murdered?"

"No. No. It is elevated but nowhere near as desolate. Anyway, they approached the van and noticed Roberto Rodriguez putting on his pants in the front seat and then they heard the victim, Sarah Bluebonnet, yell for help in the back of the van." Decker was getting more animated as he continued, "Lieutenant Richard Krumholz identified himself as the police and Rodriguez attempted to start the van to escape. Krumholz pulled him out of the van through the passenger side door. A struggle ensued as he resisted arrest and Krumholz's weapon accidently discharged striking Rodriguez in the back.

"They took Rodriquez and Sarah Bluebonnet to Cook County Hospital to be examined. Rodriquez wanted to be transferred immediately to Rush-Presbyterian-St. Luke's, and Bluebonnet went berserk, screaming and acting hysterically. She refused to be tested for sexual assault, and then she refused to bring charges."

Copelin had an astonished look on his face, thinking *this guy is shot and he doesn't like where they take him for emergency treatment.* "Sorry to interrupt again but this guy sounds a little off."

"Oh man, you have no idea." Decker continued, "Rodriguez tells the police he met the victim in a bar on Cicero and he paid some guy 25 bucks to have sex with her. They then go to another bar, drink some more and then they drive to the railroad yard and drink a bottle of Wild Irish Rose Wine and smoke some marijuana. After that they climb in the back of the van get undressed and he attempts to have sex with her." Decker now shifted in his chair and started talking with his hands as he continued. "She goes like hysterical and began to fight so Rodriguez slapped her in the face several times. Now he tries to take off her wristwatch because he figures he needs to be compensated for the money he spent to have sex with her."

"You can't make this stuff up," Copelin said. "It's too unbelievable, I'll have my guys take it from here and see if it leads to anything in the Lezkowski case. Thanks."

~~~~

Palombo and Britten read the Railroad Police report, smiled and shook their heads at the same time. They knew this was going to take a lot of busy time.

When Britten ran Rodriguez's name in the Alpha file, it came back hot. He was arrested in 1980 for impersonating a police officer. Specifically, he identified himself as an Immigration Officer to a 24-year-old white female. When she couldn't provide him with papers, he tried pulling her into his van. When he was arrested, he had papers in his possession identifying him as a patient under psychiatric care. He listed his previous occupation as a paramedic driver. He was now attending the Illinois Medical Training Center to become an EKG technician.

Britten and Palombo went to Auto Pound Seven to see his vehicle. It was a 1973 piece of shit Volkswagon van. The area below the windows was a gold color. It appeared to have had a very recent unprofessional paint job. The van had windows all around it. They took a picture.

They filed for a warrant to search Rodriguez's phone records. That would take at least a day.

Rodriguez had the title of his van in his possession when he was arrested but when Detective Britten ran his license plates and VIN (vehicle identification number) through the Secretary of State's files, he got scrambled information on the vehicle's history. The title was for a 1970 Volkswagon Kumbi Station Wagon. The owner lived in Naperville, Illinois. The plates came back to Rodriguez but with a Bollingbrook, Illinois address for a 1986 Yugo Hatchback and the car was purchased in August, not November.

Palombo said, "Everything this guy touches turns to shit, it's fucked up."

Britten looked at Palombo, "Only in fucking Chicago."

~~~~

Even though they investigated the sightings of the off-white or tan van in Lezkowski's neighborhood and it appeared to be a dead end, they decide to re-visit the two ladies who filed the report and to see if they recognized Rodriquez.

When Britten showed them his mug shot and the picture of the van, they both said the same thing, "Not him and the van didn't have windows."

They went back to Area Four to check if their warrant for Rodriguez's phone records was issued. It wasn't. Another frustrating day ended with detectives no closer to solving the Lezkowski homicide than they were when they started the day.

As they were walking out the door something was gnawing at Britten in the back of his mind. He felt he missed something, something very important. He just couldn't quite put his finger on it.

He knew he would figure it out sooner or later but the craziness of the day was catching up to him.

# CHAPTER 16

T he Ruth Lezkowski murder investigation was officially declared a cold case on December first. It was now more than seven weeks since the brutal murder occurred, but the intensity of the investigation never faltered. The arduous task of reviewing old homicide and sexual assault cases continued on a daily basis on all watches. The slightest lead was being followed up as if it would lead to a major break in the case.

~~~~

When Detective Thomas Britten returned to his desk the following morning, he was surprised and relieved. Detective Billy Rogers, the "Puzzle man," took the telephone warrant for Rodriguez's phone records and ran the six-month search. The records showed nothing out of the ordinary, but several calls to the Madden Mental Health Center triggered what was gnawing at Britten. He had read in Ruth Lezkowski's file that she had an interest in psychiatry and she may have come in contact with Rodriguez as a student in a psychiatric rotation. Rodriguez hated Cook County Hospital and immediately requested to be transferred to "Rush," the night he was shot and arrested. He had been both a medical and psychiatric patient there.

Palombo and Britten checked with the Director of Programming at Rush Medical School. Edmund Frederickson knew Ruth Lezkowski had a keen interest in psychiatry but he didn't think she was in any psychiatric learning program. He invited the detectives to a lecture on psychiatry for second year students, where Britten addressed the class about Rodriguez and his medical and psychiatric history. They showed the students his mug shot and interviewed them all. No one ever saw Rodriguez and no one thought Lezkowski was involved in any psychiatric program where she could have come in contact with him.

~~~~

They went to the campus security office and showed his picture to all the officers but nobody ever saw him. Campus police took copies of Rodriquez's mug shot to canvas the student body and said they would get back to them if they had any positive results.

As Britten and Palombo were leaving the office, they ran into the man who takes care of the school's vending machines. Roberto Ortega fills the machines and collects the money. He thought he recognized Rodriguez and that he saw him about three weeks ago at Schweppe Study Hall.

"Yes. Yes. I see him by the building where the kids study at. I remember him. I was waiting for my supply truck around three o'clock in the morning. Yes. Yes. He was walking around. You know. Looking over his shoulder. Like sneaky. Yes. Yes. I remember. It was him," Ortega said.

With renewed interest, they went to the campus bookstore where Ruth bought books, to diners where she ate and stores where she shopped. No one recognized Rodriguez from his mug shot.

Britten and Palombo also tried to locate Sarah Bluebonnet, the victim in the Rodriguez case, but she was nowhere to be found.

~~~~

Back at Area Four Violent Crimes Detective Jack Evans had just gotten off the phone with Patricia "Pat" Bass of the Serology Unit of the Crime Lab. A test of the victim's blood revealed that she was a type "O" non-secretor. The sperm found in the victim was tested. Vaginal swabs showed "H" activity, which is indicative that the sperm is from a person who is an "O" secretor.

The clothes that Rodriguez was wearing when he was shot and arrested were inventoried and sent to the crime lab to determine his blood type.

~~~~

Evans called Arnold Willard, the Administrator of Rush-Presbyterian-St. Luke's Hospital to check on the blood type of Anthony Bauer, who was still a main "Person of interest."

"Blood types are not part of a student's records," Willard said. "You know detective, here at St. Luke's we have extensive capability with regard to blood typing because of the great number of transplants we do here. I'll call Mr. Bauer and explain to him how specific we can get with blood typing and suggest that he come in to give a sample to eliminate him as a suspect in this case."

"That would be great, let me know what he does," said Evans.

~~~~

Evans went back to reviewing an old homicide case from December of 1971; Dennis Dumont was charged with beating a woman to death with a rock. He was also charged with battery for beating a woman with his fists 71 minutes after the murder. To Evans' amazement, Dumont was charged with a third crime, aggravated battery for beating a woman with a brick six hours later. He committed one murder and two brutal assaults, all within six hours of each other. At the time of his arrest, he was in possession of a large butcher knife.

He was never charged with the murder because of a lack of evidence. However, the other two women who survived his vicious attacks picked him out of the lineup. He pleaded guilty to aggravated battery and was sent to the penitentiary. He also spent time in prison for rape, burglary and attempted robbery.

Evans got a subpoena for his telephone records in an attempt to find him for questioning and blood samples.

~~~~

Detective Lee Scholl was also reviewing an old case, this one involved a residential burglary at Ruth Lezkowski's apartment building in June of 1984. Edgar Ringer struggled with the victim during the course of the burglary and stated that he fantasized raping his victims if he found them at home when he made entry. Ringer was sentenced to the penitentiary, but was paroled exactly two years later on the very date that he committed the crime, June 27th, 1986, four months before the murder of Ruth Lezkowski.

Scholl subpoenaed his phone records in an attempt to find him for questioning and getting blood and saliva samples.

~~~~

Detective Aldo Palombo was sitting at his desk typing his supplementary report about his morning at Rush Medical School when Samantha McLean walked into Area Four.

She was five feet, three inches tall, 125 pounds, long blonde hair, very pretty and on crutches with a broken leg. She was the "white woman" identified in earlier reports as being at the ALBA Homes projects on the date that Ruth Lezkowski was savagely murdered.

Palombo shook her hand and led her to Interrogation Room Three, the least intimidating room at Area Four Violent Crimes. Evans followed them in.

"How long have you known Raymond Milton?" Palombo asked.

"I met him about six years ago at a carnival on the Northwest side."

"Were you ever at the ALBA Homes projects at 1510 West 114th Place?"

"Yes, a couple of times. I first went there a few years ago with a friend of Raymond's. His name was Robert. I don't know his last name."

Palombo was shaking his head thinking *why would a beautiful woman like this go to the projects, unless she was using.* Almost incredulously he asked, "And the second time?"

"I saw Raymond at a shopping mall near my house on October 14th; he borrowed my car. I didn't hear from him for a few days and I went looking for him and my car on the 17th. I asked another friend, named Larry Seasons to take me there. I found my car in the parking lot but didn't have the keys, so I went to the lobby looking for Raymond and my keys."

Palombo rubbed his chin with his left hand and he was fiddling with his ballpoint pen in his right. "Did you find Raymond?"

"No. I talked to several strangers and then this guy, totally unknown to me, came over and gave me my keys and I left and have never been back. I can't drive anyway, because I broke my leg several days later, and have been immobilized."

"What kind of car do you have?"

"It's a 1976 Chevy Monte Carlo, two door, black with a white top. It's registered to my parents."

"Did you know that the night you were there a young medical student about your age and size was brutally murdered a few blocks from where you were?"

"Yeah, I think I heard about that," she said.

"Thanks, I think that will be all for now. We have your phone number. If we need to be in touch we'll give you a call," Palombo concluded.

"Okay, thanks."

~~~~

Evans was wrapping up his daily supplementary report when Britten, yelled, "Jack, line three, it's a Mr. Willard from St. Luke's."

What's the good news?" Evans asked.

"Not so good. I contacted Anthony Bauer and he indicated that he would take the blood test. I made all the arrangements with the proper personnel at about four o'clock this afternoon. He called back a half hour later and said he consulted with an attorney."

"What did he say?"

"He said the lawyer told him he didn't have to give blood and the police are just trying to build a circumstantial case. He went on to say that the attorney told him that he has cooperated for six weeks and that's long enough."

"He said that?"

"I told him our tests are very specific and it would help eliminate him as a suspect," Willard said.

"What did he say about that?" Evans asked.

"He asked how reliable the test would be and how specific. I told him any tests done by the Chicago Police Crime Lab would be duplicated by St. Luke's Lab to assure accuracy. He then asked me who would analyze the test at the hospital and what kind of results would be obtained and how reliable would the results be."

"Then what did he say?"

"Nothing, I gave him the name of head of St. Luke's Clinical Laboratory and told him to call him and he would be able to answer all of his questions satisfactorily. Then I gave him my home number and told him to call if he changed his mind, and I again encouraged him to take the test," Willard said.

"Thanks Mr. Willard, I appreciate your help. This guy should take the test. He's looking like he has something to hide and that's not a good thing."

"I know. I'll let you know if he contacts me."

"Thanks for your help," Evans said, and went back to his typewriter to add this new information to his report.

~~~~

At 4:45 in the afternoon, Peter Michaels was sitting in the lockup with his hands cuffed behind his back at Chicago Police Headquarters on the 11th floor. He was waiting for the station's attorney to come bail him out. He was arrested for trying to smuggle a rifle into the Branch Courthouse that is located there. The courtrooms handled cases involving illegal use of guns, auto theft, prostitution and gambling. Michaels and his partner Doug Longhini had been watching the lax security as criminals go in and out of court, especially for gun charges when their trials are up.

Police Headquarters is by far one of the ugliest buildings in all of downtown Chicago. It looks like a prefabricated rectangular structure, wider than it is tall, with its concrete exterior painted an off-white color that looked grayish. Over the main entrance big Arial font blue letters spelled out "Chicago Police Headquarters," but everyone just referred to it as "11th and State."

When you walked through the main revolving door, the elevators to the Police Department's Administrative Offices were straight ahead, but if you turn to the left, the metal detectors and security systems for the courthouse were in place. Security personnel consisted of Chicago Police Officers and Cook County Sheriff's Deputies. It's a cushy job that can become monotonous and boring, making some of the guards lackadaisical.

Longhini had already smuggled in two handguns, a six-round 22 caliber and a standard 38 Smith and Wesson. Michaels got a Colt 45 through security as well. It was when he got too bold and tried to hide a small rifle in his overcoat, that finally, one of the guards pinched him.

Paul Nagaro was on the police side of the lobby, his camera rolling all the time. He had already videoed the guns that were being used in the experiment beforehand. Nagaro caught all four of the attempts on camera, including Michaels' arrest.

Longhini didn't get caught. Michaels was waiting for his attorney in his cell when the turnkey walked by and said, "We've got your ass this time Michaels, you asshole. What a fucking stunt."

Michaels replied, "And if you would have searched me before you locked me up, you would have found the derringer I have in my sock."

Startled, he stopped immediately and pulled his keys off his belt, opened the cell door and slammed Michaels up against the wall and searched him hard. He didn't find a gun.

"You're a prick you know that?" he said.

"I was just pulling yours," Michaels responded.

~~~~

About an hour later, Sam Pfeiffer, the station's attorney walked into the lockup, looked at Michaels and shook his head. "Don't you have an off-switch?" he asked.

Pfeiffer loves to interact with reporters. He's six-foot five inches tall, with a skinny frame. He always wears a suit that looks a little too big, and his shirt collars look a little too loose. He's got wavy brown hair and brown eyes that are always surrounded by a pair brown, horn-rimmed glasses. He looks like a professor. He's witty, non-assuming and smart as a whip. All the reporters respected him and, more importantly, they liked him.

"What's up? Am I getting out of here or what?" Michaels asked.

"Yeah, I just got you out on an I-Bond. An I-Bond is an Individual Recognizance Bond, meaning no money was posted. But if you were scheduled for a court appearance and didn't show up, the court would immediately issue an arrest warrant."

"Good, I can get this on the ten o'clock."

"Not so fast! That's the deal. No story, No jail," Pfeiffer said. "You are in some real trouble here, Peter. Are you fucking nuts?"

"This is a great story!"

"Not anymore. Let's get you out of here."

# CHAPTER 17

T he first full week of December turned out to be a very busy time for all the detectives from Area Four Violent Crimes. It started off when Dennis Dumont, the man suspected of beating a woman to death with a brick in1971 and convicted of aggravated assault of two other women in a six-hour time period, walked into Area Four Headquarters and asked for Detective Jack Evans.

Evans went through his files and retrieved Dumont's criminal background information. Dumont had a concerned look on his face as Evans entered the interrogation room and told him that he was investigating the death of Ruth Lezkowski. Dumont immediately denied any involvement, and Evans immediately read him his Constitutional rights.

"I don't know nuttin' about no murder on the Westside," Dumont said. "I don't know nobody from dare. I ain't got no friends dare and I ain't got no relatives staying on the Westside. Dat's why I stays on the Southside. Everybody I know lives dare."

"Can you tell me where you were on the night of October 17th and the morning of October 18th?" Evans asked.

"I'll tell you one fucking thing, I wasn't no where's near the Westside. I don't remember what I was doing but, I sure as shit wasn't around dare."

"Would you give us a sample of your blood, saliva and pubic hair so we can eliminate you as a suspect?"

"Yes, sir. I don't know nuttin' about that murder."

~~~~

Evans drafted an authorization letter allowing them to take the samples and then he and Britten witnessed his signature. They took him to Rush-Presbyterian-St. Luke's Hospital Lab for the samples. Evans gave Dumont his card and told him not to leave town, and if he heard anything to give him a call, and then told him he was free to go. The samples were sent the crime lab for analysis.

~~~~

While Evans and Britten were at the hospital, John Morton walked into Area Four and asked to talk to a detective. Aldo Palombo came to the front desk and asked, "Who are you?"

"My name is John Morton. A patrol officer came to my house last night and said I was supposed to come here in the morning and talk to someone."

Palombo took him to Interrogation Room Two and told him he would be right back. He pulled the supplementary reports and discovered that Morton was a "Person of Interest" and was listed to be interviewed two weeks ago. When the police cadets did a new grid search of the crime scene, they found Morton's Blue Cross/Blue Shield insurance card.

As soon as he returned to the room, Palombo told him they were investigating the death of Ruth Lezkowski and read him his Constitutional rights.

"I swear to you, I know nothing about that poor woman's murder. I was never ever in that area."

"Why did we find your Blue Cross/Blue Shield card at the crime scene?"

"I have no clue. In June, I reported my car stolen to the police, but I soon found out it wasn't stolen, it was repossessed. I work at the hospital and my identification for the vehicle and my hospital ID and other stuff was in the car when it was towed away. How it got up there, I have no idea. I never got any of my stuff back either," he replied. "Look, I'm married and have two kids. I work seven days a week trying to make ends meet. I don't know nobody over here. I never come to the Westside. This a scary place."

Palombo ran his name through the Alpha file. Usually it takes a matter of minutes to get a hit on the Alpha file but if the system was busy it could take as long as an hour. By the time Palombo got a cup of coffee he had his answer. Morton came back negative. He had no criminal record not even a speeding ticket. "Would you voluntarily give us your fingerprints and palm prints?"

"I'll do whatever it takes man. I could never do anything like that. I respect life too much," Morton said.

Palombo looked at Britten and shook his head. "I am pretty sure he isn't our guy but we need to find this tow truck driver."

~~~~

Sergeant Thomas Swartz hung up the phone and yelled, "Evans get in here."

"What's up?" Evans asked.

"Your favorite guy, Anthony Bauer, is at St. Luke's. He wants to give us a blood sample and clear his name."

"No shit. I'm on my way. I'll draw up the consent forms and get over there."

~~~~

Peter Michaels and Doug Longhini were laughing about being arrested. "Man, that turnkey was pissed at me. When I told him I had another gun in my sock he wasted no time getting in that cell and searching me. I'm glad he didn't strip search me. That fucker had me cuffed the entire time I was in that holding cell. He was pissed," Michaels said.

"They were all pissed. I know we used replica guns, but man, it was easy to get them past Security," said Longhini.

"I got too cocky. I bet if we would have waited until today, we would have had a shot at getting that rifle into gun court."

"The attorneys are a little upset at us, though. Sam is pretty good with us, but he didn't think that was a good idea," Longhini said.

"Sam's a great guy. I remember the first time I worked with him. I thought, man, this guy is trying to weaken this story, but in the end it was better and it had no legal issues. I think Sam thinks I'm nuts!"

"Really!"

~~~~

"Hey, Peter, line one."

"News ... Michaels"

"You that reporter who does all those stories on the police?"

"I do my share. Who is this?"

"My name is Edgar Ringer. The police want to talk to me about that nurse lady who got killed. I don't know nuttin' about it but I'm afraid to go there."

"Well if you didn't do it, you got nothing to worry about."

"You did all those stories on police brutality, you know what they're like."

"They aren't going to beat you up, they probably just want to ask you some questions. What did you do?"

"I robbed some lady on that street where that nurse lived two years ago and I just got out of prison a couple months back. I'm nervous."

"I will meet you in the front lobby of Area Four in an hour and take you to the detectives. You'll be fine. Don't worry, nobody is going to hurt you."

~~~~

"I want to get my van back," Roberto Rodriguez insisted when he walked into Area Four Violent Crimes.

"Funny thing. I was just thinking about you. Come on in here hero and let's talk," Detective Lee Scholl said as he led him into Interrogation Room One.

The lab report on the blood sample taken from his shirt after being shot in November came back. He was an "O" secretor and he just moved to the top on the "Person of Interest" list.

"What about my van?"

"What about you answer some questions."

"What's going on?"

"Let me tell you what's going on. There are a lot of inconsistencies in your statements about your whereabouts on the night of the murder of Ruth Lezkowski, Mr. Rodriguez."

"Listen man, I suffer from depression and I'm on Social Security benefits for being mentally disabled. In the last three years alone, I have been in a dozen hospitals for it." Records showed that he was a patient at Grant, St. Elizabeth, Good Samaritan, Foster McGraw of Loyola, St. Francis Cabrini, University of Illinois, St. Luke's, Mount Sinai, Northwestern, Madden and Tinley Park Mental Health Centers.

Scholl was thinking *yeah and we pay for your sorry ass.* "We know all about that. You like to get rough with women?"

"I don't get rough with them. They like me."

"Is that why you slapped Sarah Bluebonnet around the night you got arrested?"

"Man, I paid for that sex and she went nuts on me."

"Well, when you were shot, you kept yelling that you did not have a gun, knife or stick. Then when you were arrested, you kept yelling you had no stick or no rock. How did you know about those things? They were never made public after the murder of Ruth Lezkowski," Scholl said. "Why were you at St. Luke's on October 17th, the night before Ruth Lezkowski was murdered?"

"I was visiting a friend who was having a baby."

"What's her name?"

"Juanita Torres. I'm not sure where she lives, but you can check with the hospital. I was there around dinner time and left."

"Oh, we will."

"I don't know nothing about this murder. Nothing."

"Then will you agree to giving us another sample of your blood, saliva, pubic hair and fingerprints?"

"I'll give you anything you want. I did nothing to that woman, nothing."

~~~~

"Sarge, Rodriguez has agreed to give us all his samples. We need to check with his mother, ex-wife, brother and girlfriend to verify his alibi," Scholl said.

"I'll give this to the 'Puzzle Man,' Rogers loves to do this kind of stuff," Sergeant Tom Swartz said. "We should have more answers by tomorrow."

~~~~

Edgar Ringer was sitting on a bench under the rectangular glass window in the lobby of Area Four when Michaels arrived. He was about five feet, ten inches tall. He looked shabby, wearing an old stained plaid winter coat with a knit dark blue woolen cap in his hands. His eyes looked glazed, like he was looking through a prism. His speech was slow. "Hey, man! You look skinner in person than you do on TV."

"Yeah, television does that to you. *Fuck you!* Why are you afraid to turn yourself in if you don't have anything to worry about, and why are they looking at you? Do you know?"

Ringer was nervously twisting his woolen cap in his hands, "I broke into the same house that woman who got killed lived in two years ago. I said some bad things to the woman who lived there," Ringer said.

"What do you mean bad things?"

"I told her I would love to have sex with her. I love it when a woman is home when I break in; shit like that."

"Are you nuts?"

"Yeah, I guess I am. I'm a mental patient. I just got out of Stateville earlier this year because I was being treated at the Elgin Mental Health Center."

~~~~

Stateville Correctional Center is about 50 miles from Chicago. It was built in 1925 to house 1500 inmates, but by 1986, 4,134 inmates called it home. Stateville was known as "F-House" or the "roundhouse," because it had an armed tower in the center of an open area surrounded by several tiers of cells. The maximum-security facility employs 1,300 people. It cost $32,000 a year for each prisoner. Stateville sits on 2,200 acres of land, but the actual prison occupied 64 acres that are surrounded by a 33-foot concrete perimeter with ten wall towers standing guard. The interior of the prison was painted battleship gray. It was cold and damp, dreary and depressing. Thirteen prisoners were executed by the electric chair and lethal injection. Its recidivism rate was mind-boggling.

Michaels thought, he'd better get this guy to Area Four Violent Crimes as quickly as possible. "Come on, I'll take you upstairs to the detectives. They aren't going to hurt you. I promise," Michaels said.

Walking up the steps, Ringer kept saying, "I don't know that woman. I swear I don't."

Evans looked up as Michaels walked in. "Look what we got here. Peter Michaels. What's this?" he asked.

"This is Edgar Ringer. I think you guys want to talk to him. He was nervous about being hurt if he came in alone and I assured him nothing is going to happen to him."

"We've been looking for him." Evans nodded to his partner, Lee Scholl to come over and take Ringer to an interrogation room. "What's this all about?"

"I don't know, the guy just called me. I said I would talk to him and bring him in. He's a little off," Michaels said.

"We know. Thanks. Nobody is going to hurt him."

"You got a card. If it leads to anything, I'd like to be the first to know."

"Right!"

Unbeknownst to anyone, detectives were about to learn that Ringer's daily life intersected with Ruth Lezkowski's very frequently.

Without explaining the significance of the day, Evans asked, "What were you doing on the night of October 17th?"

Without hesitation, Ringer said, "I took the bus home from work and got off at Damen Avenue and Harrison Street. I walked east on Harrison to Loomis, then I cut through the alley to get to Arrigo Park to get to my momma's house at 800 South Ada."

"What alley is that you cut through?"

"You know dat alley dat goes through the 1400 block of Harrisn and Flournoy? You know dat's close to the house dat I robbed two years ago. Dat's why I'm here, ain't it?"

Evans and Scholl glanced at each other with that knowing look—*coincidence!* Police don't like coincidences.

"Do you have a job?" Evans asked.

"I work at the Jewel over there on Racine. They don't pay me. I just be working for tips carrying peoples' grocery bags to their cars. I'm on welfare and I'm trying to, you know, get on mental disability. Since I got outta Stateville, I go to the Miles Square Health Center on West Washington," Ringer said.

Detectives knew that Ruth Lezkowski often shopped at that Jewel store and that her house is located en route to Ringer's mother's house on South Ada.

*Coincidence!*

"Do you know why you are here, Edgar? Did you ever met Ruth Lezkowski?"

"I didn't ever meet her. I don't know her. The onliest time I ever saw her was on some reward poster dat some other person who worked at Jewel showed me. He asked me if I knew this girl, man. I told him, like I'm telling you, I never saw her before," Ringer said.

"I gotta tell ya, Edgar, we're not liking some of the things you're telling us. Lot of coincidences in your life crossing paths with Ruth Lezkowski," Scholl said.

"Man, I am telling y'all. I don't know dat woman. I never met her, never saw her!" Ringer exclaimed. "What do you want me to do?"

"Well, we would like you to give us permission to get samples of your blood, saliva, pubic hairs, fingerprints and palm prints."

"I'll give you whatever you wants. I didn't do this," Ringer said.

After he signed the authorization forms, they took him to Mount Sinai Hospital's Lab and drew his blood, which was immediately brought over to the Crime Lab. By the time they got back to Area Four Violent Crimes, they found out he was an O secretor and he was read his Constitutional rights and placed under arrest.

~~~~

Lt. David Copelin had just gotten off the phone with the Chief of Detectives from Police Headquarters, and he yelled out to Sergeant Tom Swartz. "Get someone over to the Railroad property at 1039 West 111th Place. They just found a woman brutally beaten to death."

# CHAPTER 18

M
ichaels and his cameraman Paul Nagaro raced to the crime scene near the railroad property where Ruth Lezkowski was brutally murdered. Michaels was working his brick phone talking to Sergeant Bob Kennedy gathering as much information on this latest homicide so he could do a live report for the six o'clock news.

"What do we have?"

"The body of an unidentified female had been found near an abandoned area of railroad property near Ashland," Sergeant Kennedy said. "We know the victim is a 20-year-old black woman and like Lezkowski she was severely beaten to death. It's pretty gruesome, Peter."

Michaels and Nagaro arrived at the scene. Nagaro grabbed his camera and started shooting pictures. Michaels continued his conversation with Kennedy.

"When we discovered her body, it was frozen. Her death must have been horrific. She had part of her head caved in by a rock that was found close to her body. Seven teeth were laying near her shoulder. There was a pitchfork also found near the body, and apparently she had numerous wounds on her face from that pitchfork. As one last degrading bit of brutality, her hair was set on fire."

"Oh my God. It sounds a lot like the same brutal guy or guys struck again. Hey, I gotta run. I see the Medical Examiner, I need to grab a quick sound bite for the six."

Dr. Robert Crine was walking down from the crime scene when Michaels caught up to him. "Hey, Dr. Crine, you got a second for a quickie?"

"For you Peter anything."

Michaels gathered Nagaro and started the interview "What have you got here doc?"

"In the past two months, we have experienced two of the most brutal murders that I have ever seen in this city. This crime was so heinous, so extreme, so vicious, almost too hard to describe. It appears the cause of death was blunt force trauma. I will know more after the autopsy."

The live truck was set up waiting for Michaels to get in front of the camera for his six o'clock news report. Nagaro ran with his taped interview of Dr. Crine to the truck to be edited as Michaels miked up for his live shot. He put his IFB in his ear.

IFB or Interrupt for broadcast is a monitoring and cueing system used in television, filmmaking, video productions and radio broadcast for one-way communication from the director or producer to the on-air-talent in a studio or on a live remote location. So when a video package is ending the producer will count down the seconds until the talent is back on the air live.

Michaels was getting a "stand by" cue while wrapping up his live report saying, "The victim was wearing a black cloth jacket, black skirt and black shoes. It appears that she may have been sexually assaulted; her pantyhose were ripped. Ron ... Police have cordoned off the area and they are still up there by the tracks, looking for clues, footprints, evidence of any kind. That area is accessible by car, but no car was found at the scene. Ron, excuse me, but I see a couple of the lead detectives from the Lezkowski investigation walking up the path here."

Michaels broke away from his mark as the detectives approached and Nagaro instinctively unlatched his camera from his tripod and followed.

Detective Aldo Palombo was easy to spot because of the slight limp he had from his arthritic hip. "Excuse me, detective Palombo, are you here because of the Ruth Lezkowski case?"

"Peter, you know we can't talk about an ongoing investigation," Palombo responded.

"But detective, there are a lot of similarities in this brutal murder compared to the Lezkowski homicide, can you comment?"

"I have no further comment. Let us through, please. Let us through."

Michaels turned to the camera to sign off knowing that he just made some enemies back at the studio control room.

"Ron ... We have learned that every violent crime committed anywhere near the Lezkowski homicide scene is being treated as a potential lead in that investigation. There is no doubt this crime was committed with the same dark rage as that of Ruth Lezkowski. Ron, back to you in the studio."

~~~~

Michaels just totally threw the entire newscast off-schedule with his unexpected breaking news interview with the Area Four Violent Crime detectives. Show producer, David Beedy, felt like Michaels just handed him a shit sandwich.

A half-hour newscast actually has 22 minutes of news content. The other eight minutes are commercial time. That leaves 13 minutes for local and national/world news. A typical show would include four reporter "packages"—each two or three minutes long and a smattering of short anchor voiceovers and other short stories. Most newscasts end with a 20 to 30-second "kicker"—a light send-off to end the show on a high note. So, when a live shot goes long, the first place a producer looks to trim time is weather. It's the first instant escape route. Then the producer looks at trimming sports, which was certain to mean the sportscaster would storm off the set and not talk to the producer for a day or two. Talent doesn't take getting cut short of time lightly. They feel insulted and abused, and question the producer's competence managing the "game clock."

Michaels knew when he got back to the newsroom he was going to get a ration of shit and "you fucked me again" comments from both weather and sports, but he knew it was good TV, and he would do it again tomorrow if the opportunity arose.

~~~~

Detective Billy Rogers, the "Puzzle Man," was putting the finishing touches on his supplementary report after he interviewed Roberto Rodriguez's mother, brother, ex-wife and girlfriend.

Sergeant Tom Swartz walked into the Area Four Violent Crimes squad room and asked, "How'd the interviews go?"

"You can read all about it but I don't think Rodriguez is our guy," Rogers said.

"Whattaya mean, not our guy?"

"He's pretty pathetic, and he's crazy and he's a drunk, but I don't think he did this homicide."

"Why?"

"He's been divorced for three years. He still visits his ex-wife every day for three fucking years. That, in and of itself, is nuts. He even spends the night whenever she lets him. It's driving her nuts. She says he dresses in the only sport coat he owns, every single day, like he's going to job interview. He has two or three pairs of shoes that he changes every other day and she says she has never seen him wear a pair of gym shoes, ever. He just bought that goofy van in July, and she has never seen him drive any other vehicle except for his old Yugo."

"What about the mother, what does she say?"

"The mother and the brother tell very similar stories about him. He stays with either his mother or brother most of the time. He has driven the same car for as long as they can both remember. He dresses the same way every day and they have never ever seen him wear gym shoes."

"What about the girlfriend? What's her name?"

"Stella Ramirez. Now, there's a beaut! She said they were going out for about three months. She said he always carried a security badge in his wallet and he listens to police scanners all day but she said she had never seen him in a security uniform. She said they drank almost every night when she got off work. He would pick her up and they'd go to the bar. Until he purchased the van, he only drove that Yugo."

"What about the night of the 17th?"

"Stella confirmed that he went to St. Luke's Hospital to visit his friend who just had a baby during the day at about dinner time. After that she is not so sure, because she thinks they were fighting about something that night. She can't be certain because she was starting to think he was nuts. She said they lived together for three days; then she drove him to Madden Mental Health Center on October 28th. She said he went there to get out of a drunk-driving charge. She picked him up on November 3rd and broke off their relationship when she dropped him off. She says he's way out there and he has a drinking problem, but that he could never do anything like kill someone."

"Is this guy ever sober?" Swartz asked with one of those quizzical looks that only he could muster.

"Sarge, I don't know, but this guy only hangs out with people who drink, and we know that Ruth Lezkowski seldom drank and she had no alcohol in her system, according to the toxicology reports. This guy couldn't fight with anyone unless they were so drunk they couldn't stand. He's an asshole. He's a drunk. He's probably crazy, but he ain't our guy. I'm just saying," Rogers concluded.

"Finish typing that up and put it in the file," Swartz said.

~~~~

"Area Four Violent Crimes, detective Evans."

"This is Pat Fish from the Serology Section of the Crime Lab."

"Whattaya you got, Doc?"

"Anthony Bauer's blood samples came back. He's an A sector. That takes him out of the pool and his prints don't match."

"I wish he would have done this a lot sooner. It would have saved us a lot of very time-consuming work. Thanks."

~~~~

"What's that you got?" Lt. David Copelin asked Detective Thomas Britten.

"It's the report from the CTA I ordered weeks ago."

The CTA, Chicago Transit Authority operates the mass transit system in Chicago and 40 surrounding suburbs. The CTA was first started in 1947 as an independent government agency. It owns nearly 1,900 buses and 1,200 train cars. The agency provides 525 million rides a year, traveling over 140 bus routes covering 1,230 route miles, and their train cars operate over eight distinct routes, covering 222 miles of track that wind throughout the city. The CTA provides on average 1,700,000 rides on any given workday.

Detective Britten asked the CTA for the identities of any bus drivers who were operating equipment on any street in the close proximity of the Lezkowski residence, St. Luke's Hospital and the crime scene at 1500 West 15th Place. The specific routes included Ashland Avenue, one of the busiest streets in Chicago and Racine and Harrison Streets for October 17th and 18th during the time spans of 11 o'clock in the evening through 6:30 in the morning. Every bus driver who ran a route on those given times was identified and interviewed, but the results were negative. No one saw anything unusual.

~~~~

Sergeant Tom Swartz stood up and instinctively reached for his lower back. He called Evans and Scholl into his office. His desk was covered with supplementary reports, mug shots and crime lab analysis reports. He was feeling the heat from Lt. Copelin, who was feeling the heat from Commander Maurer, who was feeling the heat from the Superintendent, who was feeling the heat from the Mayor. They needed a lead.

"What's up?" asked Scholl.

As Swartz squeezed the bridge of his nose with his right hand as if releasing pressure from his headache, he handed Scholl a report from a suburban police department.

"I want you guys to run out to Aurora, they got a case with some shithead who they like for the murder of a 37-year-old female. They identified him as Willie Williams, and discovered that he had been incarcerated for rape and attempted rape in 1974 to 1978. Get this, those rapes occurred right here in Chicago, and guess what? The victims were medical personnel from the Medical Center in the 12th District. They were en route to their parked cars when Williams confronted them."

Aurora, Illinois is the second largest city outside of Chicago. Its population increased with the advent of floating riverboat gambling casinos. As Aurora grew, so did its crime rate, including murder.

"They're going to go at him at the end of December. You might want to be there when they do. Make the arrangements," said Swartz.

"You got it Boss. Right on it," replied Scholl.

"Meanwhile, I'll get someone from Records and Identifications to pull his prints, his criminal history and any pictures we have of him."

"I'll check with the Department of Corrections' Medical Section in Springfield and see what they have on Williams," Evans said.

~~~~

Peter Michaels, along with all the other reporters and producers from the UNIT-6 Investigative Team were meeting with Show Producer David Beedy. He was always assigned to the station's special projects because of his fanatical organizational skills and his writing ability.

His new project was putting together a 1986 year-end special and he was trying to decide which stories should go into the special. The "Beating Justice" series on police brutality was leading the list. It had won an Emmy and the Robert F. Kennedy Award earlier that year and it had some of the highest ratings ever recorded in the station's history.

The meeting was interrupted by a phone call. "Peter, it's for you."

"News ... Michaels."

"Petey." Peter recognized the voice of his youngest sister, Michele. And she didn't sound good.

"What's wrong?"

"It's momma. She had a heart attack." Michele, let out a sob.

Michaels turned pale as he stood up, and everyone in the room looked at him, knowing, he had just received some bad news.

"You better come home."

"I'll be there in six hours."

His oldest sister, Barbara, and youngest sister, Michele, called him "Petey." They were the only two people he would allow to call him that without getting upset. His middle sister, Mary Ann never called him anything but Peter. Michaels liked the name Peter. It was strong---Peter the Rock. Michaels was the only man left in his family. His father died 15 years ago. His sisters looked up to him, trusted his decisions and needed him home.

~~~~

Michaels was known as a tough-ass reporter who was never afraid to take on any powerful politicians, high-ranking judges, mafia figures, favored attorneys or corrupt cops. Not many people knew that he was a momma's boy. He talked to his mother every single day, at least once, to check on her and to let her know everything was alright with him and the family in Chicago. His mother was his role model. She was 86 years old and sharp as a tack. Smart, wise, witty.

Michaels had a blank look on his pale face. His smile was gone. His hands were trembling and his eyes were tearing up. The room was silent. He turned to his colleagues "I gotta go to Detroit, my mom had a heart attack. I don't know how bad it is. My sister is hysterical. I'll check in everyday."

# CHAPTER 19

P eter Michaels was driving back to Chicago on New Year's Day,1987. The ride home was easier than the drive to Detroit. It took him eight hours of white-knuckle driving to get to the hospital to see his mother. The blizzard-like conditions he was driving in were nothing compared to the anxiety he felt about his mother. He had no idea how sick she was.

When he got to Beaumont Hospital in Troy, Michigan, his mother was sitting up in bed. Her 86-year-old body looked tired. Her thin white hair had a halo like appearance from the sun glistening through her window. She was okay. She survived the heart attack. She was a tough cookie. Her face lit up with an angelic smile when her only son walked through the door. He had tears of joy tendering down his cheeks as he kissed his mother on her forehead. Michaels' sisters would always joke because momma always called Peter "the sweetest thing this side of heaven." He talked to the doctors and their plan was to implant a pacemaker because of her irregular heartbeat. That procedure was going to be performed the following day. Michaels spent every waking hour at his mother's bedside. She recovered miraculously. She was alive and well and that's all he cared about.

The roads were now dry. The sun was shining. The tires were humming, and he was driving at 80 miles an hour. He thought about the last brutal murder he covered right before he left for Detroit—*was there any connection to the Ruth Lezkowski case?* All he knew for sure was that there was a lot of pressure to solve this case and Area Four detectives hit a brick wall.

*My God* Michaels thought *There are some sick fucking people in this world.*

~~~~

Area Four Violent Crimes started off the New Year with a bang and once again, it won the bet on the first homicide of the year. Two minutes after midnight a Black Gangster Disciple was killed in a drive-by shooting. He was standing in Latin Kings' territory on the other side of Ashland Avenue. Area Four was destined to be the busiest crime area with the most murders in 1987 for three years in a row.

The Violent Crimes section had a hangover, not from alcohol but from lack of movement on the Lezkowski homicide, now 75 days old. Detectives were clearing potential Persons of Interest.

Looking for new ideas and new approaches, Commander James Maurer, Lt. David Copelin and Sergeant Tom Swartz were meeting to decide if they should call in Lt. Tom Cronin, the Chicago Police Department's newly trained criminal profiler.

Cronin was six–foot-one with a full head of curly auburn hair. He dressed exquisitely, always in an expensive suit, a starched shirt and a fashionable tie. His posture was erect. He walked with confidence. He always had a smile. He was smart.

He spent a year at the FBI's Training Academy in Quantico studying profiling. The Federal Bureau of Investigation has the most sophisticated profiling school in the world. Cronin graduated top in his class.

Commander Maurer was feeling the political heat. He knew his team was working around the clock. He needed results so he issued a citywide BOLO (Be on the Lookout). The BOLO was a request to alert every police officer citywide in the department, whether on patrol or in specialized units to shake the bushes, talk to informants and reach out to learn if anyone on the streets knows anything about the killers of Ruth Lezkowski.

For the four districts in Area Four and the 18th District that patrolled the Cabrini-Green Housing Projects, he wanted to be more specific so he issued an "All Call" alert through the Districts' C.O. book. The Command Officer Book is a two-inch thick bound book with standard size 14-inch paper that contained every special alert issued in that District. Once the information was passed on, the Desk

Sergeant would paste it in the C.O. book and initial it to verify everyone got the special alert.

Commander Maurer wanted every officer in these five districts to use every resource they had to develop information.

~~~~

The 11<sup>th</sup> District Desk Sergeant informed Sergeant Tom Swartz that Dashone Jameison was arrested on the mornings of October 14<sup>th</sup>, 15<sup>th</sup> and 18<sup>th</sup> at Ashland Avenue for smash and grabs. A smash and grab generally took at least two people. One would smash the window of the car while other would reach in and grab a purse or anything of value that the robbers would notice inside the vehicle.

Jameison was being held in the Cook County Jail and he may know something about the Lezkowski homicide. Swartz assigned it to detectives Aldo Palombo and Thomas Britten.

Britten pulled the case reports and discovered Jameison was charged with armed robbery and attempted armed robbery after he robbed a white female by smashing her car window and grabbing her purse on October 14<sup>th</sup>. He had an accomplice to the crime. On the 15<sup>th</sup>, he did the same thing, near the same corner. He smashed a white female's car window and grabbed her purse and ran.

On October 18<sup>th</sup>, a 12<sup>th</sup> District tactical officer arrested Jameison and two other black males after he observed them looking into cars that were stopped at the light at 14<sup>th</sup> Street and Ashland.

The victims of the smash and grabs picked the three of them out of a lineup and they were charged with armed robbery and attempted armed robbery.

Britten took their mug shots and called officer Daniel Starks of the Railroad Police, who discovered the body of Ruth Lezkowski and asked him to come over to Area Four to see if he could identify any of them. Starks wrote in his report that he observed a black male standing under the viaduct at 15<sup>th</sup> and Loomis before he found her body.

Starks could not identify anyone as being that person. He also said that none of the people in the lineup photos were dressed like the person he observed. "That guy," he said, "was wearing a short black leather looking jacket with a plastic shower cap on his head."

Britten had copies of Jameison's fingerprints sent to the crime lab to compare them to the ones lifted at the crime scene. They didn't match!

Detectives were starting to think their original theory of the crime that the killer or killers were adult, black males from the ALBA Homes might not be right. The Lezkowski investigation was getting a breath of fresh air and it was picking up steam.

# CHAPTER 20

E xactly 90 days after the brutal murder of Ruth Lezkowski, the investigation started to get some new life. The Citywide "BOLOs" and the Area-specific "All Calls" began producing results within days. Confidential Informants started spewing information to Gang Crimes Officers and Tactical Officers. The pressure was on and people started talking.

Area Four Violent Crimes detectives finally cleared medical student Anthony Bauer. His blood test showed he was type A not type O. He passed the polygraph test as well, and his fingerprints were no match for those recovered at the crime scene.

Although Edgar Ringer, the person who had sexual fantasies when he broke into homes, and Dennis Dumont, the person who beat two women within an inch of their lives, were both type O secretors, additional enzyme tests eliminated them as "Persons of Interest."

Further tests concluded that approximately seven percent of the population had the characteristics of the offender and Roberto Rodriguez was one of them. He was a type O secretor. Hair samples that were lifted from Lezkowski's front seat were compared to Rodriguez's head hair samples by a special x-ray machine that measures lead content and the results tended to clear him. Police still wanted an analysis of Rodriguez's pubic hair but they were starting to lean towards Detective Bill Rodgers' conclusion that Rodriguez was not their man.

~~~~

Detectives Jack Evans and Lee Scholl were interviewing Patrolman T. Wayne Purvis, of the Public Housing North Unit. Purvis, who was constantly on a diet and loved to talk, had a CI, (Confidential Informant,) who said he knew who killed Ruth Lezkowski. Purvis said he approached Leonardo Foster AKA "Rooster" and specifically asked him about the Lezkowski homicide. "Leonardo told me that a person named 'Dog' told him that Martin Darrow killed her." Martin's brother, Michael Darrow, is the head of the "Paymasters" drug operation in the ALBA Homes.

~~~~

Evans and Scholl went to the Cook County Jail, where Darrow was being held on an aggravated battery charge. Martin Darrow was read his Constitutional rights by Evans and he immediately stated, "We have information that says you killed Ruth Lezkowski."

"I don't know nuttin' about dat girl killed up there by the tracks." Darrow said.

"That's not what we hear, Martin," Evans responded.

"I did tell some people dat I did it, but I was lying. I said it bragging around my brother," Darrow said.

"Pretty stupid thing to brag about don't you think, Martin?"

"Yah, I know dat, but I didn't do it."

"Well how about you give us some blood, saliva and hair samples and how about taking a polygraph test?"

"I'll do whatever you wants," Martin Darrow said.

~~~~

Detectives Aldo Palombo and Thomas Britten were sitting at their desks when 12th District Tactical Officer Jay Reed walked over, "I may have some good information for you."

Reed had been on the job for 15 years. He was five feet, ten inches tall. He had a slim frame at 165 pounds and blonde hair. He walked with a slight limp because he got shot in the leg two years earlier chasing a gangbanger down an alley on the Westside. He could have taken a desk job but he just loved being on the street. Over the years, he had developed a long list of confidential informants.

"Whattaya got?" Britten asked.

"I pinched this guy, Oscar Miller for a robbery about a month after the Lezkowski murder. So me and my partner stop one of our informants and ask him about the Lezkowski murder. He tells us word on the street is the killer is a guy named 'Shim Sham,' whose first name is Oscar and he lives in the 1510 West 13th Street building in the ALBA Homes."

"What do you know about him?" asked Palombo.

"This 'Shim Sham' supposedly goes absolutely crazy when he smokes happy sticks and that he is a karate expert," Reed said.

Happy sticks are marijuana laced with PCP.

"Why wouldn't this informant come forward sooner and claim the reward money? It was posted on flyers all over the ALBA Homes. $25,000 is a lot of money," Britten said.

"He doesn't need money. He's a big time dope dealer and he doesn't really want to put his name out there." Reed said.

"Do you know where this guy is?"

"I can have him here in ten minutes."

"Go get him," Britten said.

~~~~

"News … Michaels."

"Kennedy here," said Sergeant Bob Kennedy.

"What's up boss?"

"You know this Lezkowski case is going nowhere and they're thinking about bringing Lt. Tom Cronin in to help."

"Who is he?"

"He's our profiler. He just finished a yearlong fellowship at the FBI's Behavioral Sciences Division at Quantico in December and just got off furlough. Here's his number. I think he's assigned to Detective Headquarters." Kennedy said.

"Thanks."

"Who was that?" Longhini asked.

"They're calling in a profiler on the Lezkowski case."

"We have to get this 'Throwaway Children' piece ready. You think you should spend more time on the Lezkowski case?" Longhini asked frustrated.

"This shouldn't affect our series. It might be a good thing to get something on the air. It's been a very long time since we had a good Lezkowski story. This shouldn't take long," Michaels responded.

~~~~

Oscar Miller was an 18-year-old black male dressed in typical Chicago gang fashion, blue jeans and a white tee shirt. Gang bangers dressed like this to throw off the police. In other words, everyone dressed the same on the street so when a description went out over police radios to be on the lookout for a black, male teenager, dressed in blue jeans and white tee shirt, everyone was indistinguishable. Gang bangers felt that it was good for them if they were arrested and had to go to court.

Evans read Miller his Constitutional rights and he immediately denied knowing anything about the Lezkowski case.

"Hey man, that ain't my name, but I do know this dude that is known as 'Shim Sham.' He's supposed to be some karate king or something. He be hanging around the karate school on West Roosevelt Road," he said.

"Do you know where he lives?" asked Evans.

"No, man, I don't but I see him a lot by that grocery store at the 1600 block of Roosevelt."

"Can you describe him?"

"Yeah, he be black, maybe 19 or 20 years old."

Things at Area Four Violent Crimes were coming alive.

~~~~

"Is Lieutenant Cronin there?" Michaels asked

"This is Cronin."

"Lieutenant, this is Peter Michaels, Channel Six News."

"What can I do for you, Mr. Michaels?"

"It's my understanding that Area Four Violent Crimes is stuck on the Lezkowski homicide case and they are calling you in to do a profile. Is that correct?" Michaels asked.

"Lt. David Copelin called me in late December. They were running out of investigative leads. They were working their asses off but getting nowhere and the heat was on to solve the case," Cronin said.

"When did you talk to them?"

"I have had several conversations with Copelin. It was too early to do a profile. You can't do one until you have a lot more information. They just had a theory that they were working off of," Cronin said.

"They've done a lot, but I think they are back to square one," Michaels said.

"The Behavioral Science Unit at Quantico has this hotshot profiler, Richard Roberts, who is chomping at the bit to do a profile of the killers. We just had some early supplementary reports, even though the autopsy was completed two months ago. We still didn't have that report. You need an autopsy report before you do any real profile," Cronin said.

"I didn't know that."

"Yeah, you remember back in the 60s, two girls who were last seen getting off the bus on Archer Avenue and they were found a month or so later, out in the Forest Preserve, naked and dead. I was recently asked to do a profile because they still don't have the killer and rapist after all this time. So I started by looking at the autopsy report that said the girls died of exposure. That's very significant because if we pinched somebody for the homicide and even if he admitted that he killed them, we probably couldn't prosecute him because the autopsy report said they died of exposure."

"That doesn't sound right," Michaels said.

"Yep, the autopsy report said they died of exposure, no violence or anything. So that's why you don't do anything until you have the autopsy report," Cronin said.

"Well, surely you have the autopsy report now. So are you going to do a profile?"

"Yes, I think we are going to come in at the end of January and do one," Cronin said.

"Thanks, Lieutenant. Do you mind if I call you if I have any more questions?"

"No problem," Cronin said.

~~~~

Peter Michaels walked into Magers office with a little spring in his step and a smile on his face.

"You look like the cat that just ate the canary. What's up?" Magers asked.

"It's been a while since we had a Lezkowski story. I have this gut feeling they're getting closer. They're calling in a profiler."

"Yep, I saw that on the rundown."

"We put together this piece for the six. Do you like the lead in," Michaels said as he handed Magers his copy.

"The Ruth Lezkowski homicide investigation that started more than three months ago has renewed life tonight. The FBI may be getting involved in the very near future.

"This is the first time the FBI has gotten involved," Michaels said. "I think they're bringing in their top guy."

"I don't recall an investigation this intense."

"In the last 95 days, detectives have worked their asses off. They've interviewed and re-interviewed some 350 people. They have fingerprinted 110 people to eliminate them as suspects. They have taken blood samples, saliva samples and hair samples from over 100 people. They have given polygraph tests to scores of people," Michaels said.

"This will just be a reader on the ten."

"Yeah, I know."

# CHAPTER 21

D etectives Jack Evans, Lee Scholl, Aldo Palombo and Thomas Britten revisited every crime reported in1985 and 1986 for every sex assault, burglary, and theft-related offense in the 11$^{th}$ and 12$^{th}$ Districts that was committed in and around the area of the Lezkowski homicide. They compiled a priority list of 28 names of known offenders. They then added 64 more names to it and ultimately assembled a list of 92 offenders with multiple violations.

With the additional flow of information from Confidential Informants, the names of Lorenzo Holmes and Marcus Broadhead appeared on numerous occasions. They discovered that Holmes and Broadhead had been arrested for breaking into boxcars on the railroad tracks where Ruth Lezkowski was brutally murdered.

~~~~

Officer T. Wayne Purvis from the Public Housing Unit North walked into Area Four Violent Crimes with a grin from ear to ear. Purvis was smiling because he was getting a steady stream of information from his CI's that the name "Dog" keeps popping up in connection with Lezkowski homicide. A few days earlier, Purvis told Evans about "Shim Sham." When Evans and Scholl met with "Shim Sham" at the Cook County Jail, the street name "Dog" also came up during their interrogation.

"One of my guys told me 'Dog' could be a violent teenager by the name of Lorenzo Holmes," Purvis said.

Now it was Evans turn to smile. He had seen that name quite a few times in the last couple of days, so he went to the card files where all the street names, nicknames and aliases of criminals that were arrested are kept on file. These card files are in each police district and area headquarters so that identifications can be made. It's an old system of known suspects' names written on three by five index cards that record: street names, nicknames, identifying marks like tattoos, scars and anything like a missing finger that will help identify a suspect.

Evans had an immediate hit. "Dog" was a common name among gangbangers. This "Dog" belonged to Lorenzo Holmes. Evans ran his name in the Alpha file and had an immediate response. He was a bad guy. He had a long juvenile record. He was violent.

Evans found that on February 3,1984, Holmes and two of his associates, Raymond Caruthers and Andrew George, were arrested for abducting an 11-year-old black child in the area of the Lezkowski murder. They first robbed him of his groceries and then forced the victim into an abandoned apartment at 1510 West 13$^{th}$ Street. Holmes had a key. Holmes pulled down the victim's pants and stuck a broomstick in his anus. All three of the offenders then placed their penis in his mouth. Caruthers beat the young boy with his fists and George urinated in his mouth. After that Holmes set his hair on fire and then beat him with a stick. They were all arrested and convicted.

Caruthers was also arrested for another sex offense. On November 19,1983, Caruthers was charged with forcing a three-year-old black child to suck his penis. Afterwards, he urinated on the victim's face. He was convicted and released within two years.

Lorenzo Holmes spent two years in juvenile detention and was released on July 29,1986, less than three months before the Lezkowski homicide.

Evans found another hit on Lorenzo Holmes. This time, he and Marcus Broadhead were arrested for possession of stolen property at 1211 South Ashland. Once again, close to the Ruth Lezkowski homicide scene. Evans then found the supplementary reports from a robbery where the stolen property was taken and the offender, looking for leniency, stated that a person named "Crazy Marcus" killed the girl on the railroad tracks. The report went on to say, however, that all attempts to find "Crazy Marcus" have failed.

Scholl then looked up cases involving Marcus Broadhead and found out that on November 23,1983 he had been arrested for shoplifting at the 24-hour White Hen Pantry located at 1524 West Taylor Street.

Scholl also ran checks on the addresses of Broadhead, Holmes, Caruthers and George, and found that all of them lived close together in the ALBA Homes.

Detectives also found Marcus Broadhead's name in a 1981 vitriol case involving a deviate sexual assault charge. Broadhead and three others were named by a six-year-old black child accusing that he was forced to suck their penis and that they beat him up. The charges were later dropped.

~~~~

Good old-fashioned police work was producing some promising results. Evans and Scholl were now like two bloodhounds sniffing on a trail that was becoming very interesting.

An attempted robbery case caught Evans' attention. On January 9,1987, as a 37-year-old white female, Marcia Ann O'Malley, entered her apartment at 922 South May Street. She was met by an intruder who told her, "I got a gun, get in the house." Petrified, O'Malley froze at the door. A second offender tried to grab her purse. The first offender then grabbed her around her waist and tried to force her inside the apartment but O'Malley screamed and fought back, creating quite a ruckus and a lot of noise.

Other tenants started opening their doors and both offenders took off running south down Roosevelt Road.

~~~~

On January 18th at ten o'clock in the evening, a tactical team from the 12th District noticed three black males walking down West Roosevelt Road carrying a VCR and a woman's coat. When they saw the police, they ran. Marcus Broadhead was arrested and brought back to the 12th District lockup.

Detective Evans got a search warrant for his apartment and two medals were recovered which belonged to Marcia Ann O'Malley. Other stolen property from various robberies in the area was also confiscated. Two of Broadhead's roommates, Oscar Miller and Willard Manson, were also arrested and charged with possession of stolen property.

Evans said to Scholl, "Is this Oscar Miller the same guy we talked to a few days ago at Cook County Jail, that Reed gave us? You know the 'Shim Sham' thing. We need to check his aliases."

The gumshoe detective work of examining all the old supplementary reports and case files was starting to come together. Evans and Scholl now knew that Holmes, Broadhead, Raymond Caruthers and Andrew George were all acquainted through crimes they committed together. Evans and Scholl went to visit Holmes. Palombo and Britten went looking for Caruthers and George.

~~~~

Evans and Scholl walked up the rear stairs at 1623 West 14th Place and knocked on door 211. When the door opened, Evonte Holmes invited them in. They paid no attention to the dirty yellow walls, the stained and worn out furniture or the filthy linoleum floors, because the first thing they noticed was Lorenzo Holmes wearing a green shower cap. Holmes matched the description of the young six-foot tall black male standing on the access road located at 15th Place and Loomis that was given by Daniel Stark, the Chicago-Northwestern Railroad Police Officer, who discovered the body of Ruth Lezkowski just moments later.

"You Lorenzo Holmes?" asked Evans.

"Yeah, what's dis all about?" he asked.

"We're investigating the death of Ruth Lezkowski."

"Who dat?" Holmes asked.

"You haven't heard about the female medical student who was killed up there by the tracks a few months ago?" asked Scholl.

"Don't know nuttin' bout that."

"Then you won't mind coming over to Area Four and talking to us," said Evans.

~~~~

Though Lorenzo Holmes was 16 years old, he looked older. He was tall, muscular and had facial hair. Lt. David Copelin told Evans to get someone from Area Four Youth Division in the interrogation room.

Detective David Hill, a12-year veteran, had been involved in many juvenile investigations. He was quiet, competent and smart. He was told by Commander Maurer to make sure this interview goes according to the book. They didn't want anything going sideways if this kid was good for this homicide.

~~~~

As soon as Lorenzo Holmes entered the room he was given his Constitutional rights.

"Man, I don't know nuttin' about dat murder. I just got outta jail in July, man. Just a few months ago. You know what I'm saying?" Holmes said.

"We know that Lorenzo. What were you in prison for?" Evans asked.

"I got all tied up with that kid thang, you know what I'm talking about?"

"Yeah, we know what you are talking about. That was a pretty violent crime."

"That was bullshit, man."

"That isn't what the evidence showed, what the victim said and what they sentenced you for. Evans paused, shook his head and continued, "Do you know Andrew George?"

"Yeah, I knows him."

"Do you know Raymond Caruthers?"

"Yeah, I knows him too."

"Do you know Marcus Broadhead?"

"No, man, I don't know no dude by that name."

Evans caught Scholl's eye with that answer and asked again, "You don't know Marcus Broadhead? Are you sure about that?"

"I don't knows what ya'll getting at."

"How could you not know him? You were arrested with him and charged with possession of stolen property on November 8th of last year, Lorenzo."

"I don't knows what ya'll are up to. I didn't kill that woman. I haven't been up by those tracks in years," Holmes said.

~~~~

Detectives Tom Britten and Aldo Palombo found Andrew George and brought him into Area Four. He did not know that Holmes was in another interrogation room. "This piece of shit knows about Lorenzo's involvement. They talk all the time, I bet," Palombo said.

"Yep. They are two violent sons of bitches," Britten said. "I'll be the good cop."

"Okay."

To both of their surprise, Andrew George had no problem giving up information.

"Thanks for coming in Andrew. Do you know why you're here?" Britten asked.

"Yeah, I know you guys are looking into that woman who got killed up by the tracks," George responded.

"I am going to read you your Constitutional rights. Do you understand what that means?"

"Yeah, I'm cool wit dat."

"Where were you when Ruth Lezkowski was murdered?"

"I was in the joint. I was incarcerated at Valley View Juvenile Detention Center at that time."

Valley View Juvenile Detention Center is located 45 miles West of Chicago near Saint Charles, Illinois in Kane County. It is a low to medium-security facility that was built to house 228 juveniles. However, it was always being criticized for overcrowded conditions, because in reality, 300 juvenile offenders were housed there.

"How well do you know Lorenzo Holmes?" Britten asked.

"I be knowing him a long time. We got caught together in that kid thing. You know what I'm talking about, the reason I was there in Valley View."

"Do you know anything about the murder of Ruth Lezkowski?" Britten asked.

"Yeah, man, one day me and Lorenzo were getting high and shit. He say to me, 'you know dat girl who was killed up on the tracks?' I say 'Yeah man, I know about that.' And then he points to himself and say 'Me, Marcus and Shakey Jake did it.'"

"He admitted that to you?"

"I say to him, 'Man I could get that $25,000 reward,' and then he say to me, 'Yeah and you could get more money because I killed Lincoln too.' I thought he was full of shit and we didn't talk about it no more."

"How well does he know Marcus Broadhead?"

"Those two motherfuckers tight, man. They be real good friends," George said.

"Thanks, Andrew, we'll be in touch. Don't you go leaving town anytime soon. Do you understand me?" Britten said.

"I ain't going no-wheres, man," George said. "I gots no-wheres to go."

~~~~

Walking back into the interrogation room where Lorenzo Holmes was sitting nervously, Evans reminded him that he had been Mirandized already and then reread him his Constitutional rights for a second time. "We have a witness who tells us you, Marcus Broadhead and a person named Shakey Jake killed Ruth Lezkowski." It was at that time that Evans noticed the maleficence in his eyes, Evans thought. *Evil!*

"I don't know no Marcus Broadhead or this Shakey Jake motherfucker. I didn't kill no woman," Holmes said.

"Then you wouldn't mind taking a polygraph examination."

"I ain't taking no fucking test. No how," Holmes said.

"How about giving us some blood, so we can eliminate you?"

"I ain't giving you nuttin'. I didn't do this and I ain't giving you shit."

~~~~

Outside the interrogation room, Youth Crimes Detective David Hill said, "We should find his mother and bring her in to talk to him. We can't force these tests on a juvenile but if the mother comes in and talks to him maybe she can change all that."

"I'll reach out to Purvis. He's been very helpful; maybe he can go talk to her and bring her in," Palombo said.

"That's the only way to do it," Hill said.

"I've got people looking for Raymond Caruthers, but so far, no luck," Britten said.

"We'll find him sooner or later," Palombo said.

~~~~

Officer T. Wayne Purvis escorted Jeanne Holmes, the mother of Lorenzo Holmes, into Area Four Violent Crimes, and introduced her to Detective Jack Evans.

"Can you tell me what this is all about?" Mrs. Holmes asked.

"Yes ma'am. We are investigating the death of Ruth Lezkowski. She was the medical student that was killed up by the railroad tracks a few months ago. Your son was named as a suspect. He won't cooperate with us. We'd like him to take a polygraph test and get some blood and hair samples. This will help clear him if he's telling the truth." Evans lied.

"Can I talk to him?" she asked.

"Yes, ma'am, please come this way. He's in room three Evans said leading her to her son.

Fifteen minutes later they both signed consent forms for a polygraph test and samples of blood, saliva, pubic hair and head hair.

Evans drove them to Mount Sinai Hospital and Jeanne Holmes witnessed the medical personnel take her son's samples. The samples were then hand delivered to the Police Crime Lab.

Lorenzo Holmes and his mother then went to the Polygraph Unit where, he was administered the examination. In the opinion of the administrator he failed the test.

Evans then drove them to an aunt's house in the ALBA Homes and advised him not to leave the area.

# CHAPTER 22

P eter Michaels tried to get in touch with Sergeant Kennedy for more than 24 hours. It was unusual that Kennedy didn't return his calls. Sources were telling him that things were at a boiling point at Area Four Violent Crimes. He reached for his desk phone to call Kennedy for the third time this morning when his brick phone rang.

"News ... Michaels."

"Hey, it's Kennedy."

"What's up? Haven't heard from you in awhile."

"I'm giving you a heads-up. We are close to breaking the Lezkowski case wide open."

"What do you have?"

"We got two guys we like a lot. They're young, not what we originally thought."

"How soon?" Michaels asked.

"We're looking for one more guy. We are pretty sure, there are at least two, and maybe a third guy involved. They're violent offenders. Real violent."

"Let me know. I'll alert the boss. We're getting ready to do our sweeps piece. I need to give them a heads-up. Thanks," Michaels said ending the conversation.

~~~~

Detective Aldo Palombo was looking for any aliases listed for Oscar Miller and Shakey Jake in the street names card file. He wasn't surprised to find out that Miller was an alias for Oscar Sampson.

Sampson had a juvenile record for sexual assault of a minor, a child really. He was also connected to Lorenzo Holmes and Marcus Broadhead through various crimes they committed.

Shakey Jake was identified as Jeremiah Hudson. He's a 25-year-old black male, dark complexion with no scars or tattoos. He was arrested in 1984 for burglary, but the case was dismissed. He no longer resides at his last known address in the ALBA Homes, but his index card noted that the name "Shakey" was painted on the walls of the lobby of 1510 West 13th Street building.

~~~~

Detective Jack Evans and Officer T. Wayne Purvis were walking out of Area Four when Palombo said, "I just realized that we've been scammed by this Oscar Miller."

"What do you mean?"

"Miller and Sampson, they are one in the same. He's been in the system so many times he really knows how to use it. We had him in our hands just a few days ago and now we can't find him. Fuck."

"We'll find him sooner or later," Evans said. "Purvis thinks he knows where we could find Marcus Broadhead."

"This looks like it's starting to come together," Palombo said.

"Hope so," Evans said.

~~~~

Officer Purvis was right. They found Marcus Broadhead at his fourth floor apartment at 1510 West 13th Street. They knocked on the door of apartment 401, "Chicago Police. You home, Marcus?"

He opened the door and let them in. The place was filthy. It looked like it hadn't been cleaned from the time he moved in more than two years ago. There was a ratty couch that was once beige but now it was a mosaic of dark stains set against a wall that looked moist and moldy. A table to the right of the couch held a shade less lamp throwing light from a 60-watt bulb. A 55-inch television set sat on top of an orange crate with a tuner on the floor connected with a series of red, white and yellow wires. The whole place wreaked of urine and cooking fat.

"You know why we're here, Marcus?" Purvis asked.

"No, man. What the fuck's dis all about?"

"It's about Ruth Lezkowski. You know, the woman who was killed up by the tracks a few months ago."

"I don't know nuttin' about dat, man."

"That's not what we hear. We have one of your buddies for it," Evans said, stretching the truth trying to make him think real hard about the questions they were asking him. "We know, you know something about it. So why don't you come to Area Four and we can talk about it. What do you think, Marcus?" Evans said.

~~~~

Broadhead was put in Interrogation Room One and was immediately read his Constitutional rights. Broadhead was a 17-year-old black male, five feet, eleven inches tall, 165 pounds, brown eyes, black hair, and medium complexion. He's been arrested four times, including the sexual assault of a minor, burglary and possession of stolen property. He could be tried as an adult.

"Tell us what you know, Marcus," Evans asked.

"I don't know nuttin' I swear," Broadhead responded.

"Okay then, why don't we do this? You're innocent, so let's take a polygraph test and some blood samples, and when you're cleared, you can go home and we forget all about this." Evans lied. "What do you say?"

"I can do dat."

"Okay, let's go over to another room and clear this up."

~~~~

The polygraph examiner was waiting for them, ready to administer the examination. Five questions. Five answers. When a polygraph examination is administered, the examiner asks two or three questions that will automatically require a truthful answer in order to establish a truth line.

"Is your name Marcus Broadhead?"

"Yes." … Truthful.

"Do you live at 1510 West 13th Place, Apartment 401?"

"Yes." … Truthful.

"Have you ever been arrested for a crime?"

"Yes." … Truthful.

On the truthful answers it's common for the administrator to look straight at the graph paper emitting from the machine. It all changes when the answer becomes untruthful.

"Do you know anyone involved in the Ruth Lezkowski homicide?"

"No" … Untruthful.

The administrator glanced at Evans and gave a slight nod. Evans knew he was lying before the last question was asked.

"Did you murder Ruth Lezkowski?"

"No" … Untruthful.

Evans concentrated on the administrator when he pursed his lips and then gave a slight grin, Evans knew they had Marcus by the balls and they could squeeze them.

~~~~

"News … Michaels"

"It's Kennedy. We're rounding up three or four guys for the Lezkowski homicide. We are really putting the pressure on one of them to implicate the others. He's at Area Four right now and they're moving fast to get at least two more. You better get over there right away."

"Great. Thanks."

Michaels' Producer, Doug Longhini, straightened up and asked, "Who was that?"

"It was Kennedy, they just broke the Lezkowski case. I'm going over to Area Four Violent Crimes. Do me a favor, talk to the boss and the show producer. I think we've got a huge exclusive for the six o'clock show. I'm going to see if I can get Nagaro to shoot."

~~~~

Evans and Purvis let Broadhead stew and worry in Interrogation Room One for 45 minutes before they came back in.

"Well Marcus, it doesn't look too good for you, man. We know you were there," Evans said.

"I wasn't nowheres near that fucking place. Man, I'm tellin' y'all."

Of all those arrested, Evans and Purvis knew that Marcus was in the system the most and he knew it better than the others. He was the type, their experience told them that was most likely to flip. Life for a few years in the big house was a good bargaining chip and knowing that he failed the polygraph test gave them even more leverage.

"Look ah' here, Marcus. We know you were there," Purvis interrupted. "You just flunked your lie test. We know that Lorenzo Holmes was there and now we know that you were with him. You know it and we know it."

Visibly shaken, Broadhead broke down. "I was with Oscar, Lorenzo and Charles," he blurted out.

"Wait a minute. Tell us, who is Oscar?"

"Man, you know. You arrested him at my place about a week ago with all that stolen shit."

"Oscar Miller is Oscar Sampson?" Evans asked.

"Yeah, that be him."

"Who is this Charles?"

"He's Lorenzo younger cousin. He live up north by the Green."

"Okay, go on," Purvis said.

"Me and Oscar, we was hanging on 13$^{th}$ and Loomis, you know. It's 'bout one in the morning. We looks up and sees this car coming down Loomis driving all crazy-like."

"What color was the car?"

"It was white or beige, you know. Lorenzo be driving the car and his cousin Charles, is holding this white girl in the back seat. I says to him what you doing and Lorenzo say he's taking this girl up by the railroad tracks. So we goes up there."

"Then what happened?"

"Lorenzo then snatches the girl out the car and opens the trunk. He grabbed some box out of the trunk and put it on the ground, and then he pulls her pants down and makes her lean over in the trunk. And then he slipped his pants down and put his dick in her ass."

Evans could feel the adrenaline pulsating through his being now, realizing they just solved the mystery.

"How long did this go on?"

"I guess about five minutes or so."

"Did Lorenzo ejaculate?"

"Shit, man, I don't know. I can't say but I don't think so. She was yelling, screaming and trying to fight. And I told him, 'Man don't you going blowing yourself off inside her.'"

"Where were you when all this was going on?"

"I was standing about ten feet off to the side," Broadhead said.

"What was she wearing?'

"She had, you know, this light-colored sweat-suit on. One leg was on and one was off. And, oh yeah, there was this dark colored coat-like thing that was just lying on the front seat. Man it was crazy."

"Then, what happened?"

"Well, when Lorenzo was inside her, Charles starts arguing with him because he wants to be next. When Lorenzo finished, he walked over to the passenger side of the car. And that's when she tried to run away. She just got a few feet and she fell down to the ground. That's when Charles went after her and started kicking her and stomping on her."

"Did Lorenzo kick her?"

"Yeah man, his shower cap fell off and he went over there and starting kicking her too. Then he reached down and found this piece of concrete on the ground and started hitting her in the face and on the head with it."

"How many times?"

"I don't know man. It was all happening so fast you know. He was like raging. Then, Charles picks her up and throws her in the car on the driver's side. Her head was over on the passenger side. Charles then pulls down his sweatpants and puts his dick in her cunt. He was fucking her for a couple of minutes."

"Where was Lorenzo when this was happening?"

"Man, that fool was looking for his fucking shower cap that was blowing away somewhere."

"What was the girl doing now?"

"Man she was bad. She making some 'wicked-ass sound,' she was gurgling and swallowing and breathing hard. Crying."

"What else happened to her?"

"When Charles was through, you know, he and Lorenzo 'adjusted' her. They like pulled up her pants. They said that way the police wouldn't suspect that she had been raped. Then, we left."

"Tell me about how you just left her there?"

"Well, Oscar he was already gone. Then me and Lorenzo and Charles walked over to the north wall, hung from the ledge and dropped down to the ground. I sprained my ankle and cut my leg. It hurt like a motherfucker. Want to see my scar?"

"Sure," said Purvis. Marcus then rolled up his pant leg and showed them the scab on his shinbone.

"I went to the clinic over on Roosevelt and Throop to get some treatment, it hurt like hell."

Purvis and Evans had to do everything in their power to control their outrage. They felt the anger building up, here this poor beautiful woman just got savagely beaten to death, and they're both thinking at the same time that *this piece of shit is complaining about a scrape he got on his shin while fleeing the crime scene.* They made a mental note to check at the clinic to see the time and date of Broadhead's visit.

"So what did you do next?"

"So we was walking away, you know, and I asked Lorenzo what he did with the lady's wallet, cause I saw it on him when we were up on the tracks. He said he just left it up there. Then I asked him, 'did you get any money?' and he tells me 'no.' then we just walked up to the 1400 block of 14th Street and we split up. I went to my sister's house and they went over to 13th Street, I guess. I think that's where Lorenzo was staying."

"We found some prints up there, but not many."

"Man, those boys knows what they are doing, you know. They up there all the time in those boxcars. They were wearing gloves and it was cold that night. I just kept my hands in my pant pockets, I didn't want to leave no prints around there. You know, I picked up that box to see what was in it, but I grabbed it with paper bags that were in the trunk. I just crumpled up the bags then threw them away. I didn't want any of my shit found up there."

"Do you know anything about her car keys? Where they are?" Evans asked.

"Oh yeah! Just last month, in December, I ran into Charles and he shows me these keys. He said, 'Remember these?' I said, 'Man, boy, you better get rid of those motherfuckers. You crazy, throw those things away.'"

"Did he?"

"I don't know, man."

~~~~

Evans and Purvis were smiling from ear to ear when they walked into Lt. David Copelin's office, motioning for Palombo and Britten to follow them in. Sergeant Tom Swartz was already there, pressing his lower back against his favorite therapeutic wall.

"We got four offenders, all teenagers. Three of them have a history of violence. This Marcus guy spelled out the whole fucking thing. Named everyone involved and basically how it all went down. We need to go pinch Lorenzo Holmes and his young cousin, Charles. I'll go with Purvis up north to get Charles and you guys go get Lorenzo."

"I can't go. I got a problem at home with my son. He got into a fight at school and I have to go to a parent-teacher conference. If I don't go my wife will come after me with a baseball bat. I can't miss this thing," Purvis said.

"Where's Scholl?" asked Copelin now standing, reaching for his iced tea.

"He's going to be pissed that he's missing all of this after all the work he put in but he had some family stuff going on. His kid is up at Northern Illinois or something and had some problem with the Admissions Office," Evans said.

"Okay, grab Don Buerline from property crimes, he's young and eager. This will be a new experience for him," said Copelin.

"I've never worked with him before," said Evans.

"I don't give a fuck, take him and teach him a few things," Copelin said sternly. "And before you go, make arrangements to get this Broadhead photographed. You know what Commander Maurer said, pictures, front, back upper torso and legs, no marks, no anything. Everything is by the book. No mistakes," Copelin said. "Good work, boys. Let's get this wrapped up. I'll go tell Maurer we got this thing figured out."

~~~~

Peter Michaels and his cameraman, Paul Nagaro, were at Area Four Violent Crimes at two o'clock in the morning. As they were walking up the stairs, Detectives Jack Evans and someone Michaels had never seen before were walking down. Michaels motioned to Nagaro by rolling his finger for him to start shooting. Holding the camera under his arm, Nagaro turned it on and nonchalantly started taking video.

"Hey Evans, what's going on?"

"I can't talk to you Peter. We're kinda busy right now."

"I understand, you got a suspect or two?"

"Can't talk," Evans said as he walked past Michaels, mumbling under his breath. *How does this prick always show up.*

Michaels walked up to the Sergeant's desk and asked to see Commander Maurer.

"Wait here. I'll go see if he wants to talk to you." A few minutes later, he came back and said, "He can't talk right now. We got a lot going on."

"I'll wait," Michaels said.

~~~~

"How does that fucking Peter Michaels find out about this stuff so fast?" Evans asked Buerline, the man he never worked with before, as they were driving to Cabrini-Green to arrest Charles Holmes.

"I don't know," said Buerline, "but some of the coppers love him and some of them fucking can't stand him."

"He's a pain in the ass but he's good at what he does," Evans said.

"It's right over there," Buerline said as they pulled up to 1160 North Sedgwick. They had to walk up nine flights of stairs to get to Holmes' apartment. Naturally the elevator wasn't working. Nothing seemed to work in Cabrini-Green. It was very dark as they walked to apartment 902 and knocked on the door. "Chicago Police. You home, Charles?"

Charles' mother opened the door and let them in. She was droopy eyed and her hair was all over the place. "Charles is sleeping."

"Go wake him up," Evans said.

Charles was dazed and tired and tried to figure out what was going on around him at 2:30 in the morning. He seemed shy. He was five feet, eight inches tall, weighed 135 pounds, thin, with black hair, brown eyes, medium complexion. He was a student at Carpenter School two blocks from his building.

"Do you know why we're here, Charles?" asked Detective Buerline.

"No, I don't know why ya'll are here," Charles responded and yawned, rubbing his eyes.

"We want to talk to you about the Ruth Lezkowski homicide."

"Who dat?"

"You know, the woman who was murdered up by the railroad tracks a few months ago.

"I don't know nuttin' about that and I don't know nuttin' about those keys."

"Charles you're gonna have to come with us." And he was read his Constitutional rights.

~~~~

Peter Michaels heard Detective Evans talking to someone walking up the stairs. Nagaro grabbed his camera and started shooting. Evans and Buerline were escorting a teenaged boy into the Area Four Violent Crimes squad room. They took him into a back room and then came out. Evans walked over to Michaels and said, "You know, Peter, you can't use any of that. The kid's only 14 years old."

Michaels knew he would have to check with Sam Pfeiffer the station's attorney about the video but more importantly, he knew that one of the suspects was just 14.

~~~~

Detectives Evans and Buerline along with Youth Officer David Hill walked into Interrogation Room Two.

"Charles, this is Officer Hill, he's from the Youth Division. He's going to be here while we ask you some questions. Okay?" asked Evans.

"Yeah, that's fine, but I don't know what you want with me?" Charles responded and yawned again.

"Well, Charles, we think you know something about this homicide," Evans said.

"I told you, I don't know nuttin' about that."

"Yes, you do," interrupted Evans. "Your friend told us you were there and we're talking to your cousin, Lorenzo. We know he was there. He flunked a lie detector test yesterday. Why did you say you didn't have any keys when we came to your house? You couldn't know anything about keys if you weren't there. You might as well tell us what you know, Charles." they said as they walked out of the room to let him stew.

When Evans reentered the room, Charles shoulders slumped even more and his chin was resting on his chest. "You ready to talk Charles?"

He looked up at Evans with sleepy eyes and in a soft voice he said, "Okay, I guess so."

"Charles, use your own words and tell us what happened on October 18<sup>th</sup> of last year," Buerline said.

"Me, Lorenzo, Marcus and Daniel was walking down the street and we was waiting at the corner of Loomis and Flournoy."

"Waiting for what?"

"We was going to do a smash and grab, you know?" Charles said. "We sees this car coming down the street and it had this lady in it. We stopped the car and Lorenzo opened the passenger side door and jumped in. Then Marcus jumped in and opened the rear door for me and Daniel. Then they jumped in the back seat."

"Okay, then what happened?"

"I grabbed the lady, like in a headlock, and pull her from the front seat into the back seat. Lorenzo gets behind the wheel and starts driving towards the railroad tracks, but he's having all sorts of problems because he don't know how to drive no stick shift."

"So what did you do?"

"I kept holding the lady and Daniel jumped in the driver's seat and started driving the car up to the tracks. Lorenzo jumps outta the car when it stops, and I did too. He runs behind the car, opens the trunk and starts taking shit out, like a metal box."

"Then what did he do?"

"He put the box down, and he went and grabbed the lady and pulled her outta the car and brought her back by the trunk. He pushed her sorta in the trunk and pulled her pants down and then he stuck his dick up her ass."

Evans was thinking about his daughters and anger was building up. He was an experienced interviewer and he knew he should show no emotion. "Keep going."

"He was fucking her and I asked him if I could be next. He started yelling at me and we started arguing, 'cause I wanted to do it too.' So he finishes and the lady ran. Me and Lorenzo caught her and brought her back to the car. He knocked her down on the ground and started hitting her in the face with a piece of concrete that was there."

"Then what happened?"

"He picked her up and threw her in the front seat by the steering wheel. I got on top of her and started to fuck her and Lorenzo pulled me off her in a couple of minutes. Then Daniel took his turn. He stuck his dick in her ass and then fucked her in her cunt."

"Then what did you guys do?"

"Well, when Daniel got done, Lorenzo snatched her out the car and threw her back on the ground and started kicking her. Daniel started like stomping on her chest and then he used his foot to see if she was still alive. She must have been, because he started hitting her with the stick."

"What happened after that?"

"Marcus and Daniel ran away and I stayed with Lorenzo. He started going through her pockets looking for money. Then we ran. Lorenzo gave me some money so I could get home."

"Did you then go home?"

"Yeah, I took a bus and then a train back to the Green."

"Okay, Charles, tell us more about this Daniel. Do you know where he lives? Where he hangs out?"

"He used to stay over on Cleveland, but I don't think he's there anymore, he moved out. Oh! He used to play in the summer basketball league at Seward."

Seward Park borders the Cabrini-Green Housing Project. It was built in 1908 on more then seven acres of land. It is part of the wealthier Lincoln Park Community Park System. When Cabrini-Green started up, there were big concerns about population density. The park has a beautiful field house with a gymnasium that hosts basketball events almost year-round.

"Can you describe this Daniel for us?"

"Yeah, he be a little older than me. He about five-foot six, about my size, you know, maybe a little bigger. He got black hair, brown eyes and he be darker than me."

"Do you know how to reach him?"

"No, sir, like I said before, he moved out. I don't know where he staying now."

"Charles, do you know anything about the lady's car keys?"

"Oh yeah, I took em'. I like keys. I put em' on my key ring. I collects keys."

"Do you still have them?"

"No, I don't. Lorenzo yelled at me awhile back and told me to throw those keys away. So that's what I did. I threw em' away. I threw away my gym shoes too. They was all worn out and shit."

~~~~

Michaels was up for almost 36 straight hours, he was tired and his eyes showed it. His makeup had a hard time covering the black shadows under them. He knew he was going to cause a news blowout with his six o'clock report that he was still preparing only minutes before airtime. He just got off the phone with Magers, who was already in the studio back at the MART. He had to keep his head down as Magers introduced him. He was gloating and he couldn't show his grin. He knew that a chain reaction was about to start in every newsroom in Chicago. The grin was gone as soon as Ron Magers introduced him.

"There is a major break in the Ruth Lezkowski murder case. Our Peter Michaels is live outside of Area Four Violent Crimes. Peter."

"Ron, our Investigative Team has learned exclusively that Area Four Violent Crimes detectives believe they may have solved the brutal murder of Ruth Lezkowski. We have learned that at least three people are now in police custody, and they are being questioned as we speak.

We were here earlier today when detectives went out and made one of the arrests. One of the offenders is a black male, 14 years of age. Police have been in and out of here all day gathering evidence and searching for people who may know something about the suspects. One other 'Person of Interest,' is still at large and a manhunt is underway to find him."

At this point Michaels knew reporters and producers in every newsroom across the city were now scrambling to get crews over to Area Four Police Headquarters. The shit just hit the fan and they were caught flat-footed. This will be a Chicago Media frenzy for the Ten O'clock News.

Michaels concluded, "We have also learned that at least two of those in custody took and failed lie detector tests. These lie detector tests are not admissible in a court of law, but they give police considerable leverage when they interrogate a suspect.

"No formal charges have been filed as of yet. I believe detectives have contacted the State's Attorneys from Felony Review to meet and discuss charges in this case.

"Ron, we'll have more for our viewers at Ten O'clock. Back to you."

Michaels, exhausted just wanted to find a place to lay down for two hours of sleep. He hadn't seen his family in over 48 hours and he knew it would be after midnight when he got home tonight to a very upset wife and two girls he loved very much. *The news business strains marriages,* he thought.

# CHAPTER 23

Daylight was fading, the temperature was dropping, and Lorenzo Holmes wasn't budging. Although he was only 16 years old, he was hard-core. Holmes had been in the system for a violent sexual assault of a minor and burglary, and he knew how to use it. He served time in juvenile detention.

Holmes couldn't hear all the commotion from the media scrambling on the floor below him. He didn't even know what time it was. He looked up when detectives Jack Evans and Don Buerline walked into the room.

"I didn't do no murder, no how, no way," he said over and over again as the detective took their third shot at him.

"We got two people who put you there, Lorenzo," Evans said.

"I don't give a fuck what they says. I say, I didn't do a fucking thing to that woman."

"You flunked the lie box," Buerline said.

"Fuck dat lie box. It ain't no good any way. You know dat don't mean shit in court."

"The Railroad Police identified you at the crime scene."

"The fuck he did, 'cause I wasn't fucking there. I want a lawyer."

It had been a long day and it was starting to turn into a longer night.

~~~~

"We have to go back after Marcus. He's got too many inconsistencies in his statement," Evans said, as he reached for his umpteenth cup of stale coffee. His mouth was dry. His lips were chapped and his stomach was aching.

"He's trying to protect his ass," Buerline said, rubbing his eyes that were bloodshot and tired. "Let's get it done."

"Marcus, no more bullshit. Your story doesn't match the other stories we got," Evans said. "Set us straight here, Marcus. If Oscar wasn't there. Who is this Daniel guy?"

"I lied, okay? I was just trying to help myself here a little bit. Here's what happened. I met up with Lorenzo, Charles and Daniel at about nine o'clock in the lobby of 1440 West 13th Street. We was going to jack some cars. So we start walking over to the Jewel (Supermarket) on Harrison Street and Racine. Me and Daniel were on the Southwest corner and Lorenzo and Charles were on the Northeast corner. We're waiting and waiting, and finally this car drives up and Daniel steps right in front of it and the lady slams on the brakes and stops. Then everything starts to happen real fast."

"Well take your time, we want to get this right."

"Okay, so Lorenzo opens the front door and grabs the steering wheel. Charles and Daniel jump in the back seat and Charles like grabs her around the head and pulls her in the back seat. I jump in the front. Lorenzo starts driving the car south on Loomis but he has trouble because he don't know how to drive no stick shift. Daniel changes places and drives now."

"What was the lady doing?"

"She was struggling and yelling. Charles found a stick in the car and put it down her shirt and started poking her with it. She starts struggling more so I grab her hands and wrist and squeeze them over her head and Charles now starts hitting her in the back of the head with the stick. Then she really got pissed and started struggling and fighting more."

"Go on."

"So now we gets up to the tracks. Charles is still hitting her, and poking her, man, then he pulls her pants down. Lorenzo goes into the trunk takes out this here metal box, puts it on the ground and pulls her out of the car, bends her over in the trunk and drops his pants and puts his dick in her ass. Everything else is pretty much like I said before. She ran, fell, they grabbed her and they kicked her and Lorenzo hit her in the face and head with that concrete. Charles wanted some and tried to get it but Lorenzo kept yelling at him, so he stopped."

"What about Daniel?"

"Well yeah, he got on top of her and fucked her. I told him, 'man hurry up we been here way too long, we gotta go.'"

"How long were you there?"

"I'd say 45 minutes."

"Anything else you can remember?"

"Charles threw that stick away, I think he threw it south, Oh! He also took a pair of coveralls that were in the car."

"Coveralls?"

"Yeah, they were in the trunk, he took em' when he left."

"Can you describe this Daniel?"

"Yeah, I think he's my age,17. He's about five-foot six, black hair, brown eyes, about 150 pounds maybe, he be darker than me. He has three earrings in his right ear and he's got a tattoo of a pitchfork, it's got the number one on each side and there is a star and a heart in the center of it."

"Anything else?"

"Yeah, when me and Daniel left the scene, that lady was still screaming, but when we got to the street her screams stopped."

~~~~

The ten o'clock news was fast approaching. Michaels grabbed his brick phone and called Sergeant Kennedy. "Anything new?"

"No. You pretty much nailed it at six. They're still questioning the suspects," Kennedy said.

Michaels did his ten o'clock story with only a minor update that police were still questioning the suspects upstairs. He was walking to his car when a reporter from another station yelled out at him.

"Nice job, you asshole."

Michaels smiled and gave him the finger.

~~~~

When Michaels got home the kids were asleep but Katie was up and she was mad but she tempered her frustration, "You're an asshole! You know that? You are married to that fucking job. The only way we know what you look like is when we watch you on TV." She stormed off to bed with tears flowing.

When Michaels walked up the steps Iris was waiting for him. Sleepy eyed, she reached around his waist for a hug and said,

"Daddy, I'm cheerleading tonight for our home game. Will you be there?"

"I'll try honey," but he knew this story had just broken wide open and it was highly unlikely that he could make it. That's why he didn't say, I promise.

# CHAPTER 24

A ssistant State's Attorney Suzanne Grande, from Felony Review, was a career prosecutor. She graduated from DePaul Law School, Magna Cum Laude six years ago, and has been with the State's Attorney's Office ever since. She was a confident woman. She was five feet, eight inches tall, slender, blonde hair, blue eyes and she had a "don't fuck with me attitude."

She's been at Area Four Violent Crimes since four in the morning, talking with Detective Jack Evans prepping for the interviews with both Charles Holmes and Marcus Broadhead.

At 7:30 am, she was on her third cup of strong black coffee. She yawned and rubbed her bloodshot tired eyes and stretched as she prepared to meet Charles Holmes for the first time. He looked tired and scared. Grande almost felt sorry for the 14-year-old, his life hasn't even started and he was facing life in prison.

Once Youth Officer David Hill walked into the room, they were ready to start. The room looked like any other interrogation room except this one didn't have the handcuff loops on the walls. The walls were painted a drab beige color and they were all scuffed up. The furniture didn't match and none of the chairs offered any comfort. It was an uncomfortable room.

Grande first read Holmes his Constitutional rights with the added caveat, "Do you understand that even though you are a juvenile there can be a hearing in Juvenile Court, after which the judge could order you to be tried as an adult?"

"Yes."

"Understanding these rights, do you wish to talk to us now?"

"Yes."

"Charles, how old are you?"

"Fourteen."

Charles was wringing his hands and he was lifting his right heel up and down rapidly. He was nervous and intimidated.

"Now, Charles, I am going to call your attention to October 18, 1986. In the early morning hours, were you with Lorenzo, Marcus and Danny, in the area of Loomis and Flournoy in Chicago?"

"Yeah."

"And were you out on the street with those guys?"

"Yes."

"What is Lorenzo's last name?"

"Holmes."

"And how do you know Lorenzo?"

"He be my cousin."

"And do you know Marcus' last name?"

"No."

"Do you know Marcus to be Marcus Broadhead?"

"No."

Charles was starting to get more fidgety. His stomach was churning and he was trying to understand what this was all about. He had never been arrested before. He wanted to see his momma.

"Now, while you were out on the street with Lorenzo, Marcus and Danny, what did you see?" Grande continued.

"A car."

"And was this a four-door car?"

"Yes."

"And what did you see the car do?"

"Stop."

"And what did the car stop for?"

"Stop sign."

"And was that at approximately Loomis and Flournoy?"

"Yes."

"And who was in the car?"

"A lady."

"Was anyone else in the car with the lady?"

"No."

"What did you do when you saw the lady stopped at the stop sign?"

"We jumped in the car and I grabbed her from behind."

Charles was starting to get animated now. It appeared that he was settling in.

"What part of the car did you get into?"

"Back seat."

"What part of the car did Lorenzo jump into?"

"The front driver's side and he unlocked the doors."

"What part of the car did Marcus get into?"

"The front passenger side."

"What part of the car did Danny get into?"

"The back of the car."

"Who got in first?"

"Lorenzo."

"What did Lorenzo do when he got into the car?"

"He grabbed the lady and Marcus grabbed the steering wheel and stopped the car."

"And when Marcus grabbed the steering wheel and you all got in the car, what did you do to the lady?"

"Grabbed her from behind."

"How did you grab her from behind?"

"Headlock." With this response, Charles demonstrated as if he were grabbing someone in a headlock with his right arm reaching out and bringing his right hand to his left shoulder.

"And after you grabbed the lady in a headlock, where did you go?"

"Up to the tracks."

"And who drove the car first?"

"Lorenzo."

"And did anyone else drive the car besides Lorenzo?"

"Yes. Daniel."

ASA Grande's adrenaline was now pumping as she got to the most important part of Holmes' statement. She looked Charles in the eyes confidently, took a deep breath to calm herself and continued.

"When you got to the tracks, what did you do?"

"Went with Lorenzo."

"What did Lorenzo do?"

"Got out of the car and went to the back and opened the trunk."

"And what did he do after that?"

"Took out a box."

"What did he do with the box?"

"Put it on the side of the car."

"After he put the box on the side of the car, what did he do?"

"Went back for the girl."

"What did he do with the girl?"

"He pulled her pants down and bent her over the car."

"What did he do after he pulled her pants down and bent her over the car?"

"Fucked her," Charles said matter-of-factly with no emotion looking straight at Grande.

"And how did he do that?"

"How did he do that? He stuck his dick in her ass."

"After he stuck his penis in her behind, what did he do?"

"I asked Lorenzo could I have some and he said no."

"What happened between you and Lorenzo?"

"We had an argument."

"While you and Lorenzo were arguing about whether you could have some, what did the girl do?"

Charles lifted his shoulders, tilted his hands with an almost boring look on his face when he answered, "Ran."

"What happened to the girl as she was running?"

"She fell."

"After she fell, what did Lorenzo do?"

"Ran after her."

"What did Lorenzo do? Did he catch up with her?"

"Yes."

"When he caught up with the girl, what did Lorenzo do?"

"Brought her back to the car."

"When he brought her back to the car, what did he do then?"

"Laid her on the ground. That's when he hit her with a piece of concrete."

"Where did Lorenzo hit the lady with the piece of concrete?"

"On the head," he said as he was nodding affirmatively.

"After Lorenzo hit the lady with the concrete on the head, what did he do with the lady?"

"Put her in the front seat of the car."

"After he put her in the front seat of the car, what happened?"

"I jumped on top of her. I was getting ready to put it in and he held me back."

Grande was getting nauseous. She was a pro but the detached way Charles was answering the questions made her think *I can't believe this kid has no feelings.* "Who held you back?"

"Lorenzo."

"After Lorenzo pulled you off the lady, what happened?"

"Daniel got on top of her to give it to her."

"While you and Lorenzo were arguing, what did Daniel do to the lady?"

"Stick his penis in her butt and her pussy."

"After Daniel stuck his penis in her butt, what happened? What happened after that?"

"After Daniel did that he got off of her."

"After Daniel got off the lady, what happened?"

He put her back on the concrete."

"Where was the lady put on the concrete?"

"Beside the car."

"Who put the lady on the concrete?"

"They did."

"Who are you talking about?"

"The lady got put on the concrete and that's when they started kicking her," Charles answered with a quizzical look on his face.

"Who kicked the lady?"

"All of them."

"Did Daniel kick the lady?"

"Yes."

"Did Marcus kick the lady?"

"Yes."

"And did Lorenzo kick the lady?"

"Yes."

"Did anyone hit the lady?"

"Yes."

"Who hit the lady?"

"Daniel."

"And what did Daniel hit the lady with?"

"A stick."

Grande was sitting straight up in her chair and then leaned forward folding her hands on the table. "After Daniel hit the lady with the stick, what happened?"

"They still was kicking her to see if she was moving."

"After they stopped kicking the lady, what happened?"

"That's when they broke and ran."

"Who ran first?"

"Marcus and Daniel."

"After Marcus and Daniel ran, what did Lorenzo do with the lady?"

"Looked for money."

"Where did he look for money?"

"In her pockets."

"And did Lorenzo find any money in her pockets?"

"Yes."

"What did he do with money he found in her pockets?"

"He used half of it to get us home."

"Where did you and Lorenzo go after Lorenzo took the money from the lady's pocket?"

"Home."

By this time Charles was totally relaxed when Grande asked, "And how did you get home?"

"On the bus and train."

"And where do you live?"

"1160 North Sedgwick."

"Now, did you take anything from the lady or from the car while you were at the tracks?"

"Yes."

"What did you take?"

"Keys."

"And what did you do with the keys?"

"I had them for a couple of weeks and threw them away because I like having keys and Lorenzo convinced me to throw them away."

"That was a couple of weeks after you took the keys, is that right?"

"Yes, ma'am,"

"Where did you put the keys when you first took them from the car?"

"On my key ring."

At this point there was no doubt in Grande's mind that she would approve charges against the young boy sitting in front of her. It never failed to amaze her how suspects dispassionately described the brutality of their actions. She grit her teeth and opened the file in front of her and reached for a picture of Ruth Lezkowski.

"Charles, I am going to show you what I have marked as People's Exhibit No.1. Do you recognize the lady in that picture?"

"Yes."

"And who is the lady?"

"The lady that we were beating up, that was beaten up by us."

"Is that the same lady you grabbed in the car?"

"Yes."

"I am going to show you what I have marked as People's Exhibit No. 2 for identification. Do you recognize that?

"That's like the stick we had beat the lady with."

"Is that similar to that stick?"

"Yeah."

Grande had just completed the main part of Holmes' statement and seemed to relax a little. Charles Holmes seemed relieved as well. The intensity eased and so did his churning stomach.

"Now, Charles, since you have been at the police station. Have you been treated well by the police?"

"Yes."

"And have you been treated well by the Assistant State's Attorney, that is me, is that correct?"

"Yes."

"And have you been given food and coffee and water to drink; is that correct?"

"Yes."

"And you have been allowed to use the bathroom; is that correct?"

"Yeah."

"And nobody's made any promises to you or threats to you in order for you to give this statement, is that correct?"

"Yeah."

"And you are giving this statement because it is the truth about what happened; is that correct?"

"Yeah."

Suzanne Grande then said, "Let the record reflect that it is now 8:00 a.m. and that concludes the statement of Charles Holmes."

~~~~

Suzanne Grande did not want to waste any time, Marcus Broadhead's statement was scheduled to follow immediately. Meanwhile, Lt. Tom Cronin, the Chicago Police Department's profiler, was having breakfast with the FBI's top profiler, Richard Roberts, at the Palace Grill.

The Palace Grill was located at 1408 West Madison Street. It was an area that has started to boom with remodeled condos and the prices for those condos were skyrocketing. The Palace Grill was a favored police eatery. It was also a big supporter of the Chicago Blackhawks and it stays open later on game nights. It was a Chicago institution that was established in 1942 with seating for 150 people. The Chicago Sun Times Food Critic labeled it the "Best Breakfast Restaurant in Chicago."

"What's good here?" Roberts asked Cronin.

"Nothing is bad here but if you want the best thing ever for breakfast, have eggs with ham off the bone. It's fucking great."

"Eggs with ham off the bone it is."

They had no idea that by the time they finished breakfast they would not be doing any profile of the Lezkowski killers.

~~~~

Suzanne Grande was in the middle of Marcus Broadhead's statement when she asked him, "What was the lady doing as you were holding her hands above her head?"

"She was screaming and calling us sons of a bitches."

"And while the lady was screaming, what did Charles do?"

"Charles had a stick pushed in her blouse," as he said this he motioned with his hand reaching straight out like he was poking someone.

"And what was he doing with his other hand?"

"He had her around the neck, pressed against the back seat."

"Was the lady able to move in the hold that Charles had her in?"

"Yes. That was when he struck her in the back of the head with a stick."

"After Charles struck the lady in the back of the head with a stick, what happened?"

"She just started—that's when she started going wild," Broadhead's eyes opened wide when he gave his answer.

"And what did Charles do with the stick at that point?"

"He still had it, but he had to set it down. We had gotten around to the middle of 14th or 15$^{th}$ Street. I got out. Charles got out. We switched seats. I got in the back seat, holding her."

"When you got in the back seat at that time. What happened?"

"Daniel was in there holding her."

"And once you got in the car, how were you holding the lady?"

"I had her by her wrists and legs."

"And what were Daniels and Charles doing to the lady?"

"They was holding her, but at the same time Charles was trying to –he poked her with the stick and struck her."

"After he poked her and struck her with the stick, what happened?"

Broadhead shrugged his shoulders like it was no big deal and said, "He was trying to take her pants off. One of her legs was out of the pants."

"Where did Lorenzo drive the car at that point?"

"We were still sitting in the car, you know? The car didn't stop."

"Where did Lorenzo drive the car to?"

"Around the 1500 block and went up the ramp to the railroad tracks."

"When you got to the railroad tracks, did anyone get out of the car?"

"Yes, I jumped out first."

"After you jumped out of the car, did anyone else get out?"

"Yes, Daniels."

"After Daniels got out of the car, did anyone else get out?"

"They were still struggling with her, trying to get her pants off. Holmes got out next to open the door."

"When you say Holmes, do you mean Lorenzo?"

Broadhead nodded affirmatively, "Lorenzo."

"Where did Lorenzo go when he got out of the car?"

"Right to the trunk. He grabbed a box."

"What did he do when he got to the trunk?"

"Opened it and got the box."

"What did he do with the box?"

"He put it on the ground."

"After he opened the trunk, did he go back inside the car?"

"Yeah, he went inside the car and got the lady who owned the car."

"And what did he do with the lady?"

"He took her back there to the trunk."

The coffee Grande had earlier was starting to upset her stomach almost as much as the person in front of her, "How did he get her from the inside of the car to the back of the trunk?"

"He pulled her."

"And how did he pull her?"

"Grabbed her around the shoulders—I mean, around the arms and neck. She was stumbling back."

"And when he got her to the back of the trunk of the car, what did he do to her?"

"He pushed her, like, pushed her back, spine, up here. He pushed her head down in the car." Broadhead pushed his chair back and demonstrated how Ms. Lezkowski was pushed in the back of the head forcing her into the trunk of her car.

Grande making sure the court record was correct on this point, said, "Indicating for the record. The defendant is placing his hands on the back of the neck, showing motion forward."

"When he pushed her in the back of the trunk, what did he do?"

"He moved her leg—her legs was still. He moved her legs with his feet."

"And after he moved her legs with his feet, what happened?"

"He flipped his underpants down, flipped his penis out and stuck his penis in her."

Grande was mentally shrugging thinking *Oh My God*. She closed her eyes slightly then asked, "What was the lady doing at that time?"

"Screaming and hollering, trying to get away."

"Did the lady ever get away?"

"She stayed for three or four minutes. Then she stumbled about five feet away and fell."

"What did Charles and Daniels do at that time?"

"They were still in the car."

"When the lady stumbled and fell, did anyone grab her?"

"Charles jumped out and grabbed her."

Recalling how Charles described the horrific rape and murder of Ruth Lezkowski, Grande had a vivid picture in her mind of how this heartless crime was committed. The black coffee she drank all morning now gave her an acidy feeling in her stomach. Her anxiety was building as she continued.

"What did he do when he grabbed the lady?"

"First he got out and grabbed her. Then he started kicking her."

"Where was he kicking her?" After she asked this question, she was amazed at the unrepentant body language of Broadhead and his shameless explanation of the brutal attack.

"All over. He was kicking and then he stomped her up in the body."

"On the front and back of her body?"

"Yes."

"Did anyone other than Charles stomp and kick the lady?"

"Lorenzo Holmes."

"And where was Lorenzo kicking the lady?"

"He was kicking her in the back."

"What did Lorenzo do after he stomped and kicked the lady?"

"He picked up a piece of concrete."

"What did he do with the concrete?"

"He hit her in the face." Broadhead responded impassively.

"Was that Lorenzo who hit her in the face?"

"Yes."

"When Lorenzo hit the lady in the face with the concrete, what happened to the lady?"

"She was—when he hit her she was on her way to getting up."

"Then what happened?"

"He hit her with the concrete. She fell back down and Charles picked her up."

"Was the brick a piece of concrete from the ground?"

"Yes."

Grande was incredulous but she could not show any emotion "After he hit her back down to the ground with this piece of concrete, where was the lady taken?"

"She was taken back in the car."

"And what happened when she—what part of the car was she taken to?"

"The front part of the car."

"Who took her to the front part of the car?"

"Charles Holmes."

"When Charles put her in the front part of the car, what did he do?"

Broadhead sat there hands folded together with a detached look on his face and answered, "That's when he pulled his jogging pants down and put his penis in her cunt."

"How long did he stay on top of her?"

"Approximately three minutes."

"What were you doing at the time?"

"I was standing right there on the side watching Ashland and Loomis."

"Why were you watching Ashland and Loomis?"

"To see if anyone was coming up."

"How far away from the car were you, Charles and the lady at that time?"

"About ten or fifteen feet away."

"After Charles got on top of the lady, did anyone else get on top of the lady?"

"Yes."

"Who got on top of the lady?"

"Daniels."

"What happened when Daniels got on top of the lady?"

Broadhead shrugged his shoulders coldly and responded, "He tried to stick his penis in her cunt, but we was telling him, 'let's go.'"

"Who said, 'let's go' at that point?"

Pointing to himself he said, "I did."

"And what did you tell everyone?"

"I told them, 'let's go, we've been here too long.'"

"How long had you been up on the tracks at that point?"

"About forty-five minutes."

"Where did Charles and Lorenzo go at that time?"

"They came behind me when I jumped. All three of them came behind me."

"Who left first?"

"I jumped down first. I limped across the field. I was about five or ten feet in front of them."

"And what did Charles and Lorenzo do after you jumped down?"

"They came behind me. I asked them, 'did they get any money?'"

"What did Lorenzo say to you?"

"Lorenzo said there wasn't no money."

"Where did you go?"

"I went straight to 1222 Roosevelt Road."

"Who lives at 1222 Roosevelt Road?"

"My brother."

"What happened to the stick?"

"The stick was thrown by Charles around the time that Daniels was trying to get on top of the lady."

"Where did Charles throw the stick?"

Broadhead looked up at the ceiling as if thinking and responded, "South of 18th."

"On what side of the tracks did he throw the stick?

"Towards South, 18th Street."

"After he threw the stick, did Charles get anything else? Did he take anything else from the lady?"

"Yes, he took overalls and keys."

"Did he take anything from the car?"

"Yes, the lady's keys from the car."

"Do you know where Charles and Lorenzo went?"

"They went to 1440 West 13th Street. That's were we met up before. Me, Lorenzo, Charles and Daniels."

Broadhead was leaning back in his chair but straightened up when Grande opened the file on her desk and pulled out a picture. She reached across the desk and handed it to him.

"I am going to show you what has been marked as People's Exhibit No.1 for identification. Do you know who that is a picture of?"

"Yes."

"Who is that a picture of?"

"The lady we murdered that night."

Grande nodded and smiled to herself … Broadhead just admitted unsolicited that they murdered Ruth Lezkowski.

"I am going to show you what has been marked as People's Exhibit No.2. Do you recognize that?"

"Yes, from a distance."

"And what does it look like?"

"Looks like the stick that Charles had, similar to it."

"Now Marcus, since you have been at the police station, have you been treated well by the police?"

"Yes."

Grande looked Broadhead over carefully to make sure he had no injuries. Her experience had taught her to be leery of suspects who have changed their original statements to police. She noticed no injuries. If she did, she would not approve any charges.

"And have you been treated well by me?"

"Yes."

"Has anyone made any promises to you or threats to you in order for you to make this statement here?"

"No."

"Are you making this statement freely and voluntarily?"

"Yes."

"Are you making this statement because it is the truth about what happened on October 18th, 1986?"

"Yes."

~~~~

"I have been doing this for the last four years, it never ceases to amaze me how indifferent these gangbangers are. Like it is no big deal that they hit this poor woman with a piece of concrete or that they beat her with a stick and kicked her. Like it's nothing." Suzanne Grande said.

"I've been the police half my life, I just shake my head." Evans said.

"What about Lorenzo. Any chance that we will get a statement from him?" asked Grande.

"Not a chance in hell. He has said three words in the last five hours. Lawyer and fuck you."

# CHAPTER 25

"N ews ... Michaels."
"Felony Review just approved felony murder charges for the three we got in custody," said Sergeant Bob Kennedy.

"What about the fourth guy?"

"He apparently is on the run. They got a manhunt going for him."

"Are they going to make a big announcement?"

"Yeah, I'm writing a release for Maurer. I think they are going to do it around five tonight. I'll be sending out an advisory in a little while. It's going to be a cluster fuck with all the stations there for their live shots."

"I'll see you there."

~~~~

Lt. Tom Cronin and FBI Special Agent Richard Roberts walked into Area Four Violent Crimes thinking they were going to start working on a profile but when they got upstairs, instead they heard laughter and saw smoke coming out of Commander James Maurer's office.

Cronin popped his head in to see his best friend smoking a cigar with a big smile on his face.

"We got' em, Tommy," Maurer said.

"Well there was so much smoke coming out of this room, I thought we just elected a new pope. We were going to meet with you and put a profile together but I guess my job is finished here. No profile. Hey meet Special Agent Richard Roberts. He's the FBI profiler I was telling you about." Cronin said.

They shook hands and Maurer said, "Thanks for coming by but we wrapped this up. The three guys we pinched are charged with Felony Murder."

~~~~

Lt. David Copelin, Sergeant Tom Swartz, Detectives Jack Evans and Lee Scholl were in Maurer's office. Copelin doesn't smoke cigars often, but he had one blazing in celebration. Smoke filled the room, smiles spread across their faces and relief was in the air, as they knew the pressure from City Hall would cease.

"You took pictures of these guys, right? I don't want anything coming back and biting us in the ass," Maurer said.

"Everything is taken care of. We got pictures of all of them. All of them failed the polygraph," said Evans.

"Now, what about the fourth guy? Do we know who he is?" Maurer asked.

"This Broadhead guy changed his story. He implicated his best friend earlier and now he says it is somebody named Daniel or Daniels. I'm not buying it but we are checking it out," said Evans.

"Okay, good work. My wife is going to be happy this case is closed," Maurer said.

~~~~

Sergeant Kennedy set up a press conference for Commander James Maurer at five o'clock so that the story would get maximum coverage by the media. Detectives had to move their desks to accommodate the television cameras. Every network and their affiliates along with every radio station in the Chicagoland area claimed a space. Reporters were elbow to elbow.

When Maurer walked to the podium he had a confident stride and smile on his face but when he began to read his prepared statement, he was all business. He wanted a full description of the case and all the work that had gone into the four month long investigation to be known to the public. He was also relieved because his wife got off his ass. She was nagging him to get the case cleared because as a medical student she was well aware of the fears and feelings of her classmates during this time. Maurer started by describing the crime scene.

"Once at the location, one of the offenders took Miss Lezkowski out of the vehicle to the rear of the auto and brutally violated her. An argument ensued between the first offender and the others over who would assault her next. At this point, Miss Lezkowski broke loose and attempted to flee. One of the offenders caught up with her, laid her on the concrete and with the entire group kicking and striking her, smashed her in the skull with a huge chunk of concrete."

Harden reporters taking notes cringed at the statement as they visualized in their minds the brutal act being played out.

"With Miss Lezkowski dead or near death, the offenders returned her to the vehicle, where the others continued to sexually assault the body. Once they were through, she was dressed and placed outside the vehicle. Personal property was taken and the offenders fled.

"It was subsequently learned that the reason Miss Lezkowski was originally victimized was because one of the four offenders needed money to get back to his home in Cabrini-Green, and the group had decided to rob someone to obtain funds.

"Since the date of the incident, we have exhausted every possible lead in an effort to bring the perpetrators to justice. Hundreds of people have been interviewed. Dozens and dozens of bits of physical evidence were examined. With all of this said, and the offer of a reward in the matter, information was scarce.

"I would be extremely remiss if I did not specifically thank and single out the members of the Area Four Violent Crimes unit. This case has been extremely emotional. The detectives involved in the details of the horrifying, day-to-day investigation have performed with a dedication unsurpassed in my career. The professional demeanor of these detectives, the members of the Public Housing Unit and Assistant State's Attorney Suzanne Grande exhibited today gives me the greatest sense of respect and admiration for these men and women."

# CHAPTER 26

Michaels and his producer, Doug Longhini, were sitting around the office setting up the last interview for their "Throwaway Children" series scheduled to air next week.

"Where's your watch?" Longhini asked.

"Oh, I gave it to a bus driver."

"You did what?"

"I gave it to a bus driver."

"Are you nuts? You'll never see that watch again and that watch wasn't cheap. Why in the world would you do that?"

"I was on the bus last night going to the train station to get home and the driver was all upset. He thought he was going to lose his job because he was running late. He lost his watch so I gave him mine."

"Peter, you'll never see that watch again."

"Yeah, I will. The guy was in trouble. I'll get it back."

"Nope, you won't."

"What about McMurry (The Public Guardian). When are we interviewing him?"

"This afternoon, then we can outline our stories. I think we lead with Tomeka, then Brian and then Roberto."

"Yep, sounds good to me. It's hard to believe people can be that brutal to kids. This is really a story that has to be told. The system is really screwed up."

~~~~

Sergeant Tom Swartz told Detective Jack Evans, "I just gotta call from Officer Purvis. He said that Andrew George is in Cook County Jail."

"We just talked to him a few days ago. What did he get pinched for this time?" Evans asked.

"Burglary, I think, go get him and get his story on the record for court and see if he knows anyone else who might have heard that our guys bragged about killing Lezkowski."

~~~~

"Andrew, I am going to read you your Constitutional rights again," Evans said. "You okay with that? I need to ask again what do you know about the Ruth Lezkowski homicide."

"That's cool," George responded.

"You know this has nothing to do with the new charges that you are now facing?"

George knew the system and he was angling at getting some help on his current predicament. He also knew that there were no guarantees he would receive any special treatment.

"Yeah man, I knows," George said.

"Where were you on October 18, 1986?"

"I was incarcerated at Valley View Juvenile Detention Center at that time," George said.

"What do you know about the Ruth Lezkowski murder?"

"I know some of those involved and I heard stuff."

"How well do you know Lorenzo Holmes?" Evans asked.

"I be knowing him a long time. Like I told you before, we got caught together in that kid thing. You know what I'm talking about. That be the reason I was over there in Valley View."

"Do you know anything about the murder of Ruth Lezkowski?" Evans asked.

"Yeah, man, one day me and Lorenzo was getting high and shit. He says to me, 'you know that girl who was killed up there on the tracks?' I say, 'Yeah man,' and then he points to himself and says, 'Me, Marcus and Shakey Jake did it.'"

"He admitted that to you?"

"I says to him, 'Man, I could get that $25,000 reward,' and then he says to me, 'Yeah, and you could get more money because I killed Lincoln too.'"

"How well does he know Marcus Broadhead?"

"Like I said, those two motherfuckers are really tight, man. They be really good friends. You know what I'm talking about," George said.

"Do you know anyone else who heard Lorenzo and Marcus talk about killing Ruth Lezkowski?"

"Yeah, my lady."

"Why didn't you tell us about that before?"

"I just remember she was hanging with me one night and everybody was talking about dis."

"Did you tell your girlfriend that you had any conversations with the police?"

"No."

"What's your girlfriend's name, and how can we get in touch with her?"

"Her name be Tereka Sears. She stays at 1440 West 13th Street, 303."

"We are going to set you up with the state's attorney and have you appear before the Grand Jury. You okay with that?"

"That's cool. Say man, you think you can help me out with this latest thing?"

"I can't go there, Andrew," said Evans.

~~~~

Tereka Sears was a 15-year-old black female freshman at Crane High School. Since she agreed to talk with Area Four Violent Crimes detectives, they needed a Youth Officer present for the interview. Her grandmother was informed of the reason the police wanted to talk to Tereka and she readily gave her permission to talk to detectives Jack Evans and Lee Scholl. Once Youth Officer David Hill got to the interrogation room at Area Four, they started.

"Tereka do you know anything about the murder of Ruth Lezkowski?" Evans asked.

"Sometime between Christmas and New Years Day, I heard Lorenzo Holmes say he did it," Tereka said.

"Can you be more specific?"

"I was at the building close to my house on West 13th Street, you know what I'm saying and, it was about eight o'clock at night. We was standing in dat landing on the third floor."

"Who is we?"

"I was with Lorenzo and Andrew's brother, Melvin and we was talking. Melvin asks Lorenzo straight out if he knew about that $25,000 reward and if he knows who kilt that girl and Lorenzo starts laughing. So Melvin asks him again if he did it."

"And what did he say and do?"

"He said several times, 'Yeah, I did it,' and then he says to me 'Hoggie' and a couple of other guys was there too.'"

"Do you know who the other guys were?"

"I know 'Hoggie' is Marcus and don't remember the other ones."

"When you say Marcus, do you mean, Marcus Broadhead?"

"Yeah, in the projects, you know, he be known as 'Hoggie.'"

I was fixing to leave and I told Melvin, 'you gonna get your ass all tied up in this bullshit and I don't want nuttin' to do with it.' So I left and went to Grandma's," Tereka said.

"We are going to have you tell your story in front of the Grand Jury. You okay with that?" Evans asked.

"If Grandma say it's okay, yeah, I'll do it."

~~~~

"This Daniel thing sounds weak to me. We need to check it out. We should work on Marcus, I think he can be flipped." Detective Tom Britten said.

"I know Vanessa Hanba," Detective Aldo Palombo said. "She is a no-nonsense, hard-ass copper who works patrol over in 18. She's very familiar with Cabrini-Green and all the gang-bangers over there, maybe she can shed some light on this Daniel or Daniels."

Police officer Vanessa Hanba stands five-eight, with a thin but toned frame. She had blonde hair, blue eyes, and a great smile with beautiful white teeth. She's been on the job seven years and she is one tough cookie. She took no crap from anyone and there isn't a copper in the 18th District that wouldn't work with her.

"Daniel's description fits more than a 50,000 teenagers in Chicago. Five-nine, black, brown eyes, black hair, medium complexion but he has two distinguishing characteristics. He is said to have three earrings in his right ear and he has a tattoo of a pitchfork on his forearm," Palombo told officer Hanba.

"Then he belongs to the Disciples Street Gang," said Hanba

The Disciples Street Gang is one of the most vicious gangs in the City of Chicago. They are just one of 73 gangs that have been identified by the Chicago Police Department. Those 73 gangs have 500 factions with 68,000 known gang members. Gang Crimes officers believe there are another 100,000-gangbanger wannabe's that work for the gangs but have not yet been identified. Chicago has more known gang members than any other city in the United States including Los Angeles.

The Gangster Disciples and the Black Disciples started in Chicago and they have spread out. The Gangster Disciples are active in 26 other states and the Black Disciples are active in 27 other states.

Chicago's gangs peddle more than a billion dollars a year worth of drugs on street corners throughout the entire city. The amount of money these gangs make and the amount of deaths attributed to them make the old Chicago Mafia look like child's play.

"Come on, let's go. I have set up a meeting with two of my confidential informants," said Hanba.

~~~~

When Terrelle Jones and Curtis Stills entered the undercover police van parked on Davison a few blocks away from Cabrini-Green, they nodded at officer Hanba.

Hanba recruited Terrell Jones four years earlier after she got him off a marijuana charge. He had on a blue down jacket that looked like it was losing a lot of its goose feathers. He was tall and skinny. He had glassy eyes, a look that comes from smoking too many joints. When he pulled off his blue Chicago Bears woolen cap his bushy black hair was matted down.

Curtis Stills had been an informant for just over a year. He started talking after Hanba let him go without charging him for a minor drug deal in one of the Cabrini-Green buildings. He was short and stocky with a round face and dreadlocks.

They both belong to the Disciples Street Gang. If it were ever discovered that they were talking to the police, they would be slowly tortured and then killed as a warning to other gang members, a fate that had them nervous when they saw two strangers, detectives Palombo and Britten sitting in the van.

"They're all right. They're working the Lezkowski homicide and need some help with an identification," Hanba said. "You okay with that?"

"Who you be looking at?" Stills asked.

"His name is Daniel or Daniels. We believe he's a Disciple. He has three earrings in his right ear and he's got a Disciple tat on his left forearm. You know him?" Palombo asked.

"Where he stay at?" Jones asked.

"His last known address to us was 1119 North Cleveland."

"Dat be Disciple territory all right. Who the other dude?" Jones asked.

"Charles Holmes. He lives at 1160 North Sedgwick. We got him charged. He's Fourteen."

They both shook their heads, negatively. Stills said, "No fucking way those two friends. Man that boy be living in 'Stones' territory. Those motherfuckers hate each other. They be fighting all the time over drug turf. No fucking way."

"Does this Daniels guy sound familiar?" Britten asked.

"I don't know nobody like him, you know what I'm talking about? I know every motherfucking gangbanger in these projects. Don't know him," Stills said.

"Me neither" said Jones.

"See what you can find out and let me know if you learn anything," Hanba said.

"Sure will boss lady," they said in unison as they exited the van with their chins tucked into their chests and their hands out waiting for Hanba to drop a rolled up 20-dollar bill in their palms.

~~~~

"Sounds like someone is feeding you a bucket of shit," said Hanba.

"Yeah, they are going to be arraigned today or tomorrow. I'm going to have a little chat with Broadhead. I think he told us the truth the first time when he mentioned Oscar Sampson and then changed his story a little after Charles started talking," said Palombo.

"Thanks, boss lady. I owe you. Let me know if I can ever do something for you," Palombo said.

~~~~

Sergeant Tom Swartz walked over to where detectives Jack Evans and Lee Scholl were meeting, he was pushing on his lower back with both hands where he had ruptured a disc four years ago. He was in pain. He told them, "I just got off the phone with a University of Illinois Campus Police Lieutenant. One of his officers arrested a guy in late November who can finger Marcus Broadhead for the Lezkowski murder. His name is Wilson Jarvis and he lives in the ALBA Homes at 1521 West 13$^{th}$ Street. Go talk to him."

~~~~

Evans knocked on the door of 404. "Chicago Police—open up."

Wilson Jarvis peeked out of the door, wide eyed as he opened it. "What dis about?" he asked.

"We need to talk to you about Marcus Broadhead. Maybe it would be better if we came inside," Evans suggested.

Jarvis was 17 and didn't need a Youth Officer present when talking to the police. He was tall, lanky, brown eyes, black hair closely cut to his head. He wore jeans and flannel shirt. His 80-pound pit bull started to bark. Evans moved his coat out of the way and exposed his holstered weapon.

"Shut the fuck up, dog." Jarvis commanded.

His mother came out of the kitchen and asked, "What's he done now?"

Evans eased his hand away from his Glock and answered, "He hasn't done anything, Mrs. Jarvis. We just have a few questions for him. We heard that he might know something about the Lezkowski homicide. He's not in any trouble. We're hoping he can help us with something. You okay with that?" Evans asked.

She nodded affirmatively. "Tell 'em if you knows something, boy."

Evans looked at Wilson Jarvis. "You know by now we locked Marcus up for the Ruth Lezkowski homicide. Right?"

"Yeah, I heard all about dat. Everybody around know bout dat," Jarvis said.

"What do you know about Marcus' involvement?" Evans asked.

"I got out of Valley View (Juvenile Detention Center) on the 16$^{th}$ of October, last year."

"We know about that," Scholl said.

"Well about four or five days later, I was in the lobby of 1510 West 13$^{th}$ Street. Marcus and Lorenzo Holmes were there too, talking, you know what I'm saying. I hears Marcus say to Lorenz, 'that broad we finished off. They offering a $25,000 reward.'"

"Then what happened?"

"Lorenzo looks at me and grabs Marcus by the arm and walks him away and they stopped talking. That's all I know," Jarvis said.

"That's critical information in a homicide investigation, Wilson. We are going to need you to go in front of the Grand Jury and testify to this information."

"Man, if they find out I could get hurt, bad."

"Wilson, the Grand Jury is a closed hearing, like a secret investigative body, your name will not surface. Now that you've told us, if you don't testify, you could be arrested for Obstruction of Justice. This is a murder investigation," said Evans.

"He'll testify," said Mrs. Jarvis. "What happened to that poor girl is just shameful. Sinful that's what it is."

~~~~

"Hey," Michaels said as he entered Magers' office.

"What's new?"

"Not much. Those suspects are going to be charged as adults. That process started today. You should have seen those fuckers in court. They had no remorse. They were almost smirking when the judge was talking to them. I was shaking my head."

"Yeah, I know sometimes it can be very callous,"

"It amazing though, those coppers are not stopping with the arrests. They're looking for more collaborating witnesses to go in front of the grand jury. I think they have found three or four already."

"You think their case is weak?"

"It looks pretty strong to me but you never know. I cannot find out about the blood stuff yet. Even Kennedy is holding that shit close to his vest but I think he would tell me if he knew."

"What about the other guy?"

"They've got every copper in 11 and 12 looking for him."

"They'll find him."

"Yeah, they will."

# CHAPTER 27

A rea Four Violent Crimes detectives had been searching for their fourth suspect Oscar Sampson and for two weeks he's managed to elude them. A 12$^{th}$ District Tactical Officer spotted him twice, but he fled to avoid arrest. Sampson also had outstanding warrants for burglary from two suburbs.

Detectives stopped at 15 locations where Sampson was known to live or hang out but came away empty-handed. Witnesses also told detectives that Sampson knew the police have been looking for him since the time that Marcus Broadhead and the others were arrested.

One informant told police that Sampson said that the police were "coming after me next" once he saw the others had been arrested on TV three weeks ago.

~~~~

The WMAC Newsroom was abuzz, as Michaels finished his series on "Throwaway Children," he walked off the set and over to the other reporters who were gathered in front of the rows of television monitors mounted on the wall.

The fourth suspect in the Lezkowski homicide case, Oscar Sampson, turned himself into Channel Eight General Assignment Reporter, Ross Elder. Elder was a genuine guy, who had a flare for the dramatic. Many black suspects have turned themselves into the police with Elder at their sides. They would say they were afraid of being beaten and Ross would bring them in untouched. Channel Eight was playing it for all it was worth. The station had two or three cameras at the Third District Police Station on the City's Southside where Elder brought in Sampson. They were getting the exclusive footage that would run over and over again on their Newscasts during the next few days.

"You got your ass kicked on that one, Michaels," Reporter, Paul Hogan said with a smile on his face, getting in the dig.

Hogan was one of the best reporters in Chicago. He was an exceptional writer who had an incredible talent for weaving the facts of a story into prose. He was about six-foot-two-inches tall, thin, with a full beard that was always neatly trimmed. He wore designer suits, shirts and ties. He looked like he should be in GQ magazine. They were good friends. Michaels was godfather to his only daughter.

"Why you busting my balls, Hogan? Do you know how many suspects have turned themselves in with Ross at their side. This has to be the third one this year," Michaels retorted.

~~~~

"News … Michaels."

"Hey, they're transporting Sampson from the Third District right now. If you hurry, you might get a shot of him in the rear of the 11th District," Sergeant Kennedy said.

Michaels grabbed the nearest cameraman and ran out the door. They were 15 minutes away from Area Four if traffic was clear. It was going to be another long night.

They got there seconds before the Third District Transport arrived and got about 15 seconds of useable video of Oscar Sampson being shuffled into the cellblock.

Michaels got out his "Brick Phone" and dialed. "Hey, Hogan, kiss my ass," he said with a smile.

~~~~

Oscar Sampson was escorted into Interrogation Room One with his hands cuffed behind his back. Detectives Jack Evans and Lee Scholl were preparing their strategy for this crucial interview. Evans picked up his three-inch thick file on the Lezkowski homicide and entered the room.

Sampson was five feet, ten inches tall, brown eyes, black hair and he had a medium complexion. He was built like a high school sprinter. He was dressed in blue jeans and a red plaid flannel shirt. He looked tired.

Evans read him his Constitutional rights and explained to him that he was a suspect in the Lezkowski homicide.

"I don't know nuttin' about dat murder," Sampson said.

"Do you know Marcus Broadhead?" Evans asked.

"I been knowing him a long time. He like a brother to me."

"Do you know Lorenzo Holmes?"

"Yeah, I know him."

"Do you know Charles Holmes?"

"Nope, don't know that dude at all."

"You know Lorenzo Holmes but you don't know his cousin? They are inseparable, and you don't know him? He lives in Cabrini-Green. You sure about that?" Evans asked again.

Sampson was slouched down in his chair with an indifferent look on his face, he turned his head slightly to the left and said, "and I don't know no fuckin' Charles Holmes."

"What were you doing last October when Ruth Lezkowski was murdered?"

"Shit man, I don't remember. I didn't have nuttin' to do with it."

"Where were you?"

"I was staying on the Southside."

"Where?"

"I don't remember."

"You haven't been at the ALBA Homes?"

"No." He answered smugly.

"Where were you then?"

"I don't remember."

"Why were you running from the police?"

He leaned forward and folded his hands on the table and said with a smirk on his face, "Somebody told me, youse' guys were looking for me."

"Who?"

"Somebody was saying."

"Well if you didn't do anything, why were you running?"

"You knows how youse' guys are."

"Oscar, you were running before we even knew you were involved. Why?"

"I was told you was looking for me."

"And you don't know where you have been living. That doesn't sound too good. Do you understand what I'm saying here, Oscar?"

"I was staying at 1510 West 13ᵗʰ Street, apartment 207."

"That's vacant, isn't it?"

"Yeah, I gotta key."

"When's the last time you spoke to or saw Marcus?"

"I went to see him at Cook County Jail twice and he called me once at his place on 13ᵗʰ while I was staying there."

"You know, Oscar, Marcus told us that you were up on the tracks at the same time Ruth Lezkowski was killed."

"Dat's fucking bullshit, man, Marcus would never do me dat way. No fucking way."

"Well, I'm telling you, your friend put you there."

"Fuck you, man, Marcus would never do that shit to me. He and me be like brothers. He'd never do that."

"Why don't you want an attorney, Oscar?"

"Dat would screw up the plan."

"What do you mean screw up the plan?"

"Man, I'm done talking wit ya'll." Sampson said.

"We'll take a break. Sit tight Oscar. Don't go anywhere."

~~~~

Lt. David Copelin was at his desk leaning on his elbows, rubbing his eyes with both hands. His iced tea was sitting on a piece of water stained paper next to a stack of files on his desk. The tea was thin from its melted ice cubes, tasteless, tepid and unappealing. His ashtray was full and the air in his office smelled like smoldering cigarettes—disgusting. The dark circles around his eyes made him look tired but he was smiling, because this case was finally about to be "cleared."

"Whattaya got?" he asked Evans and Scholl.

"We like Sampson as the fourth guy. He was running before we even knew he was really involved. His story is all over the place. He was stunned when we told him his best bud, Marcus, gave him up and he said, 'that's fucking bullshit, Marcus would never do that.' We're letting him stew a little. We'll go back at him. He was there. He and Marcus were always together. He said they were like brothers."

"See if he'll take the polygraph. Let's see what that tells us," Sergeant Tom Swartz said from his perch against the wall he always leaned on. "If he was involved he'll slip up."

~~~~

"News … Michaels"

"We like this Sampson for the fourth guy. His story is filled with inconsistences. We might have some real solid stuff by tonight," said Sergeant Bob Kennedy.

"Did he break?"

"Not yet, we think he'll take a polygraph later."

"Thanks, I'll talk to the 'Powers that Be.'"

~~~~

"So you don't know anything about the Lezkowski homicide?" Evans asked again.

"I told you I don't know what you all are talking about." Sampson said.

"Then you wouldn't mind taking a polygraph test to clear it all up for us, would you?"

"I'll take that polygraph. I know I'd pass it with flying colors."

"How about you give us some blood and hair and saliva samples while you're at it?"

"I do dat … too."

"Good, we'll make the arrangements. Sign this release form giving us permission and we'll get right on it."

# CHAPTER 28

A t three-thirty in the morning, detectives Jack Evans and Lee Scholl entered Interrogation Room One and woke up Oscar Sampson, who had been asleep across three chairs. Armed with the new information that he failed the polygraph examination, they once again read him his Constitutional rights.

"You want a cup of coffee, Oscar?" Evans asked.

"Hey man, what time is it? When am I getting outta here?"

"You ain't. You got some problems, Oscar."

"What you mean, problems?"

"You failed the polygraph. You flunked it, Oscar. You're not telling us the truth," Detective Lee Scholl said.

"I didn't do none of dat, man, I swear."

"That's not what your best friend says, Oscar. Marcus puts you at the scene of the murder. He says you were there." Scholl countered.

Scholl wanted to come at him hard. *He ran for a reason and when people run generally they are guilty as sin.* Scholl had learned from experience.

"Dat's bullshit, man. I don't believe a word you says."

"Okay, you don't have to believe us; here, read this," Evans said as he handed Sampson a copy of the first statement made by Marcus Broadhead. "Go ahead and read it."

Evans shut his eyes and rubbed his temples, he knew they were close. He felt that *Marcus changed his story about Daniel to protect his longtime friend.* Evans was good at reading people. He watched Sampson closely as he read the report.

Oscar Sampson put the report down on the table, rubbed his eyes and picked it up and read it for a second time.

"Dat's bullshit Marcus would never do me that way."

Evans knew they had him thinking hard, wondering if Marcus turned on him. "You know, Oscar, we found two hair samples on the front driver's seat of Ruth Lezkowski's car. We also found sperm inside her. You and Charles were the only ones who fucked her in the front seat, Oscar. How long did Charles fuck her, Oscar?"

"For only a couple a minutes," Oscar blurted out.

Evans looked at his partner with that knowing look that only partners working a homicide case could communicate without saying a word. They were not surprised that he admitted he was there when Lezkowski was brutally sexually assaulted and murdered.

"Do you realize that the hairs we found on the front seat may be traced to you and Charles?" Evans asked.

"Yeah, I realize dat," Sampson responded.

"Do you want to start telling us the truth about what really happened up there?" Scholl asked.

"I want time to think about it," Sampson said.

Evans and Scholl stood up, knowing that Oscar Sampson just admitted to participating in the crime. Walking out the door, Evans turned to Sampson, "Knock on the door when you are ready to tell us the truth about what happened that night."

"Okay," Sampson said.

~~~~

At five o'clock in the morning, Detective Jack Evans called Assistant Cook County State's Attorney Suzanne Grande at Felony Review. "Hey, Suzanne, Sampson just told us that he was there. He admitted that Charles assaulted her for two minutes. I don't know if he'll make a statement or not."

"I'll be there around seven. Let me wrap up a few things here," Grande said.

At eight o'clock sharp, Detective Jack Evans and ASA Suzanne Grande entered Interrogation Room One and woke up Oscar Sampson. They handed him a cup of coffee with double cream and three sugars.

"I am Assistant State's Attorney Suzanne Grande. I'm going to read you your Constitutional rights again before we talk." After reading him his rights, she confronted him with the inconsistencies in his statements. "How can you not know where you were for the last six months?"

"I was staying on the Southside."

"Where?"

"You know, here and dare."

"Not good enough. Where, Oscar?"

"I ain't saying shit, man."

"Why were you running from the police before they actually started looking for you?"

"I told them. A friend told me they was looking for me."

"How would that friend know anything about it when the police didn't even identify you as a suspect yet? That doesn't make any sense."

Sampson didn't respond. He just glared at her.

"How about your good friend, your brother, Marcus Broadhead, implicating you? You read the statement, didn't you?"

"No fucking way Marcus do dat. I didn't do nuttin."

Detective Jack Evans interrupted, "You just told me that Charles fucked her for two minutes and that you knew those hairs from the front seat of the car could be yours. Now, you could only know that if you were there."

"It don't matter dat I said it. It don't prove nuttin'," Sampson said.

"Your admissions put you there, Oscar," Evans said.

"It don't mean shit. I'll be outta here, anyway, the next time I go to court. I'm not sayin' another fucking word."

"That's okay, Mr. Sampson, the next time you're going to court will be this afternoon for your arraignment," Grande said. "The State's Attorney's Office is charging you with felony murder, aggravated criminal sexual assault, aggravated kidnapping and armed robbery."

~~~~

The snow flurries were blinding as Peter Michaels drove to New Buffalo, Michigan, about an hour's drive from downtown Chicago. The temperature was a freezing 15 degrees, but the wind chill factor made it feel more like ten below. Visibility seemed like 20 feet as the car's defroster and wipers worked overtime to keep the snow from accumulating and forming ice on his windshield.

This weekend trip to New Buffalo was planned months ago with a group of people who were teaching him how to sail. Michaels needed some time with his wife Katie. They were starting to have arguments about his long working hours and time away from home. Neighbors were watching the kids and they needed a little time together. They all planned to meet at the "Stray Dog," A well-known hangout that served a very good Bloody Mary. You may see people across the country wearing a "Stray Dog" Tee shirt with its logo on the back "Sit-Stay."

As Michaels pulled off of Interstate 94 on Exit One in Michigan, his brick phone rang. "Hello. It's Peter."

"Hey, it's Kennedy. Where are you?"

"Buffalo City, that's how the sailing group referred to New Buffalo. What's going on?"

"I think they're going to arraign Sampson over in Branch Court 66 later this afternoon."

"Anything new?"

"Yeah, he failed the lie box."

"I figured that. Did any of the four pass it?"

"Nope. A tremendous amount of work went into this investigation. There was a lot of heat from the mayor's office."

"I bet. Where does it go from here?"

"They are following up on some leads. They want a few more witnesses to conversations admitting they killed her."

"Is there something wrong with Charles Holmes? He seems a little odd or something."

"He has a very low IQ. He admires the ground his cousin Lorenzo walks on," Kennedy said.

"If he didn't, he probably wouldn't be in the situation he's in now. Anyway, thanks. I'll call the newsroom with the update. Hey, thanks again. Let's have a beer next week."

"Sounds good. Enjoy your weekend."

~~~~

The snow had stopped and the plows and salt trucks were hard at work clearing the road that lead into downtown New Buffalo. "It looks like a Christmas card when everything is so white," Katie said.

"It's nice around here. Not to far and you're here in an hour. Let's enjoy this time together. Dial the newsroom for me, please. I've got to give them some instructions and then I am incognito for the rest of the weekend.

"Channel Six News, assignment desk."

"Hey, it's Michaels."

"Hey, what's up, asshole?"

"Nice. Hey, listen. They're probably going to arraign the fourth guy in the Lezkowski case later today."

"Yeah, it's on the wires."

The wires are news information networks. City hall and the police department notify all the news outlets in the city using press releases filled with information of events they hope to get covered.

"I think you can basically run the same story I did last night but put in that the I-Team has learned Sampson flunked his polygraph test.

"Got it, thanks. Have fun this weekend."

"There's a lot of beer with my name on it at The Dog."

# CHAPTER 29

With the Lezkowski homicide case "Cleared and Closed," Area Four Violent Crimes detectives were getting back to normal. However, in the busiest crime area in the City of Chicago, nothing is normal. It is hectic and chaotic every day. The 50 Violent Crimes detectives have caseloads that consist of all violent crimes, not just homicides. They cover all shootings, stabbings, beatings, non-fatal assaults and unsolved homicides. It was not uncommon to have a homicide a day in the summertime in Area Four. There were so many aggravated assault cases in the Area that detectives used to say, "The difference between aggravated assault and murder is marksmanship."

~~~~

Detectives Jack Evans and Lee Scholl were assigned two new homicide cases as soon as they returned to work from a week of furlough to rest after 115 days of intense pressure. Though these new cases would take up a lot of their time, they still reached out to Gang Crimes Specialists and Tact Team Officers to find more witnesses to bolster the Lezkowski case.

Property Crimes Detective Don Buerline, who worked with Evans for the first time the night they arrested Charles Holmes, walked over to Evans and signaled he needed to talk to him by putting his thumb and baby finger to his ear and whispering, "It's important."

Buerline had been pulled into homicide duty several times because of the high body count in Area Four. He had been on the job for seven years. He looked like a typical detective, suit from J.C.

Penny, button-down blue oxford shirt, striped red tie, knees stretched out on his pant legs from getting in and out a car too many times a day. Buerline was well liked. He always had a smile on his face and he knew everything in the record books about the Chicago Blackhawks. He was very good at his job; that's why previous supervisors recommended him for detective. In all police departments, being a detective is considered an honor.

Evans motioned "just a minute" as he cradled the phone to his ear. When he finished the call he said, "What's up?"

"Got some information you need to check. I had this assault and burglary case and the victim told me he had information on the Lezkowski homicide. Said he heard some guys talking about it, and he's very specific," Buerline said.

"Who is he?" Evans asked.

"DeSean Bryant, he lives in the ALBA Homes at 1459 West 13th Street, apartment 909."

~~~~

The stairway up to the ninth floor was typical for this time of year. Black snow was caked in the corners of each step. The center of every step was either damp or wet from the melting snow, and the filthy handrail was half attached. Apartment 909 was also typical of an ALBA Homes apartment: dirty, pale yellow walls, worn out carpet at the door, scuffed up wooden floors, linoleum floor in the kitchen; neither floor has felt a mop in a long time.

DeSean Bryant was 23 years old. He was six feet tall and thin. His dreadlocks were pulled in a ponytail and his brown eyes darted from side to side when he spoke. He was unemployed and on welfare.

"What do you know about the Lezkowski homicide?" Scholl asked.

"Well shortly after you arrested those three boys for killing her, I was at the building next door talking with Oscar Sampson and Kendall Marshal. We was on the second floor in the hallway. I say to Oscar, man, you better turn your ass in. He say, 'I ain't going to turn my ass in because I didn't do nuttin'.'"

"So what does that mean, if he said he didn't do anything?"

"I say to him, man come on, everybody in the neighborhood knows you was up there with Hoggie."

Even though Evans and Scholl suspected who 'Hoggie' was, they had to ask, "Who's 'Hoggie'?"

"You guys know 'Hoggie' be Marcus, you know what I'm saying?"

"Yeah, go on."

"Then, Oscar kept saying, 'I was up there with Marcus but I didn't do nuttin'. I was just watching.' Then I asked him, 'what the fuck you doing out that night, anyway?' He say they were waiting on a bus at Taylor Street to take Charles home but there was no buses running."

"What else did he say?" Evans asked.

"Then, he say Lorenzo was the first one to make the 'Rambo move.' He say Lorenzo jumped in the driver's seat and then Charles got in. Then Lorenzo yell out to Marcus and Oscar, who was up on the other corner, to get in. So they gets in the back seat. Then they drove the broad up to 15$^{th}$ Street. Then he say that Lorenzo and Charles were doing things to the broad and he and Marcus was just standing there watching."

"Then what happened?"

"Then he say that Lorenzo said he was going to make the broad pay because she ran. He said the woman tried to run away and Lorenzo caught her and hit her with a brick in the face. He say, me and Hoggie was trying to see who was messing with her in the car. Oscar told me that Lorenzo said, 'We're going to kill the the bitch for running away.'"

"What time did this conversation take place?" Evans asked.

"It was about six or seven o'clock. Oscar was just standing there talking away, you know what I'm sayin'. He was smokin' a joint and drinkin' a can of beer" Bryant said.

"You know, DeSean, you're gonna have to testify in front of the Grand Jury. This is valuable information," Evans said.

"When do I have to do dat?"

"Soon. We'll get back to you when we set up a date and time. Don't go anywhere."

"I gots nowhere to go, you know what I mean?"

"Yeah, I do," said Evans.

~~~~

Marshall was a neat freak. He worked as a janitor for the Chicago Housing Authority. His gray uniform was neatly pressed and his shoes were polished. Marshall was 20 years old, six feet, trim, brown eyes and his black hair was styled in a buzz cut with a number two trimmer. He came to Area Four Violent Crimes after work on Thursday, April 23, 1987.

Detectives Jack Evans and Lee Scholl escorted him into Interrogation Room Three and sat him down. "We'll be right back," Evans said.

"I am starting to think a lot of people know more about this case than we know. I think these shitheads were actually bragging about doing this crime," said Scholl.

"Yeah, I'm starting to think that way as well."

"That fucking Lorenzo is not talking. He only says 'lawyer and fuck you.' He's going to be our biggest headache. He really knows how to work the system for a young kid."

"We'll see what Kendall knows and if he can lead us to more witnesses" Evans said.

"Kendall, you are not in any trouble here. We just want to talk to you about any knowledge you have concerning the death of Ruth Lezkowski. DeSean Bryant told us you heard a conversation with DeSean and Oscar Sampson," Evans said.

"Yes, sir, I did," Marshall said.

"Why don't you start and tell us about what you heard?"

"Well, a few days after ya'll arrested Marcus, Lorenzo and that young kid, I was at home painting my apartment door. A friend of mine, Travis, he was inside the apartment helping me clean the bathroom. He didn't hear any of the conversation. So anyways, Oscar and DeSean was there and Oscar called out for DeSean to come out to the hallway. They was about ten feet away. I really didn't see them but I could hear them pretty good, most of the time. Sometimes they was talking low and I couldn't hear some of the shit they was sayin', but what I heard, I heard."

"You couldn't see them at this point, but you could hear them. Are you sure who was saying what?"

"Oh, yes, sir. I be knowing those guys for a long time. I'm sure. Man, DeSean comes right out and asks Oscar if he was there when they killed that girl up by the tracks, you know? Oscar said that he and Marcus was up there, but that he didn't do anything, because he was just watching. DeSean told him, 'man you should turn yourself in,' but he said he didn't want to right now, that he was going to be running for awhile."

"Did they say why they were there?"

"Yeah, he said they were trying to get money to get the young kid back to Cabrini-Green. He said that Lorenzo Holmes was the guy who drove the car up to the tracks and it was Lorenzo doing most of the stuff to that girl."

"Did he say what he meant by 'doing that stuff' to the girl?"

"Yes sir, he said that it was Lorenzo who hit the girl with a brick. Oscar said he thought the girl was unconscious, but that he didn't know she was dead."

"Do you remember anything else about the conversation? Oh, by the way, what time was it that this conversation took place?" Scholl asked.

"It was after five o'clock. I got off work at four and then came home and got ready to paint my door," Marshall said.

"Okay, thanks. Do you know anything else?" Evans asked.

"I guess, I should tell you that Marcus called my apartment a number of times. I remember because they was collect calls. He was in Cook County Jail."

"What were the calls about?" Evans asked.

"He wanted my momma to lie for him. He wanted her to say that he was at the social club at a party on the night that girl was killed."

Evans looked at Scholl with a slight grin. Their case was getting stronger and stronger. The more witnesses like this the better off they would be.

"We need to talk to her. When will she be home?" Evans asked.

"She's probably home now. She gets off work at 3:30. You want me to call her?"

"Yeah, if she's home, we'll take you there. Now you have to go before the Grand Jury with this information," Scholl said.

"When is that?" Marshall asked.

"We will set it up and give you plenty of notice," said Evans.

~~~~

Latrisha Marshall worked at George Washington Elementary School as a lunchroom attendant. She was a woman who liked to be involved in her community. She ran the "Chicken Bakes" at the ALBA Homes Social Club once a month.

Latrisha Marshall, 40, had four children she raised on her own since the divorce. She looked tired, her brown eyes sunken and surrounded by darker skin. She wore her black hair pulled straight back, giving her face more definition. Her five-foot-six frame seemed heavy, the blousy dresses she favored hung to the floor. She was reluctant to talk to detectives Evans and Scholl when they first arrived.

Evans sensed immediately that Mrs. Marshall *didn't trust the police very much.* He needed to be firm and threatening if he had to be. He looked her straight in the eye and asked, "Mrs. Marshall, this is a murder investigation and you need to tell us about the phone calls you received from Marcus Broadhead."

"What's this all about?" she asked.

"You know that we've already talked to your son. He told you that already so you know we're investigating the death of Ruth Lezkowski. The woman who was killed up by the tracks."

"Yeah, I knows. Ya'll arrested some boys for that already, didn't you?"

"Yes, we have four suspects in custody and we know there are a lot more witnesses who know something about this case. Your name came up. That's why we are here. If you know something, you need to tell us." Evans paused for effect and looked her straight in the eye. "Do you?"

"Well Marcus called me a few times after you guys arrested him for the murder of that white girl. He asked me to lie for him. He wanted me to tell the police that he was at the social club at the party on the night that girl was killed. He wanted me to say he was at the party from eight o'clock at night until two o'clock in the morning."

"Did he want anything else?" Evans asked.

"Yes, he did. He said he wanted me to tell his attorney that he was there and he wanted me to testify in court for him," Mrs. Marshall said.

"Are you going to? You know if you lie in a courtroom that's perjury and that's up to seven years in prison," Scholl said.

Evans felt that Mrs. Marshall had talked to the police before. She was wringing her hands when the interview first started but now she was adamant and became demonstrative. "I ain't going to jail for nobody, no how, no fucking way," she said.

"That would be a very wise thing, Mrs. Marshall," said Evans.

~~~~

The phones were ringing off the hook in the WMAC newsroom. Peter Michaels and the Unit-6 Investigative Team just finished a series of reports on the dangers of radon gas in homes. Viewers were calling non-stop since Monday night when Michaels first broke the explosive story. Reaction from the State was swift and that is what prompted the final story.

~~~~

APRIL 23,1987

Michaels was sitting on the set next to Ron Magers who was reading his intro to their newest blockbuster story on radon gas. He knew this was going to hit every viewer in their most delicate spot … their home.

Ron Magers began, "Two State Agencies are calling for new legislation requiring all new homes and homes that are for sale to be tested for radon gas. Peter Michaels and the Unit-6 Investigative Team have been reporting on the dangers of radon gas all week. Peter is with us now with the latest. Peter."

While the camera was on Magers, Michaels took a deep breath, exhaled to relax and was cued to camera three.

"Ron, the Illinois Environmental Protection Agency and the Department of Consumer Affairs want stricter laws enacted immediately to protect consumers from radon gas."

The director cut to Michaels pre-recorded package and Michaels looked over to Magers and said, "this story is going to piss off every viewer we have."

The news package continued; "Radon gas is a colorless, odorless, tasteless radioactive gas that is present in homes in every county in the State of Illinois. It is dangerous because it is the second leading cause of lung cancer in the United States. Radon gas is formed from the breakdown of uranium in soil, rock and water. It's every-where and it releases through the ground and can seep into your home through cracks and holes in the foundation. Radon can also contaminate well water.

"It is measured by what is known as a picocurie. Any amount over four picocuries can be dangerous to your health.

"The I-Team measured radon gas in seven counties in our viewing area. Here's what we found;

"In Cook County ... 15% of homes had dangerous levels of radon gas of over four picocuries.

"In DeKalb County, it was 35%

"In Du Page County ... 36%

"In Kane County ... 42%

"In LaSalle County ... 47%

"In Lake County ... 27%

"And in Will County, it was 41%

"Real Estate agents have been critical of this radon gas revelation because it was affecting home sales. Radon gas is easy to measure. Consumers can buy measuring kits at any hardware store. It's simple to use. You place a hockey puck size canister in your basement for 48 hours or up to 96 hours. A long-term test takes 90 days. These kits give the homeowner an accurate reading. Once a homeowner knows the radon gas level in their homes, simple mitigation methods can be made."

Michaels with the most sincere look he could muster was cued to camera two and wrapped up, "There is no need to panic. Radon gas tests will be required when the legislature enacts these new laws. Smokers who live in homes with radon gas increase their risk of lung cancer."

As they went into a commercial break the phones started ringing, Michaels looked at Magers and said, "Here we go."

Producers, writers and all the people on the assignment desk were answering the calls. The radon story hit a very big nerve in the community. When the value of someone's home is called into question, people react.

"Michaels you prick, we don't need this right now," someone on the assignment desk yelled over all the noise and clatter.

"These phones are non-stop," Michaels said as his telephone lit up with another call. He grabbed the receiver and pressed it to his ear.

"News ... Michaels."

"Hey, it's Kennedy. Great story. Now you have every fucking homeowner in the Chicago area wanting to kick your ass," said Sergeant Bob Kennedy.

Michaels couldn't help but laugh, shaking his head, "You know when I do a story about the police, all the coppers hate me. When I do a story about politicians, they all hate me. Now all the real estate agents in the state hate me. I can't win. To what do I owe the honor of this call?"

"Thought I'd let you know that Evans and company have found seven or eight circumstantial witnesses to bolster the case in the Lezkowski homicide."

"When do you think the first case will go to trial?"

"Six months, probably. The State's Attorney's Office is starting to interview these witnesses soon."

"Who do you think will be first?"

"Probably the ones with the confessions. So Charles Holmes and that shithead Marcus Broadhead."

"Thanks, let's have a beer soon," Michaels said.

# CHAPTER 30

B y mid-September, the Cook County State's Attorney's Office was busy getting ready for the trials of the four suspects in the Ruth Lezkowski homicide. Charles Holmes would be the first one to be tried. He celebrated his fifteenth birthday in the Cook County Jail. He would be tried as an adult. The charges were felony murder, aggravated sexual assault, aggravated kidnapping and armed robbery. Prosecutors would seek a sentence of life in prison without parole.

Assistant State's Attorney, Michael Pangborn, was named to First Chair of the Prosecution Team. Two other assistant state's attorneys were appointed to assist at trial. Pangborn, a career prosecutor with 20 years of experience was known as the go to guy in the state's attorney's office for major cases in the last ten years. He's sharp, smart and aggressive. The Magna Cum Laude Notre Dame Law School grad stood five-foot-ten inches tall, ran marathons and prided himself on being physically fit. He dressed in dark blue or black suits only, tailored to perfection, lying across his shoulders like the suit was part of his skin. He wore only white shirts, heavily starched. His tie was in a half-Windsor knot. His suspenders never clashed with his tie. He believed looking sharp made your mind sharp.

Melanie Wantuck was named Second Chair on the team. She was smart, quick-witted and aggressive. Another career prosecutor, Wantuck worked at the State's Attorney's Office for 15 years. She lived in Chicago all of her life, educated in Catholic schools and graduated from Northwestern Law School. For the last seven years, she worked out of 26th and California in Felony Court. She relished the opportunity to work with her mentor, Michael Pangborn.

Wantuck was five feet, nine inches tall, weighed 131 pounds of solid muscle. She worked out four or five times a week. She dressed in tailor-made pantsuits. When she went to trial, like her mentor, she wore only dark blue or black suits and white or off white silk blouses with conservative necklines. She walked with confidence and when she entered a room every man's head turned. She was stunningly beautiful. She had long, dark brown hair, green eyes and a natural beauty mark on her right eye that she darkened with an eyebrow pencil to accentuate it even more. Her fingernails were always manicured to perfection, and she wore simple jewelry. Though she was married, she didn't wear a wedding ring on her left hand.

Devante Jackson, the third member of the team, worked in Felony Prosecutions for the last three years. He was an up-and-comer in the state's attorney's office. Jackson graduated from Marshall Law School in Chicago ten years ago. He was smart, aggressive and eager to learn. This case would be the first time he had been teamed with Michael Pangborn. He wanted to take full of advantage of the experience.

Jackson, a handsome African-American, stood six feet, two inches tall. His handshake was firm and his smile was warm. His easy-going manner disguised his attention to detail and his intensity. Unlike Pangborn and Wantuck, his suits were not conservative. Jackson never wore a white shirt and his ties were all unique and colorful. His designer shoes were always polished. He shaved his head, which gave him a domineering and confident appearance.

~~~~

Pangborn walked around his desk and threw his souvenir Cubs baseball in the air whenever he was deep in thought. His preparation for trial was always meticulous and detailed. He already made up his mind in what order he would try the suspects. His prosecution team entered his office for their first meeting to discuss the witness order for the Charles Holmes trial that began next month. Normally his secretary would hold all calls when he discussed trial arrangements, so when the phone rang, he knew it must be important.

"Pangborn here."

"Hey Mike, it's Detective Jack Evans."

"Hey, Jack. We were just going through our witness list. What's up?"

"One of the Tact guys gave me the name of a suspect who may give you some leverage to flip Marcus Broadhead."

"What do you mean?"

"He was intimidating one of our witnesses, Kendall Marshall. He said he won't implicate Marcus, but from what I hear, it may be good for the case. Me and Lee are about to interview him. I'll call you when we finish."

~~~~

Corey Wallace was arrested for aggravated battery and intimidation on March 18,1987 for attacking two people. One of the victims was Kendall Marshall, a circumstantial witness in the Ruth Lezkowski murder case. Wallace started yelling at Marshall, and threatened him to change his testimony against Marcus Broadhead. Wallace wanted him to say that Broadhead was at the party all night at the time of the Lezkowski murder.

"Fuck you, man. I ain't going to jail for some sorry-ass killer," Marshall said.

Wallace went after him with a baseball bat and his friend Martavis Thomas stepped in and tried to stop him. Wallace hit him in the head with the bat.

Thomas is in Cook County Hospital with a concussion and Wallace is in Interrogation Room One at Area Four Violent Crimes in deep shit.

~~~~

Corey Wallace was 22 years old, five-eleven, 160 pounds, black hair, brown eyes and a dark complexion. He has had some minor incidents with the law and this, by far, was the first time he was facing real jail time. He was ready to bargain.

While Detective Jack Evans read Wallace his Constitutional rights, his left foot was bouncing up and down a mile a minute in a nervous fit.

Evans felt Wallace had to know something about the Lezkowski case because of his nervous reaction to being questioned. He went after him hard. "Obstructing justice is a pretty big charge that we can tack onto that aggravated assault and intimidation charge, Wallace."

"I knows some stuff man, but I can't bring Marcus into this. You know what I mean? I know shit about that white girl getting killed up there by the tracks but I ain't saying nuttin' about Marcus at all."

"You tell us what you know and we'll see what we can do. What do you know?" Evans asked.

"On October 17th, we was having this here party at 1510 West 13th Street, in apartment 207 on the second floor. I was the DJ. This girl named 'Chocolate' was living there at the time. She hired me and we was charging a dollar at the door to get in. You know what I mean? We was gonna split the money, you know?"

"Yeah, so what happened?"

"Around eight o'clock Lorenzo Holmes and Oscar Sampson comes in but they don't stay too long. They leaves and comes back around ten. I don't know this Lorenzo guy but Oscar does and I think they did some shit together. You know what I'm saying? There was this younger dude with them too, at first, but when they comes back he ain't with 'em."

Evans was thinking, *this can't be a coincidence these pieces are all starting to fit together. We need this in writing.*

"What were they dressed like, do you remember?" Evans asked.

"Yeah man, I think Lorenzo had on a dark jogging suit.

"Was he wearing a hat, a shower cap or gloves?"

"No man, I didn't see any shit like that. Oscar had on a gray sweater, blue jeans and British Knight Gym Shoes."

"So what time does this party end?"

"The party ended after two in the morning. We was all standing around and something was going on down the street. Police cars were everywhere, spotlights looking for something and blue lights flashing and shit. Oscar comes back to the place after four. I say hi to him and then I goes home. You know what I'm saying?"

"Okay, so what?"

"Well, I don't hear about the murder until the next day. I saw it on the news. I don't make the connection at the time. I know that Oscar and Marcus be doing some robberies north of Roosevelt Road for months. They would always bring their shit back to Marcus' place. You know what I'm saying?"

"So what?" said Evans.

"They kept robbing peoples after that girl was killed. So when they get arrested, I say 'shit man.' I see them on TV and that night I run into Oscar and I starts talking to him. He's acting all kind of strange and shit, you know what I'm saying? So I ask him, 'What's wrong with you, man?' He says right away that 'the police will probably be looking for me next.' He says then that he and Lorenzo were the ones who killed that white girl up on the tracks."

"He admitted that to you?" Scholl asked.

"Sure did! He said he was going to avoid the police for as long as he could. Right before he finally turned hisself in, I saw him up by DeSean's place. I remember, DeSean he just moved in and he was painting his door and Kendall Marshall was up there with them. I walked over there and they were drinking some beer and I saw Oscar sitting on a rail outside the apartment. That was the last time I saw him."

"Then what happened?" Evans asked.

"I sees Marcus' brother and he says, 'Marcus said he wanted me to get some people to change their story and say he was at the party all night that girl was killed.' I says, 'man I don't know and here I am, in deep shit.'"

"Corey, you are going to have to make a statement to the state's attorney but I also want you to make a written statement for our files. This verifies what a lot of others have told us."

"Man, can you do anything for me?"

"The only thing I can tell you is, I'll talk to the state's attorney and they may be able to help you. I can't promise you anything," Evans said.

~~~~

ASA Michael Pangborn was pacing and tossing his Cubs baseball in the air and thought about the leverage he now had to pressure Marcus Broadhead into cooperating. The meeting with Corey Wallace was very brief and to the point. "Mr. Wallace, we are going to schedule you to appear before the Grand Jury. They are going to ask you similar questions like I have and like detective Evans did. Do you understand?"

"Yes, sir."

"And you understand that I may call you as a witness during trial?"

"Yes, sir."

"And if I call you, you are expected to tell the truth?"

"Yes, sir. Is you going to be able to help me with these charges?"

"I'll talk to my boss and the other witnesses. I make no promises. Do you understand?"

"Yeah."

# CHAPTER 31

R on Magers loved it when his office was busy with reporters and producers coming and going before any newscast. Everyone trusted his opinion on the most serious story of the night or the funny kicker that would end the show.

On the night before the first trial of the Lezkowski Four, Peter Michaels walked in and said, "Big day tomorrow for the prosecution."

"They're doing the kid first?"

"Yeah. He had his 15th birthday in county. The kid is facing life without parole. He's fucked. I can't imagine thinking that you are never going to walk the streets again."

"Isn't Judge Albanese sort of the 'Judge Roy Bean' at 26th Street?"

"Yep, they call him the hanging judge but Pangborn feels they have a very solid case with Charles Holmes confession, all the witnesses they have and with the medical examiner's testimony, it will be absolutely devastating. How do you like the lead in for tonight's show?"

"Looks good. Let's put this thing to bed," Magers said as he and Michaels walked into the studio to do the ten o'clock newscast.

~~~~

Cook County's Criminal Courts Building, also known as 26th and Cal, first opened its doors on April Fool's day in 1929. At that time, it cost $7.5 million to construct. It replaced the stone-heavy Otto Matz Courthouse that was built in 1893 on Hubbard Street in downtown Chicago. That courthouse was totally remodeled and is now being used by lawyers for their offices. The classic play "The Front Page" got its flavor from its gallows hangings in the courtyard.

The Cook County Criminal Courts Building is located on 96 acres of land, which is said to have been owned by the family of Anton Cermak, the mayor of Chicago, who was assassinated in Miami in 1932, when a bullet intended for President-elect Franklin D. Roosevelt hit Cermak instead. The assassin was Giuseppe Zangara. Alternative accounts suggest the bullet was actually meant for Cermak. There were many theories as to why Cermak would have been assassinated, but in the book, *Frank Nitti: The True Story of Chicago's Notorious Enforcer,* the author contends that Cermak was corrupt and that the Chicago Outfit hired Zangara to kill Cermak in retaliation for his attempts to murder Frank Nitti.

The building is faced with Bedford limestone from Indiana. The top floor windows were adorned with eight tall stone reliefs sculpted by Swedish-born sculptor, Peter Toneman, that depict the human form of ideals such as law, justice, liberty, truth, might, love, wisdom and peace. The building houses 31 courtrooms, which on any given day can have as many as 12 murder trials going on at the same time. Each judge had as many 300 cases on his or her docket at one time. There were 22,000 felony cases tried in a year.

The case of Charles Holmes will be tried in Courtroom 404.

~~~~

The doors of Courtroom 404 were ten feet tall and made of heavy, dark oak that open outward with a grunt and a heave. They reminded you of an entrance to a Cathedral or Basilica. The courtroom's vaulted ceilings are 20 feet high and adorned with figures of stars, moons and scrolls tied with ribbons along with the symbols of justice, truth and peace. The tiled floor is glossy with decades of polish burnished into it with hand held buffers. The walls are wood-paneled with two feet wide windows that start midway up and go to the ceiling on one side of the room. The 15 rows of ornate church-like pews are made of heavy dark wood, separated by a ten-foot wide aisle providing seating for at least 300 people in the gallery or the "hard seats."

The judge's eight-foot dark mahogany bench was like an altar, four feet higher than anything in the courtroom. It was the focal point of the well. The well of the courtroom is the area where the state's attorneys and defense attorneys conduct their trials. The three-by-five-foot prosecutor's table was to the right of the judge and the defense attorney's table was to the left. Both of the tables' tops were scratched and scarred from years of writing with ballpoint pens pressing into single sheets of paper as attorneys frantically took notes. Each table had four chairs that didn't match.

The witness box sat one step up from the floor, to the right of the judge and to the left of the prosecutors. The court reporter with her stenographic machine, sat directly in front of the witness.

The jury box had 14 blue vinyl padded chairs laid out in two rows. The seven front-row seats were one step higher than the floor, and the back row was two feet higher, so each juror had a clear view of the witness box and the well. The jurors were seated in the order that they were selected. The two alternates sat in seats seven and 14, the furthest away from the witness box.

~~~~

When Charles Holmes entered Courtroom 404 for the first time, his eyes were wide with amazement and filled with fear at the same time. They darted back and forth, up and down, taking in the atmosphere that surrounded him. He was bewildered and nervous, and his hands were shaking. He felt sick to his stomach. He was dressed in the only suit he ever owned. He would never wear it again after his trial. He took his seat at the defense table and shyly glanced at the jury of six men and eight women. He didn't know that two of them were alternates. Seven were Black, three men and four women. Five were White, two men and three women. Two were Hispanic, one man and one woman.

~~~~

Judge William Albanese entered the courtroom as if on cue. The proud Chicago Italian wore a black robe that hid his five-foot, nine-inch muscular frame. As a high school All American defensive linebacker, he went on to earn straight A's at the University of Notre Dame. He was a fan in college, not a player. He graduated with honors from Notre Dame Law School. He worked first with the Cook County State's Attorney's Office; for seven of his 15 years as a prosecutor he supervised "Special Prosecutions." He was elected to the bench on his first try in 1980. He was a scholarly, no-nonsense jurist, who has never been overturned in the Appellate Courts. His gavel brought the courtroom to order as everyone took their seats.

~~~~

There was tension in the packed courtroom on Tuesday, February 2,1988, the Cook County Clerk of the Court announced The People of Illinois versus Charles Holmes. Judge Albanese had already denied a Motion to Suppress Holmes' statement that implicated him in the murder of Ruth Lezkowski. His defense attorney, Steven Roberts filed it immediately after the jury had been selected.

Roberts was a high profile and highly priced criminal defense attorney who had practiced law for more than 20 years in both, state and federal Courts in Illinois. He was appointed by the court but was offering his services Pro Bono in this highly publicized case. A graduate of John Marshall Law School in Chicago, Roberts was a very skilled litigator. Though only five-foot, seven inches tall, he glided across the courtroom with an air of confidence and decorum. He was a student of criminal law. He was quick to his feet with an objection and sharp with his words on cross-examination.

~~~~

Michael Pangborn never took his eyes off the jury when he delivered his opening statement. He was looking for any reactions as he focused on the grisly, brutal, heinous murder of Ruth Lezkowski. As he highlighted the three tragic ways that she could have died from blunt force trauma, he could read the reactions on their faces. He then set the stage for his final witnesses, Cook County Medical Examiner Robert Crine. Pangborn knew that Dr. Crine's blunt and medically specific detail of all the injuries that Ruth Lezkowski received when she was savagely beaten to death would be the last thing the jury would hear from the witness box before the defense presented its case. When Pangborn took his seat at the prosecutor's table, he was full of confidence that he had them hooked.

Steven Roberts' knew he had an uphill battle for his client. He was hoping to paint a totally different picture of Charles Holmes in his opening statement. As Roberts looked at the jury, he saw a more defiant group. They all sat straight up and looked at him directly as if to say, *this better be good*. He described Charles Holmes as a young teenager who was tricked into confessing to the crime that he now says he didn't commit. Looking for sympathy, Roberts described Charles as a kid with an IQ of 65, that he was a "Special Ed student," and that he didn't comprehend the gravity of the situation he was in.

"Can you imagine the police coming into your house at 2:30 in the morning? Wouldn't you be confused? This simple-minded boy was confused and scared." Finally, Roberts told the court that Holmes was tricked by a promise of a "McDonald's Egg McMuffin and that he could go home if he told the police he killed Ruth Lezkowski."

~~~~

Ninety-nine times out of a hundred the first witness in a murder trial is one that is referred to as a "Proof of Life" witness. This witness will establish the victim as a living person on or about the time he or she was killed. Michael Pangborn's first witness was Ruth Lezkowski's mother, Violet.

Clutching a damp handkerchief, wet from wiping tears from her eyes, Mrs. Lezkowski looked straight at the jury box, as she talked about her beautiful baby girl, her only daughter, and what she did the morning before she was brutally murdered on October 17,1986.

"Ruth was so excited about taking her final exams of that semester. She was looking forward to spending Thanksgiving Day with her family at home," she said, before she broke down. "And now I'll never see my daughter again. I'll never hug her or hold her. We will never have a Thanksgiving or a Christmas," she whispered as ASA Melanie Wantuck ran to her aid and tried to console the grieving mother.

The women on the jury cried with her. The men were choked up. Most of the people in the courtroom had tears in their eyes and their heads were bowed. It was a very emotional moment. The "hanging judge" called for a ten-minute recess and walked to his chambers with a lump in his throat thinking about his 22-year-old daughter.

~~~~

A very aplomb and proficient Area Four Violent Crimes Detective Jack Evans testified for most of a day, outlining the homicide investigation in detail. Evans was a seasoned detective who testified in many homicide cases but this case he took personally and he worked tirelessly for five straight months on it. He was well prepared as he told the court that detectives worked night and day for more than three months, and that they eliminated nearly 100 witnesses that were questioned and then cleared. He said that he and Detective Don Buerline, whom he never worked with before, arrested Charles Holmes at 2:30 in the morning because that was when the whole case came together. He testified that Charles Holmes confessed by his own free will and that he knew things about the crime that only someone who was there could possibly know.

Under intense cross-examination, Defense Attorney Steven Roberts, accused Evans of tricking Holmes into his confession by offering him a McDonald's Egg McMuffin. Evans retorted "We give all suspects coffee and food if they're pinched in the early morning hours." He also told the court that no one laid a hand on the witness or threatened him in any way.

~~~~

Three witnesses placed Charles in the company of the other defendants before the homicide occurred. The extra effort of detectives to find other witnesses was paying off. Members of the jury shook their heads almost nodding in agreement but the fourth witness did the most damage to the defense's case. DeSean Bryant placed him in Lezkowski's car and at the murder scene. Bryant described it as the "Rambo move" when Lorenzo Holmes jumped in the car and then Charles got in and they drove up to the railroad tracks. He testified "Oscar Sampson told me that Lorenzo Holmes and Charles were the ones who killed the woman up by the tracks."

The jury at this point was spell bound.

~~~~

Scientific evidence can be confusing to a jury but Chicago Police Crime Lab Specialist, Patricia Bass was a master at simplifying serology testimony. She had been on the witness stand many times and on this day she was the 13th witness called by the prosecution. Her testimony proved to be very damaging to Charles Holmes. Bass testified "Charles Holmes' blood was consistent with the semen recovered from the body of Ruth Lezkowski. More specifically 37% of the population could have donated the semen that was recovered from the victim."

~~~~

Michael Pangborn's 14th witness sat on the bench outside Courtroom 404 waiting to be called. The Cook County Medical Examiner did not know why the Lezkowski case made him reflect so much on his miserable childhood. Clutching his medical files leaning his head against the wall he thought back to his senior year in high school and being the town's sports star and his last soccer game of the year. Soccer was his passion and he was very good at it. His high school team won state championships and his club team won national championships. His coaches told him "You can go pro." *My parents didn't give a shit about any of my abilities on or off the field*, he thought. *Everyone I met was always so kind to me and I imagined they thought I led a charmed life. What a joke. If they only knew how many times I was beaten by my drunken parents.*

"Hey doc, you're up," the sheriff deputy said, bringing Dr. Crine back to reality.

"Dr. Crine," Pangborn said standing at the prosecutor's table, "You performed the post mortem examination of Ruth Lezkowski, starting from the head. Could you tell the jury, what you noticed about the head and face of Ruth Lezkowski that was so significant?"

"On the head and face, the first thing I noticed was that all the facial bones had been crushed or fractured," Dr. Crine began. "There was a large gaping laceration that extended from the eyebrow down to the lip. All of the sinuses and all of the nasal bones and the upper jaw had been fractured. There were multiple abrasions and scrapings of the skin; multiple bruises all over the face. There were multiple lacerations or tears of the scalp located on both sides of the forehead and on the back of the left side of the head. There were lacerations on the right side of the head about the ear."

"What about the neck?"

"On the right side of the neck extending to midline there was a large area where the skin had been scraped off. This area had turned leathery and was black in color. Beneath this and below this there was a large area of bruising and all the tissue was hemorrhagic and swollen. There were also small scratches noted on the left side of the neck."

"Did you notice anything about the stomach area?"

"Yes, on the chest and upper stomach there were multiple bruises noted: many of them were oval in shape. In the center there were small reddish circular bruises. On the right side of the chest there were long linear bruises that had a central pale area. There were also multiple small abrasions and very tiny puncture wounds. On the lower chest there was a large bloody footprint."

The jury and most of the spectators sitting in the crowded courtroom including Judge William Albenese were mesmerized by Dr. Crine's riveting testimony.

Pangborn then took autopsy pictures of the body and presented them as State Exhibits, asking Dr. Crine to identify them. One by one the pictures showed the extent of the injures that he had just described in his testimony. The jury could view these Exhibits entered as evidence, if they decided to look at them.

"Dr. Crine you not only performed an external examination, you also preformed an internal exam. Is that correct?"

"Yes."

"Doctor, after making the incision for the autopsy, what did you notice from your internal examination?"

"There was a small amount of blood noted in the abdominal cavity. There was a small amount of hemorrhage or bleeding around the left kidney as well as some hemorrhage and bleeding around the rectum, which is part of the large bowel. I also noticed there were multiple rib fractures."

"Did you notice anything in the head area?"

"There was bruising of almost the entire scalp region. And also there was hemorrhaging into the two temporal muscles on each side of the scalp. The damage to the facial bones and the sinuses had caused some of the bone at the base of the skull to be pushed upward into the brain of the frontal region."

"What about the neck?"

"My examination of the neck revealed extensive hemorrhage and swelling of all of the tissues of the neck. There was also a fracture of both the right and the left side of the Adam's apple and the hyoid bone was fractured at the midline."

"Based on your experience in the field of pathology and your autopsy of Ruth Lezkowski, did you come to a conclusion as to the cause of death to Ruth Lezkowski?"

"Yes."

"What was that?"

"She died as a consequence of the multiple blunt force trauma injuries."

~~~~

The final witness for the state was almost anti-climatic after the spellbinding testimony of Dr. Crine. Suzanne Grande, the assistant state's attorney who took Charles Holmes' statement was sworn in as the 15th prosecution witness. Dressed in a conservative black suit and white blouse she sat erect and looked at the jury.

"Ms. Grande, did you take the statement of Charles Holmes on the morning of April 28th, 1987 at 7:50 am?" asked Melanie Wantuck.

"Yes, I did."

"Did you read Charles Holmes his Constitutional rights?"

"Yes, I did."

"Was anyone else present when you took Charles Holmes' statement?"

"Yes. Detective Jack Evans and Youth Officer, David Hill were there."

"Did Charles Holmes give his statement willingly?"

"Yes, he did."

Knowing that her next question would be critical in any appeal, ASA Melanie Wantuck walked from the witness stand to the prosecutor's table and picked up Holmes' statement in dramatic fashion. She knew all eyes were on her, as she seemed to peruse the document. She looked directly at her witness. "Did you observe any injuries on Charles Holmes while you took his statement?"

"I did not see any injuries nor did he complain of any injuries."

"Were any promises made or any threats made to Charles Holmes to give his statement?"

"There were no promises made or threats made to Mr. Holmes."

"Thank you, Ms. Grande, that will be all."

Wantuck waited for Suzanne Grande to exit the witness stand then she walked over to the bench and handed the Charles Holmes' statement up to Judge Albanese and said, "Your Honor the State would like to submit the statement of Charles Holmes taken on April 28, 1987 and mark it as State's Exhibit 78."

"Your honor, the state rests," said Pangborn.

~~~~

Between the afternoon of Tuesday, February 9th, and following day, the defense called ten witnesses to the stand. Charles Holmes was not one of them, as he chose not to testify on his behalf.

Defense attorney Steven Roberts knew he literally had no chance for an acquittal. When he cross-examined Dr. Robert Crine he made a colossal mistake. His questions just re-enforced the brutality of the murder. He had a suffocating feeling from the jury.

The first witness was Charles' mother, Helen. She was wearing a blue, loose fitting dress and clutching a white handkerchief. She told the court that Charles was a "special needs child," and he was "a slow learner who struggled in school." She stated that he was never in trouble before, and that he was "a good and kind boy who could not do such a thing as murder an innocent woman."

Nine other people, friends and family members, took the stand briefly and described Charles Holmes as a nice young man who wouldn't hurt a fly, and that he was not capable of murder.

Roberts rested the defense's case shortly before noon.

Before Judge Albanese dismissed them for lunch, he asked both the prosecution team and the defense team, if they had any rebuttal witnesses. They did not.

~~~~

After lunch, Judge William Albanese assembled the jury and gave them their instructions. He told them "review the instructions, I just gave you and apply them to the facts of this case during your deliberations." The jury was then escorted to the jury room and began their deliberations.

The jury room was plain and bland and tired. Years of use took its toll. The white paint on the 12-foot high ceiling was turning gray. Six, eight-foot-long fluorescent lights strained and hummed as they produced light that made anyone in the room look unwell. The walls were painted a pale yellow, dull and dinghy. The thick wax on the tile floor could no longer hide the scuffmarks from shoes and chairs being pulled in and out from the old wooden table that sat in the center of the room. It looked worn out. The twelve wooden chairs were mismatched, eight mahogany and four pine, beat up and old. The chalkboard against the far wall resembled a movable chalkboard from a grade school classroom. Its slate was no longer black. It looked exhausted. A juror had to strain to read anything written on it. Its eraser could hardly wipe off old writings. A water cooler sat next to the doorway on the right side as the jury walked in. Eight ounce plastic cups in a box laid across the top of the water jug. Two bathrooms were on the left side of the room. The men's seat was always up. Both of them were very clean.

Three hours and fifteen minutes after they entered the room, they announced to the judge that they had reached their verdicts. Charles Holmes' statement, which contained his confession, the testimony of Dr. Robert Crine and Crime Lab Specialist, Patricia Bass sealed his fate.

The jury found Charles Holmes guilty of felony murder, aggravated criminal sexual assault and aggravated kidnapping, but not armed robbery. Judge Albenese accepted the verdicts and set a 30-day date for post-trial motions and sentencing. He then adjourned the court.

~~~~

Charles Holmes stood up. He was shocked that the verdict came back so quickly and stunned as the jury forewoman announced the guilty verdicts of the charges, one after another. He felt no relief that he was found not guilty of armed robbery because he realized at that moment that he would probably spend the rest of his life in prison. His shoulders were sunken, his chin was in his chest, and his eyes were red. He was crying as sheriff deputies led him out of the courtroom and back to the Cook County Jail. His life was over before it ever really got started. He was just 15 years old.

# CHAPTER 32

T he Cook County State's Attorney's office is the second largest prosecutor's office in the United States. It's a political position. Richard M. Daley won with 66% of the vote when he first ran for the position in 1980. Naturally all Democratic. Though Daley never tried a case, he surrounded himself with 800 very competent attorneys.

His first assistant Kevin Benedetti was a career prosecutor for 20 years. Benedetti was a boss in most of the criminal units in the State's Attorneys Office. He could care less about politics. He just liked to put criminals in jail.

The Office has four suburban districts assigned to criminal courts. The criminal bureau has the most prosecutors. The office also has an appeals unit, a juvenile unit, a civil unit and a first municipal court's unit along with a traffic court unit.

Benedetti hand picked Michael Pangborn to head up the Special Prosecutions Unit in the criminal bureau.

~~~~

Pangborn was sitting behind his dark brown mahogany desk that was covered with court transcripts and Chicago Cubs memorabilia. His office had picture windows that let in the natural light even on gloomy days. His view consisted of California Avenue and an island of green grass and weeds nine months a year. He had his feet up and crossed on his desk tossing his Cubs' baseball confidently thinking about the victory in the Charles Holmes case two weeks earlier. His thoughts were interrupted when two Cook County Sheriff Deputies escorted Marcus Broadhead and his attorney, Jacqueline Oliver into his office.

The court appointed Oliver and she didn't really want to be there. Her willingness to work with the prosecutors was her only satisfaction.

Detectives Jack Evans and Lee Scholl worked Broadhead hard to flip him as a state witness for the prosecution. They knew he was a career criminal who had worked the system and their experience told them he was the type that would turn on his friends for an easier sentence. They weren't wrong and the purpose of this meeting was to make it official. Pangborn knew his case against Lorenzo Holmes was weak and Broadhead's testimony was what he needed to strengthen their position. He was ready to deal.

Broadhead was dressed in his orange prison jumpsuit with CCDOC stenciled on its back (Cook County Department of Corrections). Broadhead was now 19-years old and 15 pounds heavier from starchy prison food and lack of drugs in his system.

"Have a seat, Marcus," said Pangborn. "I want to talk to you about your plea deal."

"Yes, sir."

"You are charged with felony murder, aggravated sexual assault, aggravated kidnapping and armed robbery which carries a life sentence. Your attorney tells me that you are willing to testify for the State in return for dismissing some of the charges. Here's the deal, you plead guilty to aggravated kidnapping. If you testify truthfully, the state will dismiss all other charges and recommend a sentence of 12 years in the state petitionary with the possibility of getting out in six years if you behave yourself. Do you know what this means?"

"Yeah, I knows."

"You must testify truthfully. You have confessed to your involvement in the murder of Ruth Lezkowski already. As you know we have six witnesses that put you at the crime scene and in the company of all the other defendants. We also have a witness that says you intimidated her to lie for you. These are all very serious crimes. You understand?"

"I knows. I knows."

"You are getting the deal of a lifetime. Your homeys are going away for life. You understand that don't you?"

"Yeah, I do."

~~~~

On the day Charles Holmes was sentenced, the Honorable Judge William Albanese's courtroom was not as crowded as it was just five weeks earlier, when the jury found him guilty of felony murder, aggravated criminal sexual assault and aggravated kidnapping after just three hours and15 minutes of deliberation. Every media outlet in the city was present though. Every reporter in courtroom 404 knew Holmes would be sentenced to life.

With the slam of his gavel and his powerful voice, Judge Albenese brought the courtroom to order and proceeded with the Sentencing Hearing of Charles Holmes. At the conclusion of it, Charles Holmes was asked if had anything to say. His shoulders were slumped, his head was down and his prison jumpsuit looked two sizes to big for him.

His spirit broken with his voice almost in a whisper and barely audible, he said, "I didn't do nuttin', your honor. I don't understand all of this."

Judge Albanese looked down at Charles Holmes and said, "The jury has found you guilty as charged. The evidence against you was overwhelming. Ruth Lezkowski suffered a horrible death at your hands. Your acts were brutal, heinous and shocking. Your acts were unconscionable. You are serious risk to this community. I cannot imagine the pain and suffering and agony that Miss Lezkowski went through before she died. And for those reasons I sentence you to prison for your natural life for the murder of Ruth Lezkowski. I also sentence you to 30 years in prison for the aggravated criminal sexual assault of Ruth Lezkowski. Furthermore, I sentence you to 15 years imprisonment for the aggravated kidnapping of Ruth Lezkowski. These additional terms shall run concurrently with the natural life imprisonment term."

With that, Judge Albenese gaveled the proceeding to an end and stood up. Emotionally drained, he shook his head as he walked through his chamber's door.

Cook County Sheriff Deputies lightly grabbed Charles Holmes by his elbow and turned him around to lead him out of the courtroom when his mother, Helen wailed, "My baby. My baby." He looked down at his feet as he shuffled out of the courtroom, tears flowing down his cheeks.

Violet Lezkowski sat in dead silence grasping her handkerchief, shoulders slouched and heaving as she cried silently for her baby. Her only daughter. The daughter that made her life worth living. The daughter she would never see again. Violet Lezkowski was present for every single court appearance, no matter how insignificant they were, she suffered through every one of them. Today she felt relief but she also felt enormous sorrow.

She had two more trials to endure. She wanted justice for her daughter.

~~~~

State's Attorney Michael Pangborn scheduled Lorenzo Holmes' trail as the last. He told fellow prosecutors that they had less than 50 percent chance for a conviction. That's why Broadhead was such a critical witness. Lorenzo Holmes has steadfastly refused to give any statement about his involvement in the death of Ruth Lezkowski. He continued to deny that he had anything to do with it no matter how many witnesses the prosecution would put on the stand. Prosecutors had no physical evidence that directly tied him to the crime. He had a violent past as a juvenile but that could not be introduced at his trial. All the witnesses that will be called to the stand however would testify that he was basically the ringleader in the brutal rape and murder of Ruth Lezkowski.

# CHAPTER 33

May 4,1988 was a miserable day. Thunderstorms, lightening and chilly 35-degree air greeted everyone as they walked into the Criminal Courts building at 26th and Cal. The revolving doors could not keep out the dampness that crept into the lobby as defense attorneys, detectives and reporters went through security. The building's heat only added to the humidity making those who shook the water off their raincoats and tapped their umbrellas on the wet terrazzo floor made everyone sweat even more profusely.

The media was there for the trial of Oscar Sampson, the second of the four suspects in the Ruth Lezkowski murder.

Sampson would appear in the courtroom of Judge Robert Genirs.

Courtroom 504 was exactly the same as courtroom 404 with two exceptions. The jury seats were black vinyl instead of blue and the well and gallery were separated by a dark mahogany railing with two gates that swung in both directions allowing access and regress to and from the well.

Judge Genirs, a 52-year-old, six-foot one man, who always stood erect, with his shoulders back and head held high. His dark brown hair was turning gray at the temples. His dark blue eyes could stare down any defendant, lawyer or prosecutor who appeared in his courtroom. He was handsome, confident and smart. His Catholic education began at St. Vincent's Grade School in River Forest, Illinois. Then, he went to Fenwick High School, a college preparatory school that has very high academic standards. Almost every graduating student gets into the college of their choice every year. Known as the Friars, Fenwick's sports teams were always competitive and fierce. Robert Genirs was an all-state baseball and basketball player. He was offered a full scholarship to play at St. John's University in Jamaica, Queens, New York. He had to make a choice between baseball and basketball after his freshman year. He chose basketball.

After St. John's, he went to Notre Dame Law School where he graduated with honors. He was immediately hired by the Cook County State's Attorney's Office where he worked for 14 years. He was appointed to the bench in 1982. He had the reputation of being a fair minded and honest jurist, who was known as a student of the law.

~~~~

A jury of eight women and six men was empaneled for the trial of Oscar Sampson. Seven women were black and one was white. Three of the men were black and three were Hispanic. One black woman and one Hispanic man were the alternates. At exactly ten o'clock in the morning Judge Robert Genirs called his courtroom to order and the clerk of the court announced the case of The People of the State of Illinois versus Oscar Sampson.

Michael Pangborn's 33-minute opening statement was clear, concise and brutal. He described the savage beating Ruth Lezkowski endured before she died from her injuries. He told the jury that they will hear from a total 17 witnesses who will detail Sampson's involvement in this heinous murder. He told them that they would visit the crime scene where she was killed. Pangborn very slowly and dramatically paced as he told the spellbound jury that when the trial was over there will be "no reasonable doubt" that Oscar Sampson was guilty of felony murder, aggravated criminal sexual assault, aggravated kidnapping and armed robbery.

~~~~

Attorney Craig Hill was one of the top Cook County public defenders. His resume included some of the most high-profile cases ever tried in the Cook County Criminal Division. His long graying hair hung over his shirt collar and covered his ears. His blue eyes were intense and absorbed everything that was happening around him. His stomach was an indication of how much he loved his red wine and rare steaks, a taste he acquired, while working at one of Chicago's most prestigious law firms. Although, he was a partner at Carlin and Miller for ten years, he felt a calling to become a public defender to help the poor. Hill was overweight but he moved smoothly and gracefully around the courtroom with ease and confidence. His nickname was "Easy." He was a very competent lawyer.

~~~~

Hill's opening statement was pure, simple and short. He stated to the jury that, "the State's Attorney's Office had no case, with no credible evidence linking his client to the murder of Ruth Lezkowski." He called most of the circumstantial witnesses against Oscar Sampson "criminals that cut deals with the prosecution to get out of serving time for crimes that they committed." As Hill closed his dramatic 22-minute opening statement, he looked each juror in the eye and said his client was "not guilty of this horrible crime."

~~~~

Again Ruth Lezkowski's mother was the first witness. Her testimony was heartbreaking, Pangborn's second witness was Detective Jack Evans, who led the Lezkowski homicide investigation from the very beginning. Evans confidently laid out in precise detail the 115 days of investigative work performed by Area Four Violent Crimes detectives. "Oscar Sampson was running from the police before we even identified him as the fourth suspect," Evans said. "We looked for him for more than four weeks."

Sampson sat next to his attorney seething. He was shaking his head saying to himself, *you fucker*. Hill sensing his client's tenseness and mood tried to settle him down by patting his hand.

Evans could care less. He felt deep in his heart, *I have no doubt Sampson took part in the death of Ruth Lezkowski.*

"How did you find out that Oscar Sampson knew about the murder of Ruth Lezkowski?" Pangborn asked.

"When we were interrogating him, we told him we found hair samples on the front seat of Ms. Lezkowski's car and that we found sperm inside of her. Other defendants told us that he and Charles were the two, who raped her in the front seat. Then I asked him how long Charles was raping her and he blurted out, 'for about two minutes.' That was consistent with what other defendants told us and unless he was there, he would not know that," Evans said.

"Did he make any other admissions to you, detective?"

"Yes, he did."

"Would you please tell the court, what that other admission was?"

"We asked Mr. Sampson if he realized that the hairs we found on the front seat of Ms. Lezkowski's car could be traced back to him."

"And what did he say?"

"He said, 'Yeah. So what.'"

Sampson now was burning holes through Evans with his eyes. The jury noticed his reaction and could almost sense the hatred. Hill was still tapping his left arm with his right hand. "I am going to rip him a new ass on cross," He whispered to Sampson.

"Then what did you do?" Pangborn asked.

"Then, I asked him if he wanted to start telling us the truth?"

"And what did he say?"

"He said, 'I want time to think about it.'"

"And did he think about it?"

"Yes, and he told us to go fuck ourselves."

"Objection, your honor," roared Hill.

~~~~

Hill sprang to his feet and moved in front of the witness box before Pangborn got to his chair and sat down. On cross-examination, the public defender tried to discredit Evans, saying he tricked Oscar Sampson into believing that police had evidence that linked him to the crime.

"I asked him if he realized the hairs could be traced to him, I never said they did," retorted Evans. "He is the one that said that Charles Holmes was raping Ms. Lezkowski for 'about two minutes.' That was consistent with other information we had developed."

Evans enjoyed the banter. He had faced Hill before and he was totally prepared for any blistering question that the public defender would throw at him. Evans never looked at Hill, his eyes were locked on the jury and his confidence was never inhibited. He was enjoying himself.

~~~~

Pangborn felt his eighth witness would be damaging to Sampson, because not only did he have his testimony, he had a signed, handwritten statement that verified what he told the police. Corey Wallace was the DJ from the party at the ALBA Homes, the night Ruth Lezkowski was killed.

"Did you see Oscar at the party on October 18th, 1986?" Pangborn asked.

"Yes, he was in and out a few times."

"Did you see him at two in the morning?"

"No, it was later than that, 'bout four."

"Did he say anything at that time?"

"No, not then."

"When did he say something?"

"When the police arrested those three boys, I saw Oscar and he was acting strange and stuff, you know what I'm saying? So I asked him, 'What's wrong with you man?'"

"And what did he say then?"

"He said right away that 'the police would probably be looking for him next.'"

Sampson sat rigid and was staring through Corey Wallace and with a defeated grin shook his head side to side. He knew what was coming next and he buried his forehead into his right hand, still shaking his head.

"Then what did he say?"

"He says that 'he and Lorenzo were the ones who kilt that white girl up on the tracks.'"

"Objection, your honor. Hearsay!" roared Hill.

"Your honor, this is not hearsay. This is a statement made by the defendant to Mr. Wallace," Pangborn responded.

"Objection overruled. This is a statement by the defendant therefore it is not hearsay," Judge Genirs ruled.

~~~~

DeSean Bryant was Pangborn's ninth witness. He told the court that he met with Oscar Sampson shortly after the three defendants were arrested.

"What did you tell Oscar to do?" Pangborn asked.

"I told him, he should turn his ass in. Excuse me, your honor," said Bryant.

"What did he say?"

"He say, 'I ain't going to turn myself in cuz I didn't do nuttin'.'"

"Then what did you say?"

"I say, 'Man, come on, everybody in the neighborhood knows you was up there with Marcus.'"

"Did he say … he was there?"

"Yeah, he said that he was there but that he was just watching."

"Did he say how they got there?"

"Yeah, he said Lorenzo told him to get in the car and they drove up there and then Lorenzo started hitting the woman."

Pangborn then approached the bench and handed the judge Wallace's handwritten statement and asked that it be entered as State's Exhibit #68.

~~~~

The third day of the trial was Friday, May 6th, 1988. Pangborn called his 15th witness, Chicago Police Crime Lab Serology Analyst Patricia Bass to the stand. Bass told the court, "I excluded Oscar Sampson as a donor of the semen taken from the body of Ruth Lezkowski." She then testified, "The blood types of Lorenzo and Charles Holmes were consistent with the semen."

This testimony corroborated the testimony of DeSean Bryant and Corey Wallace which linked Sampson with them participating in the death of Ruth Lezkowski.

~~~~

The 16th witness was Analyst Richard Zolinski from the Chicago Police Department's Crime Lab. Zolinski was an expert on trace evidence. He testified "The hair samples we collected from the front seat of Ruth Lezkowski's car were consistent with the samples taken from Sampson."

Pangborn was tightening the noose in his case against Oscar Sampson.

~~~~

Cook County Medical Examiner Dr. Robert Crine sat outside courtroom 504 waiting to be called to the witness stand and he was smiling. He had no idea what made him think of the fart story and how he took a severe beating. It was like he was reliving it when he was nine years old as if it was yesterday. *The normal beating after I farted at the kitchen table was a lesson well learned, DON'T do it at the table. At dinner a month or so later I had to do it again so I left the room and went into the hall and farted. I knew no one heard me. I went back to the table to finish my meal and my sister started laughing, then so did I. Mom asked what was so funny? So I told her, thinking I did the right thing. Apparently not, she came up behind me and hit me in my right ear with a cupped hand. I thought I was going to go deaf. Then she got the belt and really beat me.*

Dr. Crine awoke startled, no longer smiling but sweating. His nightmares were frightening. As he stood to enter the courtroom he reached into his back pocket and pulled out his freshly ironed handkerchief. He wiped the sweat off his forehead and grinned as he thought of his children and how he never raised his voice to them.

Dr. Crine was the 17$^{th}$ and final witness for the prosecution. Once again he outlined the horrible beating that Ruth Lezkowski received. The jury was spellbound as he wrapped up his two hours of testimony.

"There was also hemorrhaging into the muscles on both sides of the scalp, and when we examined the brain you could see that the bones of the face and the sinuses had been fractured so that the floor of the skull in this region was fractured and it had been pushed up, crushing the bottom part of the brain itself.

"These were all blunt trauma injuries; these aren't stab wounds or cuts. These are the kind of injuries that come from blunt trauma, being hit with something or falling onto something."

"Doctor, I will show you first of all what has been marked People's Exhibit No. 22-C, for identification. It has been identified as a piece of concrete.

"If Ruth Lezkowski were struck in the face with that piece of concrete, would it result in injuries consistent with the ones that you saw on her face, the gaping injury across her face?" Wantuck asked.

"Yes, it would," Dr. Crine responded.

~~~~

The defense decided not to cross-examine Dr. Crine. In the case against Charles Holmes, the cross examination of the Medical Examiner proved to be a disaster and helpful to the prosecution.

Judge Genirs surprised the jury as he announced that they were taking a field trip.

"Ladies and gentlemen of the jury, you have now heard all the testimony that you are going to hear for the day. The day is not quite over for you, though. At this time the court is of the opinion that a visit to the scene of the crime and perhaps one or two other locations is in order."

The jury was all a buzz, talking nervously about the unusual trip of going to the scene where the victim was actually brutally beaten to death. They viewed some of the gory crime scene photos, which revolted the women jurors. They were all anxious to board the buses that would take them there.

"Whatever belongings you have, I guess you could take them with you. We will return you to 26ᵗʰ and California but you will not have to come back to this courtroom.

"We will recess then for the weekend and we will begin this case on Monday morning at ten o'clock sharp. Thank you, and with all things going well we should be able to wind this case up by Monday or the latest Tuesday morning, so prepare yourselves," Judge Robert Genirs ordered.

~~~~

The 14-person jury, the judge and all the attorneys got into Cook County Sheriff transport buses and drove to Loomis and Flournoy. They all got out and ASA Michael Pangborn did a walk around explaining how a "Smash and Grab" of a car worked. He pointed out the general area where the kidnapping took place and motioned towards South Loomis indicating the direction of the desolated railroad service area where Ruth Lezkowski was murdered.

The bus ride up the narrow tree lined road showed the jury how quickly one could disappear into this isolated area from a very busy city neighborhood. Once everyone exited the buses, Melanie Wantuck painted a picture of the gruesome murder. "This is where Ruth Lezkowski's body was found." She walked slowly and pointed to the ground, "Her head was pointing in this direction and her feet were situated like this." She used both hands to illustrate the direction of her feet. "Her car was parked right here," she paused for effect and then once again pointed to the exact spot and continued, "and investigators found the murder weapon next to her battered body right here."

With that final illustration, she quoted the last line of Railroad Police Officer Daniel Starks' report, "The blood was still dripping from Ruth Lezkowski's car door."

The bus ride back to 26th and California was quiet and somber, Judge Robert Genirs once again reminded the jury to be back to his courtroom no later than 9:45 Monday morning. The jury had two and a half days to think about what they just saw and how the pieces of this dark rage puzzle would come together.

# CHAPTER 34

R on Magers was holding court in his office as Peter Michaels and Doug Longhini were putting the finishing touches on their script.

"How often does a jury take a trip to the crime scene?" Magers asked.

"It happens but not very often," Michaels replied. "They took the same route that was laid out at trial and I can't even imagine what those jurors felt when they got to the scene of the murder."

"That had to be pretty eerie," Longhini added.

"I'll tell you what, the defense must feel fucked with the jury sent home for the weekend with the impression of that crime scene, fresh in their minds," Michaels said.

"I wouldn't be surprised if the jury came back in less time than the last trail," Magers said. "You guys ready for the ten?"

"Yep," Michaels answered. "Let's do it."

~~~~

ASA Melanie Wantuck appeared before Judge William Albanese with a Motion for a Plea Agreement for Marcus Broadhead. The State's Attorney's Office negotiated a deal of a reduced sentence for Broadhead if he testified against Lorenzo Holmes, truthfully. The charges of felony murder, aggravated criminal sexual assault and burglary would be dropped and he would be charged with only aggravated kidnapping, which carried a minimum of 12-years imprisonment with his cooperation.

The State's Attorney's Office agreed to the deal because Lorenzo Holmes was their weakest case and they considered him the ringleader of this brutal murder. The State's Attorney had to present the Plea Agreement at least 30 days before the start of Lorenzo Holmes' trial to give the defense time to prepare.

The motion took five minutes. Then Melanie Wantuck went up one floor to Courtroom 504 and the trial of Oscar Sampson.

~~~~

At exactly ten o'clock, Judge Robert Genirs' Courtroom came to order and Public Defender Craig Hill called his first witness. Scott Blanchard was an independent expert in trace materials. Blanchard, a former police officer from Oklahoma City, worked in the crime lab for 25 years. After retiring from the police department, he formed his own company. Now he works for the defense charging a thousand dollars a day as an expert witness. In addition, he charged $600 a day for his lab work.

Hill's primary purpose for calling Blanchard to the stand was to create reasonable doubt in the minds of the jurors.

"Mr. Blanchard you heard the testimony of Richard Zolinski, did you not?" Hill asked.

"Yes, I did."

"Do you agree?"

"Yes, I do."

Hill feigned a surprised look and asked quizzically, "What do you mean by that?"

"Well, Mr. Zolinski testified that the hair fragment recovered from the car of the victim could have originated from Mr. Sampson, but there is no way of knowing that for sure. The 'could have' does not mean 'it did.' There is no exact science, at this time, that can positively tell us that the hairs recovered at the scene and that of Mr. Sampson are exactly the same," said Blanchard.

"Thank you, Mr. Blanchard."

~~~~

Dennis Defranco had been a Chicago police officer for 22 years. He was shot in the kneecap and retired with a medical disability pension. He walked with a noticeable limp and he couldn't run. He has been a private investigator for the last seven years. He had a strong work ethic and a solid reputation.

"Mr. Defranco, you heard the testimony of Corey Wallace and DeSean Bryant did you not?" Hill asked.

"Yes, I did."

"Have you talked to these two men before?"

"Yes, I have."

"What did you discover in conversations with them?"

"That they were lying."

"Objection, your honor," said Pangborn, jumping to his feet. "That's his opinion but the truthfulness of a witness is the job of the jury to determine. I ask that the answer be stricken and the jury be instructed to disregard."

"Objection sustained, the jury is instructed to disregard," Judge Genirs said.

Hill called five witnesses to the stand, like an assembly line production trying to improve the character of Oscar Sampson. One said, "he shoveled the snow off my sidewalk" and another said, "he carried my groceries all the time." None of them offered anything about his character or reputation. Their testimony took a little more than an hour. Then the defense rested its case.

~~~~

The prosecution's closing argument began after the noon lunch hour. Melanie Wantuck in precise detail went down the witness list, summarizing the poignant points of all 17 witnesses the state called to the stand.

Detective Jack Evans' testimony was very strong, relating that Oscar Sampson knew things about the crime that no one who wasn't there could know.

Serologist Patricia Bass' testimony tied Sampson directly to Lorenzo Holmes and Charles Holmes

Wantuck particularly spent time on Dr. Robert Crine's autopsy testimony detailing the horrible, despicable torture that Ruth Lezkowski endured before her death.

Then she walked the jurors through the crime scenes they visited, pointing out where her body was found savagely beaten.

~~~~

Public Defender Craig Hill started telling the jury, "The case against Oscar Sampson is strictly circumstantial. The prosecution did not have a shred of evidence that definitively ties Mr. Sampson to the murder of Ruth Lezkowski as horrible as it was."

He went down the list of prosecution witnesses and tried to discredit every one of them. However, he did not mention the testimony of Ruth Lezkowski's mother.

He called Detective Jack Evans' testimony a sham, saying "Detective Evans put words into Oscar Sampson's mouth. Other than two utterances as a result of trickery and hours of relentless questioning, Mr. Sampson knew nothing about the crime as it happened."

Hill reminded the jury that his private investigator testified that two of the state's witnesses were "lying" and that "they were looking for a deal. That's why they testified for the prosecution only to get out of going to jail for crimes that they committed after the Lezkowski homicide."

Hill also pointed out to the jury that Scott Blanchard, his Independent trace expert contradicted the testimony of the Police Department's trace expert Richard Zolinski.

In Hill's summary, he called the prosecution's case a trip to "Fantasy Island." He approached the jury box and placed both his hands on the railing and in a soft pleading voice proclaimed, "There is no hard evidence linking my client to this horrible crime but there is plenty of reasonable doubt to find Mr. Sampson not guilty."

~~~~

In rebuttal, lead prosecutor Michael Pangborn told the jury "No witness is going to commit perjury and risk going to jail for a murderer, like Oscar Sampson." He paced slowly in front of the jury box as if he was in deep thought and then turned toward them and said, "Remember, Oscar Sampson was on the run from the police before he was even named a suspect." He shrugged his shoulders and raised his hands, palms out for emphasis and asked, "Why would he do that?" He paused for a theatrical moment lowered his head and then he brought his eyes to theirs and asked, "Why would any innocent person ... run? If he wasn't guilty? Think about that, ladies and gentlemen ... only the guilty ... act guilty."

The entire courtroom was silent—mesmerized. Pangborn paused briefly and once again he began to pace dramatically, left hand in his pocket, right hand slowly rubbing his chin. Every juror followed him intently and when he stopped abruptly directly in the middle, he knew they were totally focused on him and he said, "Mr. Hill would have you believe that this case is a trip to 'Fantasy Island.' If his idea of 'Fantasy Island,' is being violently kidnapped, brutally raped and savagely beaten to death then I guess, he is right. But, I know you don't believe that. No! This case is about the brutal, savage murder of a 23-year-old woman, who had her life in front of her, working hard to become a doctor, only to have that life taken from her because she was in the wrong place at the wrong time. The state has proven beyond any reasonable doubt that Oscar Sampson is guilty of felony murder, aggravated criminal sexual assault, aggravated kidnapping and armed robbery. We ask you to find him guilty of all these horrible crimes. Thank you."

~~~~

When judges give the jury their instructions, they are very precise. They don't want to provide any opportunity of a mistrial. It's not that they work off a script but they do have proven methods and verbiage that they use to prevent anything that may raise issues at a later time.

After the closing arguments and a short recess, Judge Robert Genirs gave the jury their instructions on the law as they applied to this particular murder case. He told them, "During your deliberations, review the instructions, I just gave you and apply them only to the facts of this case." The courtroom sheriff then escorted them to the jury room to begin their deliberations.

Jury room 504 was a carbon copy of 404 with a few exceptions. The fluorescent lights didn't hum as loudly, the plastic water glasses were in a dispenser on the wall next to the water cooler and there was a white grease board with black and red markers instead of a chalkboard.

In less than three hours, the jury announced it had reached a verdict on all counts. They found Oscar Sampson guilty of felony murder, aggravated criminal sexual assault, aggravated kidnapping and armed robbery. Judge Genirs accepted the verdicts reached and then polled the jury.

Polling the jury is a last ditch effort by the defense to give a juror a chance to change his or her verdict. Judge Genirs asked each juror if that was their verdict in the jury room and is it still your verdict now. No jurors changed their minds and with that Judge Genirs thanked them for their service and dismissed them.

Judge Genirs then set a 30-day date for post-trial motions and sentencing. He then adjourned the court.

~~~~

Oscar Sampson was shaking as he stood up. He was shocked that the jury reached its verdicts so quickly and stunned as the jury foreman in a deep baritone voice announced the guilty verdicts of all charges, one after another. It finally hit him that he would probably spend the rest of his life in a prison cell. He had been in juvenile detention before but now he knew he was going to the big house. His eyes darted back and forth searching for an impossible rescue, a miracle that would not come on this day.

Sheriff Deputies led him out of the courtroom and back to the Cook County Jail. Oscar Sampson was 19 years old.

# CHAPTER 35

Oscar Sampson was sentenced on Friday, June 10th, 1988, on the same morning that the final jurors would be selected for the trial of Lorenzo Holmes. Almost every seat in the courtroom of the Honorable Robert Genirs was filled. It was exactly 30 days since the jury found Sampson guilty of felony murder, aggravated criminal sexual assault, aggravated kidnapping and armed robbery after three hours of deliberation.

Judge Genirs was soft spoken but his gavel was thunderous, as he brought his courtroom to order for the sentencing hearing of Oscar Sampson. It didn't matter what motions were filed, what any witnesses had to say, Judge Genirs had been pondering his actions for a month. Three hours later at the conclusion of the hearing, he asked Sampson if he wanted to say anything before he was sentenced.

His orange prison jumpsuit sagged on him. He looked dejected, but he was defiant when he told the judge, "I didn't kill no-one."

Judge Genirs sat with his fingers interlaced, leaning forward with his elbows on his bench. He looked down at Oscar Sampson. "The jury has found you guilty as charged on all four counts. The evidence against you in this trial was overwhelming. Your acts were unconscionable. Ruth Lezkowski suffered a horrible, brutal death at your hands. Your acts were heinous, unthinkable and shocking. Your vicious acts bordered on the unbelievable. You are a serious risk to this community. I cannot imagine the pain and suffering that Miss Lezkowski went through before she died at your hands. And for those reasons, I sentence you to prison for the rest of your natural life for the murder of Ruth Lezkowski. I also sentence you to 30 years in prison for the aggravated criminal sexual assault of Ruth Lezkowski.

Furthermore, I sentence you to 30 years for armed robbery and 15 years for the aggravated kidnapping of Ruth Lezkowski. These additional terms shall run concurrently with the natural life imprisonment term."

Judge Genirs was emotionally drained. No matter how many times a judge sentences someone to life in prison it takes its toll. He was exhausted and he still had a full day of jury selection ahead of him for the trial of Lorenzo Holmes.

~~~~

County Cook Sheriff Deputies grabbed him by his elbow and led the defiant Oscar Sampson out of the courtroom. As he shuffled away, he looked to see if anyone he knew was there, but nobody came to see him before he would go behind the walls of Stateville Correctional Center on the next prisoner transport bus. He was 19 years old and on his way to the penitentiary for the rest of his life.

~~~~

Pangborn's prosecution team wanted as many women on the Lorenzo Holmes jury as they could manage. Besides the brutal way Ruth Lezkowski was killed, the prosecution was going to concentrate heavily on the brutal rape she endured. This was the weakest case of the three.

Since his arrest, Lorenzo Holmes basically said three words to the police and prosecutors "lawyer" and "fuck you." There was no real hard physical evidence linking him to the Lezkowski homicide. But the testimony of Marcus Broadhead was a game changer and it greatly improved the State's chances for a conviction.

By four o'clock, a jury of eight women and six men was convened. Five of the women were black, two were white and one was Hispanic. Three of the men were black and three were white. One black man and one white man were the alternate jurors

~~~~

Lorenzo Holmes' attorney was Ronald Myers. He was a very well known and high-priced criminal defense attorney in Cook County. He was a partner in the prestigious firm of Myers, Byers and Janis. Myers was a graduate of John Marshall Law School. He was in the top ten percent in the class of 1964. He was an assistant state's attorney for five years before he started his firm in 1971. Everyone in the firm had at least five years of experience as a prosecutor. Their firm grew rapidly as they defended some very high-profile drug dealers.

Myers was six feet tall, 188 pounds, had a muscular build and hazel eyes known for their confidant glare. He was an expert shot with his 12-gauge shotgun versus clay pigeons and his 40 caliber, Smith and Wesson versus paper targets. He also loved to fish for bass, smoke cigars and drink bourbon with his close friends. He was a worthy opponent in the courtroom. He took this high-profile case Pro Bono. He was the ultimate competitor.

~~~~

Knowing that the prosecution planned to call 19 witnesses in this case, Judge Robert Genirs told everyone in his courtroom to be ready to proceed at exactly nine o'clock on Monday morning.

~~~~

Ron Magers' office was busier than most days on this Friday night of June 10,1988. If he had a revolving door it wouldn't have stopped spinning, people were coming and going every few minutes

"Your day looks as busy as mine was," Michaels said as he walked in.

"It's been a crazy day. What's up?"

"It was nuts at 26th street. Genirs spanked Sampson. I've never seen him react that way. He must have a daughter Ruth's age. Man he was wound up. Then he had jury selection and Pangborn got his perfect jury."

"Monday's trial is the tough one, right?"

"So far they're batting two for two but with Marcus Broadhead's testimony it just made their case stronger. I don't think they had a fifty-fifty chance of winning without him."

"He wants to keep his ass out of jail."

"Yep. Hey look at this lead-in for the ten."

# CHAPTER 36

"Proof of life" witness Violet Lezkowski was in the box for the third and final time. She looked frail, tired and cried out. There were no more tears left. Her heart was aching. Her voice was soft, just above a whisper. All the women in the jury box were wiping their eyes. All the men had a lump in their throats. Lorenzo Holmes was the beast, the ringleader. It took all the courage she had left in her being to look him in the eye, her mind asking, *How could you?*

~~~~

Detective Jack Evans took the jury on an investigative journey of the Lezkowski homicide. Because of his experience, Evans was assigned as the lead detective from day one. He was present at every major suspect interview. He had instant recall of hundreds of pages of supplementary reports. He was a terrific witness for the prosecution.

"Now, on April 27th, 1987, did you recall having a conversation with Marcus Broadhead?" asked ASA Melanie Wantuck.

"Yes, I did. That day was the turning point of the entire investigation," Evans said.

"What happened on that day?"

"Marcus Broadhead confessed to his involvement in the murder of Ruth Lezkowski. He also implicated three other defendants."

"Was Lorenzo Holmes, one of them?"

"Yes. He said Lorenzo Holmes is the one who jumped into Ms. Lezkowski's car and drove it up to the crime scene. He told us that Lorenzo Holmes initiated the first sexual attack and that he was the first one to strike Ms. Lezkowski in the face with the concrete block."

Everyone in the jury box was riveted on Evans' testimony, barely moving a muscle, almost statuesque.

"Broadhead told us after Lorenzo raped Ms. Lezkowski, he walked over to the passenger side of the car and that's when she tried to run away. She just got a few feet away and she fell. Charles Holmes caught her, then started kicking and stomping her."

"Did Lorenzo Holmes kick and stomp Ms. Lezkowski?"

"Broadhead said, Lorenzo's shower cap fell off and he was angry. He said he went over to Ms. Lezkowski and started kicking and stomping her. He said, Lorenzo Holmes found the piece of concrete and began hitting her in the face and on the head."

"Did Mr. Broadhead ever change his testimony?"

"Yes, he did. The second time we interviewed him he changed the name of the fourth offender. At first he identified Oscar Sampson but changed the name to Daniel. After that his confession was exactly the same as the first time we talked."

~~~~

Criminal Defense Attorney Ronald Myers declined to cross-examine Detective Jack Evans immediately after his testimony telling the court that he would call Evans as a defense witness.

~~~~

As Marcus Broadhead entered the courtroom, Lorenzo Holmes' body went rigid and he glared at him with hate in his eyes. If looks could kill, Broadhead would have never made it to the witness stand. Holmes never took his eyes off of him. Anger flared through him. His attorney Ronald Myers touched his arm in an attempt to calm him down. The tenseness in his muscles however never eased, he knew that Broadhead's testimony would doom him.

ASA Michael Pangborn methodically and dramatically guided Broadhead through his testimony. "Describe for the court what happened after you arrived up by the tracks?"

Impassively and emotionless Broadhead responded, "Lorenzo pulled her pants down and then he dropped his pants and put his dick in her. She was crying and struggling. While he was in her, you know, Charles starts yelling he wanted to be next, you know what I mean?"

"What happened next?"

Shrugging he said, "When Lorenzo finished, you know, she tried to run away. She fell a few feet from the car. That's when Charles catches up to her and starts kicking her. Lorenzo be all pissed off cuz his shower cap blows off. He was mad when he got to her and he started kicking and stomping on her. After that he finds this concrete block and starts beating her in the face and then on the head. Then they drag her back to the car and Charles tries to you know, fuck her." Shifting in his chair, he continued "She didn't move much, she was making some sounds, you know? She be crying, then gurgling or something and breathing hard. She was in a bad way, you know what I'm saying?"

The jury was mesmerized, shaking their heads and some of the female jurors placed their hands over their gasping mouths. Holmes however was fuming. Hatred glazed his eyes. Tenseness gripped his body as he clenched his fists.

"Then what happened?" asked Pangborn.

"When Charles finished with her, Lorenzo said, 'Let's adjust her,' so they pull up her pants and he sez, 'the police wouldn't know she was raped.' Then we left and I went home."

Broadhead never looked over at Lorenzo Holmes. His eyes were focused on the jury or Pangborn just as he was instructed to do. His testimony was devastating to Holmes.

Defense Attorney Ronald Myers stood up, buttoned his suit coat and went on the attack. "Mr. Broadhead, you are testifying here today because you got the deal of a life time, correct?"

"I'm telling the truth," he replied.

"Sure, you are. Are you getting a lesser sentence in exchange for your testimony?"

"I don't know what I'm getting. All I know is, I have to tell the truth."

"When you gave your confession, did the police threaten you?"

"No."

~~~~

On day three of the trial the prosecution called five witnesses, who testified in front of the Grand Jury that they had heard Lorenzo Holmes tell them he was involved in the murder of the white girl up on the tracks.

"Now Mr. George, what did Lorenzo Holmes say to you?" asked ASA Melanie Wantuck.

"One day me and Lorenzo was getting high. He says to me, 'you know that girl who was killed up there on the tracks?' I say, 'Yeah man,' and then he points to hisself and says, 'Me, Marcus and Shakey Jake did it,'" said Andrew George.

"Do you know anyone else who heard Lorenzo Holmes admit his involvement in the Ruth Lezkowski homicide?"

"Yeah, my lady."

~~~~

"Sometime between Christmas and New Years, I heard Lorenzo say he did it," Tereka Sears told the court.

"Could you be more specific? Where were you when you heard Lorenzo Holmes say, He did it?" asked ASA Wantuck.

"We was at the building next to where I stay, you know? It was about eight o'clock at night and we was talking."

"Who do you mean by we?"

"Me, Lorenzo and Melvin. Melvin be Andrew's brother. So Melvin asks him straight out if he knew about that $25,000 reward and if he knows who kilt that girl and Lorenzo starts laughing, you know what I mean?"

"What happened next?"

"So Melvin asks him again if he did it? He said yes, several times, 'Yes, I did it,' and then he says to me 'Hoggie and a couple of other guys was there too.'"

"Do you know who the other guys were?"

"I know 'Hoggie' be Marcus but, I don't remember the others."

"By Marcus, do you mean Marcus Broadhead?"

"Yes."

~~~~

"I heard them say they killed her," Wilson Jarvis told the court."

"Mr. Jarvis, when did you hear this and what was specifically said?" asked Michael Pangborn.

"About four or five days after that girl was killed, I was in the lobby of 1510 West 13th Street and Marcus and Lorenzo be there too. I hears Marcus say to Lorenzo, 'that broad we finished off. They be offering a $25,000 reward.'"

"Then what happened?"

"Lorenzo looks at me and grabs Marcus by the arm and takes him away. They stopped talking about it."

~~~~

Corey Wallace, the DJ the night/morning of the Lezkowski homicide told the court that Lorenzo Holmes, Oscar Sampson and a younger kid came to the party at 1510 West 13$^{th}$ Street.

"Were they there all night?" asked ASA Wantuck.

"No. They were in and out a couple of times. The young dude was only with em' once."

"What time did the party end?"

"Around 2:30, in the morning."

"Did you see the defendant Lorenzo Holmes after that?"

"No. I saw Oscar Sampson around four or so, maybe a little later."

"When was the next time you saw Oscar Sampson?"

"The night those three boys got arrested and he was acting all kinda strange. I says to the man 'what's wrong with you?' He's all nervous and shit and says that they'll be coming after him next. Then he says that he and Lorenzo were the ones who killed that white girl up on the tracks."

"He admitted that to you?"

"Yes, ma'am, he sure did."

~~~~

DeSean Bryant was the last witness of the day called to the stand.

"Now, Mr. Bryant will you please tell the court exactly what Oscar Sampson told you about Lorenzo Holmes' involvement in this case?" asked Michael Pangborn.

"Oscar says to me that Lorenzo was the first one to make 'the Rambo move.'"

"'Rambo move,' what did he mean by that?"

"You know, he says he makes this 'Rambo move' that he was the first one to jump into the lady's car. He said then everybody gets in and they drives up to the tracks. He say they were doing things to the broad but that he was just watching."

"What kind of things were Lorenzo and Charles Holmes doing to the victim, Ms. Lezkowski?"

"He said that Lorenzo said he was going to make the broad pay because she ran. He said that after she ran when Lorenzo got to her that he started hitting her in the face with a concrete brick. Oscar told me that Lorenzo said, 'He was going to kill the bitch for running away.'"

~~~~

The 19th and final prosecution witness was Dr. Robert Crine, the Cook County Medical Examiner. His testimony like the two trials before was riveting, as he described the massive injuries that Ruth Lezkowski endured.

"Now, Doctor, after you saw the bruises and injuries on the outside of the chest, did you perform an internal examination?" asked ASA Melanie Wantuck.

"Yes, there were several fractured ribs on the front of the chest, on the right side ribs—5, 6, 7, and 8 were fractured, and on the left side of the chest ribs—3, 6, 7 and 8 were fractured. When I examined the lungs, blood had been aspirated or breathed into the tissue lining of both lungs. Also some blood had gotten into the stomach."

"Doctor, where were the broken ribs in relation to the footprint on the chest?"

"The ribs on the right, 5, 6, 7 and 8, and 6, 7, and 8 on the left would have been beneath the bloody footprint."

"Would these injuries be consistent with her lying down on the ground and being stomped or kicked from above?"

"Yes."

"Doctor, did you perform an examination of the vaginal area of Ruth Lezkowski?"

"Yes. That examination showed that there was bruising around the entire entrance of the vagina as well as a small tear of the tissue itself. There was a small amount of blood mixed with the mucous material around it."

"And that injury to the vagina, was that consistent with forcible penetration?"

"Yes," Dr. Crine testified.

~~~~

Although Defense Attorney Ronald Myers vigorously cross-examined every prosecution witness except Mrs. Lezkowski, he also chose not to cross-examine Dr. Crine as well. He made the decision that it would just hurt the defense.

The State rested its case on the fourth day of trial.

~~~~

Judge Robert Genirs announced that buses were ready to take everyone to the crime scenes. He said the trial will more than likely conclude tomorrow and instructed the jury to take all their belongings with them because they did not have to return to the courthouse.

The crime scene where Ruth Lezkowski car was taken and the scene where her brutal murder occurred would be the last thing the jury of eight women and six men would see before they went to bed.

# CHAPTER 37

The defense called Detective Jack Evans as their first and only witness. Defense attorney Ronald Myers knew he would be given some leeway from Judge Robert Genirs when he went on the attack to try to discredit the confession and testimony of Marcus Broadhead.

"Now, detective Evans didn't you lie to Marcus Broadhead when you brought him in for questioning?" asked Myers.

"No."

"You didn't arrest him under false pretenses?"

"No."

"Didn't you tell him that you were interested in him for robberies?"

"We were. That's how we started connecting him the Lezkowski homicide."

"Did he not change his confession from the first time you spoke to him?"

"Yes."

"Don't you find that curious?"

"No. It happens often. His first confession made sense because he named his life-long friend Oscar Sampson. In his second confession, he named another person, Daniel as the fourth offender."

"Don't you find that odd?"

"Not at all. During the course of our investigation when he decided to cooperate, he told us, he would not testify against Sampson. Also other witnesses came forward and tied Sampson and Broadhead to the crime."

"You didn't allow him a phone call, did you?"

"We read him his rights. We told him, he had a right to an attorney and if he wanted to call anyone he could."

"Didn't he continually deny he had anything to do with the death of Ruth Lezkowski?"

"Yes. We told him he could go home if he took a polygraph test. He signed consent forms for blood samples and the polygraph. He failed the lie test and that's when he confessed to his involvement in the death of Ruth Lezkowski."

"You threatened him, to get him to take that polygraph test, didn't you?"

"No. No police officer or detective laid a hand on him."

"You kept him confined for over 24 hours, you just wore him down didn't you?"

"He had food, water and coffee, if he wanted it. He agreed to take the tests while he was in custody. He was never ever mistreated."

The aggressive questioning took over an hour but Evans, a seasoned detective, was cool, calm and collected throughout his testimony and finally Myers announced he was finished with the witness.

~~~~

Michael Pangborn on re-direct asked detective Evans, "Did you mistreat Marcus Broadhead in any way?"

"No. We did not. We even took full frontal body pictures to make sure that he had no injuries."

"When he was admitted into Cook County Jail did he have any injuries?"

"No."

"Nothing further, detective. Your honor the state would like to enter into evidence, Exhibit No. 81, the Medical Intake Report of Marcus Broadhead that shows no signs of any physical injuries on his person."

"Mr. Myers?"

"No objection, your honor."

"Any other witnesses, Mr. Myers?"

"No, your honor. The defense rests."

~~~~

Judge Robert Genirs instructed the jury on all four charges against Lorenzo Holmes right before lunch. The two alternate jurors were dismissed and the eight women and four men retired to the jury room for lunch and started their deliberations. While eating their box lunch sandwiches from the courthouse cafeteria which were just awful, they elected their foreperson, a 50-year-old black woman, who was the food manager of the Walnut Room Restaurant at Marshall Field's on State Street in downtown Chicago.

Each juror has an opportunity to communicate with the judge, but it is the foreperson that must do the communication on their behalf. She is also the one responsible for signing and presenting the verdict to the court. There were no real legal issues that the jury had to ask the judge and by 3:30 that afternoon, they reached a verdict.

Judge Genirs went down the list of charges asking the jury foreperson "How say you?"

"Guilty." She answered.

After polling the jury, Judge Genirs turned his attention to Lorenzo Holmes and asked him if he had anything to say.

"I didn't do it," Holmes defiantly declared.

Judge Genirs then thanked the jury for their service and dismissed them. He then scheduled a sentencing hearing in 30 days. Lorenzo Holmes in his orange prison jumpsuit was led out of the Courtroom. Shuffling in his leg irons, he looked around for his mother, who yelled out, "Don't you worry baby, we gunna' appeal," and Lorenzo Holmes disappeared through the prisoner door.

~~~~

Monday, August 15,1988, ASA Melanie Wantuck appeared before Judge William Albenese along with Marcus Broadhead and his attorney Jacqueline Oliver. She liked to be called Jackie. She was 5-foot two, athletic and ran marathons in her spare time. Jackie had short dishwater blonde hair and blue penetrating eyes that took in everything around her. She had a scholarship to George Mason University Law School, where she graduated in the top five percent of her class. She was a Prosecutor in Buffalo, New York for six years until she met her husband Michael, who lived in Chicago. She soon became an Associate Partner at the prestigious law firm of Carlin and Miller. Oliver was appointed by the court to represent Marcus

Broadhead. She did not like her client, but was glad to work with ASA Michael Pangborn to flip him to testify against Lorenzo Holmes.

"Your honor, we appear before you today to recommend a 12-year prison term for Marcus Broadhead who testified for the prosecution in the case against Lorenzo Holmes. We are recommending that he be charged with only aggravated criminal kidnapping for his involvement in the death of Ruth Lezkowski. He testified truthfully at the trial against Mr. Holmes," said Melanie Wantuck, as she handed the judge the plea agreement.

"Ms. Oliver did you explain everything to your client about this plea agreement and are you sure he understands it?" Judge Albenese asked.

"Yes, your honor."

"Mr. Broadhead do you realize that you pled guilty to the felony of aggravated criminal kidnapping and that I am not bound by this plea agreement to give you 12 years in the penitentiary. I could give you more. Do you understand that?"

"Yes, I do your honor" Broadhead responded.

"Ms. Wantuck said you cooperated fully with the state attorney's office, therefore, I am going to agree with that sentence. I hereby sentenced you to 12 years in the penitentiary to be served at Stateville, with your time at the Cook County Jail considered as time served."

~~~~

Judge Robert Genirs was not in the best of moods at the sentencing hearing of Lorenzo Holmes. He had heard enough testimony and denials during the last three hours when he asked Lorenzo Holmes if he had anything to say.

Standing there is his orange prison jumpsuit, Holmes looked dejected but once again he was defiant when he told the judge, "I didn't kill no-one."

Judge Genirs sat on the edge of his chair knowing that he would have given Holmes the death penalty but he couldn't because he was a teenager. "The jury has found you guilty as charged on all four counts. The evidence against you in this trial was overwhelming. You are the last chapter in this book of horrors. The evidence showed that you were the ringleader in the Lezkowski kidnapping and murder. You were the author of this book."

Genirs, who had never imposed capital punishment as a sentence, leaned forward and said, "If I could I wouldn't hesitate for a second to give you the death penalty and rid the world of your very existence. If there was ever a case that cried out for the death penalty, it was this one."

Judge Genirs sentenced Holmes to life imprisonment and added 60 more years for aggravated criminal sexual assault and armed robbery to be run consecutively with the life sentence and then he added 15 years for aggravated kidnapping to be run concurrently. "I want to make certain that you never ever walk the streets of this city or any other city again."

~~~~

Assistant State's Attorney Michael Pangborn, who never talked to the media during any of the three trials finally broke his silence after the last sentencing took place during a press conference in the lobby of Criminal Courts Building. Surrounded by TV cameras Pangborn approached the microphones and told reporters. "A lot of dreams ended the day Ruth Lezkowski was murdered," he said. "We think we have brought those responsible for her horrific, painful death to justice this year."

Peter Michaels raised his hand. "How important was Marcus Broadhead's testimony in the trial of Lorenzo Holmes?"

"Broadhead's cooperation was vital to the conviction of Lorenzo Holmes. Holmes did not cooperate with police at all. We had no confession and no physical evidence tying him to the crime. Our prosecution team felt we had less than 50 percent chance of conviction without Mr. Broadhead. So his testimony was very important. He placed Lorenzo Holmes at the scene and he named him as the ringleader of this vicious crime. Remember, Broadhead confessed that he was there and now he is going to prison for 12 years."

~~~~

This was the last day Violet Lezkowski would spend in a courtroom in Chicago. She was there everyday for the trials of the three people convicted of killing her baby girl. "We're glad it's over. Our son is getting married next month and this won't be hanging over us," she told a group of reporters gathered in the lobby of the Criminal Courts

Building. "As brutal as they murdered, we think they should be locked up for life."

"Mrs. Lezkowski," Peter Michaels asked. "You have been in this courthouse everyday for all three trials and you have maintained an incredible amount of composure throughout all this testimony. Can you tell us about that?"

"You know, Peter, after you cry for a year and think about it for a year, you just get so you don't cry easily anymore. It hardens you, I guess," Mrs. Lezkowski told reporters. "She was a wonderful daughter. You know, she would have been 25 years old, today."

# PART TWO

# CHAPTER 38

The only thing that didn't appear to change in the last 15 years was Chicago's evocative murder rate. The world was transformed at the speed of light, literally by technology.

In 1990 the Hubble Space Telescope was launched, followed by the explosion of the Worldwide Web that expanded the internet and lead to the invention of this new thing called email.

The United States of America entered the Gulf War and the first SMS text message was sent in 1992. Peter Michaels exchanged his old Motorola, pound and a half brick phone for a Nokia with a colored screen that weighed less than three ounces and it was half the size of a pack of cigarettes. It could fit in his back pocket.

Peter Michaels got divorced.

The Chicago Blackhawks and the Chicago Bulls got a new home. The $170 million construction of the United Center began with 3,500 tons of steel making it the largest arena in the United States. The old Chicago Stadium or the "Madhouse on Madison" with its rafters that vibrated when the National Anthem was sung was torn down in 1994.

The Appellate Courts affirmed all three convictions of Lorenzo Holmes, Charles Holmes and Oscar Sampson.

The crime-fighting tool, called DNA analysis, was becoming increasingly more sophisticated. It quickly became an important tool to identify criminals for the police and it provided proof beyond reasonable doubt for convictions by prosecutors. It also became a new weapon for defense attorneys to clear their clients in wrongful conviction cases.

Marcus Broadhead served his prison term for aggravated kidnapping at Stateville only to return one year later, this time for robbery.

The war on worldwide terrorism was accelerated after the September 11, 2001 terrorist attacks on United States soil. The attacks were vicious. Suicide planes bombed the Twin Towers of the World Trade Center in New York City and the Pentagon. The fourth plane that was headed for the U.S. Capitol Building was downed in a field in Pennsylvania after heroic passengers overpowered the terrorists and sacrificed their lives to save thousands of others.

~~~~

"News ... Michaels."

"Hey, Peter, it's Jose Aguilera."

"Hey, brother what's up?"

"Same-O, same-O, but hey, I just wanted to give you a heads up. I'm filing a report in federal court tomorrow that I commissioned in conjunction with my lawsuit for Alvin Lewis and Adrian Rawls"

Lewis and Rawls were exonerated after spending nine years in prison for a rape that DNA indicated they didn't commit. Aguilera was a successful criminal defense attorney and he made a bigger name for himself after his successful trial for the wrongful convictions of Lewis and Rawls.

~~~~

Jose Aguilera was a gifted child. He graduated from St. Ignatius High School, a college prep school run by the Jesuits on Roosevelt Road, when he was 16-years old. He graduated from Loyola University on Chicago's North side by the time he was 20. He got into DePaul Law School immediately and passed the Illinois Bar when he was 24. Though his name was Aguilera, he taught himself how to speak Spanish, Italian and German. Spanish was never spoken in his house growing up. His father was 100 percent Mexican and his mother was half German and half Lithuanian.

His criminal defense work started slow but accelerated quickly. He set up his first law office in a storefront on Ashland Avenue in the Pilsen neighborhood to represent poor Latino residents in 1986. He quickly caught the attention of gangbangers, drug dealers and a mafia kingpin.

When Aguilera first started practicing the Lezkowski Four were on their way to prison. It never crossed his mind that he would one day represent them until he got a single page letter from Oscar Sampson that caught his attention. In a few simple sentences, Sampson volunteered to take a DNA test to prove he didn't rape Ruth Lezkowski.

Aguilera was just getting started with wrongful convictions and remembered the Lezkowski case like it happened yesterday. He was a brilliant attorney, who loved the law and he hated corruption and wrongdoing.

~~~~

Michaels perked up. He almost knocked his coffee cup over as he scrambled to get his feet off his desk and started taking notes.

"What's in the report?" Michaels asked.

"It's very critical of the forensic testing and it's use at trials. It is particularly focused on Patricia Bass' work. This report may not exonerate every defendant whose cases are mentioned, but it does imply forensic fraud may be more serious than originally believed. We found evidence that Dr. Bass' blood work in the nine cases that we studied showed that she misrepresented the significance of that blood work either directly or by omission."

*If that were true then a lot of defendants might be about to go free,* Michaels thought. He wasn't sure how he felt about that.

"Who did the study?" Michaels asked and then he heard Aguilera shuffle some papers. He was clearly on a speakerphone.

"We hired Dr. James White, a DNA analyst and Edward Kelly, a forensic scientist. Their report stated, 'the nature of her errors are such that a reasonable investigator, attorney or fact finder would be misled. And she always offered an opinion that was most damaging to the defendant.'"

*That's her job*, Michaels thought as he shrugged his shoulders. *That's what she's suppose to do*, then he asked, "She's over in the Illinois State Police Crime Lab now, isn't she?"

"Yes, she and about 40 others, who worked at the Chicago Police Crime Lab. They moved over there about six years ago, but now she is a supervisor making $76,000 a year as the chief of the biochemistry section of the lab."

"How many guys have gotten out of prison so far … a dozen?"

"Thirteen inmates on Death Row have been recently released. I'm going to petition the court to vacate the judgments against Lorenzo Holmes, Charles Holmes and Oscar Sampson."

"When?"

"Soon. I got this very simple, one full-page letter from Oscar Sampson stating that, he and the others are willing to give DNA samples. After 15 years in prison, they still claim they are innocent in the Lezkowski homicide."

Michaels rubbed his forehead and sat up straighter and thought. *Could this be right? I read all the evidence and that shit was overwhelming. I was sure they were guilty.* He shook his head. *I was at every trial. I didn't miss a word. I stared at them, their faces, their body language. I had no doubt they were guilty.*

"Jose, most criminals deny they did it, don't they? Those guys were all convicted in less than a total of eight hours of jury deliberations. As I remember it, those cases were very solid."

"Yeah, but DNA is changing the landscape of the criminal justice system. What they had back then was primitive compared to today. I'd bet my life that if they had DNA in 87, those boys would never have been charged. That's what makes this Patricia Bass stuff so important. She was involved in all of the cases we studied. So far we are batting 100 percent on exonerations with more to come, I'm sure."

# CHAPTER 39

J oliet Correctional Center was built in 1858 before the Civil War. The limestone used for construction was actually quarried on site. Both prisoners of war and criminals were housed there during the Civil War. By 1872 the prison population reached record highs for any prison, 1,239 inmates.

There was no running water or toilets in the cells in 1910. Joliet Correctional Center was slow to modernize. Correction officials thought that Joliet would close in 1925 after Stateville Correctional Center was built but that never happened. Both prisons operated simultaneously for the rest of the 20th Century. Joliet was the oldest penitentiary in the United States in 2001.

Nathan Leopold and Richard Loeb served life sentences after their attorney Clarence Darrow successfully negotiated away the death penalty in the case known as "the crime of the century." Leopold and Loeb were convicted for the kidnapping and death of Robert Franks.

More than 20,000 inmates a year were processed and assigned to other prisons throughout Illinois. In 1975, members of the notorious street gang the Almighty Black P. Stone Nation and other Chicago street gangs took over a cellblock and held several correctional officers hostage to negotiate for better living conditions.

One of the most violent street gangs in Chicago's history, The Black P. Stone Nation ran their criminal enterprise from Joliet Prison and they controlled a large number of inmates. Correctional officials started transferring gang members to other prisons and that was the primary reason for the riot. One inmate who worked with the

administration offices to bring about change was murdered and
shortly after the riot was resolved.

By the year 2001, Joliet Correctional Center housed 1,180
prisoners. Charles Holmes was one of them.

~~~~

Charles Holmes was considered a "model prisoner." He turned 29
years old behind bars. He found religion. He was shy and soft
spoken. Correctional officers and the Warden protected him and they
believed that he was not capable of committing murder. He had
several opportunities to escape because gates nearby where he was
working were often left open and unattended. He never took
advantage of the opportunity.

~~~~

Assistant Cook County State's Attorney Amy Wilson was assigned to
work specifically with Jose Aguilera on the new post-conviction Ruth
Lezkowski investigation. From the start it was beginning to look like
the DNA from the evidence recovered at the scene in 1986 was not
going to match any of the four original suspects. The state's attorney's
office pledged to fully support the new investigation.

Ms. Wilson was a very competent attorney. She was born and
raised in Chicago. She went to Catholic grade school, high school
and college. She entered DePaul at age 17 and graduated in three
years. Law school was easy for her, she graduated with honors,
passed the Illinois Bar on her first try and was hired by the Cook
County State's Attorney's Office immediately. After spending ten
years working her way up the ladder, she was transferred to the
Special Prosecutions Unit. Under the tutelage of Peter Di Donato, the
head of Special Prosecutions, she became even more organized,
detailed and quick witted.

Wilson looked like Meg Ryan, the movie star. Her lithe muscular
body was the result of spin classes, running and a vegan diet. She
dressed the part as well with custom tailored suits, blouses, and
stylish heels from Nordstrom's. Her natural blonde hair was cut in
layers and fell exactly at her collar line. Her blue eyes could pierce
through any defendant that she was interviewing or cross-examining.
Her mind was photographic and quick; she remembered everything
like it just happened. She was the perfect person for the job.

~~~~

ASA Amy Wilson and Jose Aguilera appeared before the honorable Judge John "Jack" Green on a Motion for Buccal Swabs from the four Lezkowski defendants. Aguilera's first two attempts to get swabs from Lorenzo Holmes and Oscar Sampson were denied but after the state's attorney's office decided to cooperate with the new investigation, Judge Green granted the swab for Charles Holmes and then for all the defendants.

Judge Jack Green was known as a prosecutor's judge, fair and honest and by the book. He'd been on the bench for 22 years and hoped to retire soon. Green spent 16 years in the state's attorney's office. He was a first chair prosecutor for 10 years before he became a judge. He looked the part of judge, white hair combed back with a neatly trimmed full beard. His five ten frame was slender but his running days were over because of arthritic knees. He moved slow but with purpose. He was a student of the law.

One of the easiest and fastest ways to a get a DNA sample is with a buccal swab. A saliva sample is taken from the mouth on a sterile white cotton stick and immediately sealed in an evidence bag. Once obtained the DNA is compared against other evidence. The waiting period for the analysis is two to three weeks. Aguilera was certain it would free his clients.

The state's attorney's office presented a small piece of cloth from Ruth Lezkowski's jogging pants to Aguilera for the analysis. The groundwork was already prepared for a cooperative working relationship between the two parties.

"I'm assuming that a full scale investigation is about to get underway once we get the results back from the lab?" Judge Green asked.

"Yes, your honor, the state's attorney has ordered that we get all the evidence together to expedite a new investigation," said Ms. Wilson.

"Your honor my office is currently analyzing all the police reports and we are preparing to file a Petition to Vacate Judgment for my clients. I will be presenting that to the court once we have the DNA results," Aguilera said.

~~~~

Peter Michaels was a meticulous note taker and it took him some time to gather all his old Lezkowski notes from 15 years ago. He was feeling the years creep up with a knee that was bone on bone from years of tennis and sailing. His hair was getting thinner and graying at the temples. He and anchorman Ron Magers were the same age and for the first time he was thinking about calling it quits. The Lezkowski case re-energized him. If Michaels wasn't a reporter, he probably would have been a cop.

He got to know Detective Jack Evans during the initial investigation and was convinced he was a painstaking investigator and this new development was going to devastate him.

~~~~

APRIL 27, 2001

Ron Magers was sitting at his desk with his feet up reading the newspaper when Michaels walked in.

"Here we go again. Do you believe it after all this time?" Michaels handed him a copy of his script.

"These wrongful convictions are going to use up a lot of airtime. This DNA stuff is a lot faster now and more sophisticated."

"Yeah. Aguilera is convinced he'll get all four of them off. DNA just doesn't go away unless it is washed away with bleach and even then they just need one microscopic dot."

"I was just reading in the paper about a cop in Detroit who planted a knife on a suspect that he shot. When the crime guys analyzed the knife, they found a tiny bit of hair. It turned out to be his cat's hair. He was indicted for first degree murder," Magers said, shaking his head.

"Aguilera said the first samples came back negative for his clients. He'll get more samples out soon."

"What about that one guy that testified against one of the defendants?"

Michaels shook his head slowly and said with a slight smile, "Broadhead, what a piece of work, he is. Remember, he was sentenced to 12 and got out in six. He has been arrested 14 times since he was released in 1992 and now he's back in the shithouse again. He'll probably get exonerated as well."

"What about this forensic fraud stuff?"

"Aguilera is challenging the entire police investigation that lasted more than 115 days and accumulated over 3,500 pages of supplementary reports, lab analysis and medical reports. Some 110 witnesses were questioned, scores of polygraph tests were given and over 100 samples of blood and saliva were analyzed.

Two of the defendants that confessed are now recanting and saying they were coerced. Marcus Broadhead claimed his confession was beaten out of him. Charles Holmes is now saying that he was tricked into confessing."

Magers had a habit of rubbing his right earlobe when he was thinking. He said, "It sounds like this case is falling apart."

"Aguilera is alleging that the homicide investigation was flawed from the very beginning." Michaels was sitting back in his chair but now he scooted forward put his forearms on his thighs and he stared at the floor. "He claims the time line for the crime doesn't make any sense. The crime began at one o'clock in the morning according to the confessions and all the police reports."

Michaels got up from his chair and walked to the door, but paused. "Dr. Edward Radney last saw Ruth alive after they finished studying and she drove him home. He said that she was going straight home because they were going to study again in the morning for a pathology exam. Police reports stated that her murderers kidnapped her at approximately one in the morning and took her to the desolated area immediately."

Magers perused Michaels' copy, "This is very interesting. The contradictions about the stuff at the scene when she was discovered."

"Yeah. The railroad cop finds her body at approximately 4:30 that morning. His report states that 'blood was still dripping from her car door' when he approached the crime scene. Aguilera hired this private medical examiner guy, who concluded that would be impossible to happen if the murder occurred shortly after one in the morning. The dripping blood would seem to indicate that the murder occurred closer to four not one."

"Script looks good."

"Thanks, see you on the set."

# CHAPTER 40

D etective Jethro Richard Corley was sitting at his desk in the Cold Case detective squad room in the old Sears Warehouse on the city's near Westside. It was known as Homan Square.

The Chicago Police Department purchased the property and it took two years to remodel. It now houses all of the Department's Special Operations Units like S.W.A.T., Organized Crime, Gang Enforcement, Narcotics and the new crime lab. The four-story structure was built on a full city block. You could literally ride a bicycle from one end of the building to the other. It was a maze of organized chaos.

Corley was investigating a serial killer/rapist and he had 13 different case files on his desk some dating back 16 years. Corley was intense. He loved a good mystery and re-investigating was his forte. He and Detective Bill Rogers "the puzzle man" from Area Four Violent Crimes were best friends and they shared the same love of golf. Unlike Rogers, Corley never smoked a cigarette in his life. He was physically fit, his five-foot, ten-inch frame was solid muscle, all 155 pounds of it. An avid runner and health food enthusiast, Corley was very regimented. He required only four hours of sleep a night and his mind was constantly in a state of motion, particularly when he was investigating a case that had a lot of questions but not a lot of answers.

He hated the name Jethro and was in a constant battle with himself to spend the money and energy to legally change his name to just Richard.

~~~~

"Cold Case Squad, this is Corley."

"Hey, Dick. It's Phil."

Philip Cline was just promoted to the Chief of Detectives. His 30-year career provided him the opportunity to serve in just about every unit of the Chicago Police Department. He was a Sergeant in Narcotics and a Lieutenant at Area Two Violent Crimes, the Commander of Area Five Detectives and the Deputy Chief of Organized Crime before his new promotion. He had a photographic memory and he could recall the slightest detail of any case he was ever involved in. A cop's cop and a prankster who giggled at all the gags he pulled on his friends. He was always very informal with his friends even though he out ranked them but when it came time to be serious no one would bear down with truer grit.

One would never guess that Phil Cline was a policeman. He loved good food, especially Italian, but he seldom drank alcohol. He was as round as he was tall. He had to buy larger suits to fit around his stomach and then have them tailored to fit his short arms. The same was true for the shirts he wore. He loved to ride his bicycle and he was surprisingly fast in a foot chase.

"What's up boss?" Corley asked quizzically not expecting a call from the Chief of Detectives.

"I hate to do it but I am reassigning you to the state's attorney's office to handle the Department's interests in the post-conviction investigation of the Ruth Lezkowski homicide."

"Why? What's so important?"

"DNA doesn't match the bad guys we got. Not even close from what I've been told. We are going to start from square one. You'll be working with Assistant State's Attorney Amy Wilson. I want fresh eyes on it immediately."

"You're the boss. Do you have this Amy Wilson's number?"

~~~~

The 15 years brought about many changes in Peter Michaels' life as well. His mother passed away in 1991 when she was 91 years old. He also separated and eventually divorced his wife Katie. His older sister almost died from a ruptured intestine and his two other sisters had breast cancer. He was becoming quite the sailor and he even did a Solo-Mackinaw race.

The Chicago to Mackinaw Island race is the longest fresh water race in the world, 333 miles. His partner for 16 years Doug Longhini took a new job with a different network.

Michaels was sitting at his desk talking with his new producer.

Dave Beedy was a newscast producer for years but wanted more of a challenge to work on long-term projects. He replaced Doug Longhini.

Longhini had an offer he couldn't refuse, the CBS Network hired him as an Investigative Producer. Longhini could speak and read several languages. He was assigned to work out of the 48 Hours Show. Michaels told everyone at his going away party that he was going to miss the sight of Longhini pulling at his hair when he was reading or concentrating on something.

Beedy was a workhorse. He embraced the opportunity to join the I-Team not only because he loved new challenges but he was also burned out as a show producer. He was an exceptional writer and very organized. The Investigative Unit was now being used more on daily stories as well. If the news department got beat on a big story, they would call in the I-Team to catch up and take over the story. This had its genesis when Michaels broke all the stories of the Lezkowski homicide. As the world was changing so was television news. It was going in a new direction, a direction Michaels didn't like.

~~~~

"News … Michaels."

"Hey, Michaels, it's Corley."

"What's up, Jethro?"

Michaels was one of the few that called Corley "Jethro" and he only did so in private conversations. He knew that Corley hated the name on the first day they met.

The "Cold Case" television show was such a hit that the news director wanted Michaels to do one cold case story a month. Michaels had a good rapport with Lieutenant Mark Leonard who was in charge of the Cold Case Unit.

Leonard was a religious man, who went to Mass every day before work. He had the nickname "Deacon." He despised corruption and bad cops. He took a liking to Michaels after his "Beating Justice" series years ago about police officers that had multiple charges of brutality filed against them. He became a major source of information to Michaels ever since. Leonard set up the first meeting between Michaels and Corley.

Corley was close to solving a six-year-old murder of a Hegewisch man and a news story might jolt some results. Steven Luzinski was shot in the back of the head three times and was found in a nearby park where he ran his dog at Wolfe Lake. Luzinski was an odd looking man who had an IQ of 79 and walked with slight limp. His brother and Corley were positive his young girlfriend plotted to kill him because he amassed $565,000 in his bank account.

Amanda Blankenship was 20 years younger. One of her brothers had a drug problem and another had an arrest record. None of them had a dime to rub together until Luzinski died. The day after his murder, they were at the bank making a withdrawal.

Hegewisch is an ethnic community located on Chicago's far south side. It has one of the lowest crime rates in the city. Hegewisch has more undeveloped land than anywhere else in the city. The community consists of 375 acres of single-family homes. Hegewisch also contains Chicago's only trailer park.

Luzinski's murder shocked the entire community. After Michaels did the story, the Blankenship family sued him and the station for eight million dollars. The lawsuit is still in the Cook County Civil Court system and the relationship between Michaels and Corley was cemented.

"You know you are the only person that I allow to call me Jethro?"

"What's happening?"

"I just got reassigned to the state's attorney's office. I'm heading up the new Lezkowski homicide investigation. We just got the first DNA test back and it don't match the four guys in the shithouse."

"Can I go with that?"

"Sure. Your stuff has been right on target so far. You just, didn't hear it from me."

"I'll call Aguilera too."

~~~~

Two days later Detective Dick Corley met ASA Amy Wilson for the first time and he was taken aback by her beauty. He was also very impressed by her work ethic. They hit it off instantly as she handed him a copy of the first DNA test results. Two samples were used, one from Lezkowski's panties and another from a vaginal swab. The report stated "Two different and highly discriminating DNA profiles were obtained from the evidence. One profile originated from the spermatozoa on the vaginal swab and on her panties. This profile was designated as originating from Unknown Male #1. The second profile came from the sperm found only on the panties and it originated from Unknown Male #2."

"So Lorenzo and Charles Holmes, Oscar Sampson and Marcus Broadhead are excluded. That's pretty definitive! Are you thinking of more DNA tests?" Corley asked.

"Yep. We are in the process now of gathering more evidence samples. Aguilera told us he would be back in court with a petition to include more evidence therefore more testing. I'm sure you know that DNA was used in medical research for years and years. The technology has gotten better and better for criminal cases and now with PCR things are not only getting better, they're getting faster and faster. A few years ago it took weeks to test a sample. PCR changed everything." Wilson said.

"PCR?"

"Polymerase Chain Reaction is now used to reproduce and amplify selected sections of DNA for analysis. In the past, amplification of DNA involved cloning segments of interest into vectors for expressions in bacteria, and it took weeks to test a sample. But now, with PCR, its done in test tubes and it takes only a few hours."

"What lab do you use?"

"We use one in Baltimore, Maryland and another in Burlington, North Carolina. Aguilera uses one in Toronto, Canada. They are all very respectable."

"What's next?" Corley asked.

"We are going to do DNA test on all the original suspects or 'Persons of Interest' and lots more I am sure," Wilson said.

~~~~

MAY 15, 2001

"It ain't them," Michaels said as he walked into Magers office. "They do know now that there are at least two bad guys but it isn't the Lezkowski four."

Magers got up out of his chair and stretched "ugh" he sighed. "Their case is really falling apart."

Michaels had a pined look on his face. He always felt the case against the Lezkowski Four was strong and now he was beginning to doubt his convictions. "I just got off the phone with Aguilera he said there is absolutely no DNA evidence linked to his clients. None! And get this—the two confessions where they claimed they kidnapped her at the stop sign at Flournoy and Loomis, there is no stop sign there." Michaels made a mental note to question Detective Jack Evans about that obvious mistake.

"I bet Aguilera is chomping at the bit and can't wait to sue them."

"He is really pissing them off though with the charges of prosecutorial and police misconduct."

"What's the state's attorney's office saying?"

"Not a lot right now but Di Donato told me they're probably going to order another batch of tests.

"DNA evidence has turned this case into a disaster."

"You got that right," Michaels said as he handed Magers a script. "See if this works for you. I'll see you on the set for the ten."

# CHAPTER 41

J
ose Aguilera's law office was now located in the Monadnock Building. The historic building sat kitty corner from the United States Federal Courthouse in Chicago's South Loop at 53 West Jackson. The skyscraper was built in 1891 and designed by the firm of Burnham and Root. It was the tallest load bearing brick building ever constructed. Its decorative staircase represents the first structural use of aluminum in building construction. The building was divided into professional offices from 250 square feet to 6,000 square feet. Aguilera's firm occupied 3,500 square feet and his interior decorator had very expensive tastes. His law practice grew with his reputation. His clients included organized crime figures, art thieves, gangbangers and the Lezkowski Four.

Aguilera sat behind an eight foot by four foot, hand craved mahogany desk. His handmade office chair had vibrators to sooth his lower back pain. His desk and chair sat on a $30,000 antique Persian Serapi rug. He preferred his Mont Blanc fountain pen with blue ink compared to any of his Mont Blanc ballpoint pens. Law books adorned his walls in hand carved bookshelves that match his desk. Criminal defense work had been very good to him.

Peter Michaels was a frequent visitor because Jose Aguilera was not only a good source of information but they also sailed together on summer weekends out of Burnham Harbor and they drank beer year round in downtown taverns.

"When are you going to file your Motion to Vacate?" Michaels asked.

"Look Peter, this thing had been fundamentally wrong from the get go. I don't believe for a second that those boys carjacked her. She was abducted from behind her apartment and the police blew it."

"What do you mean?"

"First of all, by all accounts, Ruth Lezkowski was very security conscious. She always locked her car doors. Always! The police reports mention this over and over again. No way those guys could just open that door and climb in because she would have run them over to get away from them.

Aguilera struggled in his chair, twisting his hips to relieve the pain is his lower back. He tilted his head and said, "Secondly, the only things missing from the scene were her car keys and the stick her brothers gave her for protection. According to the confessions, Charles Holmes threw that stick away somewhere near the crime scene and then he kept the keys for a souvenir but eventually tossed them. Don't you think it's a little bit convenient that the police never found either of those items?"

Aguilera reached for a crime scene photo. "Look at this picture. You see that bloody footprint. It's as wide as her waist. Detective Jack Evans found a footprint that matched that behind Lezkowski's apartment. Their Crime Lab guy Landis identified it as the same type found on the body. That footprint evidence, Peter, never made it to the trials. That lead went nowhere other than asking if some 'Persons of Interest' ever wore gym shoes. Nothing places the Four in that alley and that's where I theorize she was taken."

Michaels finished looking at the picture and handed it back to Aguilera, who continued, "Finally, an off-duty police officer who lives right behind Lezkowski told police, he thought he saw her car a little after one in the morning but he couldn't be totally sure because of the glaring headlights. He didn't give it another thought until the police questioned him the following day. My bet is that's where she was grabbed."

"Yeah, I read all those reports and I wondered why the footprint was a dead end," Michaels said. "But that investigation was massive. There has to be more than 3,500 pages of reports and evidence analysis and shit like that."

"The footprint may have been their best lead in the case but they literally ignored it. At first police kept going back to the people who knew her. The people she studied with, the doctors. They even had a profile that stated she 'knew the person that killed her and had a relationship with him for awhile.' The police over time were able to eliminate those who knew her because of alibis, polygraph tests and serological tests. Then they developed a theory that the killers were adult black males, from the ALBA Homes and boxcar thieves. They kept going back to that theory."

Aguilera shuffled a stack of crime scene photos when he got to the one he wanted, he reached across the desk and handed Michaels the picture he selected.

"Look at this picture of Lezkowski's car. There is no evidence of any smash and grab—none. Look at the windows nothing broken, no evidence of forced entry, nothing! Marcus Broadhead's confession stated that their motive was robbery but look at this evidence list of things found at the scene, her purse, her backpack, and her wallet. She was even still wearing her wristwatch. Both those confessions are contradicting the police theory of robbery."

Michaels flipped through the pages in his notebook and when he found what he was searching for he said "I remember after the first of the year back in 87 there was tremendous pressure to solve this case. TV, the papers, radio stations were all over it."

"Yeah, that's it, all conventional leads were exhausted and all of sudden there was a dramatic shift in the investigation. They turned all their attention to old cases from that area and started concentrating on young black males with criminal records living in the ALBA projects. That theory came from a top FBI criminal profiler, a guy by the name of Robert Richards. He was brought into it by a former student."

"Yeah, Tom Cronin. I interviewed him at the time. He said there was no profile because the day he brought Richards to Area Four, they had already solved the case." Michaels scratched his head and had a quizzical look on his face. He pursed his lips. "I remember him saying that distinctly."

"Bullshit." Aguilera reached for a book and opened it to the marked pages and handed it over to Michaels.

"Yeah, well, Richards wrote about it in his book, *In Search of Demons*. It's right here. He talks about how they were young gangbangers looking to rob someone. How the killers lived close by and that they were familiar with the area. He also says that anal assaults convinced him that one or more of the killers probably served time because that happens a lot in prisons.

We believe the police used Richard's profile as the script for the crime and, they force fed that information to Broadhead and Charles Holmes."

"Are you sure about that? As I remember it, Cronin had breakfast with him and by the time they got there, Charles Holmes was already confessing. Cronin told me when they went upstairs there was so much smoke coming out of Commander Maurer's office that he thought they just elected a new Pope. That's why I remember it so vividly."

"Look Peter from the evidence in this homicide, at the time, there was no way of knowing if there was one killer or two or three or four. That profile planted the idea that it was more than one person," Aguilera said.

~~~~

"That's a fucking lie! There was never a fucking profile. We had the guys before, I even met Richards." Maurer screamed.

James Maurer was a source of Michaels for a long time and he sensed this phone call was going to set him off but he didn't expect such a visceral reaction. He could picture Maurer's face turning beet red and he smiled. Michaels was very familiar with how Maurer reacted when he got pissed off. He knew that Maurer always stood up from his desk chair to vent. Then he would start to pace around his office and if he was on the phone he would stretched its cord to its maximum length.

Maurer was promoted to Deputy Chief of Patrol. Chief of Patrol was one of the most coveted jobs on the department. The Patrol Division is the heart and soul, the backbone of any police department. Police officers that most people come in contact with are from patrol.

"Listen, I'm just telling you what they're saying. It was that lead that led them to take this case." Michaels said.

"I'm telling you, Peter. That never, ever happened. Cronin set it up because we were going nowhere fast. Then all these new leads started coming in and by the time Richards got here, it was over. We had our suspects and one of them was with the state's attorney from

Felony Review giving us his confession when Richards came into
Area Four Violent Crimes."

"Well it's in his book, *In Search of Demons* or something like
that."

Maurer's face was turning red with anger, "Then the book is as
full of shit as Richards. I don't care about his fucking book. It never
happened. Every FBI profile has to be on file. I'm tell ya', it's
mandatory. There is no official FBI profile on file. The guy is a liar
pure and simple. It never fucking happened."

"He said, he gave it orally," Michaels said.

"That's bullshit too. He never did a profile for us and he never
delivered any profile in any form to the FBI."

"What do you think about the new DNA evidence that appears
to prove the four didn't rape Ruth Lezkowski?"

"DNA may prove they didn't rape her but it doesn't prove they
didn't kill her. Listen, we had two confessions and remember what
they said? They didn't ejaculate in her. They all knew stuff about that
crime and unless you were up there it would be impossible for them
to know those things. The cases we developed were the result of
good solid police work. The juries believed the cases. Hell, they
found three of them guilty in record time," Maurer said.

"Well, they are recanting their confessions. Broadhead says you
beat it out of him. Charles Holmes said he was tricked."

Maurer was calming down. He regained his composer and
stated, "Listen, those guys were in police custody for less than 24
hours and they were confessing. No one was beaten. I would of fired
any detective that would of fucked up this case. It meant too much
for the department and the city. Pictures were taken of everyone. No
one laid a hand on any of them. Intake records at Cook County Jail
show no evidence of beatings. That's bullshit, Peter! These guys knew
too much not to be involved," Maurer said.

"Well, the Chicago Bugle Editorial reamed you a new asshole,
didn't it?"

Maurer returned to his desk and sat back down. "Fuck them too!
You know me. I am not afraid to talk to any reporters but they took
me out of context, used half quotes and omitted so much of what I
told them. It's outrageous! Do you really think that I would want to
put the wrong people in jail for life if we didn't have the evidence to

convict them? Look at that letter to the editor I wrote, it was never published. Look at the top of page two where it begins;

> You have decided that because I do not agree with your one-sided version of events, and do in fact believe that the four individuals in prison for the Ruth Lezkowski murder are guilty, that I should be categorized as being more interested in upholding a bogus conviction than making sure I get the actual killer. I find that conclusion as illogical as it is reprehensible. I also said that absence of seminal evidence means that the perpetrators didn't leave any seminal evidence. And the absence of seminal evidence did not mean that these four did not kill her. This statement you categorize as 'new theories so far-fetched even armchair sleuths educated by Andy Griffith and Barney Fife would laugh.' Once again you chose to misrepresent my statement and leave out explanatory information.

Maurer settled back in his chair, put his feet up on the desk to get his blood circulating. He rubbed his forehead as he often did and said, "Remember my now ex-wife was a medical student. She put a lot of pressure on me to solve that case and not to fuck it up. I had every one of those detectives do everything by the book. If they messed up I would've sent them to the farthest end of city from their home to work. Listen, the Ruth Lezkowski murder was one of the most horrific crimes I have ever been involved with."

> Maurer's letter went on: The brutality, the visions of horror that must have gone through that young woman's mind, and most of all the unbridled, cold ruthlessness provided by the un-coerced confessions, demanded nothing but the most professional response by my Detectives. The personnel involved in this investigation were relentless in their search for the truth. They played by every rule in the book and certainly would not have done anything to jeopardize a just, proper and righteous conviction. To suggest

that my personnel or I would have settled for anything
less than the true killers is outrageous. And, for you to
report these latest developments as deliberate
misconduct on the part of the Police and Prosecutor,
while at the same time placing unquestioned
credibility in everyone except the authorities,
especially four killers, is even more appalling. Your
reporters allegedly have reviewed the files thoroughly.
If they have, they know far more about the character
and past history of the four than I am allowed to go
into. Your paper was not prohibited from printing that
information, yet you chose to portray these thugs as
misunderstood, learning disabled, naïve young kids.
You know that is not the case. For that you should
also be ashamed.

"Peter, I told you this earlier and I am saying it again, those four
individuals knew too much about that crime scene not to be
involved."

"Do you mind if I do a story on your letter?"

"If you have the balls, I'd love it."

# CHAPTER 42

A SA Amy Wilson and Detective Dick Corley were meeting with Peter Di Donato, the supervisor of Special Prosecutions for the Cook County State's Attorney's Office to discuss the 43 people they wanted to get buccal swabs from, and compare them with both the Illinois and Federal CODIS databases.

CODIS was the acronym for the Combined DNA Index System and was the generic term used to describe the FBI's program of support for criminal justice DNA databases as well as the software used to run these databases.

Di Donato, normally easy going, was agitated at the moment after getting off of the phone with his boss Kevin Benedetti. Though the state's attorney's office wanted to get to the bottom of this new investigation, yesterday there was a feeling surfacing that this was not going to bode well for the office. As soon as the phone hit its cradle, he snapped. "I want swabs from everyone in the original investigation that had an O blood type and everyone who was an O secretor. I want swabs from any violent person that we identify. We also need samples from Dennis Dumont that crazy fucker who beat all those women within 45 minutes of each other and Edgar Ringer the guy that whispered in the ear of his female victims that he wanted to 'fuck em' after he robbed them. They were both O secretors," Di Donato said.

~~~~

Di Donato had been with the state's attorney's office for 22 years and the supervisor of Special Prosecutions for the last eight. He expected to get an appointment to the bench within the next year. He was five feet, nine inches tall and prematurely bald. What hair he still had, he wore long, touching the collar of his handmade white heavily starched shirt. His Armani suits were all conservative and dark in color. His neck blended into his trapezoid muscle. His chest looked like a barrel. His arms were thick from lifting weights. He was strong and smart and a student of the law known for being, a no-nonsense prosecutor who would put his own mother in jail if she broke the law.

Di Donato, perused the report on the DNA results, his reading glasses perched on his nose, "There were no CODIS hits on the unidentified Male #1 or Male #2 profiles obtained through the original DNA samples of Lezkowski's vaginal swab and panty's swab. We are now gathering new samples of her clothing, her jacket, her shoes, her jogging suit; we're including scrapings from her fingernails. We are also going to have the pubic hair we found at the scene analyzed."

"We are going to court on Friday to officially hand over the evidence Aguilera requested and we are going to send them to our lab in Maryland for analysis. When the results come back, hopefully within 30 days, we will all share the same information and go on from there. I've got to say this arrangement with Aguilera is working well. He is a very competent attorney and I think he is going to sue our office and the police department when this is over," Amy Wilson said.

Di Donato shook his head, though he agreed to the arrangement, it didn't mean he had to like it. He also knew that Aguilera would sue anyone connected to this case and that pissed him off.

~~~~

Corley looked tired. The circles under his eyes betrayed him. His tie was askew and his pants were wrinkled from the long plane trip from the west coast. He was methodically working his way down the list of suspects he had to get buccal swabs from. He was a little irritated but happy he felt he had *eliminated two more suspects.*

"I just got back from California and Reno, Nevada. We found a former lover of Lezkowski, Dennis Monroe. Monroe told me he met Ruth Lezkowski in Germany in the summer of 1986. Monroe and her brother served in the U.S. Army together and were stationed there, that's how he met her. He said they had consensual sex a couple of times during her visit. Monroe learned of her death from her brother when he flew back to the United States for her funeral. He gladly volunteered to give us a buccal swab."

Corley shuffled the paperwork he had in his hand and continued, "Dr. Edward Radney is practicing in San Pedro, California. He consented immediately to the buccal swab. He said he tried not to think about this case anymore. It was such an awful time in his life."

"The lab has both his samples now but I don't think we'll be talking to him anymore. I am running the fingerprints of everyone we talked to through AFIS but so far no hits."

AFIS stands for automated fingerprint identification system. It's a computerized database that contains fingerprints of anyone ever arrested.

"I also found another boyfriend from when she attended the University of Illinois in Champaign. I'll go see him or send one of the other investigators," Corley said.

~~~~

Jose Aguilera was sitting in his handmade office chair having his lower back massaged as he answered Peter Michaels' questions. "When are you going to file your Motion to Vacate?"

"We're getting close. The second batch of DNA testing came back and once again nothing matched my clients. We are going to court the day after tomorrow to get more evidence to be DNA tested at the state's attorney's lab. I am totally confident that it will exonerate my guys and then I will file it. I think Mr. Di Donato knows we've got them by the balls."

"So by August you'll be ready?"

"Yep. Late August for sure. I am reviewing the Patricia Bass stuff again."

Aguilera pushed himself forward to the file on his desk, "It was her work that got the original detectives to start taking blood and saliva samples. She found, of course, that the semen recovered from Lezkowski's body was from a person with type O blood who secreted his blood enzymes into his bodily fluids. That is what started it all. They eliminated suspect after suspect because of this information. She also eliminated those crazy fuckers Dennis Dumont and Edgar Ringer even though they were type O secretors but their enzymes didn't match those of Lezkowski's attackers. She even eliminated Broadhead and Sampson but Lorenzo and Charles Holmes were type O non-secretors and she failed to eliminate them. I don't understand that," said Aguilera.

Michaels forever flipping through his notebook looked up and said, "From what I understand the police department and the state police crime lab people all stand by Bass but I think they are starting to feel the heat from all the press coverage this is getting. They said, she does 'a great job.' And it's my understanding that she was dropped from that civil suit filed by Alvin Lavis and Adrian Rawls."

Craig Hill, the Public Defender testified that Dr. Bass' testimony at the criminal trial excluded Lavis from having contributed the semen found on the vaginal swab and that was 'the most favorable testimony a scientist could offer and that her testimony did not contribute to the conviction.' That doesn't sound to me that she's all that bad," Michaels said.

~~~~

Producer David Beedy had a sincere look of concentration on his face while he read a document that he was holding as Peter Michaels walked in the I-Team office. "What's that, Dave?"

"It's a letter I got from the City's Corporation Council's Office. Man, I thought Aguilera was a hot-shot attorney but if, what is in this letter is true, he might be walking on some thin ice."

"What do you mean?"

"My sister-in-law's sister works in the Corporation Council's Office. She got this for me. Talk about forensic fraud these guys Aguilera hired sound like quacks. Read this, it's a letter being sent to the network. They're thinking about doing a documentary on the Lezkowski case. It's pretty compelling."

~~~~

Chicago's City Hall is the official seat of government. The 11-story building houses the Office of the Mayor, all 50 of the Aldermen Ward Offices, the City Treasurer, the City Clerk's Office and Streets and Sanitation. The symbolic City Council Chambers where legislation is passed with the wink of an eye, has also been the scene of numerous public protests.

City Hall's main entrance off of LaSalle Street features four relief panels sculpted in granite representing the four principle concerns of city government: schools, parks, playgrounds and water supply. Elaborate marble stairways and bronze tablets that honor the past city halls of Chicago from 1837 adorn the walls. The building was dedicated on February 27,1911.

A 39,000 square foot roof garden was being installed as a pilot project to assess the impact green roofs would have on the environment with Chicago's climate. In all, 20,000 plants from 150 different species, including shrubs, vines and two trees can be seen from 33 taller buildings in the surrounding area.

~~~~

Chicago's Law Department was located on the ninth floor of city hall. Rosemary Ravalli, an assistant corporation council was sitting in her office when Peter Michaels walked in. She stood and shook his hand and Michaels was like a little schoolboy stunned by her beauty. Almost six feet tall, thin, trim and striking. She had auburn hair, green eyes and red lips. Her form fitting black dress accentuated a figure that was sculpted from hard work in the gym. Her voice was soft but raspy and confident. "What can I do for you Mr. Michaels?"

"I would like to talk to you about this letter regarding Patricia Bass."

"Where did you get that?"

"You know; I can't reveal my sources."

"What do you want to know? I can't say much but Dr. White is certainly not what he appears to be."

"You mean expert?"

"I mean his credentials are questionable. Dr. White has never held any position at a prestigious public crime lab, but instead he operates his own unaccredited three-person laboratory. He operates that laboratory without any written quality assurances or quality control standards and no written protocols."

This was the first time Michaels ever talked with Ravalli and he wasn't too sure how hard to press. She could be a valuable source in the future when Aguilera sued the city. "What about him calling the evidence in the Lezkowski homicide 'forensic fraud'?" Michaels asked.

"Scientific fraud is the term he often uses. Dr. White has made accusations of scientific fraud against a number of other scientists, not just Dr. Bass. In fact, he routinely makes that allegation against any scientist that disagrees with him. He even keeps information on scientists who disagree with him in a two-volume binder which he has labeled 'Whores I' and 'Whores II.' Furthermore, at least one government office in Dr. White's home state has directed its lawyers not to use Dr. White on any of their cases."

Michaels frowned, "Does he have any real credentials?"

"Not really, although he portrays himself as a premier DNA expert, he is not a member of the Scientific Working Group for DNA Methods ('SWGDM'), the premier group of DNA experts who write the national standards on DNA. Dr. Bass is a member of SWGDM."

"Why hasn't any of this come out?" Michaels inquired.

"You're the reporter. You tell me. Listen, we finally got him to submit to an examination under oath about his accusations against Dr. Bass and the glaring weakness in his report became clear—most surprising, he had never read Dr. Bass' lab notes, lab reports and full testimony in all of the cases which he criticized."

"Come on, seriously?"

"As a matter of fact, Dr. White's report wasn't even written by him. His assistant Edward Kelly wrote the report. Mr. Kelly conceded that he had no idea about Dr. Bass' motives, yet he claimed that Dr. Bass should have read the minds of the lawyers and answered the questions that were not asked."

"Does this Kelly guy have any credentials?"

She smiled sarcastically, pursed her red lips and mocked, "He certainly doesn't have any advanced degrees. Shortly before joining Dr. White's unaccredited laboratory, Mr. Kelly was the subject of a 16-day challenge to his own expertise in which it was revealed that Mr. Kelly made errors in proficiency tests designed to demonstrate his expertise. He was barred from conducting certain serology tests in the 1980s. At the time of that hearing, Dr. White had had a contract with Mr. Kelly's laboratory to supervise his work, and therefore the attack on Mr. Kelly's work was also an attack on Dr. White's supervision."

"What happened?"

"At the end of the 16-day hearing, the court noted that Mr. Kelly's testimony was 'disturbing' and that perhaps his most outrageous comment was that he could 'do DNA in a barn' and that Mr. Kelly 'barely qualified' as an expert."

"The report seems so, what do I want to say, so legitimate" Michaels said with a perplexed look on his face.

"Well in our opinion it used outdated and questionable theories. The Kelly/White report was based on the 'quantitation' theory, which is neither scientifically sound nor generally accepted in the scientific community. Labs rejected this 'quantitation' theory across the country in the 1980s. Mr. Kelly and Dr. White and those who prop them up have leveled accusations against Dr. Bass in connection with other convictions, only to have those accusations fall apart when DNA showed that the person convicted had in fact committed the crime."

It was evident to Michaels that Ravalli was in Dr. Bass' corner and she would defend her work steadfastly when she cynically said, "You know Mr. Michaels, Dr. Bass has been the subject of a media campaign by lawyers who have an agenda guided by money and publicity rather than the truth."

"Wasn't Dr. Bass investigated by the FBI?"

"Yes. She and another serologist were investigated by the FBI and guess what? The other person was found to have committed wrongdoing whereas Dr. Bass has never been found to have committed any wrongdoing. She was exonerated."

# CHAPTER 43

T he Cook County Clerk of the Courts office on the fifth floor of the Criminal Courts building at 26$^{th}$ and Cal was humming with activity on the morning of July 1, 2001. The clerk's office stores all the court records of the cases heard in the courthouse. Tens of thousands of files are arranged by the dates of their proceedings in the sprawling 25,000 square foot area on two floors. The files are saved until the appellate court confirms or overturns the convictions, in other words for up to ten years before they are moved to a warehouse.

Conference room 501 was typical of any room used thousands of times each year. The floors were scarred and scuffed. The black linoleum floorboards were separating from the beige painted walls that were faded and dirty. A third of the fluorescent ceiling bulbs were burned out but the main source of light came through a large twenty by ten foot double paned storm window that made up most of the east wall. The window blinds were bent, twisted and unworkable and they were staggered at different heights because the cords to raise and lower them were no longer functional.

The once highly varnished five by ten-foot conference table in the center of the room was battered, marred and bleached by the sunlight. It was now covered with 35 pieces of new evidence that will be hand delivered to an independent laboratory for DNA analysis.

Detective Dick Corley spent two days in the property room gathering and sealing the materials in evidence bags. A legal chain of evidence had to be established as the exhibits were placed in the sealed bags for transportation. Corley packed the exhibits that included more pubic and head hair samples, different parts of Ruth Lezkowski's clothing and more scrapings from her fingernails.

Prosecutors, defense attorneys and investigators were examining the exhibits to make sure they were satisfied with the new evidence. Both sides would appear before Judge John Green first thing in the morning where what is called an 'Agreed Order' would be signed. It ordered Diagnostics Labs of Maryland to conduct serological tests for the presence of any bodily fluids on the new exhibits and if found to be preserved for further testing if necessary.

Detective Corley thought that defense attorney Jose Aguilera was a *gormless little prick,* after he over-heard him say to his partner, Mark Middleton, "I have no doubt our guys will be out by the end of the year and we are going after these fuckers for prosecutorial and police misconduct."

ASA Peter Di Donato saw that Corley was agitated and said, "This evidence will be examined by both sides. It will be scrutinized very closely as we continue our investigation. The sophisticated technology we have today was not available in 80s. We want to take advantage of these investigative tools and we will have to wait and see where it leads us."

~~~~

Ron Magers looked up from his computer screen when Peter Michaels walked into his office and was startled by his appearance. "You look like shit Mage. When's the last time you shaved?"

Magers had been out of work for a few days with the flu and he hadn't shaved. Normally he had to use a razor twice a day, his beard was so thick. "I know. I didn't do the six but I am doing the ten. What's up?"

"I just wanted you to help me re-write your lead into my piece tonight. Aguilera is going to court tomorrow to have more evidence analyzed and I think that will be the coup de gras. I don't think there is any question that his guys are getting out. It is just a matter of when."

"What's the state's attorney say?"

"They are avoiding me like the plague. I think they know. They're looking for a way to avoid egg on their face."

"That poor family has to go through this again after all these years. I just can't imagine."

"Yeah. I talked to Mrs. Lezkowski earlier. She is pretty shaken by it all but she is a strong woman and she told me, she 'didn't want the wrong people to be in jail.'"

"I just can't imagine. Okay I'll look this over and see you on the set," Magers said as Michaels left his office.

~~~~

The early morning hearing in Judge John Green's courtroom was just a formality to get the DNA analysis moving. It took longer for the attorneys to assemble in the courtroom than it did for the "Agreed Order" to be approved.

ASA Peter Di Donato and Amy Wilson left the courtroom, shook hands with Aguilera and went to Di Donato's office to go over the status of their investigation.

"It sure looks like these guys are going to get out very soon," Wilson said.

"Yeah, it does. That Peter Michaels is driving me nuts. He calls three times a day, every day. They smell blood," Di Donato said.

"Actually, he has been pretty good. He seems to want to know both sides of this story. I know he is tight with Aguilera though but we need to keep our door open too."

~~~~

While they were in court Detective Dick Corley was in the air flying to Maryland with more evidence. He took the first flight out. He was upset because it was the day before the Fourth of July. He wished it could have waited until the following week but he was used to working holidays and holy days.

Impromptu meetings in Di Donato's office were not unusual after a court appearance. It was his way of staying organized.

"Corley is on his way to Diagnostics with the new evidence as we speak. He should be back tomorrow but I think he's a little pissed. It's been a long time since he's had a day off." Wilson said as she put her files on the front of his desk and took a seat.

"He'll get over it," Di Donato grunted. "Where are we?"

"It's back to old fashion gumshoe police work. Corley subpoenaed all the visitor logs from Joliet and Stateville looking for anyone who had been in contact with the four over the years. He also wanted to talk to all their cellmates in the last 15 years. He's boring in on anything that can produce some leads on our Unknown Males, #1 and #2," Wilson said

Di Donato stroked his baldhead as he looked over the report on the last DNA analysis that identified the unknown offenders. "Yeah, Corley should request a CERTS search for all the existing biological evidence on file for violent sex offenders."

The CERTS system are computer records of all sex offenders filed with the Clerk of the Courts. The records are public but one would have to physically go the clerk's office and look up each individual case.

"If any evidence exists that hasn't been destroyed, it might be a great tool to lead us to these unknown males," Di Donato said. "He has already put all the information into CODIS but so far no hits there. This Corley is really good. He is on top of it. He already accessed our SOA Promise Computer."

The SOA Promise Computer is a database that contains information from fact sheets of criminal prosecutions. Prosecutors forward letters to the Illinois Department of Corrections so that their files on convicted felons are also updated. It is a great resource for investigators to access violent crimes that have similar MO's to crimes like the Lezkowski homicide or any violent crimes that were committed in a reasonable time frame or location of the Lezkowski homicide.

~~~~

Peter Michaels and Dave Beedy were on a speakerphone in their office talking to Jose Aguilera. Pressure was building to hold public hearings on the conduct and methods used to identify evidence in the Illinois State Police Crime Lab. All media outlets were relentlessly doing stories on forensic fraud.

"You know the city, the police and the Illinois State Police Crime Lab are still backing the reputation of Patricia Bass?" Michaels rhetorically asked Jose Aguilera.

"You know Bass blew it, Peter. Our investigator just interviewed a highly thought of forensic scientist from McHale and Associates from St. Charles. Do you know the process to identify semen on clothing has not changed in almost 70 years?"

"I didn't know that. Seventy years? Wow!"

"Yeah. Bass either missed it or ignored it. The first thing they do is a visual inspection of the clothing and if there are any possible stains, they are tested. They look for an enzyme in high concentrations of the semen. If it's positive, it would require more testing. There were more than a dozen semen stains on Lezkowski's clothing. Could she miss all of them?"

"I don't know," Michaels conceded.

"Look, it could be that she just missed them but if she is as good as they say, I doubt it or she just didn't look hard enough or she's lying. We are going to get these guys out of jail soon." Aguilera promised and hung up his phone.

Peter Michaels and Dave Beedy were looking forward to having some fun with family and friends at the fireworks off of Navy Pier. Michaels would be on a sailboat laying on the deck looking up at the stars. He had a new girl friend but his interest was already flailing. Beedy was looking forward to fireworks with his two sons and wife at a park just down the street from his house. When the phone rang, it broke their train of thoughts. It was Beedy's cousin from the Corporation Council office with a phone number he had requested.

Michaels took the number and smiled as he dialed.

"Yes, this is Jack Evans."

"Detective Evans this is Peter Michaels from Channel Six News."

"Look Peter, I'm retired. I've got nothing to say."

"Listen, I know you put your heart and soul into the investigation years ago. What do you think about all this DNA stuff?"

"I'll have more to say in the future. I am sure there will be lawsuits and accusations flying all over the place. I have nothing to say at this time. I talked to you back then and I will tell you one thing 'off the record' agreed?"

"Yep."

"I don't care what the DNA shows, those kids were at that crime scene. They knew way too much about how she was killed. They'll deny everything but I'm telling you, they were there!" Evans said and hung up the phone.

"What he say?" asked Beedy.

"He says he doesn't care what the DNA shows. It doesn't show him that those kids weren't there."

"What do you think?"

"I might be the only son of a bitch in the media that is at least willing to think that there is the possibility that two different crimes were committed over a period of four hours. Remember that Dumont guy? He was accused of murdering one woman and beating two others in a ninety-minute time frame. This is Chicago, Dave."

# CHAPTER 44

T he Chicago media was unyielding with its coverage of the new findings of DNA evidence in a number of cases including Ruth Lezkowski's. Several other convicted murderers and rapists were released from prison as a result of post-conviction reversals because of DNA.

Even though serologist Patricia Bass was dropped from two civil law suits filed against her, pressure was mounting about her work product. A House Special Committee on Prosecutorial Misconduct was investigating the ramifications of this new phenomenon of "forensic fraud" and what effect it would have on hundreds of cases already adjudicated. The hearing was held in the James R. Thompson Center in downtown Chicago.

The Thompson Center in the North Loop is a spectacular glass building. It is one of Chicago's biggest attractions. Major motion pictures like *Running Scared, Music Box, Miracle on 34th Street and Switching Channels* have been shot in the towering structure. It draws worldwide attention and more than two million visitors a year.

The views are captivating from inside and out with its spacious ground floor Atrium lobby that reaches to a remarkable angled skylight. It is a multiple purpose government building that combines state agencies and commercial shops and restaurants.

The special hearing was called by Democratic State Senator Edward T. Devlin and was being held in one of the Assembly Hall annexes. Devlin from the 26th Ward was serving his second term. The former pipefitter won his state senate seat easily the first time he ran for office. He lived in a predominately union ward and his Irish-Scotch heritage made him a shoo-in with the backing of the majority whip in Springfield. Devlin gained 50 pounds on his five-foot-eleven-inch frame since he retired. He hated to wear a suit and tie but at the hearing it was a requirement. His suit coat was unbuttoned and his necktie hung loose around his 19-inch neck. He couldn't button his collar.

The Director of the Illinois State Police was the center of attention. Bob Bowe was appointed to the state's top cop job two years earlier. He was a Chicago Police captain with 25 years on the job when he was offered his new position. He was five-nine and bulky but he didn't look fat. He did look like the police in his gray suit, white shirt and yellow power tie. He sat erect at the center of the table with the department's lawyer at his right. He opened his briefcase and took out a prepared statement and expressed total confidence in the Illinois State Police Crime Lab.

"Our crime lab is one of the best in the world. We have not been accused of this so-called scientific fraud. We have and continue to do a superior job with all of our analysis."

Senator Devlin sat wringing his fingers and fidgeting as Bowe read his opening statement. After Bowe concluded his remarks, he glanced at each member of the panel before him, except Devlin, "If you have any questions, I will do my best to answer them."

Devlin wasted no time. He was chomping at the bit, "What about this Patricia Bass? Her work has been challenged time and time again as fraudulent."

"Her work is not fraudulent at all. She has all the professional credentials and experience in the world and I stand by her 100 percent. She is a great analyst and no-one works harder."

"She is being sued by at least three people who just got out of jail because of her work and false testimony," Devlin pointed out.

Bowe was expecting a confrontation with Devlin. He was sitting straight in his chair and glared at the senator. "Anyone can file a lawsuit senator. It is my understanding that she has been dismissed from those suits at this time. Listen, after she came to us, she was promoted to chief of the biochemistry section. She handles all our DNA testing now and she has done an outstanding job. As a safeguard we go through hundreds of internal tests and audits by quality assurance specialists to guarantee that our test results are accurate. I am very proud of what we have accomplished over the years."

Bowe wanted to get in one more jab at Devlin before he ended his testimony. "And by the way, I am sure you are aware senator that our crime lab system is the third largest in the world and we have consistently been accredited by the American Society of Crime Laboratory Directors."

After two hours the hearing ended. Devlin was convinced that Patricia Bass had to go. He was receiving a lot of pressure from a number of prominent attorneys who were also big contributors to the Democratic Party.

Reporters and camera crews swarmed around director Bowe as he exited the center stage platform. He steadfastly backed Patricia Bass but he knew they had to take some sort of action because he was feeling the heat as well.

~~~~

Detective Dick Corley's trip on July 3rd to Diagnostic Labs in Maryland to drop off the new evidence was uneventful except he got lost driving in the unfamiliar surroundings which really pissed him off. He spent his Fourth of July with his family but they weren't real happy because he only got to spend the one-day with them. Since he was chosen to be the lead detective in the new Lezkowski investigation he had spent little time at home which played havoc on his personal life.

He didn't like to fly but he had crisscrossed the country locating 27 former suspects to get new buccal swabs for DNA comparison. The 28th person he wanted to interview was a former boyfriend of Ruth Lezkowski. While he fought traffic on the drive to Elkhart, Wisconsin, he was listening to a Chicago all-news radio station. What he was hearing he didn't like, more criticism of the police and prosecutors. He had just finished qualifying with his firearm at the shooting range in the basement of the 11<sup>th</sup> District. He got on the Ryan Expressway heading north. Traffic was heavy, he was tired and his investigation was not looking good.

He was on the phone with ASA Amy Wilson, who was not optimistic about the new DNA results. "We just got out of a meeting with the State's Attorney, Thomas Porter. He is not a happy camper."

Porter was just elected to his second term as Cook County State's Attorney and the last thing he wanted was negative press but recently his office has been bombarded. Newspapers, television and radio news ripped his office and the police almost every day.

~~~~

Corley got out of his puke green unmarked squad car in front of Tom Conroy's house in Elkhart Lake, Wisconsin. The entire block was ranch style homes built in the late 90s. Trees lined the street and wrapped around a small lake. Corley stretched his legs and back then bent over to touch his toes.

Conroy answered the door immediately, as he expected his visitor. He was 39-years old, six foot with long disheveled curly blonde hair and deep blue eyes. His red "Wisconsin" tee shirt was not tucked in his faded Levi's. "You must be Detective Corley? Come on in."

"Yeah and you are Tom Conroy? I just need a few minutes of your time."

"Sure. What do you need to know?"

"What was your relationship with Ruth Lezkowski?"

"We met at the University of Illinois in Champaign in our junior year. We had a sexual relationship that lasted half way through our senior year and then we became good friends. She was focusing on medical school. I helped her move to Chicago on Flournoy Street in the spring of 1985. She was very excited about medical school, as you can imagine."

"Did you see her after that?"

"Like I said we were good friends. It all ended on a positive note. I came back to U of I and she started living her dream."

"I'd like your consent for a buccal swab for DNA. Do you have a problem with that?"

"Not at all. I'll do whatever it takes to catch these monsters."

~~~~

Michaels was sitting at his desk drinking a cup of coffee reading the Wall Street Journal nursing a hangover when his phone rang.

"News … Michaels."

"Hey it's Jose. We just finished taking Charles Holmes' recantation. Quite a story how they tricked that poor kid."

Michaels stood up and started pacing. "Tell me about it."

"The kid was sound asleep and four detectives came and grabbed him at 2:30 in the morning pulling him out of bed. He said, 'they threw me against the wall, searched me and yelled at me saying I killed some woman on Loomis Street. I said, I didn't kill nobody. I don't know what you're talking about.'"

"Jose, I don't know of any criminal that says 'I did it' when they get arrested. Are you saying they did something improper because they pinched him at 2:30 in the morning?"

"I'll email it to you. It's not very long. Let me know what you think."

Later, in his office, Michaels pulled up the email on his computer and began reading.

> They brought me over to the police station and kept asking me why I did it. I kept saying did what? They kept sayin' I killed that lady. I said, I didn't kill no lady. I didn't kill nobody. I don't know what this is all about.
>
> Once we got there, I was put in this small room with a table and a chair and left alone in there for what seemed like a long time. I wanted to see my momma. I was scared.
>
> Then two policemens comes back into the room and started askin' me about the murder up on Loomis Street. I said I don't knows what you are all talking about. I kept tellin' em' I'm innocent. They says come on Charles your cousin Lorenzo says you were there with him and you guys starting hitting and kicking that woman and killed her.
>
> They had a yellow pad in their hands and they kept sayin' this is how Lorenzo said it happened and you were there. I kept sayin, I don't know why Lorenzo would be saying shit like that because I don't knows what you all are talking about. If Lorenzo be sayin' that he ain't telling you the truth. He's lying man. I didn't do nuttin'.
>
> I then told the police that I wanted to see my momma. They got mad at me and started yelling at me. The one guy threatened to slap me in my damn

mouth. I got very, very scared. I didn't know what they were talkin' about. The officers then left the room and let me sit there alone for a long time.

When the police comes back in the room and says they would let me go if I put everything back on Lorenzo. I asked them if that meant I could go home and they told me yes. All you have to do is cooperate with us and we'll let you go. Then they asked me if I wanted an Egg McMuffin. I says okay.

The two policemens came back in the room and told me to read and study what they had written down on this yellow pad. I said okay and I was there a long time reading what they wanted me to say. They asked me a bunch of questions and then they said there is a lady here who wants to hear your story. I asked them once I told my story can I go home. They says yes. So I told the story to this lady.

When I finished they said they were going to get me an Egg McMuffin but first I had to get finger printed and have my picture taken. I went downstairs and the man was there to take my picture and the policeman says "Smile Charles you're going home." So I asked if I'm going home now and he tells me, 'No, you're going to the Audy Home.' That's when I realized they tricked me. I started to cry. I knew I just signed my life away.

~~~~

Michaels printed the statement and put it on his desk and started to think, *This case has really unraveled.*

Dave Beedy walked in the door and asked, "What's up?"

Here read this. "Aguilera is putting his ducks in line. He is almost ready to file his petition. He's prepping Broadhead for his recantation and the one you're reading is Charles'. Once they get this final DNA stuff back it won't take him long. Those guys are gonna walk."

"Does that bother you?"

"No. I remember when this first happened. These coppers didn't have a single doubt that their four guys where there. DNA is pretty convincing though. Hopefully. There will be some answers soon."

# CHAPTER 45

P eter Michaels and Dave Beedy were sitting at their desks reading the six-page recantation transcript of Marcus Broadhead's confession and shaking their heads. "This is hard for any rational human being to believe," Beedy said.

"Mohammed Ali or George Foreman would not be able to stand or walk if they took the punishment he described," said Michaels. "From the time he got out of jail with a reduced sentence for his testimony against Lorenzo Holmes in 1992 until now, this lowlife has been arrested 21 times and forfeited his bond 12 times for not appearing in court," Michaels said, as he handed Beedy, Broadhead's rap sheet. "Look at this prick and he's on his way back to prison."

"This guy really knows the system well and he knows how to use it. He just got out of jail. That's why it took so long for Aguilera to get his statement." Beedy said.

The statement began: Chicago Police Department Detectives Evans and Purvis arrived at my mother's apartment at 1510 West 13th Street, Apartment 401 at 9:30am on January 27, 1986. (it was 1987) There may have been additional police officers but I don't remember their names. I was about to leave for school. Officer Evans stated that they wanted to talk to me about a burglary at the station for about five minutes. My mother and my probation officer, Tim Morrison were at the apartment when the police arrived. I agreed to go with the police. Morrison agreed to take my mother to my school to explain my whereabouts. I was not placed in handcuffs. I left with the detectives. No conversation took place in the car. The police never mentioned anything about a murder.

At the Area Four police station the police took me to a room with a table and some chairs. The room had a solid door and no windows. The room also had a ring on the wall. The detectives instructed me to sit down at the table. An officer took a picture of me sitting at the table. He said that the picture would be used in a photo lineup. The police never mentioned anything about a murder. I realized later that the purpose of the photo was to show that I had not been beaten and that I was treated okay.

After taking the picture, Evans attitude changed and he ordered me to strip off all my clothes. He stated that he wanted to 'test the clothes.' I removed my pants, shirt, jacket, socks and shoes. Evans ordered me to take off my underwear, which I did. He then handcuffed my left arm to the ring on the wall. He kicked my clothes out the door of the room and shut the door.

After I was handcuffed to the wall, Detective Evans and Purvis started to talk to me in an angry voice. Evans stated 'Tell us who was with you when you killed that woman.' I stated, 'What woman are you talking about?' Evans responded, 'The white woman up by the railroad tracks.' As Evans asked me this question, I noticed Purvis put on leather gloves on his hands. I felt he was trying to intimidate me.

Evans next stated that 'You know you and Lorenzo Holmes had something to do with it.' I responded by stating, 'Me and Lorenzo ain't done nothing, we ain't killed nobody.'

Evans struck me with a closed fist to the face. I was unable to avoid the blow because it took me by surprise. Evans continued to state 'I know Lorenzo and you did it.' Each time he said this, I responded that 'We did not kill her' he would punch me in the face.

Outside the room, I thought I could hear my mother's voice but she didn't know I was in the room.

Evans then left the room and an officer came into the room to remove the table and chairs in the room.

"Do you really believe the dicks would go through the trouble of taking the table and chairs out of the room? Impossible! That would have tipped off Maurer and I know he would have transferred anyone who messed up this investigation." Michaels said.

"So far he says he's been hit several times in the face and head," said Beedy.

Purvis remained in the room. He stated 'Do you want to keep getting beat? I can keep him away from you if you tell me what happened.' I responded, 'I didn't kill nobody.' Purvis stated, 'I was afraid you would say that.' Purvis than began hitting me in the face and in the neck with closed fists. I tried to avoid his punches by ducking and covering my face but he then started to hit me with knees and kicks to the stomach and legs.

As Purvis beat me, about four or five other white police officers, not wearing uniforms came into the room. One stated that, 'it sounds like a fight in here, is he still not talking?' By this point, I was hit approximately 30 times by Evans and Purvis and was bent down near the floor. I was bleeding from my nose and mouth.

"I can't believe this. This guy would be unconscious if he was hit 30 times. Unbelievable," Beedy said.

The officers that came back into the room gathered around me and continued to punch and kick me. One officer stated 'Stand up so we can get a good shot.' I was crying and pleading for them to stop. I was trying to protect myself as best I could. The officers hit me in my stomach, my chest, my neck, my face, my back, my arms and my legs. During the beating, Evans stated, 'We want to know who else was with you, we know Lorenzo was with you.' As they beat me, different people kept coming into the room to watch. I overheard someone state, 'That's him, that's the rapist and murderer.'

Officer O'Reilly then stated, 'I want to be alone with him.' All the officers except O'Reilly left the room. O'Reilly was very big. O'Reilly gave me the worst beating. He punched and kicked me so hard that I was knocked off my feet into the wall. I begged him to stop. He ignored me. He hit with a punch directly in the face that smashed my nose. He punched and kicked me in the face and in my stomach while repeatedly called me a rapist and a murderer.

After O'Reilly left the room, I was alone for a long time. My face was numb and bloody. Blood covered the walls and the floor in the room.

"I can't believe Aguilera believes this shit," said Michaels. "This guy must have seen all five *Rocky* movies. So far he has been hit in the face and neck more than 60 times."

Evans and Purvis returned with a mop bucket. They closed the door behind them and threw a piece of carpet or blanket at the base of the door. Evans told me to stand-up. He then dumped the bucket of water over my head to wash the blood off of my body. The water was cold and dirty.

Evans then stepped out of the room and returned with my clothes. He un-cuffed my arm from the wall and told me to get dressed. He also gave me some tissues and told me to 'pack' my nose. He stated, 'We are going to take you downtown for a polygraph.' They put me in handcuffs and took me out to the car. We drove for approximately 15 minutes. The officers parked in the back of the police station on State Street underneath the EL tracks. They took me through the back door. We took the elevator up. We went to a room where a man hooked me up to a polygraph machine. He asked me questions about the murder. I said, 'I didn't do it.' After a short time, Evans and Purvis led me out of the building through the back door to their car. As we drove away in the car, Evans told me that I failed the polygraph and was lying.

Evans and Purvis took me back to the Area Four police station. At the police station, they took me back to the same room. The room had been cleaned. Somebody had tried to remove the blood from the floor and the walls. There was no water or debris on the floor. The desk and chairs were in the room again. Evans handcuffed me to the wall. I was very scared and began to plead with the officers not to beat me again. Evans stated, 'We are going to take your black ass to the dark room and kill you, and since we already told your mom that we released you, nobody will ever come looking for you.' I believed that they would kill me and hide my body.

Evans and Purvis left me alone for a long time. I was in and out of consciousness. The door opened and an officer came into the room. I lifted my head. I couldn't see what he had in his hand. Without saying a word, he hit me in the head with a large book that I think was a phone book. I was then kicked in the mouth so hard that it broke several of my teeth off.

Evans and Purvis then returned to the room. They asked if I was ready to cooperate. I pleaded with them that I did not do it. Evans slapped me across the face. I pleaded with them to let me use the bathroom. One laughed and said, 'No way.' Evans and Purvis then left the room.

Evans and Purvis returned every few minutes. They continued to punch me in the face and the stomach. Later O'Reilly returned and started to punch me again. At that point I just gave in. I said, 'O.K., I will say what you want.'

O'Reilly left the room and Evans and Purvis returned. Evans had a yellow pad in his hand. He stated, 'We know how the crime happened.' He said,

'You, Lorenzo, and Lorenzo's cousin Charles did it.' I did not know who they meant by 'Charles.' At that time, I did not know Lorenzo had a cousin named Charles. I knew that Lorenzo had a cousin named Kareem who was about our same age. I thought that the police were mistakenly saying 'Charles' but actually meant 'Kareem.'

Evans showed me the pad in his hand. All the details of the crime were hand written on the pad. He said, 'We want you to read this and remember it. If you don't, we will keep beating you until we kill you.'

I read the writing on the pages and said, 'Whoever told you all how this happened, they must have done it.' Evans and Purvis started to punch me again. They hit me five or six more times in the face and in the back of the head until I said, 'I would say whatever they wanted.'

They made me read the writing on the pad out loud to them. Evans told Purvis that 'There can't be just three guys, we need four.' These three guys are too small.' Purvis had a photo of Charles Holmes. He stated, 'This guy is pretty young, how big is he.' I said, 'I don't know.' Evans then stated, 'He will work.'

The statement said that we jumped in the car when it stopped at a stop sign on Flournoy and Loomis. I knew there was no stop sign at that intersection, but I went along with their story.

The victim's name was not on the pages. Evans and Purvis were acting like they were writing a script to a play. They left me alone with the statement for about 20-30 minutes. When they returned they took the pad away and one of them said, 'Tell us what happened.'

The paper said that Charles was driving but they realized that Charles could probably not drive a stick shift or any kind of car so they had Lorenzo drive. They did not know that none of us could drive a stick shift.

I repeated to the detectives what I read from their pad. As I read, the detectives told me to change some things. They told me to say that on the way to the tracks that I jumped out and switched seats with Charles because he was not big enough to hold her. If I made a mistake they punched or kicked me.

After a number of hours of practice, I was ordered by the police to give a recorded statement to the state's attorney's office. After I made the recorded statement, the detectives told me to make certain changes. The changes that I made were false as well as the original statement.

As a result of the beating my eyes were swollen, my face and whole body were bruised, and my teeth were chipped. I was taken to Cook County Jail after I gave the statement. I remained in County Jail for 21 months before anything was filed for me in court.

All of the statements that I made in my testimony at Lorenzo Holmes trial concerning the commission of the Lezkowski murder by me, Lorenzo Holmes, Charles Holmes and Oscar Sampson were false.

"The only thing this guy said that was true was that he was in Cook County Jail for 21 months." Handing Beedy a document, Michaels said, "Dave look at this. It's his jail intake report. Check out the bottom right—no injuries listed. If he got hit more than 60 times he'd be in Cook County Hospital not jail."

"Aguilera's medical expert is also saying that Broadhead had blood in his saliva when he was swabbed and tested at Mt. Sinai Hospital. You know as well as I do that if he was beaten that badly doctors at Mt. Sinai would have made note of that and reported it," Beedy said.

Michaels got up from his desk to stretch. He liked to walk when he was thinking. "So Jose is saying that blood in his mouth is consistent with being hit in the mouth in his Petition to Vacate because it is going to independently corroborate all Broadhead's recantation."

~~~~

Suzanne Grande now specialized in medical malpractice and product liability law. Her seven years in the courtroom with the state's attorney's office made her a very seasoned litigator.

"I thought I'd be hearing from you guys sooner or later. What can I do for you Mr. Michaels?"

"I just read Marcus Broadhead's recantation. It's pretty unbelievable. He says he was beaten, hit in the face and head more than 60 times."

"That's utter nonsense. When I took his statement, he had no bruises, no black eyes, nothing. If they beat a confession out of him, it was after he talked to me. I would not jeopardize my career or our case against any one of those defendants."

"He said the police prepared a script for him and Charles Holmes."

"Even though I felt nothing for Broadhead he did not look like he took a beating. I felt sorry for Charles. He was scared and nervous but with his IQ, I guarantee you he could not have memorized what he told me in that short of time. I was convinced he was a participant. You know defense attorneys will stretch everything they can for their clients and this DNA stuff that I am reading about gives this kind of thing credibility in court no matter how outrageous it may sound."

# CHAPTER 46

A s Detective Don Buerline read Marcus Broadhead's recantation statement, he smiled and rubbed his chin, "I can't believe this guy. It's six pages of bullshit," Buerline said as detective Dick Corley walked into the office.

Buerline first worked on the Lezkowski case when he was an Area Four property crimes detective back in 1987. He went with Jack Evans to arrest Charles Holmes. He now works with the state's attorney's office of special investigations and hopes to retire in two years with 30 years on the job. Over the years, his work ethic increased and he started buying his suits at the Men's Warehouse. He and Corley never worked together although they knew each other for a long time.

"Yeah, I know, pretty amazing. I've known Evans for years and I'm telling you he was too good of a detective to risk his career on some shithead, he would never do anything like that," said Corley.

"Unfortunately the DNA will overshadow this bogus shit and it will be allowed into evidence."

Corley and Buerline had already taken 33 buccal samples from the original suspects and they talked to all but two of the original grand jury witnesses that testified. They reverted back to good old gumshoe police work. They were getting nowhere and they knew it was just a matter of time before the Lezkowski Four would get out of jail.

"The computer spat out 16 names of some really wicked people that we need to rundown and get buccal swabs from," Corley said. "All of them had been convicted of crimes with similar MO's as those arrested in the original Lezkowski investigation. I can't believe some of the sick fucks that live in this city."

Buerline reaching for the printout said, "Let's see what have we got here?"

~~~~

Delvin Curtis was trying to get paroled from Stateville. He didn't have a chance. In 1986, he lured three women at different times to a hotel room using the same story. He targeted young women that worked at places like Burger King or Wendy's. He offered them the job of a lifetime with a chance of advancement. He told them that he could get them clerical positions at Water Tower Place and that he could help them build their resumes. He lured them to his hotel room on the fourth floor and threatened to throw them out of the window if they didn't have sex with him. He made them strip, covered their eyes with tape and performed oral sex on them. He then forced them to do the same to him. Afterwards he would bite them hard on their breast leaving teeth marks. His third victim saw him walking with another woman and called police. He ultimately was arrested and charged with kidnapping, criminal sexual assault and battery. He was sentenced as a serial rapist to 30 years at Stateville penitentiary.

~~~~

Reginald Fleming was another serial rapist who liked young high school girls. He sought victims that were walking alone and who were vulnerable. On two different occasions on January 9,1987 he raped two girls. The first one was 14 years old. She was walking down an alley on her way to school. She thought Fleming was walking a dog and paid no attention to him. He grabbed her and said he had a gun and if she cooperated she wouldn't get hurt. He then pulled her into a vacant building. He taped her eyes, mouth and wrist and pulled down one of her pant legs. He than pulled the tape off her mouth and hands and forced her to perform oral sex on him. He then forced her down on the ground and he performed oral sex on her. After that, he raped her. When he was finished he told her not to tell anyone because he knew where she lived and knew people who would do worse things to her.

He targeted his second victim that same day two hours later. At 17, she was on her way to high school. He did the same thing to her.

The 14-year-old told her mother who called police and Fleming was arrested a month later when he was in the act of raping another teenager.

The 14-year-old girl identified him in a lineup and said, "That's him" and she lost all composure and had to be held up by detectives in the room she was so distraught and hysterical.

Fleming was charged with four felony rapes, aggravated criminal sexual assault, unlawful restraint and aggravated kidnapping. He was sentenced to 30 years in the penitentiary.

~~~~

Brendon Smith, Billy Roman, James Davis and Dennis Duval were arrested for aggravated sexual assault, aggravated kidnapping, kidnapping, unlawful restraint and aggravated battery in a public way.

On August 20,1988 the four gangbangers offered to give a 16-year-old girl a ride to her girlfriend's house but instead they gang raped her, forcing her to engage in vaginal, anal and oral intercourse. After they finished the first time, they drove to another location and gang raped her again. The brutal rape caused great bodily harm to the young girl along with severe psychological damage.

A Chicago Police Sergeant who caught the four in the act, said "If I didn't interrupt them surely the young girl's corpse would have been found in the dense brush along the railroad tracks at 47th Street."

They were all sentenced to 30 years.

~~~~

Leroy Franklin was a psychopathic rapist, who was charged with kidnapping, aggravated kidnapping, unlawful restraint, robbery, armed robbery, home invasion, arm violence, residential burglary and criminal sexual assault.

On August 5,1988 he broke into the home of a 29-year-old mother of four through the kitchen window. As the children slept in their bedrooms, Franklin held an iron to the mother's head and forced her into the bedroom were he ripped off her bra and panties and raped her. He tore a golden chain from her neck and pushed her into another room and forced his penis in her mouth and then he shoved her over the couch and had anal sex. She dared not to scream because her children were asleep in the next room. He threatened to kill her as he left. This incredible violation lasted more than one hour.

A month later she saw him walking down the street but he had shaved his head to alter his appearance. He had a face that she would never forget. She called police and he was arrested, convicted and sentenced to 25 years in prison.

~~~~

Derek Russell abducted a 15-year-old girl at gunpoint in front of her house. Russell showed the teenager what she thought was a badge to stop her on the street then he pulled out a pistol and prized her into his car. He fired two rounds in the air to scare the girl. He then forced her to have oral sex with him and then sexual intercourse. He told her not to tell anyone or he'd come after her because he knew where she lived. He said he knew her aunt and that is why he forced her to have sex with him.

All of this was witnessed by a neighbor, who called police and gave them Russell's license plate number and a very detailed description of him. He was arrested and charged with aggravated criminal sexual assault, aggravated criminal sexual abuse, aggravated kidnaping and aggravated unlawful restraint. He will be 58 when he gets out of prison. His parole was denied.

~~~~

Elliot Dell, nick named "Poo-Poo," Jamaal Howard, Leroy Bell, Travis Allen and Ameer Jones were cold-blooded killers. Four of the men, dressed like ninja warriors on September 10,1988 came upon a 20-year-old woman who was walking with her father down the street and announced a stick up. They ordered the father and daughter to strip. Jamaal Howard went through their clothes and found $13.00. While the robbery was taking place Elliot Dell forced the woman to perform oral sex on him saying, "Why don't you suck Poo-Poo's dick or I'll kill you."

The four gangbangers then fled the scene only to come back within minutes because a fifth member of the gang, Ameer Jones said the father had more money and ordered them to go back and get it. When they returned, the father, who had just gotten dressed, fled and was shot in the back four times.

During the homicide investigation, detectives ran the name "Poo-Poo" through the Alpha file and identified Elliot Dell. Shortly after his arrest, he confessed hoping for leniency. All five were charged with first degree murder, armed robbery, aggravated criminal sexual assault, armed violence, attempted armed robbery, criminal sexual assault, aggravate unlawful restraint and all but Jamaal Howard were charged with unlawful use of weapon by a felon. They were sentenced to 60 years and parole was never considered even though they asked for it.

~~~~

A 29-year-old woman and her boyfriend were making out in her car on September 20,1990 when Freddy Trout, Noah Robinson and Marcell Donaldson approached the car and announced a robbery. Trout had a gun, Robinson had a knife and Donaldson had a small baseball bat. Robinson and Donaldson ordered the boyfriend out of the car and hit him with the bat and kicked him in the stomach and ribs and then they took his wallet and money. Trout opened the door and threatened to shoot the woman if she didn't perform oral sex on him. When he was finished the other two did the same thing.

A patrol car came upon the scene and the three defendants fled. Trout was pinched a block away and was immediately brought back to the scene where he was identified as one of the assailants. Once at Area Four Violent Crimes he instantly gave up his two accomplices.

They were all charged with aggravated criminal sexual assault, armed robbery, criminal sexual assault, aggravated battery in a public way and aggravated unlawful restraint and sentenced to 30 years in the penitentiary.

~~~~

After reading the preliminary reports, Corley and Buerline decided to split the workload. "I'll take all those at Stateville and you take the ones at Joliet," Corley said. "I'll have Amy set up the interviews assembly line fashion with the wardens. It shouldn't take 15 minutes per person unless they have something to hide but first we have to see what evidence is still around from these old cases before we interview them."

"What about cellmates of the original four over the years? Did you put together that list?"

"Yeah, Amy did. It's not that long and we should be able to do all of it in two or three days, max."

"This isn't looking too good."

"Yeah, I know. These dogs are some of the worst of the worst but I'd be surprised if their DNA matches our unknown males #1 or #2."

# CHAPTER 47

F irst Assistant State's Attorney Kevin Benedetti called ASA Peter Di Donato and Amy Wilson along with lead detectives Dick Corley and Don Buerline into his fifth floor office. He had a concerned look on his face as everyone walked in. He held his hands in a steeple position almost as if he was praying as he waited for everyone to sit down. "It looks like we have exhausted every means of DNA testing. We knew from the first round that the DNA didn't match our guys. We just now got the final test results. These guys are going to walk."

"I am pretty sure Aguilera is going to file his Motion to Vacate very soon. He has given me a draft copy. He'll finish it with the new results," Wilson said. "I'll turn over the results as soon as this meeting is over."

"The last pieces of the puzzle were the hair samples. They also don't match our guys," said Corley.

"What else do we have?" Benedetti asked.

"I am sure you read Broadhead's recantation statement, that dog ass is going back to prison. He will be in Branch 22 tomorrow on a new theft charge and he's on parole. He'll be back in the joint when the others get out," Wilson said.

"He's a career crook. How can anyone believe any of his bullshit?" Di Donato said.

"Me and Buerline have 16 inmates with violent backgrounds that we have to interview. We are gathering the evidence from their old cases and we'll go talk to them and get swabs. I am not sure if we will get it all done by the time these guys get out."

Benedetti stood up and stretched indicating that the meeting was over. Benedetti was five-foot nine, stocky and strong. His black hair was cut short, almost military. He loved to cook and it was starting to show. He was built like a linebacker, which he played on his high school football team. He wasn't very happy. "I'll meet with the state's attorney after lunch. Mr. Porter is not a happy camper."

"We're doing everything we can, boss," Wilson said.

~~~~

Jose Aguilera was leaning back in his handmade chair. His phone was on speaker and he was very relaxed, even smiling as he answered Peter Michaels first question. "They'll be freed on December fifth if everybody does the right thing. I just got the final DNA test results back. They're free."

"What makes you this positive?"

"The last thing they could hang their hat on was the pubic hair and head hair found on her clothes and in the blood samples. It didn't match. It's over. The evidence is now undeniable and overpowering."

"Have you talked to your clients?"

"As a matter of fact I have. We went to see them this morning. They are in good spirits but they're shocked that they'll be getting out so soon. They became men in prison."

"Yep, a lot has changed."

"They are amazed at things like the internet and cell phones. Those things were basically non-existent when they went to jail as teenagers."

"I imagine that must be pretty scary to them. I assume they are pretty angry?"

Aguilera got up from his chair and he started to pace around his office. His speakerphone had an omnidirectional microphone. "Yeah, do you blame them? They are angry at the criminal justice system that wrongfully convicted them. Yeah, they're pissed. I don't blame them."

"How did you like working with the state's attorney's office?"

"I'll tell you, I was a little apprehensive at first but they did a great job. They realized that mistakes were made and they wanted to correct them. Amy Wilson was great to work with. She is a fine attorney. I'd hire her in a heartbeat, if she ever wanted to leave the office."

"Yeah, she's a pretty smart woman. I am guessing you will file a civil suit?"

"Yes, without a doubt but that can wait. We just want to get them out. They spent a long time in prison for a crime they didn't commit. I am also going after the police, prosecutors and Patricia Bass in particular when all the dust settles."

~~~~

Amy Wilson took a seat in one of three chairs in front of her boss Peter Di Donato's desk. Her black suit neatly pressed, her white blouse opened at the neck. She had an apprehensive look on her face. "Now that Thanksgiving is over, I've got to call the family and let them know that these guys are getting out in less than two weeks," Wilson said.

"I'll make the call if you want me to," said Di Donato.

"No. No. I have a rapport with Mrs. Lezkowski. I know this will be devastating to her. She is such a loving soul."

"Good luck with that. Where are we?"

"This investigation is getting as big as the original one. Corley and Buerline have already taken 33 buccal swabs and have interviewed 47 people. They are going to interview all of their cellmates and 16 others we have found. I know there will be more before this is all over but right now we are running on a treadmill and getting nowhere."

~~~~

Retired Detective Jack Evans was beside himself. The acid in his stomach boiled, he could feel the bitter regurgitation in his throat as he paced around his outdated kitchen. He more than 30 years on the job and nothing like this had ever happened to him. He was agitated as he talked to Detective Dick Corley.

"Jack, you are not going to like it but these bastards are going to be freed pretty soon. This DNA stuff doesn't match any of the four. I hope you can get your head around this," Corley said.

Evans coughed and cleared his throat, "It's all I have been thinking about since that newspaper editorial against Chief Maurer for defending our case."

Corley had his feet crossed on his desk and the phone cradle between his chin and shoulder. "I know this is going to be hard for you. I know how much work you guys put into this investigation. I have read over 3,500 pages of reports and lab analysis. Did you hear about Broadhead's recantation saying he was beaten within an inch of his life and that you threatened to kill him?"

"I don't care what that fucking dog says. We never laid a hand on that prick. Maurer would have transferred me to Hegewisch on the far Southside if I did anything like that. No dog ass is worth that or my pension," Evans said as he rubbed his forehead and grimaced. "I don't care what that DNA says, I'm telling you, those guys knew too much about that murder not to have been there. Lorenzo is one wicked son of a bitch. I don't have any doubt in my mind that he killed that poor woman. Not a doubt. In my opinion, all that DNA says is that they didn't ejaculate."

~~~~

If Amy Wilson smoked she would have devoured a pack of cigarettes by now. Her stomach did flips and she had a lump in her throat and her hands were shaking as she dialed Lezkowski's home phone number.

Every time Violet Lezkowski reached for her phone she saw a picture of Ruth. "Hello Amy. How are you?"

"I am fine Mrs. Lezkowski. This is a very difficult conversation for me but I need to tell you that the three men in prison for killing your daughter are going to be set free very soon. We now have new scientific evidence that wasn't available back then and it says they didn't do it," Wilson said.

"I have been expecting something like this after reading all the newspaper articles the last few months. Are you saying they didn't do it?"

"All I know is that the new DNA evidence does not connect them to the crime."

"I would not want the wrong people in jail if they didn't do it. Those judges back then were so positive, so profound. The police and the prosecutors all thought those men were guilty. Now, I don't know what to think. This has been torture."

Violet Lezkowski was now 70. Her eyes were stinging but she wasn't crying. Her hands trembled as she held the phone close to her right ear. Her voice was soft, a little louder than a whisper.

Amy Wilson tried to keep her composure. Her hands were also shaking. She respected Mrs. Lezkowski and though she couldn't see her, Wilson could sense the woman's helplessness at this moment. She wanted to make her feel as comfortable as possible with what she was about to say, "I can assure you that we are doing everything we can to find those responsible. We even have the FBI involved with our top investigators. They have been working very diligently to bring this case to a conclusion. I know you want closure and I can assure you, so do we."

"Will you keep me informed Amy?"

At the mention of her name, Amy Wilson's heart seemed to stop. She closed her eyes and took a deep breath, "Yes, I promise, I'll keep you updated. You should know that my boss is going to have a news conference in the next day or two and announce that he expects these men to be released."

After Wilson hung up the phone, she put her face in her hands and began to weep. "Oh, my God! Oh, my God give me strength," she prayed as tears filled the palms of her hands.

~~~~

This was one press conference the Cook County State's Attorney Thomas Porter would rather not have. Unlike other state's attorneys, Porter liked to be in the courtroom whenever possible, even though he was elected, he was a very accomplished trial lawyer. He was a partner in the prestigious law firm of Porter, Shannon, Victor, Gargiulo and Borruso.

All of Porter's suits were handmade. Every inch of cloth was smooth across his back and shoulders. His white starched shirt, his highly shined shoes and his red power tie in a half Windsor. He was dressed for action. His hazel eyes were always focused. He stood erect, shoulders back and he looked up at the multitude of cameras and reporters in front of him.

"Tomorrow, attorneys from my office will go to court and recommend that all the charges against Lorenzo Holmes, Charles Holmes, Oscar Sampson and Marcus Broadhead be dropped. Six months ago we re-opened the Ruth Lezkowski investigation as the

DNA results started pointing away from those convicted. We are currently seeking a match for two unknown male DNA profiles that we have developed. Our investigators have interviewed scores of people in ten different states as part of a completely new and exhaustive investigation. This office acted in good faith 14 years ago, based on the evidence that existed at that time. But the evolution of DNA has produced new evidence that renders questions of those verdicts. In addition, several key witnesses have recanted their testimony. As a result, we have no case against these men and we will drop the charges."

As soon as Porter finished his prepared remarks, Peter Michaels jumped at the chance to ask the first question, "Why did your office work so closely with defense attorney Jose Aguilera?"

"This case was a real failure of the system. This is certainly a big reminder to all of us that we are not perfect. We wanted to find out whether or not we had the right guys in prison. We cannot be afraid to admit that we made a mistake. Mr. Aguilera came to us with some new evidence that showed there was no DNA match. We want to do everything possible to make sure that those responsible for this hideous crime are put in jail and we want to bring closure to the Lezkowski family. They have suffered long enough."

~~~~

"Tomorrow is going to be a shit storm," Ron Magers said as Michaels and Dave Beedy walked into his office.

"I guess. I'm telling you there had to be 25 cameras there from all the networks. This DNA stuff is national news now."

"You think they'll get out tomorrow?"

"Without a doubt. Court will only take a few minutes in the morning. Then it will be a circus as everyone tries to keep up with Aguilera and his entourage. He told me today that he rented a big van to pick these guys up and you better believe he will milk every ounce of publicity he can muster out of this. Here, take a look at this lead in. I'll see you in the studio. I gotta go to make up. The boss always yells at me because I try to skip out on that stuff."

"See ya on the set."

# CHAPTER 48

O
n December 5, 2001, Chicago's temperature was hovering at zero degrees. When ASA Amy Wilson walked into 26th and Cal, her nose was red and running, her feet were cold, her hands were numb and she was later than usual but all she really had to do in front of Judge John Green was say "The state has no objection, your honor."

At precisely ten o'clock that morning Jose Aguilera presented the court with his Motion to Vacate. The entire proceeding took less than five minutes for Judge Green to declare that Lorenzo Holmes, Charles Holmes and Oscar Sampson were free men. Wilson also asked him to vacate the sentence of Marcus Broadhead who was given a lighter sentence for cooperating with the prosecution.

Marcus Broadhead would be walking into Stateville Correctional Center at almost the same time two of his buds would be walking out. It was the third time he went to prison since he was released in 1992 for his part in the Ruth Lezkowski case.

~~~~

Jose Aguilera stepped into the nice warm oversized van he rented to pick up his clients as they walked out of the prison's gates. It was a well-choreographed television event. Twenty TV news crews and scores of reporters that resembled the paparazzi chased his van and he loved every minute of it.

When the police walk a suspect by television camera crews it's called a "Perp Walk" but Aguilera called his the "Free Man Walk." He was doing it in grandiose style that would have made Barnum and Bailey very proud.

It took more than an hour to get to Stateville. Traffic was heavy and streets were wet. The temperature was warming up, icy spots on the roads were melting and potholes were sprouting up like spring flowers. The driver knew precisely where to park the van to allow total access by the media to Lorenzo Holmes and Oscar Sampson as they walked out of prison for the first time in 15 years. They were dressed exactly alike in gray sweaters, black corduroy pants, and shiny black shoes. Aguilera bought them the matching outfits. He wanted to make sure everything was perfect. The sun was now shining and the temperature was getting tolerable. The smiles on their faces were like reverse rainbows – ear-to-ear and bright.

Technicians set up a make shift staging center with a podium that had a single microphone connected to a sound box where all the crews could plug-in to the sound system. Every detail was planned.

Holmes and Sampson nervously approached the microphone and reached inside their coat pockets for the written statements they prepared during the last few days. Holmes had tears in his eyes and couldn't speak at the moment so Sampson went first. "It is obvious that a great miscarriage of justice was committed against us and a greater injustice was committed against the family of Ruth Lezkowski. I have always said I didn't do this horrible thing. We are finally vindicated and I am glad to be a free man. I am angry with the criminal justice system. I never admitted any involvement in this crime. I wasted 15 years of my life for something that I did not do."

"What do you want to do now?" a reporter shouted out.

"I want to eat some food that ain't penitentiary food as long as it is a big dish of something really good. I'd like to go to a Popeye's Fried Chicken place and get me some wings. I want to see my momma and my family."

"How was your last night?" A radio reporter asked.

"I was so excited I couldn't sleep at all. I got notes and congratulations from a bunch of the guys." Holmes facial expression changed from happy to a mad frown and tears welled in his eyes. "Prison life is brutal. I hated every minute I was locked up. I am bitter about that no doubt. Nothing can make up for those last 15 years of living in a jungle."

"What about you Mr. Sampson?"

"I had trouble sleeping too, you know what I'm saying. I couldn't believe I was getting out. I feel I was robbed of a good part of my life.

I never want to go back to prison. I hated every minute of it but I knew I didn't do anything to that woman and when I found out about DNA testing I wrote Mr. Aguilera and prayed he'd read my letter. Thank God he did and now here we are and free."

"What do you want to do?"

"I wanted to use a cell phone and I did for the first time today," said Sampson. "I called a lady friend. It was cool." He nodded his head in a backward motion to the prison behind him and continued, "I've read about them in there and now I finally got a chance to use one."

The next stop was Joliet Correctional Center about 20 minutes away. When Charles Holmes walked out of the gate, the warden and a few prison guards watched and smiled and said good-bye to him. Correctional officers often become cynical to the hard luck stories of inmates like "I didn't do it," and "I never killed no one," but to them Charles was not that type. They believed he couldn't hurt a fly. They liked him. They felt sorry for him. They wished him the best when he was released.

Charles had everything he owned in a box; a fan, a bible and pictures of his childhood. He was smiling from ear to ear as he walked into the arms of his cousin Lorenzo and Oscar Sampson. "Long journey, man," he said.

"I told you to hold on brother. I knew this day would come," Lorenzo Holmes said.

As reporters and camera crews swarmed around Charles Holmes, he said, "I have dreams. I want to become a minister. I knew God would free us. I found Jesus and if anything good has come from this, it is that."

"Are you angry?"

"I am trying to find forgiveness but those prosecutors tried to kill me. That life sentence was just like the death penalty. It was like they just put me under the rug and forgot about me. Fifteen years is a long time, I thank God I am finally free. I can't wait to listen to Ladysmith Black Mambazo."

"Why?"

"Because that is what led me to Jesus. That was how I found religion."

Ladysmith Black Mambazo is a South African all male choral group that became popular after singing with Paul Simon on his 1968 album *Graceland*. The group has won five Grammy Awards and dedicated years to teaching people about South Africa and its culture.

~~~~

The next and last stop was a pizza party at Jose Aguilera's office. He had organized a family reunion of sorts with family members and friends. Many of them stopped visiting the three in prison ten years ago.

The office was adorned with banners stating; **Welcome Home** and **Free At Last.** The entire office staff clapped as they entered the master conference room.

Charles' mother and one of his old grade school teachers were wailing when he walked in the door. She hadn't seen him in seven years. "My God! My baby! My baby!" she howled as she grabbed her only son. "Come over here and let me hold you, child," she cried. "I knew you were innocent. I knew God would answer my prayers. Oh! My baby! My baby!"

The joyous occasion got serious when Peter Michaels asked the freed men their thoughts about Marcus Broadhead.

"I know the police put a lot of pressure on Marcus. I know he would never turn on me like they said he did," Oscar Sampson said.

"Yeah, I forgive him though at the time I was filled with hatred. I know that the police was all over him." Lorenzo Holmes said.

"I really didn't know him. All I know is they scared me something awful. I really didn't understand what was going on at the time. I was young and scared," said Charles Holmes who was now 29.

~~~~

Jose Aguilera announced that he would file a civil rights suit in Federal Court on Friday. "I plan on suing the Police Department and the State's Attorney's office for misconduct. I want to take this case all the way to trial in front of a jury. I want the citizens of Chicago to know how the police and prosecutors handle these kinds of investigations. We now know that the confessions were false and coerced. We are going to set the record straight once and for all. This is abuse of power if I ever saw it. It should never have happened. This kind of misconduct should never happen again."

"What kind of money are you talking about?"

Before Aguilera could answer, Lorenzo Holmes bellowed, "Shaquille O'Neill kinda money." O'Neill had just signed one of the largest NBA contracts in basketball history with the Los Angeles Lakers.

Everyone laughed but then Aguilera said, "You better believe we are going after more money than the Alsip Heights Four got. We will be aggressive."

In 1989, four men who were wrongfully convicted of a double murder received $36 million in a Federal Court settlement.

"Since we took over this case a year and a half ago, we have spent $250,000 and consumed over 800 hours of time researching and investigating it. All I can say as you can see, it was time and money well spent," Aguilera said. "Four men are now free and have their lives back and I just feel wonderful."

~~~~

Ron Magers was straightening his tie when Michaels and Beedy walked in his office before the ten o'clock news. "Quite a day you had out there."

"It was interesting to say the least," Michaels said as he eased into his chair. "You should have seen the look on Charles Holmes' face when he picked up a real knife for the first time in 15 years. He turned it around in his hand like it was sterling silver jewelry."

"It sounded like that Sampson guy is bitter?"

"He is very bitter. You know, he was stabbed 14 times in prison. He's got this big-ass jagged scar on his head."

"That usually means its gang attack, doesn't it?"

"I am trying to get their prison intake records. You know if inmates were in a gang they are pretty honest about listing their right gang affiliation. The correctional system wants to separate rival gangs from going to the same prisons. That's why Stateville may have a lot of Gangster Disciples and Joliet has Black Gangsters. It's really a way to control gang fights."

"You reported that the warden and some prison guards wished Charles good luck. That's pretty unusual isn't it?"

Michaels started to turn the pages of his reporter's notebook looking for some quotes. "He found religion in jail. He might have been in the wrong place at the wrong time in all of this. He said, 'Anytime you take a child and you force him into the wilderness, he's going to turn into a beast or he is going to learn there is a higher power.'"

"That's pretty profound from a person who is supposed to have an IQ of 65." Magers said.

"Yep. He also said, 'Sometimes you have to go through certain things for God to work in your life and bring you to a certain point.' He's a pretty interesting person."

"Did the suspected ringleader say much?"

"No, Lorenzo is a very angry man. I'll tell you, he had a violent background as a juvenile but that never came out in court. Now Sampson, he was a talker. He said, 'There is no apology that would restore the time they took from us or wipe away the trauma we all went through.'"

"These guys are going to make a lot of money."

"They can file immediately for $150,000 from the State Court of Claims and they will get that money in a week or so. Aguilera however is going for much more in his civil rights suit. Sampson knows it and he said, 'I think they know what's coming—they know a big storm is on the way.'"

"I gotta go to make up. See you on the set," Magers said.

"I'm right behind you."

# CHAPTER 49

"**S**on of a bitch," Peter Di Donato screamed as he slammed the newspaper down on his desk disrupting all of his Cincinnati Reds baseball paraphernalia he had on display. He was livid at Jose Aguilera's comments about prosecutorial misconduct and criminal behavior.

Amy Wilson was startled as she walked into his office. "Who shit in your cornflakes this morning?"

"Do you believe after all we did to help Aguilera in this case, he is now saying our actions were criminal? I can't believe this. On one side of his mouth he praises us for our cooperation and paying for all these DNA tests and then he attacks the shit out of us."

"Did you see that the governor is placing a moratorium on all capitol punishment cases?" Handing Di Donato a manila folder, Wilson continued, "I did some research this morning. Did you know that nationwide with the Lezkowski Four, 98 cases of murder and/or rape have been overturned because of DNA testing? This DNA issue has a lot of momentum."

Di Donato moved his red designer reading glasses from his nose to the top of his bald head and said, "Hey, I am glad we have DNA testing available to us. It will help us eliminate this wrongful conviction problem in the future. Where are we in the new investigation?"

"We have a major mystery on our hands. The guys we are looking for could already be in the system but we didn't start keeping DNA files until 1995. At this point we don't have any idea who belongs to this DNA, but we are turning over a lot of rocks." Wilson stood and reached across the desk to gather the file she gave her boss. "Corley's team has interviewed at least 63 people already and they have all volunteered their DNA. So right now all we have is the original evidence and no suspects."

~~~~

Former ASA Michael Pangborn just won a multi-million-dollar product liability lawsuit for a well-known hotel chain in federal court. He was now a partner and the chief litigator in the law firm of Carlin and Miller. He was very familiar with reporters chasing him down and asking him questions. He was surprised but not shocked that not a single reporter asked him a question about saving $100 million for his client.

"What is your reaction to the Lezkowski Four being freed?"

"I felt those defendants were guilty then and I think they are guilty today. We were required to prove them guilty beyond a reasonable doubt. We did that. It was a very strong case."

"What about the DNA saying it wasn't them?"

"If the DNA is matched to another individual that in and of itself would not permit charging that person with murder. It proves they raped her for sure but without a confession one could argue they didn't murder her. Look, O.J. Simpson was not convicted in criminal court because reasonable doubt was established. He was overwhelmingly convicted with the same evidence in a civil trial. It's just a lower standard of proof. No matter what though, remember, a jury does not find people innocent—they find them guilty or not guilty."

"What about the recantations?"

"To say they were beaten half to death is just utterly preposterous. There is absolutely no evidence of that at all. A judge held a hearing and heard all of those arguments and motions to suppress the confessions before trial on these same grounds and he found them to have no merit. Those statements were taken by a civilian court reporter and that person is required by law to report any brutality if they suspect it. That never happened—never ever happened. It just didn't. The jury returned guilty verdicts based on the evidence presented and the lack of reasonable doubt. Period."

~~~~

Retired Detective Jack Evans was sitting at his kitchen table drinking his fourth cup of coffee that was making him sick to his stomach. For 30 years he never had a blemish on his record as a police officer. Now he was reading stories in the newspapers and watching news reports on television saying he was about to be sued. He wanted to throw up but the phone interrupted his thoughts.

"Detective Evans this is Peter Michaels. Got a minute?"

"I told you I don't want to talk to you or any other reporter."

"Come on Jack, you have known me a long time. I think what you have to say is very important. Your side of this story should be told."

Evans took a deep breath and rubbed his forehead with his left hand and said, "I swore an oath to serve and protect, apprehend criminals, intervene in criminal activity and save the citizens of this city from jeopardy. That means I would sacrifice my life to honor that oath. I have watched 92 Chicago Police Officers give their lives to honor that oath in the last 30 years." He stopped for a second took another deep breath and slowly exhaled "To suggest that there is some human being or some situation so significant that a police officer would deliberately and knowingly attempt to charge a person with a crime that he or she didn't commit is not only outrageous, it's despicable. No human being or situation is worth my reputation or my freedom and my pension. I would not tolerate that kind of conduct from any police officer nor would I participate in that type of activity myself. Now leave me the fuck alone."

~~~~

Oscar Sampson and Charles and Lorenzo Holmes were anxious to put their lives back together but they were nervous, scared and doubtful. Jose Aguilera arranged for three of his former clients to meet with the recently released men and offer them some good and friendly advice.

Donte Chester, Mario Custer and Wendell Bridges were all clients of Jose Aguilera. They were convicted of rape, spent at least nine years in prison and they were also exonerated through DNA. They were glad to help their new friends get back on their feet.

The breakfast meeting started out with hot pancakes that Charles Holmes devoured and fresh fruit that Lorenzo Holmes and Oscar

Sampson picked at. The mood was contemplative and the conversation was soothing.

"The world now moves quickly like the speed of the internet. It will take you awhile to get accustomed to cell phones," said Donte Chester, who was sitting at the head of the table and directing the meeting. Chester was studying to be a paralegal. "You should always dress sharp to make a good-impression." He was wearing a gray suit with a conservative tie.

Oscar Sampson said, "I want to go to law school and become an attorney." While Sampson was in prison he started to consume books. He read everything from military history to philosophy. He was especially interested in law books and he studied his own case.

"This will be a very big adjustment. You guys probably don't even know how to drive," said Mario Custer. They all nodded in agreement. "Don't hide your prison background. If it comes up in a job interview, explain that you were exonerated. There are employers out there that will give you an opportunity if you are qualified."

The Holmes cousins and Sampson had their eyes locked on their new acquaintances trying to take in every word. "You are celebrities now. Your names and pictures are all over the papers. You are going to hear from people you haven't seen in years. People will want to hang out with you because they know there is going to be a big settlement coming your way," Wendell Bridges said. "Be careful who you trust. Don't go back to your old environment. Don't hang with peoples who can bring you down. Remember the police will be looking for you. They know you was exonerated and they'll try to arrest you for the littlest thing. You know what I'm saying."

They all nodded their heads in agreement and all three said at the same time, "I know about that."

"I know what I am about to tell will be hard, but you need to be careful about your anger. Don't dwell on it. You suffered for 15 years, let it go. Don't let resentment fester about the system that convicted you," Chester said. As he looked at them one at a time, he leaned forward and softly said, "You must not let it be like a cancer. You cannot let it grow."

All of them had a thoughtful look on their face. Charles said, "God got me this far. I can do that. I just want to get on with my life."

Aguilera came into the room with a big smile across his face. "Come on guys let's go get you some clothes for your new life." They left and walked down State Street and started a two-hour shopping spree.

# CHAPTER 50

T erry G. Hillard was the city's top cop, Superintendent of Police. He just looked military. An ex-marine, five-nine, he stood erect and he was fit and trim. He always dressed to perfection. His shirt, belt and zipper were always in perfect alignment. He had a folksy manner but he was always focused. He loved being the police and he hated when the police were not being the police.

The Chicago Police Department committed itself to a community-policing concept they called CAPS—Chicago's Alternative Policing Strategy. Hillard recognized that Black ministers in Chicago had developed into not only a strong religious community force but also a strong political force. So he formed a task force of 20 religious groups, community groups and business leaders to address issues that affected the Black community.

Community activists were criticizing Mayor Richard Daley for not taking a stand on the wrongful convictions of the Lezkowski Four. The activists claimed that Daley owed the Black community an apology because he was the State's Attorney when they were convicted.

Hillard called a meeting of his newly formed task force and promised to root out bad cops. They were calling on him to minimize racial profiling and police brutality. Hillard promised that any police officer that didn't abide by their oath would be held accountable.

The group also called for the entire judicial system to be held accountable for each of the deliberate mistakes of sending innocent people to jail.

~~~~

Detectives Dick Corley and Don Buerline just finished processing 16 more buccal swabs for DNA testing trying to match that of Unknown Male #1 and #2. They weren't expecting any hits. The convicts they interviewed were very violent men but they also didn't hesitate to give swabs. Their guts told them these guys weren't their guys.

Buerline was standing by the computer waiting for a printout. He was tired, his eyes burned and his head ached. They had been putting in 12 to 14 hour days for the last two weeks. They developed a comprehensive list of 146 individuals and their forensic identifiers that they wanted to run through CODIS to identify their DNA.

"Shit! This is going to be impossible to identify any trace to our unknown males if we don't have anything on file. They're probably in prison now," said Corley.

"Yeah, but we do have new information on this list of 146," Buerline said. "I'll start cross indexing them."

"How are you doing with the new grand jury subpoenas?"

"They'll be here today or tomorrow."

They also wanted grand jury subpoenas to question some of the original circumstantial witnesses from the original case. Two had recanted their testimony however the other five basically said, "What I said back then, I say today." They knew they had a mystery to solve but they also knew that they were not even close.

"This is like finding a needle in a haystack," Corley said. "It is going to boil down to someone stepping forward. That's how we are going to crack this case."

~~~~

January 10, 2002 was very cold, minus 10 with the wind-chill factor. Michaels still had on his woolen cap and was rubbing his hands together on the elevator on his way to Jose Aguilera's office. He couldn't wait for a hot cup of coffee.

Aguilera was at his computer when his secretary escorted Michaels into his office. He turned, stood up and shook hands. "I'm filing the civil suit later this afternoon."

"That's fast, isn't in?"

"I'm naming every cop who signed a supplementary report, every cop who was a boss, every evidence technician particularly Patricia Bass and every prosecutor who touched this case. We want to show the public a blueprint of how a case like this was manufactured," said Aguilera as he handed Michaels a copy of the lawsuit.

"Did you always want to do this? Be a liberal anti-police, anti-prosecutor attorney?"

"I am a die hard Republican. I love guns. I love God and I love apple pie. I grew up in Appleton, Wisconsin. I'm conservative to the core. I actually wanted to be a policeman when I was a kid."

"Come on!"

"No. I'm not kidding you. When I first practiced law, I wanted to be a products liability—medical malpractice attorney. When I opened my first office on Ashland Avenue, clients just started coming in the door and it has never stopped since. You know Peter, you might find this hard to believe but I am not against capital punishment, but now I have my doubts that everyone on death row is guilty."

"I'm going to look over this lawsuit. We will probably lead with it at six o'clock."

~~~~

Mayor Daley's Office filed a brief statement in which he apologized for the wrongful convictions of the Lezkowski Four. It read in part: "At the time, we did not have DNA testing, as we know it today and the case brought before us was very solid. I sympathize with the Lezkowski family and I hope we can give them closure soon."

~~~~

Ron Magers motioned Michaels to come into his office. He had a grin on his face, shaking his head he said, "Man, Aguilera didn't pull any punches with this suit."

"Have you ever seen anything so uncharacteristically scathing with that kind of bitter language in a lawsuit? He's named more than 30 people."

"It doesn't say how much he's going after."

"Nope. He got 36 million in the 'Alsip Heights Four' suit. They were wrongfully convicted with the kidnapping and murder of a suburban couple. I think he is trying to make a statement."

The suit claimed: The police knew the four men were innocent but framed them by violently forcing them to sign confessions they knew were false; prosecutors knew the men were innocent but went along with the frame-up; and that evidence technicians knew they were innocent but fabricated evidence to frame them.

The plaintiffs were center stage in one of the greatest frauds perpetuated in a Chicago courtroom. The plaintiffs watched as every single one of their civil rights was trampled by a prosecution so cynical and corrupt as to betray every principal of a fair trial.

Defendant Michael Pangborn was captain of the ship in the conspiracy to maliciously prosecute the four plaintiffs for a crime they did not commit. Pangborn knew the defendants were innocent of the Lezkowski homicide.

"What did Pangborn say?"

"I have never seen anyone so enraged. Obviously he called all of the allegations completely and totally false. He said 'He is more convinced than ever before that the guys are guilty because when you revert to lying like that you are really digging your hole deeper and deeper.' Mage, he was pissed."

"I bet. Did Porter's office say anything?"

"They're going to fight it tooth and nail. I talked to Di Donato. He said, 'We believe that the prosecutors who tried this case back in 1987 acted in good faith based on the evidence at the time and we will support and defend Mr. Pangborn and this office at trial.'"

"Your script looks good. Let's go do this thing," Magers said as they walked to the studio.

~~~~

Michaels was locking his desk drawer getting ready to go to Blackie's for the best burger in the city when his phone rang.

"News ... Michaels."

"Say! Lookey here. You dat guy who works for Ron Magers. You just finished a story about those boys who got off for killin' that white girl?"

"Yeah, that be me. Whose is this?"

"I be Reggie Russell. I knows who kilt that girl. You know what I mean?"

Michaels froze in his tracks, slide his coat off and sat down in his chair and reached for his notebook. "How can you be so sure?"

"I knows who did it. I been carrying a heavy heart for a long time. I be seeing these newspaper articles and you on TV and I say to myself I got to do something. You know what I'm saying?"

"Yeah, I do. Something like that can gnaw away at you. Can I come talk to you?"

"Sure. Tomorrow. The place be closed tonight."

"Where are you?"

"I'm staying at Apple River."

"What is that?"

It be a treatment center. I'm trying to sober up. Been using for a long time."

"Where is it?"

"It be in Lemont, Illinois."

"I can be there in the morning."

"I ain't going no wheres."

Michaels stood up put on his coat and thought, *the cold winter air just warmed up. That Blackie's burger is going to taste very, very good tonight.*

Michaels buttoned up his coat, wrapped a scarf around his neck, pulled his woolen cap down over his ears and skipped out the door with a smile on his face. *Finally, closure.*

# CHAPTER 51

M ichaels was very tired Saturday morning as he drove to the Apple River Treatment Center in Lemont about 26 miles from downtown Chicago. He didn't sleep well. He was anticipating this visit all night and it made him restless. It snowed hard through the night. Although the I-55 expressway was cleared, the driveway to the treatment center was not. The trip up the winding road was picturesque. The sun's rays sparkled through the leafless tree branches that were covered with heavy fresh white snow. The pavement was waiting for a plow. It was not packed down but his tires had no problem with traction, not many cars went before him. He thought he was driving through a Christmas card. It was that pretty. It reminded him of his mother. He said a silent prayer.

~~~~

Reggie Russell was waiting for him at the kitchen table of the Portage dormitory, which was a separate cottage on the east end of the campus. A cold cup of stale coffee sat in front of him. He looked dingy. His braided hair was clumpy and matted. His old plaid shirt had stains. His blue jeans were faded, baggy and hung on his plump body. He was overweight. He looked depressed.

Michaels researched Apple River the night before and discovered that it was psychiatric treatment facility that specialized in drug rehabilitation and depression treatment. He extended his hand. "I'm Peter Michaels.

"I told them, you'd be coming," Russell said.

"You okay?"

"Like I told you last night. I have a heavy heart. I've been depressed. I've used drugs for as long as I can remember. I have been carrying this burden for 15 years."

"Tell me a little about yourself?"

"I be 39-years old. Back in the 80s, I used to live up there in the ALBA Homes with my girlfriend at 1210 West 12<sup>th</sup> Street, apartment 1208."

Michaels' mind was racing. That was close to the building that Marcus Broadhead lived in. *Could this be a coincidence? Was there a connection?*

It was my girlfriend's place, you know what I'm saying? I knows who kilt that white woman up by the tracks. I saw all the posters back then that they had up all over the fucking place. Two of my 'associates' did it but I was not involved. No sir."

"Who are they?"

"First, I want to tell you, I wants money, $3,000 and if that $25,000 reward is still on the table, I wants that too."

"I can talk to the police. I am not sure about how that works but I'll do everything I can to get you the money. Everybody wants closure to this murder. Why are you so sure you know who they are?" Michaels persisted.

"A short time after the murder, I was walking with my 'associates' and those posters were up. You know what I'm saying. One of dem looks at me and says, 'You know that poster dat's up. We did her. She was a hard bitch to kill.'"

~~~~

When Michaels left Apple River his heart was racing so fast, he felt like he just finished a marathon. His hands were shaking as he reached for his cell phone. He found Jethro's number and hit the dial button.

Corley answered on the third ring, "Corley here."

"Hey Jethro."

"Fuck you Michaels. Why aren't you in some warm toasty bed with a woman getting laid on a cold Saturday morning?"

"We gotta talk. I found someone who knows who killed Ruth Lezkowski. I'm not shitting you. I feel it in my guts. He knows."

"Where are you?"

"Driving back to the city from Lemont, see you at Pete's in a half hour."

~~~~

Pete's coffee shop was part of the Maxwell street redevelopment project. It had strong coffee and quiet corner tables. The paved patio, that provided tables, and seating in the warmer months was now covered with snow. A six-foot wide path was shoveled to the front door. Parking was always a problem in the area unless you had a police car. Michaels didn't. Corley was sitting at a corner table, his hands wrapped around his warm porcelain cup when Michaels walked in.

"I hate fucking coming here because of parking," Michaels began.

"Sounds like you had a productive morning," Corley said grinning. "Tell me all about it."

Michaels filled him in on his conversation with Reggie Russell. "I believe this guy. I think he may be related. That's why I am positive that he knows something."

"You know Pete you can't go with any of this." Corley knew Michaels hated to be called Pete the same way he hated to be called Jethro but he did it for effect. "If you report this you will drive the bad guys further underground. I promise you, I will give you plenty of lead-time on anything that can help you with this story in the end but please don't put this on the air. We need to get these guys."

Michaels became reflective as a serious look crossed his face. He began to think. "I'll talk to my boss. I have an ethical problem making deals like this with the police or anybody else for that matter."

"Think about the Lezkowski family. They need closure and we need to get these bastards. You talk to your boss and I am going to talk to Reggie. Do the right thing here."

~~~~

Michaels lived in the South Loop, an area that was exploding with new development and remodels. His condo on South Michigan had 25-foot ceilings, two bedrooms and two baths. It overlooked Grant Park, the museum campus and Lake Michigan. He walked straight to the fireplace, turned it on and called Phil Rivers his news director at home and told him what just happened. "What do you think?"

"Philosophically I hate to make deals with anyone but in this case I think we have to. You've known this Corley guy for a long time I take it?" Rivers asked.

"Yep."

"You trust him. He's not going to fuck you, right?"

"No. He's good people. He'll honor his word."

"Here's what you should do. Get a script ready with all the info you know. Have Beedy go through the library and gather any video and pics you may need. Have a piece ready to go so we don't get caught with our pants down. Hopefully Corley comes through for us."

~~~~

Corley went back to his office at 26th Street and ran Reggie Russell's name. It came back with his arrest record. He was pinched 19 times, mostly for drug related crimes nothing violent. He had four aliases. He had done time and he clearly had a drug problem.

Corley called Amy Wilson and filled her in. "I've got to go talk to this guy right now."

He called Reggie Russell who said, "Come on over, I've gots nowhere to go."

It was 2:30 in the afternoon when Corley walked into the dormitory kitchen. Russell had a cup of warm coffee in front of him. Two other people were sitting at a table in the opposite corner. They appeared to be catatonic. Their arms were crossed in front of their chests and they were leaning forward and back-wards in perfect rhythm. They were in some place no one else could enter. Corley knew they would not be a problem.

Russell told Corley everything he told Michaels then added, "I have an attorney but I don't want him to be part of our conversation."

"What do you want?"

"I want a legal paper that guarantees me the $3,000. I want to be re-located with my family, so we be safe and I want the $25,000 hospital reward if you convict these two boys. You know what I'm saying?"

"How are you so sure you can identify these guys?"

"They's not from the ALBA Homes but they been around there lots, promise you dat. These boys are not part of any of those other four guys who was arrested earlier. This be on my mind a long time now. I saw one of them a while back and I says to him, 'You know if your friend get caught up doing something, he may flip on your ass for this here murder.' Man the dude just look at me like I am some kinda fucking crazy fool and he don't say nuttin' but I knows he's thinking about it. You know what I'm saying."

"I can't make any promises but I'll see what I can do, you got a social security number. I'll get everything started.

"You knows I have been arrested before. I have a few aliases that I've used in the past. Next time you comes back here bring the papers and I'll gives you the killers."

# CHAPTER 52

T he mood was very optimistic in the Chief of Special Prosecutions' office on Monday morning, January 14th. It was the first time Peter Di Donato smiled in weeks when it came to discussing the Lezkowski investigation. Detectives Dick Corley and Don Buerline were sitting with ASA Amy Wilson trying to figure out how to go about getting the $3,000 reward money. Everybody was thrilled about this new development.

"I don't think this has ever been done before. We get money all the time for confidential informants on drug cases. I've never heard of it in a murder case but Cline is a pretty progressive thinker when it comes to innovative ways to get things done, I'm sure he'll do it," Corley said.

"Call him and let's get this ball rolling," said Di Donato.

~~~~

"Tell me something good, Jethro," Chief of Detectives Phil Cline said.

"Boss, I need $3,000 for a reward and I am positive we can solve the Lezkowski murder." Corley said.

Cline was leaning back in his chair when he answered the phone. Now he was resting his elbows on his desk, rubbing his chin and thinking. "This has never been done before but I don't see why we couldn't get this approved. We get CI money for drug informants. This is really no different. It's my contingency fund. I like the idea but I gotta run it past the boss. I'll get back to you shortly."

"Thanks boss. Call me on the cell."

~~~~

Superintendent Terry Hillard was sitting at his desk.

His blue suit jacket was neatly hanging on the valet near the entrance to his private washroom. His white starched shirt had French cuffs and gold cufflinks and his red tie was in its usual half Windsor. He was on the phone but motioned Cline into his office. Cline sat down in one of the four chairs in front of his desk and waited until Hillard hung up the phone.

"What's up Phil?"

"We have an interesting issue," Cline said as he explained the reward money problem. "I don't see this as any different than drug money for a CI."

Hillard had his fingers together like a steeple. He looked up at the ceiling for a few seconds, "If we can solve a murder. It's your money, make it happen."

~~~~

Cook County State's Attorney Thomas Porter called his number one man, Kevin Benedetti and Peter Di Donato into his office for the update. Porter was a White Sox fan through and through. He was tossing an autographed baseball up in the air that he got when he went to the Sox fantasy camp last year.

"No fuckups. I want this thing fool proof. No appeals. No mistakes. Everything by the book. Make it air tight," Porter demanded.

"I got off the phone with Corley a half hour ago. Cline approved the funds for the reward money. Pete and I have gone over how to draw up the agreement to make it legal and binding. No results. No money," Benedetti said.

"And if this DNA doesn't match Reggie?"

"The agreement is null and void," Di Donato said.

"Pete get this done. The next time I go in front of the media on this case I want to make sure we have closure with the family and with all the critics.

~~~~

Amy Wilson was sitting at her desk when Corley and Buerline walked in. They were both smiling.

"It never ceases to amaze me how so many of these cold cases get solved by someone coming forward. I bet this guy is related to Reggie in some way," Corley said. "I told you Cline would come through."

"Best boss ever," said Buerline.

"So how are you going to handle this agreement thing?" Corley asked.

Amy Wilson might be the only prosecutor who didn't have baseball paraphernalia all over her office. She loved the Chicago Blackhawks. So she had an autographed puck by Bobby Hull on her desk. It was even functional as a paperweight.

"Simply put, the agreement has to contain four specific things. First, the DNA has to match one of the unknown Male suspects identified in the DNA tests we already conducted. Secondly, if it leads to the arrest, prosecution and conviction of the murderers, the state's attorney's office agrees to seek the original reward of $25,000 from St. Luke's. Thirdly, the state's attorney agrees to re-locate Russell and his immediate family including his wife, children and mother because he told Corley he is afraid of retaliation. Finally, if it turns out to be Reggie he gets nothing but jail time."

"We also need to get a hair sample," Corley said.

"I have already included it in the consent form in our package."

~~~~

Dr. Bruce Chambers is a Forensic Psychologist who has been practicing for more than 25 years. His thick brown hair turned gray at the temples and the gray filtered down into his stubby beard. He speaks softly and reassuringly.

His office was typical. Two comfortable chairs sat at a slight angle giving the patient the feeling of eye-to-eye contact but not in an overbearing or imperious way. He didn't have a sofa. His desk was ten feet away from the chairs. His bookcases are filled with books about every form of criminal behavior imaginable. He has testified as an expert witness hundreds of times across the country.

Michaels had met Dr. Chambers for lunch a year or so ago after he testified at the murder trial of a guy who was arrested for 13 armed robberies and one of them ended in the murder of an 89-year-old man. They shook hands and Dr. Chambers motioned for Michaels to take a seat in one of his chairs.

"Doc are there studies that show armed robbery can lead to murder?"

"Peter, there has been a great deal of recent research that has provided methodologically sound tools for prediction of violence and studies regarding violent crime including armed robbery. In armed robberies murders can occur without pre-meditation. For example, a victim may suddenly pull a weapon in self-defense, leading the perpetrator to fire a weapon he was not planning on using. However, there are many armed robberies where murder is pre-determined, or the perpetrator commits murder without remorse."

Dr. Chambers smiled often when he spoke. He was very reassuring making whomever he was talking with feel very comfortable.

"What are the findings regarding repeated armed robbery offenders?" Michaels asked.

"The careers of armed robbers can be seen as a progressive scale, with particular characteristics varying as more robbery offenses are committed over time. Beginning as amateurs, offenders tend to be younger and less experienced, that is they do not have extensive prior records, and tend to rob individuals. A large proportion of amateur armed robbers are not likely to go on to become regular robbery offenders."

Michaels picked up his tape recorder to check if it was working. This information was getting a little technical and he wanted to make sure he was getting it all, then he asked, "But what about those who rob to get money for their drug habits?"

"That changes the dynamic somewhat because they can get very careless. They are not really professional robbers. They commit crimes of opportunity but they can become cavalier and insensitive. They may make stupid choices. That's the kind of person who will not become a career robber but a convict. Those who do continue committing robbery offenses will become more professional as their career continues. They will be older, become more likely to rob commercial establishments and have more extensive prior criminal records. As their careers continue, offenders become more likely to commit more robberies, engage in better planning and be motivated by their narcissistic needs."

Michaels wriggled a little in his chair trying to get more comfortable. "I don't think these guys are professional thieves. They are more like thugs but what about armed robberies where murders take place?"

"This also is seen as progressive and associated with personality traits. If one continues to engage in armed robberies, despite the negative consequences they may have previously experienced, the odds are that they have what psychologists describe as a failure of empathy, a trait associated with anti-social personalities, and to some extent, narcissistic personalities."

"Some of these guys feel that if the person they rob is a woman and they don't have any money, they'll rape them because they want to get something out of it. They feel like they're going to get caught anyway?"

"There are a lot of very sick individuals out there, no doubt about that. They get to a point where they don't care. In essence, these individuals are unable to put themselves in their victims' shoes—so that they cannot appreciate the terror or pain that their victims experience. There is no 'behavior thermostat.' There is no feeling of empathy or remorse stopping them. They are quite capable of committing cold-blooded murder."

"Doctor, would a rapist have the same criminal profile as an armed robber?"

"Generally speaking, yes. The dynamics and pathology are quite similar."

Michaels struggled with his notebook flipping pages until he found his notes on confessions. "Doc, what about false confessions?"

"False confessions are consistently one of the leading, yet most misunderstood, causes of error in the American legal system and thus remain one of the most prejudicial sources of false evidence that lead to wrongful convictions."

With an inquiring expression on his face Michaels asked, "Why do people make a false confession?"

"There is no single cause of a false confession, and there is no single logic or type of false confession. Police are more likely to elicit false confessions under certain conditions of interrogation, however, individuals with certain personality traits and dispositions are more easily pressured into giving false confessions."

Michaels again shuffled through some pages of his notebook until he found what he was looking for, "Fifteen years ago, Marcus

Broadhead and Charles Holmes confessed, now Broadhead said they beat him and Holmes said they tricked him."

Dr. Chambers rubbed his chin, looked up at the ceiling and thought for a moment, "Look, there are three distinct types of false confessions; voluntary, coerced-compliant and persuaded. Most voluntary false confessions appear to result from an underlying psychological disturbance or psychiatric disorder. Individuals volunteer false confessions in the absence of police questioning for a variety of reasons: a desire for notoriety or fame, the need to expiate guilt over imagined or real acts, an inability to distinguish between fantasy and reality, or a pathological need for acceptance or self-punishment. But voluntary false confessions need not be rooted in psychological maladies. A person may, for example, provide a voluntary false confession out of a desire to aid and protect the real criminal, to provide an alibi for a different crime or to get revenge on another person."

"Well Broadhead confessed and testified against Lorenzo Holmes but he would not testify against his best friend Oscar Sampson."

"Yes, but didn't he also get leniency?"

"Yep, he did."

Dr. Chambers got a concerned expression on his face as he leaned forward, "Look, a compliant false confession is one given in response to police coercion, stress, or pressure to achieve some instrumental benefit—typically either to terminate and thus escape from an aversive interrogation process, to take advantage of a perceived suggestion or the promise of leniency, or to avoid an anticipated harsh punishment."

Dr. Chambers settled back in his chair, smiled and continued, "There are several reasons that suspects give compliant false confessions. In the pre-modern era of American interrogation, physical coercion, the so-called third degree, was the primary cause of such confessions. Innocent suspects knowingly falsely confessed to avoid or end physical assaults, torture sessions, and the like. In the modern era, psychological coercion is the primary source of compliant false confessions. Psychologically oriented interrogation techniques are just as capable of eliciting a compliant false confession as physical ones."

Michaels shrugged his shoulders and turned his hands outward and sardonically said, "Cops lie all the time. They trick people by walking another suspect past a person they are interrogating and say things like, 'the first one to talk gets the best deal.' Don't they?"

"Yes, that is common. Look! Detectives seek to persuade a suspect that he is indisputably caught and that the most viable way to mitigate his punishment and escape his otherwise hopeless situation is by confessing. Its been well documented, American police use interrogation techniques that are designed to convince a suspect that he is caught and that it is futile for him to deny the crime. They also use techniques that are designed to convince the suspect that it is in his or her interest to confess."

Michaels leaned forward and checked how much time he had left on his tape recorder and asked, "Is it illegal for cops to lie about no existing evidence?"

"Peter ... Promises and threats are neither standard nor legal; rather, they are regarded as coercive in both psychology and the law. It is not hard to understand why such threats and promises in combination with standard interrogation techniques, such as repeated accusations, attacks on a suspect's denials, lies about nonexistent evidence, pressure, and inducements, may cause a suspect to confess knowingly to a crime he did not commit. Put simply, the suspect comes to perceive that the benefit of confessing will outweigh the cost of denial."

Michaels sat up straight in his chair and slowly shook his head, "I guess I still find it hard to believe that someone would confess to a crime they know they didn't commit."

Chambers raised his eyebrows and continued, "You have to remember most of the time these defendants have been in a crime ridden environment all their lives, so although psychological coercive threats and promises may be the primary sources of compliant false confessions, they are not the only ones. Stress and police pressure are also causes. Custodial interrogation is inherently stressful, anxiety provoking and unpleasant."

Dr. Chambers shifted in his chair and leaned forward to give emphasis to his complicated and technical answer, "The interrogator's interpersonal style may also be a source of distress: he or she may be confrontational, insistent, demanding, hostile, overbearing, deceptive and manipulative. His accusatorial techniques are also designed to induce distress by attacking the suspect's self-confidence, by not permitting him to assert his innocence, and by causing him to feel powerless and trapped."

"It seems to me that these types of confessions normally take place over a long period of time," Michaels said rubbing his forehead as he tried to process it all.

"Typically these interrogations may span hours, as often occurs with compliant false confessions, weakening a suspect's resistance, inducing fatigue and heightening suggestibility. Facing an overbearing interrogator who refuses to take no for an answer, the suspect may reason that telling the interrogator what he wants to hear is the only way to escape."

Dr. Chambers stood up, "Do you want a cup of coffee?"

"Do you have any diet pop?"

"Water."

"Great."

Dr. Chambers handed Michaels a bottle of cold water and returned to his chair, "I only have a few more minutes. I have a patient coming in soon."

Michaels unscrewed the water bottle took a sip, turned on his tape recorder and asked, "Persuaded false confessions sound just like the term?"

"Yes, well kind of but it boils down to persistence. This gets a little complicated but persuaded false confessions typically unfold in three sequential steps. First, the interrogator causes the suspect to doubt his innocence. This is characteristically a by-product of an intense, lengthy, and deceptive accusatorial interrogation in which the interrogator repeatedly accusing the suspect of committing the crime, relentlessly attacking the suspect's denials and repeatedly confronting the suspect with fabricated evidence of his guilt. The innocent suspect thinks that his interrogators are genuinely mistaken but they wear him down. They won't listen to his denials and evidentially he gets convinced maybe he did commit the crime but he has no memory of it."

Michaels reached for his water and pointed his index finger to suggest he wanted to say something. Dr. Chambers smiled and nodded affirmatively with a look in his eyes that said, *Go ahead and ask your question.*

Michaels nodded "Do the interrogators supply the suspect with a plausible reason that suggests he committed the crime and can't remember it?"

"Exactly," Dr. Chambers said nodding his head. "They must supply him with a reason that satisfactorily explains how he could have done it without remembering it. This is the second step in the psychological process that leads to a persuaded false confession. Classically, the interrogator suggests one version or another of a 'repressed' memory theory. He or she may suggest, for example, that the suspect experienced an alcohol-or drug-induced blackout, a momentary lapse in consciousness, or perhaps most commonly, that the suspect simply repressed his memory of committing the crime because it was a traumatic experience for him."

Michaels interrupted again. "I still can't believe you can convinced someone they committed a crime like murder when they didn't. I still can't fathom it."

"The police are not going to grab just anyone off the streets and convince them they killed someone. No, that's just not realistic. If the suspect knew the victim or was somehow associated with the crime scene; something has to connect him to the crime for him to be a suspect in the first place. The suspect can only be persuaded to accept responsibility for the crime if he regards one of the interrogators' explanations for his alleged amnesia as plausible. Despite his lack of memory, once the suspect is over the line, he is ready for the third and final step in the making of a persuaded false confession: the construction of the post admission narrative."

Michaels was still shaking his head, perplexed but Dr. Chambers continued, "Once a suspect accepts responsibility for the crime, the interrogator pushes him to supply the details of how and why he did it. He may believe that if he thinks hard enough, searches his mind, he will somehow be able to remember it. Instead, the suspect either guesses or confabulates about how the crime could have occurred. He repeats the details that the police have suggested to him and knowingly makes up a story to fit the crime."

"Do these persuaded confessions happen a lot?"

"No ... persuaded false confessions appear to occur far less often than coerced-compliant false confessions. They also tend to occur primarily in high-profile murder cases. Once the accused is removed from that environment and its accusatory influences and pressures, the persuaded false confessor typically recants his confession. Some recant even before the interrogation terminates. Regardless, ordinary police interrogation is not strong enough to produce a permanent change in the suspect's beliefs."

"Doc ... I gotta tell you, this has been very enlightening, though confusing in a way."

"I know, Peter, the mind is a funny thing. That's what keeps me in business."

# CHAPTER 53

"Y ou got my money?"

Corley looked over to his partner Don Buerline and ASA Amy Wilson slightly shaking his head and thought *Judas*.

"Well it doesn't quite work that way, Reggie. Here, look this over," Corley said as he handed him the document. "It's a legal agreement. We will give you the money if we arrest and convict the people responsible for killing Ruth Lezkowski. We will need your cooperation as well."

The post-conviction team had already discussed that Reggie may have to wear a wire. They all thought it would be the final nail in the coffin if they could get the suspect on tape admitting to the murder.

"Yeah, dat be good by me."

"Sign here for the agreement and here is a consent form that we need so we can get your DNA."

Russell signed the forms, opened his mouth and Corley swabbed him and put it in an evidence bag. They got a hair sample and fingerprinted him.

ASA Amy Wilson was fidgety and anxious as she watched Reggie Russell clean the ink off his fingers. "Okay, Reggie, who killed her?"

Russell threw the hand-wipe into the wastebasket and ambled over to his chair and sat down. He leaned forward and placed his forearms on his thighs then lowered his head and sighed. After a thoughtful moment, he slowly lifted his head and looked directly at them with sad eyes. "One of them is my brother Douglas and the other guy is Clayton Cranston, his good friend. I wants you to know I was not there and I didn't have no part of this. When Douglas and Clayton saw those posters that was up, Douglas said, 'We did it. She was a hard bitch to kill.' You know, he say, 'we' so I know he was talking about the two of them because he pointed at Clayton when he said we."

"How do you know this Cranston?'

"We all worked together on the newspapers trucks as helpers. Douglas got me the job but I didn't work that long with em." Russell starting shaking his head and looked like he was about to cry, "That motherfucker got me hooked on drugs when I was just 14. It be hard for me to do this but it's been heavy on me all these years. I was scared at that time but I gotta do the right thang. You know what I'm saying?"

"Yeah, we know."

~~~~

Corley and the others were all smiles and couldn't stop talking about what a colossal break this was while they were driving back to the city. "I knew none of those early suspects did this. I spent a lot of time on airplanes. My gut just told me, all those people we interviewed didn't hesitate a second to be swabbed."

They dropped Wilson off at 26th and Cal and took the evidence bags to the crime lab. "Shit, we should have gotten two swabs from Reggie so we could get it Mito-typed."

Mitochondrial DNA testing is so sophisticated that you can analyze a microscopic speck. A millionth of a gram, molecular weight can produce positive results. Every cell has mitochondria that you inherit maternally. Siblings from the same mother will inherit the exact same mitochondrial DNA profile.

When they got back to the office Corley took Douglas and Buerline took Cranston and they started working up criminal profiles.

Douglas Russell was arrested 35 times during his criminal career, three of which were for aggravated criminal sexual assault and four for armed robbery. Corley printed multiple copies of his picture. Cold case detectives discovered that he lived in a basement apartment in the 1800 block of West 69th street and was immediately put under surveillance. He was positively identified three hours later leaving his apartment.

Clayton Cranston was arrested 30 times, once for criminal sexual assault and once for armed robbery. Most of his arrests were drug related. Crack ruined his life. The last time he was seen was in Joliet, detectives theorized he was probably homeless.

When they finished the background checks, they returned to Apple River. Reggie identified the photos of Douglas and Clayton. "How old do you reckon Clayton is?" Corley asked.

"I believe he be a little younger than my brother. I think around 40." Reggie's face lit up, "I just remembered when my brother was about 15 or 16 he beat the shit out of a girl; hurt her bad."

Corley just finished his background check and recalled his criminal history but not the teenage stuff because it doesn't appear on the adult record. "When was last time you saw your brother?"

"I saw him around Christmas or New Year's, I said to him, 'If your friend gets caught he may flip on your ass,' but Douglas said, 'I ain't worried about that shit.'"

"Well we may have to jog his memory and have you meet up with him soon. I need another sample of your salvia."

"Anything you need. When do I get my money?"

"After we convict Douglas and Clayton."

~~~~

Lt. Mark Leonard from the cold case squad had 30 detectives at his disposal. He had half his team hunting down Clayton Cranston or someone from his family. They already had Douglas Russell under surveillance and discovered within the first day that he was running a minor drug operation out of his basement apartment. He was not going anywhere.

Leonard was sitting at his desk in what looked like a meditative state when Corley walked in.

"Any news on Cranston?" Corley asked

"We found out he has been in and out of rehab numerous times. He's got a bad habit. Do you think Reggie will have a problem doing a sting on his brother before we pick him up?"

"He wants the money. He'll help us, I'm sure."

"I got a call from Peter Michaels. He's a little antsy about the arrangement you made with him."

Corley let out a little sigh and rubbed his chin, "I told him we would take care of him when the shit hit the fan. I would give him a little something more than anyone else had. We gotta take care him. If he does a story it will blow this entire thing."

"He won't. I told him he'll have plenty of lead-time. We'll figure something out."

# CHAPTER 54

D etective Don Buerline knew his partner was getting good news from the smile on his face. Corley hung up the phone, reached across the desk and high fived Buerline. "It's certain, Douglas Russell (the short one) is unknown male #1."

"That means Cranston (the tall one) has to be #2."

"Yep. They are absolutely certain that it's Reggie brother. The analytical results show a 99.9% probability that a full sibling of Russell is the source of the sperm found in the victim's panties."

"What about the mito-typing of the hair?"

"We'll get those results probably later today. I don't have a single doubt that one of those hair samples will show the same results. We got our guys!"

"Now all we have to do is find Cranston."

"We'll find him," Corley said as he reached for his phone to call ASA Amy Wilson.

"We got em."

Wilson jumped out of her chair and raised her arms like Rocky. "I'll call the boss and start the arrest warrants."

~~~~

Lt. Leonard put the phone in its cradle, gave a fist pump and reached for his Rolodex cards to look up the number of his counterpart at the FBI.

Bob King had been with the bureau for 20 years. He was a Rocky Marciano look-alike except he had light brown hair and a square chin. He loved working in Chicago. He investigated everything from the mob to bank thieves. There was a never-ending supply of crime.

"What's up Mark?"

"I need to borrow one of your safe houses for a wire. We positively identified the killers in the Lezkowski homicide. We'd like to see if he incriminates himself."

"I am sure that shouldn't be a problem. We have one set up down south near 55th Street. The video and audio is set up on the third floor with a flick of a switch. The furniture is clean but old. The neighborhood is bi-racial. Does that work for you?"

"That would be perfect. That's just about a mile from where our guy lives. It shouldn't be hard to get him over there."

"When do you think you'll need it?"

"A week or so."

"I'll get the paperwork started."

~~~~

Detectives Corley and Buerline were in their ugly green unmarked squad car driving to the 6100 block of Martin Luther King Drive. They found Clayton Cranston's mother.

Emma Blackwell was in her early sixties but she looked older and tired. Her eyes were empty. Her heart was broken. Her son was an addict. She didn't know how long he had abused drugs and she knew he was using again. He checked himself out of a rehab center run by Northwestern Hospital five months ago.

"I haven't seen him in … I don't know how long … maybe months. He's got a bad habit with drugs and he drinks a lot."

"I know. We are concerned for his safety," Corley lied. He could care less for this murderer. They just wanted to find him. "If he turns up in the morgue and we don't know who he is, he'll just be passed through as a John Doe. You'll never even know that he died."

"How can I help you?"

"Well, the best way to help is to give us a swab of saliva and we'll run a DNA sample."

She agreed and signed a consent form and Corley swabbed her gently twice and put the samples in evidence bags. "Do you know where Clayton is?"

"I haven't seen him in a long time. He could be homeless for all I know. He stayed in various places in the past. He did have a girlfriend."

"Do you know her name?"

"One of them was Shannae or Shanniqua Farnsworth, I think but I'm not really sure. If you find him tell him to come see his Momma."

"Sure," Buerline lied. *The only people he is going to see are fellow inmates, Corley thought.*

They took the swabs to the State Police Crime lab and fed-exed one of them to the mito-typing lab they used in Philadelphia. In a few days they would have their answer but they already knew it would come back positive.

~~~~

Reggie Russell checked out of Apple River and was escorted into the office of Lt. Mark Leonard in the Cold Case unit. Leonard's office was bland but it had one window. The walls that were once white are now scarred and dirty. "Wanted" posters were pinned to the wall to his right. Stacks of files filled his desktop. His black phone had 16 lines. Four of them were blinking.

"Have a seat. Want some coffee?"

"Yeah, that be cool. It's fucking cold outside."

Leonard didn't like the F word. He also didn't care much for Reggie Russell but he needed him. "I want you to call your brother and tell him you need to talk to him. Tell him your counselor has set you up in this house on 55th Street until you can find a permanent place to live."

"What about my wife and kids?"

"Tell him they'll be joining you in a couple of days."

Leonard got up and shut his office door and sat back down. He picked up his phone, silenced all the other lines and dialed Douglas Russell's number and handed the phone over to Reggie. On the third ring Douglas answered.

"Hey, brother what's up?"

"How you doing motherfucker?"

"I don't know, man, shit I need to talk to you I'm afraid some shit is happenin' and I don't want to get caught up in it."

"Whatchew talking about nigger?"

"Some people was askin' a bunch a questions while I was in rehab. I don't want any that shit I was involved in robbing those trains and shit back in the 80s. They made a number of us give sperm samples. I am worried about what could be coming back. You know what I'm sayin' man."

"Don't be talkin' on no motherfucking phone. I be by to see ya'll tomorrow."

"Yeah, you right bout that shit man. I'll see ya'll tomorrow."

"Well? What did he say?" Leonard asked.

"He say, he'll be by tomorrow."

"Did he say what time?"

"No. He be there probably in the afternoon fur sure. Dat motherfucker never do anything in the morning. I be sure of dat."

~~~~

The Chief Judge of the Cook County Criminal Division was sitting behind his modern desk in his chambers when detective Corley walked in with the affidavits for conventional overhears (wiretaps).

Judge Michael Hook had his black robe hanging on his light brown pine door. He was in shirtsleeves with his tie as always tight around his neck. Hook was a scholarly looking man. At five nine he was a little plump. He had a pleasant smile that ingratiated people around him. He loved his snacks and vodka. His white hair was neatly trimmed around his collar and his blue eyes studied everyone who came before him. His fellow judges elected him three times and he planned to retire as the Chief Judge.

His chambers were located on the first floor of 26th and Cal behind courtroom 101. The chamber itself was bland and boring. The ten-foot ceilings were adorn with new LED lights that kept the room bright. It was always very busy. Basically his office reviewed every case that flowed through the criminal courts. He had three law clerks, two secretaries and two administrative assistants. All of their offices connected to his.

He barely used his courtroom that was also big and modern and uninteresting. Surprisingly, Judge Hook held most of his proceedings at his desk. His decisions were quick, decisive and fair. He looked up over his Dollar Store reading glasses as Corley walked in.

"Do you guys finally have these bastards?"

"No doubt about it, your honor. DNA is a perfect match with Douglas Russell. I am sure we're going to have a perfect match with the second guy as well."

Judge Hook read the petitions for the wiretaps and signed them. Besides using the safe house, the team intended to wire the cell where they would place Russell and Cranston.

~~~~

Don Buerline and Amy Wilson were discussing the arrest warrants in her office. She was twirling her Blackhawk hockey puck in her fingers. "We have to get a BOLO out on this girlfriend of Cranston. I don't think he is living under Michigan Avenue."

"You're right about that. We have patrol going through every homeless camp under lower Wacker and they haven't found him. The girlfriend is our best shot. I'll call Lt. Leonard and get that started. We are going to get the results back shortly and I know he's the other guy."

"I don't have a single doubt about it. Make the call."

# CHAPTER 55

L t. Mark Leonard, Detectives Dick Corley and Don Buerline along with the CPD and the FBI's electronics guys were having a cup of coffee with Reggie Russell. They were going over the final details of the meeting with his brother. He had never been involved in a wiretap operation.

Three television monitors and two tape recorders were set up on a desk in the front bedroom of the house's third floor. The equipment was checked three times while they were giving final instructions to Russell. There was tension in the air although Reggie himself showed no signs of nervousness and that concerned the lieutenant.

"Don't be pushy on the Lezkowski case. Let it come out gradually. Don't make it the first topic of your conversation. You okay man?" Leonard asked

"Yeah, I be fine. Don't worry about me. I can handle this shit."

The safe house was a typical Chicago three flat that was 25 feet wide and 70 feet long. Three flats make up about 25% of Chicago's housing stock. Many are red brick or limestone with a cornice of stone decorating the roofline. They characteristically have a small entry porch to one side with a bay window. The grassy front yards are postage stamp size and five-foot gangways run between these closely spaced buildings. They generally have one bathroom whether they have two or three bedrooms. This safe house had three bedrooms.

Leonard stood to stretch when his phone rang "What's up?"

"He just came out of the apartment and he's heading to his car. I think he's on the way."

"That was the surveillance team. Game time. You ready Reggie?"

"Yeah, I'm cool."

Ten minutes later Douglas parked his car in the open spot made available by the investigative team. It was three cars away from the safe house's front porch. He rang the doorbell for the second floor apartment and Reggie buzzed him in. The electronics guy pushed record. Russell walked up the stairs and stomped his snow-covered feet in the hallway and blew warm air into his hands as he entered the room.

"It's motherfucking cold, man shit."

"You wanna cup of coffee man?"

"These motherfuckers takin' some good care of your black ass, boy."

Reggie handed his brother a cup of coffee with three sugars. "I be glad we didn't talk no more on the phone, yesterday. You were right, you know what I'm saying," Reggie said.

"Yeah, never knows whose listening on the fucking phone, man. What's up wit you?"

"The reason I'm askin' you that cause the bullshit, man. I had them robberies and shit, man, when I was fucking around in the 80s on the buses and shit on Ashland. And you know, you and me having the same fucking daddy and shit, can they fuck around and put some shit on me?"

Detective Corley was rolling his eyes and Lt. Leonard was shaking his head. They were trying to understand what seemed to be another language with fuck being the most used word in the Russell family's vocabulary. Leonard's ears were turning red. He was saying a few prayers under his breath.

"No. The only thing, man, if your sperm show up—come up in the old girl's pussy," Douglas replied.

"I'm sayin' my DNA; my DNA cause I never ain't never did no shit like that."

"You ain't got to if your sperm in the motherfucker and they come up with it then that's what you got. Your sperm is just like your face; only one motherfucker got that. That's you. That's how they see ya'll."

"You know, what I'm worried about, that shit you told me about you and Clayton."

"Clayton. Shit man."

All eyes immediately went to the television monitors. Leonard snapped his head and zeroed in on the picture in front of him. Corley and Buerline stood up, goose bumps on their arms. The moment of truth had arrived. Everyone was rigid.

"Cause if that shit come up, because you know we got it generically in our inheritance. What if that shit come up? What if I gotta take a lie detector test or something, man?" Reggie said.

"Lie detectors ain't shit, man. You can turn them down any motherfucking way. Whether you take a lie detector test or not, they still gonna charge you," Douglas responded.

"Charge me with what, fucking murder? What if they try to hook me up with-with-with that white bitch, man?"

"No, if they try to hook you up with that white bitch then … they'll come at you with six years. Then you're gonna have to do three years and you can't beat it."

"That's why I asked you about Clayton. What if he get catched on something."

"Man. I'm going tell you something. That shit was so far back, I don't think they still have it, his sperm sample. And if they do, fuck him. If they do, I mean—cause that nigger like this here man. Whoa, whoa he fittin' to go. He fittin' to go out like that."

"The only thing I be worried about is the sperm shit. But, you say I don't have to take no lie detector test?"

"No. The sperm shit gonna get you. It's gotta be mixed. I mean two motherfuckers fucking. It's gotta be mixed. It's going to be hard, you know with that shit all mixed and shit. You know what I am saying. If that motherfucker all mixed, then they really got no case cause it's mixed."

Bingo. They all smiled. This asshole thinks that DNA can't be separated if sperm is mixed. Before Clayton Cranston's DNA came back, they knew who their second guy was. Just then something miraculous happened. Peter Michaels came on the air with a report on the Lezkowski Four filing a civil lawsuit for their wrongful convictions. The volume on the television was low, almost muted, while they were talking so Reggie stood and turned it up.

After watching the report, Reggie said, "See there, man. That's what the fuck I was trying tell your ass. Those boys who were convicted of that murder they got off."

"They gotta pay those motherfuckers."

"That's why I was worried about that sperm shit, man."

"Your sperm is different than everybody's. That shit different. You ain't have to worry about that white bitch. But every motherfucker sperm be different. That's why we all had different kids and shit."

~~~~

Corley and Buerline wanted to run down the stairs and pinch Douglas Russell at that moment but Lt. Leonard stopped them. "We are not going to arrest him until we find Cranston. I want to get them at the same time."

"Have they found Cranston yet?" Corley asked.

"No. We're getting close but not yet."

"Well that couldn't have gone any better. It looks like they didn't know the original Lezkowski Four," Buerline offered.

"Yeah, looks that way. I know a lot of the guys that worked the original case. They were all very good detectives. They still feel that those four were at that crime scene. I'm not saying they didn't trick those kids but I know Evans and Scholl, God rest his soul. I know one thing for certain, they didn't beat those kids up," Leonard said.

Lee Scholl had a massive heart attack two weeks after he retired. He was honored at the Police Department's Recognition ceremony held last month.

"Chief Maurer would have transferred them to the moon if they screwed that case up. He still firmly believes those kids were there in some capacity."

"Aguilera is really going after all of them. It's going to be interesting," Corley said.

~~~~

Michaels walked into Ron Magers office with a look of concern on his face. "I am starting to think about retiring. I don't know, this business is changing and I am still wondering about my decision to cooperate with the police."

"It's a thin line but I know you have done it before and it worked out for you. You talked it over with Phil, right?" Magers asked.

"Yeah, I know. I don't think Corley will screw me. I believe it was the right thing to do. I'd love to see closure for the Lezkowski family. I would hate for these guys to get away."

"Well at least those kids got off."

"I don't know after reading the recantation of Broadhead. I just don't believe that happened. He needed to do that because he is part of that civil lawsuit. He couldn't keep the confession out there. What he said those cops did to him was outrageous. I don't believe for a second that he was beaten like that.

"You might be the only person in this newsroom that feels that way."

"I know. There is no question that the DNA didn't match the original four but it also doesn't prove they weren't there. Corley told me that they got the guys. They just haven't rounded them up yet. I am going to start writing the story and fill in the blanks. It's going to happen real soon," Michaels predicted.

# CHAPTER 56

D etectives Dick Corley and Don Buerline left Homan Square heading to the Northwest side of Chicago after a team of cold case detectives found Clayton Cranston. His girlfriend Shanniqua Farnsworth had a short arrest record for minor drug charges. Her address hadn't changed in the last five years but Cranston had only been living with her for a few months.

Her six flat building had been neglected for decades. Suburban slum landlords didn't spend a lot of money for heat, water pipes or tuck-pointing on their depressed Chicago area properties. The building had a single entrance. The two concrete steps leading to the front door were disintegrating from age and years of winter salt. A three-story hallway with worn thick wooden stairs connected each of the flats. The apartments' doors were tired and warped. They were barely connected to the hinges that kept them upright in their frames.

Corley knocked on the door that displayed 2 0, the three fell off long before Shanniqua moved there in 1998. "Chicago Police open up."

Two wide brown eyes peered through a slight opening a minute later "What's dis bout?" she managed to say in a frightened voice.

Corley flashed his star that was displayed in a black leather carrying case about the size of a large wallet "We need to talk to Clayton Cranston. Is he here?"

"Sure is," Shanniqua said timidly as she opened the door to let them into her unhappy living room. The daylight that was left outside had a hard time finding its way through the dirt streaked windows that hadn't been cleaned for a decade. The shades were torn and half drawn. Corley thought *inoperable*. The walls were filthy and mold smothered the darken corner furthest away from the front window. The furniture was sparse and mismatched but a 65-inch color Samsung television hung on the wall directly in front of the musty, old and faded lavender couch. The picture was clear and bright as Ron Magers delivered the five o'clock news.

Corley smiled, *almost an inside joke*, he thought. Just then Clayton Cranston entered the room. He was six foot seven and thin. His ear lobes were about the same size as the top of his ears, odd looking. Corley noticed the white gym shoes he was wearing immediately and guessed *size 13 or 14*. Cranston's hair was closely cut and receding, revealing a very high forehead. He was wearing a thick black and white plaid flannel shirt with a gray tee shirt underneath. His blue jeans hung on his boney frame. His skin had an anomalous tone, light olive green. *Cancer* Corley thought.

"What's dis about?"

"We need your help with an old murder case we're working on," Corley lied.

"Don't know no nuttin' about no murder, man."

"Well, we think it may involve someone in your family," Buerline said. "We need you to come downtown with us. We have some questions."

"I ain't fucking goin' nowheres," Cranston said as he started to back away.

"Listen Clayton, you can do this the easy way or the hard way. You are coming downtown with us."

"Man. Shit. I didn't do nuttin'."

"We believe you," Buerline lied. "Come on grab your coat. It's cold outside."

Cranston walked back to the bedroom and put on his thick black winter coat and followed Buerline out the door. Corley walked behind them with his hand ready to reach for his Glock.

It was February 4th, 2002. The tall one was the first to be arrested.

~~~~

Lt. Mark Leonard was reading a report of the mitochondrial DNA analysis of Clayton Cranston's mother. It was a 99.25% familial match to her son. Cranston was positively identified as unknown male #2. Leonard put the report down when his phone rang.

"Where do you want us to take Cranston?" Corley asked.

"Did he say anything yet?"

"Not a word, other than I don't know shit."

"Take him to Area Four and put him in a room and let him stew for a couple of hours. The techs are still wiring cell three for video and audio." Leonard said. "Get him printed as soon as you get there and get his prints over to the lab."

"He's being printed and photographed while we speak. When will Reggie be over there?"

"He's with me now. I will go over everything with him and send him over there. Bring him in the back door."

"Is the plan still the same?"

"Yep, we'll go at him in about three hours. If he doesn't talk, we'll take him to cell block three."

~~~~

Clayton Cranston was mumbling to himself when detectives Corley and Buerline entered Interrogation Room One. He was thinking *what do they know?*

Sticking to the prearranged plan, Corley asked, "Do you know why you are here Clayton?

"I don'ts know a fuckin' thing, man. This is bullshit."

Corley read him his Constitutional rights and then asked, "What do you know about that white woman who was killed up by the tracks near the Alba Homes back in 1986?"

"I don't know what the fuck ya'll talking bout. I don't know nuttin' bout that, Man come on, man. That be a long time ago, shit."

"Come on Clayton. We know you know something about that. It's better that you tell us now what you know."

"I told ya'll. I don't know shit. I have no idea why ya'll brought me here. I haven't been feelin' no good for a while. You know what I'm sayin'?" Cranston said, as he slouched down in his uncomfortable chair, stretching out his long legs and crossing his feet.

"We're not a 100 percent sure yet but we got some biological evidence that we are testing," Buerline said. "We'll know more for sure in a few days."

Cranston pulled his feet in and he immediately sat up. "What's you talkin' bout? Evidence? Evidence bout what?"

Corley leaned over the table almost in his face with his two fists on the table. He could smell Cranston's foul breath and with a mordant look on his face, he said, "We know it was someone in your family. We are not sure who yet," Corley lied. "If it turns out to be you it would be better that you tell us now rather than later."

"I don't know a fuckin' thang bout that shit, man."

"Stand up," Buerline ordered.

An astonished look flashed across Cranston's face and he hesitated. "Where you takin' me?

"Jail," retorted Corley. "Now standup shithead."

Cranston didn't want to stand up but he slowly got to his feet. He now had a flabbergasted look as Corley said, "Put your hands behind your back." Corley reached up and gripped his left shoulder firmly and authoritatively and slowly walked behind Cranston holding his left wrist. He reached behind his back and pulled his handcuffs from its holster and slapped them hard across Cranston's wrist and tightened them. "Let's go," Corley said as he led him out of the room.

A dozen detectives sitting at their desks in the open squad room looked up as the door opened and Cranston was led out. They all had simpers on their faces, as Corley moved him through the area, and down the back stairs to the cellblock that was already wired for video and sound.

~~~~

ASA Amy Wilson was sitting at her desk talking to Lt. Mark Leonard. "What's next?" she asked.

"We're putting Cranston in the wired cell. We are bringing in Reggie Russell to set him up. We are certain he's going to give it up."

"When are you pinching Douglas?"

"As soon as Cranston says he did it. We have him under 24-hour surveillance. He's not going anywhere. As soon as we pinch him, we'll bring in his girlfriend and see what she has to say."

"I want to do the statements. I want to look these bastards straight in the eyes. I want to see it for myself so I can tell Mrs. Lezkowski that we've got the right ones. I feel just awful for all that she has gone through."

"This will move rapidly once Cranston admits he did it. It will be like that," Leonard said with the snap of his fingers.

~~~~

Clayton Cranston was sitting on a dull battered steel bench with his forearms on his thighs and his head hanging low between his knees when the sound of a key in the lock of the cellblock door startled him and brought him back to consciousness. His eyes were drooping and tired. All he saw was a silhouette of a man as a uniformed police officer opened the gray barred door and led Reggie Russell in, "They'll be coming for your sorry ass in a little while."

Cranston got a dumbfounded look on his face once his blurry vision cleared and he saw the familiar face of a man he hadn't seen in over ten years.

"Whatcha doin' in here nigger?"

"The police they, they just caught me up and said I had somethang to do with that murder up on those tracks back in the 80s. Fuck man, I didn't have nuttin' to do with that shit man."

Cranston got up and went to the cell's bars and put his face as close as he could to explore up and down the cellblock to see if anyone was lurking. Once satisfied he turned and walked within an arm's length in front of Russell and asked, "What they fuckin' tell you, man?"

Reggie following the plan laid out to him by Lt. Leonard put a worried look on his face, started rubbing his forehead and paced around for effect. "They says they got some fucking evidence test or some shit that they're waitin' for and they says they be sure it will come back to me or somebody in my inheritance. You know what I'm sayin."

All eyes in the office where the recording equipment was set up turned to the monitor sitting on top of the lone desk in the room. It was a black and white wide shot of the cell. They could not remotely zoom in on Cranston's face. They didn't have to. Russell positioned himself exactly where he was told to stand. Cranston got an apprehensive look on his face. He pursed his lips and said, "Shit, motherfucker, you gots nuttin' to worry about man. You weren't there. Have you talked to your brother? Have you seen that motherfucker? What's he sayin?"

"Yeah, I talked to that nigger two days ago. He be sayin' if dat sperm shit is mixed they ain't got shit, he say that shit be old and mixed and shit. He say when two motherfuckers be fucking that shit gets all mixed up and when its old, he say they can't separate it. You know what I'm sayin."

"Yeah, they told me they was runnin' some kinda fuckin' tests too. You weren't there. You gots nuttin' to worry bout. We was. Fuck man."

With that Lt. Leonard smiled and thought *Gotcha*. Then he gave the order to place him under arrest for the murder of Ruth Lezkowski. Detective Dick Corley's heart was pumping fast but he was also smiling. He made hundreds of arrests during his career but this one would be the most unforgettable. *This guy has no way out*, he thought.

Reggie Russell was standing with his back against the cellblock bars and Clayton Cranston was sitting with his head between his lanky legs shaking his head back and forth when Corley and Buerline walked in smiling. Corley walked up to him put his hands on his knees, got directly in his face and read him his Constitutional rights. "Get up," he commanded and at the same time Buerline pulled Cranston's hands behind his back not hard but with authority and cuffed him. They then led him back to Interrogation Room One.

As they were walking away, Cranston looked back over his shoulder and noticed that Reggie Russell was going in the opposite direction with the same police officer that had brought him to the cell. They were laughing and Reggie wasn't cuffed. Cranston realized what had just happened and said to himself, *I'm fucked.*

# CHAPTER 57

C layton Cranston was slouched in his steel gray chair with his right arm draped over the back of it, his legs were stretched out with his feet crossed. He reeked because he hadn't washed in at least 36 hours. That's how long he was in police custody. His breath ponged from eating McDonald's and drinking coffee with three spoons of sugar.

As ASA Amy Wilson walked into the interrogation room Cranston's droopy eyes started to focus. Was a movie star sitting down in front of me? He asked himself. *Who is this fine looking bitch?*

The interrogation rooms at Homan Square were different from those at the Area Headquarters. These rooms were 12 by 12. The paint was still fairly fresh and clean. The fluorescent lights didn't strain to brighten the room. The three military style desks were in a tee shape configuration.

Cranston sat at the center of the adjoining desks. Wilson was on his left and Detective Dick Corley on his right. The stenographer sat behind Wilson and the police videographer was directly in front of him.

As Wilson sat down she lowered her purse to the floor and gagged. The stench emanating from Cranston was revolting. It almost made her sick to her stomach. She felt nauseous. The heat in the room didn't help the odiferous warm air.

Sweat appeared on Cranston's upper lip just above his Errol Flynn type mustache that adorned it. His nerves were taking hold of him and he tried to stop his hands from trembling by interlacing his fingers as if in casual prayer. He was oleaginous with detectives Corley and Buerline just two hours before as he admitted his part in the Ruth Lezkowski homicide. He was very obliging, pointing the finger at Douglas Russell as Lezkowski's killer.

"Clayton Cranston, I talked to you earlier and you told me about the murder of Ruth Lezkowski. At that time you said in summary that you and Douglas Russell back in October of 1986 forced a woman into her car and took her to an area near the railroad tracks. And both you and Douglas Russell forced her to have sex and Douglas Russell hit her in the face with a brick. Is that correct?" asked Amy Wilson.

"Yes."

"I am going to read you your Constitutional rights again."

~~~~

Lt. Mark Leonard had just returned from Police Headquarters where he met with the Chief of Detectives Phil Cline. Cline always thought outside of the box. He approved the CI money to get Reggie Russell to cooperate with the police.

Cline was sitting behind his desk in shirtsleeves. He had a pile of files on the left side of his desk. His desktop calendar was filled with notations and reminders of all his meetings. Being the Chief of Detectives was a 24-hour a day job and Cline loved it.

"Look Mark, we've never tried this in a homicide case before but I want you to get these mutts to do a videotaped walk through of the actual crime."

"You mean like a re-enactment?"

"Exactly, the defense strategy will certainly be that we charged the wrong guys the first time around why should the jury believe beyond a reasonable doubt that these guys are guilty."

"Boss, we got all the DNA. I am sure that palm print is going to come back to one of them."

"The DNA proves they raped her. Cranston is already pointing the finger at Russell to get the murder off his back. These mutts will do anything they can to help themselves. Go talk to them. If they don't agree I'll buy you lunch at Tuscany's."

~~~~

Leonard walked into the room with a two-way mirror. Detective Don Buerline was sitting there watching and listening to Cranston's statement when he looked up to see Leonard enter.

"What's up?"

"Go get Russell. Forbes is on him at his apartment, take him with you. Make sure there is no way out the back. Get him over here and put him in three."

Buerline shot to his feet with a smile on his face "You got it boss."

Leonard took the empty seat and watched as Wilson methodically walked Cranston through the abduction up to the point where they got to the desolated area.

"What was the girl doing?"

"She was sitting there still shivering and crying, you know. And then I told her, 'You know, everything will be okay.' She said, 'I'll do whatever you want me to just, you know, don't hurt me.' And Douglas said, 'Well, okay, we're going to have a little party, you know.'"

"Did you know what Douglas meant?"

"Yes, I did."

"What was that?"

"He said, we're gonna have sex with her then let her go."

"Now when Douglas said, 'we're going to have a little party,' what happened?"

"She said, I'll do whatever he say. Just don't hurt me, you know. And then after she said that, Douglas said, 'Well you in the back, you go first.' And I proceeded to unzip my trousers and took her pants off."

Wilson tensed and her nerves tightened. She took a deep breath ... slowly exhaled and continued, "How did you take her pants off?"

"Just pulled them down, that's it. She had on like stretch pants, something like stretch pants."

"And were you still seated in the back in the seat?"

"Yes. Then she got on top of me and I had sex with her."

Wilson hated to ask some of these questions but they had to get everything right this time. No mistakes. "When you say you had sex with her, what do you mean by that exactly, Clayton?"

"I had intercourse with her. I, you know, I put my dick in her pussy and had sex with her. She sat on top of me facing me."

"Were you up against the seats at all with her facing you?"

"I was sitting back. The front seat slides up. I pushed it all the way to the dash. That what gave me room."

"What was she doing while you were having sex with her?"

"She was just sitting there with her eyes closed, still shivering."

Wilson closed her eyes trying to picture the incredible scene of this poor woman being brutally raped and this demon sitting in front her thought nothing of it. He was phlegmatic. He explained it like he was putting a cigarette out in a filthy ashtray. She inhaled as the intensity of the moment ebbed. "Could you see if she was crying or not?" She wanted to add *You fucking bastard.*

"Well, shivering, she had a few tears coming out of her eyes, you know."

The answer sent chills down Wilson's spine and she managed the next question without hesitation, "Did she say anything?"

"No, she didn't."

"Did you come when you had sex with her?"

"Yeah."

Wilson once again closed her eyes looking for strength. She shook her head ever so slightly, looked up and asked, "What happened after you came having sex with this woman?"

"I grabbed a hold of my shirt and her's and just wiped myself off."

Wilson cringed and tenderly bit the inside of her cheek, "When you say, wiped yourself off, where did you wipe?"

"I wiped my penis off. And when I wiped my penis off, I like pushed her over to the side here and I zipped my pants thing up and I proceeded out of the car on the right hand passenger side. And then Douglas got in the back with her."

Wilson was disgusted by the nonchalant matter of fact answer and continued, "Was she still undressed?"

"Yeah."

"Then what happened?"

"He got in the back of the car and got on top of her and had her legs up in the air."

"Could you hear anything from where you were at?"

"Yeah. I hear her start hollering and screaming saying, 'it hurts, you know, stop.' And he was hurting her and he was in there quite a long time."

"And you could see her legs?"

"Yeah like touching the ceiling."

"At some point did you hear her stop hollering?"

"No. Through the whole thing she was hollering 'it hurt.'"

Wilson closed her eyes and shook her head trying to gather her thoughts. Her stomach started to ache. "Then what happened?"

"Then they—it was over. And he got dressed, she got dressed. And they got back in the front seat of the car."

"Then what happened?"

"Well, he was up there talking, he told her to, give that to him. And she reached and had—it was money because I—the motive was to rob, you know."

"What did she say when she handed over the money?" Wilson asked.

"She said, 'Okay, I did my part' this and that, you know, 'let me go.' And I guess he had changed his mind then she reached and grabbed him or either scratched him. And he, 'you bitch,' you know. And the next thing I noticed the car door opened and he reached down and grabbed an object. It looked like a stone, a brick, you know."

"How big was that object, the stone or brick?"

"It was pretty big size cause I could see it hanging out his hand. And he was holding her with his right hand and he took his left hand and just smacked her in the face with the stone."

Wilson gritted her teeth and she asked, "Did you hear that when he smacked her in the face?"

"Yeah, I heard it. Then I came up to the car and said, Man, what are you doing? You know, I said, you crazy or what? He was like, Man, 'fuck you. Look what she did to my face.'"

"Could you see the young woman then after she got hit in the face with the stone?"

"I seen blood coming all down."

"Could you see where the blood was coming from?"

"No. Not exactly. Her whole face, like her whole face had been busted." Cranston looked down at his hands and shook his head. It was the first time he showed any emotion through the interview.

"When you heard this, tell me, what did it sound like?"

Still looking down at his hands, he continued, "It sounded pretty loud cause I heard—it sound like something hitting a wall or something, you know. It was pretty loud."

"What did she do after she was hit in the face?"

"She was crying. She had her hand up like this." Cranston leaned back slightly and demonstrated turning his head to the side and putting his right hand up like warding off another hit. "Like she trying to protect herself. And I asked him, I said, 'Man, what are you fucking crazy?' I said, 'Man, I'm not fitting, I'm not fitting to be part of this here.' And then he's like, 'Fuck you, man.' And then when he said that, I just got scared and nervous and I, I started going down the hill."

"Now, when you left him," she began to ask and Cranston interrupted the question, his nerves where on edge and he said, "I heard her steady hollering and screaming. I started walking faster. I don't know if he hit her again or what. I didn't see it. I just tried to get away from there."

"Who did you recognize to be hollering and screaming?"

"She was screaming and crying and he was hollering, telling her to shut—shut the hell up."

When Wilson was satisfied that she covered all of the relative points of the investigation and documented all the semen evidence on Lezkowski's clothing, she asked, "Has anyone forced you in any way at all, Clayton, to give this statement?"

"No. I'm doing it on my own free will. Free, to free my conscience."

*You have no conscience,* Wilson thought.

~~~~

Detective Ed Forbes was sitting in a battered dirty old undercover car that everyone knew belonged to the police. It was parked four doors down from Douglas Russell's front door. He had a clear view of his basement apartment. The car's heater was cranked up and working hard to keep him warm but it barely kept pace with the freezing temperature on this fifth day of February 2002. Forbes had a pair of winter rubber boots over his shoes but his feet were still cold.

Don Buerline slid into the passenger seat rubbing his hands, "Fuck its cold out there."

"No shit. I have been sitting here for three hours. My coffee got cold before I had a chance to take the lid off. I don't think this prick gets up until noon."

"Well let's go give him a wakeup call. Lou wants him at Homan ASAP. I'll take the front. You go around back and make sure he doesn't rabbit."

They both exited the car and pulled their stocking caps over their ears. Buerline signaled Forbes to go around back and 15 seconds later pounded on the front door with his fist. "Chicago Police ... open up."

A woman with shadowy eyes cracked the door open about six inches, "What's dis bout?"

Buerline flashed his star and asked, "Is Douglas Russell here?"

Douglas Russell was there when Buerline knocked but he was pulling on his thick winter coat as he tried to exit the back door. Detective Forbes greeted him with his Glock pointed directly at the middle of his forehead.

"Mornin' Douglas. Going somewhere?" Forbes asked smiling. "You're under arrest for the murder of Ruth Lezkowski. Put your hands behind your back."

He shrugged his shoulders, "Fuck man."

~~~~

Lt. Leonard walked into the interrogation room and shook hands with ASA Wilson, then walked over to Cranston and said, "We would like you to do a crime walk through this afternoon."

"What's dat?" he asked.

"Whoa. What are you talking about lieutenant? Walk through!" Wilson interrupted.

"Just so we get everything straight. I would like Cranston to go through the crime on the street and tell us in his own words what happened that night. We are going to videotape it. Think you can do that Clayton? It's for your own good because your buddy already agreed to it," Leonard lied.

"I don't think my boss is going to like this. I've got to check with him." Wilson said.

"You go ahead and check. We're the police and Chief Cline wants to do this to make sure we seal everything up nice and tight. So, we are going to do it. One of your guys can go with us but we're doing it." Leonard was standing his ground defiantly. Cline already got the videographer lined up to shoot it.

Wilson was already dialing her boss Peter Di Donato. She handed the phone to Leonard "Hey Pete! What's up?"

"You want to do fucking what?"

"I am going to take Cranston to the scenes of the crime and have him re-enact what actually happened and document it on video tape."

"Are you nuts?"

"No. We think it will actually help the case. If you want, to have someone there to monitor it, that's fine with us. If they want to ask any questions that's fine too. Cranston has agreed to do it and I am sure Russell will too."

"Let me talk to Amy."

Leonard handed the phone back to Wilson. She took it, turned and walked a few feet away and said, "It's really not a bad idea. I'll go with them and monitor it. I've worked with these guys before. They know what they're doing. I won't let anything interfere with our case."

Wilson turned to Leonard and asked, "When are we doing this?"

"We'll meet in my office at 2:30 to strategize then go to Roosevelt Road where it all started."

# CHAPTER 58

P olice Officer Jan Kuzniar had been on the job for 12 years. She loved being the police. For the last five years she had been assigned to a very active gang unit on the Southside. Every young cop on the Chicago Police Department wanted to be assigned to gangs, narcotics or a tactical team. That's where all the action is every single day. High speed chases, busting down doors, drive by shootings. Adrenalin constantly flows. As a Gang Specialist, Kuzniar saw her share of dead bodies, stinkers, floaters and burn victims. Like many police officers they see so much mayhem, brutality and death that they learn how to compartmentalize it. Kuzniar was no different. She was surprised when Lt. Mark Leonard called and asked her to be at his office at 2:30 for a special assignment.

"What's up?"

"We're going to do a walkthrough demonstration on a murder investigation. I'll explain when you get here. What kind of car do you drive?"

"I have a Nissan sedan. Why?"

"That's perfect for our demonstration. See you at 2:30. Don't be late. Bring your car."

~~~~

Detective Dick Corley walked out of the cold case office, looked over his shoulder, flipped opened his cell phone and dialed a familiar number.

"News ... Michaels."

"It's me, Corley."

"Hey Jethro. Give me some good news."

"We got them. They're both in custody. DNA's a perfect match."

"Names?"

"Not yet. Tomorrow night at six, you can go with it. I'll fill you in. By ten o'clock the shit will hit the fan."

Michaels shot to his feet and started pacing with his desk phone pressed hard to his ear, "Fuck Jethro! This just isn't right. I held off, man."

Corley rubbed his forehead with an aggrieved look on his face, "I know but listen to me. We are going to do a walkthrough demonstration of the murder around four o'clock this afternoon. Get a crew and be at Roosevelt and Racine. You'll see all the activity. You can shoot it from a distance but don't let anyone see you. If you do, it'll fuck up everything. We have never done this video stuff before but Lt. Leonard convinced the state's attorney that it would augment the case."

Michaels was now bending over his desk writing in his notebook as Corley continued, "We'll do the same thing tomorrow but you'll have video already so you can put together your story. You'll have your exclusive with video but you didn't hear any of this from me."

Michaels started to grin but then turned serious, "You know I would never give you up, Jethro."

"Oh, by the way, you remember Apple River where you interviewed Reggie?"

"Yeah. What about it?" Michaels started to pace again and he knew Corley had a grin on his face. He was going to deliver on his promise of another exclusive story.

"The feds are hitting it next week. They found a fraudulent billing scam for care not given and falsifying reports. They're probably going to close them down within a couple of weeks."

"Thanks, man."

"So now are you happy? You'll have two exclusives and you should write the part you played in all of this in your stories. Thanks for trusting me, Pete. I'll get back to you tomorrow."

Journalist say they don't make deals with sources in ethics seminars but Michaels knew that was bullshit. It doesn't happen often but reporters will agree to hold off on a story if it's going to pay off for them. Michaels didn't want to delay the story of finding Reggie

Russell but he also knew that putting the story on the air could put two rapist/killers in the wind. *I did the right thing,* Michaels thought.

~~~~

Jose Aguilera had Lorenzo and Charles Holmes along with Oscar Sampson in his office outlining a series of speaking engagements for them. He wanted them to go out to high schools and talk to students from Western Springs, Hinsdale and Elmhurst in the western suburbs.

"Why you want us to go out there and not in the city?" asked Lorenzo.

"Quite honestly, for a few reasons but most of all, these students are from affluent areas and they will be America's future leaders. It will make a big impression on them and their thoughts down the line on how the police and prosecutors operate and I think the publicity would be good for our lawsuit."

All three shook their heads affirmatively in unison. Oscar Sampson was becoming more serious about his future and wanted to become a paralegal at some point. He asked, "How are the lawsuits going?"

Aguilera got up from his chair and started to walk behind his desk, "I am setting up depositions now for the three of you. That's another reason I wanted you guys in here. My assistant will start prepping you on your responses and body language."

"How long will that take?" asked Charles.

"No more than a day for each of you but if we need more time we'll do whatever we have to do," Aguilera said.

~~~~

Jan Kuzniar arrived a half hour early and walked over to the coffee pot, dropped a quarter in the Folgers can and poured herself a cup of hot black coffee. She noticed an odd looking tall man sitting in a conference room. *He has funny looking ears,* she thought.

The way he was buried deep in the couch made his legs look too long for his torso. His plaid shirt was unbuttoned and his sleeves were rolled up revealing a tattoo on his right arm that spelled out the name BO. His left arm had a tattoo that looked like three hearts with some names inscribed.

"Who's that?" she asked as she entered Leonard's office and took a seat in front of his desk.

"That's Clayton Cranston. We got him for the Lezkowski homicide."

"Why am I here?"

"Jan. You are basically the same size and weight as Ruth. We are going to do a re-creation of the murder. We are going to videotape it as he demonstrates what they did. You are going to become Ruth. Can you do that?"

Kuzniar got an apprehensive look on her face "I'm sure I can handle it."

Leonard was rolling a pen in his fingers staring straight at her, "He's going to grab you and push you and lay on top of you. You okay with that?"

Holding her coffee cup with both hands, she closed her eyes and thought about this assignment and asked, "How long will all this take?"

"No more than an hour."

"I'll be fine."

~~~~

Detectives Dick Corley and Don Buerline were in Interrogation Room Three with Douglas Russell. He sat at the end of the table with an uneasy look on his face.

"What da fuck dis bout man?"

"Dis about your jizz, Douglas, your sperm, the sperm that matches the sperm on the clothing of Ruth Lezkowski. You know the stuff you told your brother that was too old and to mixed up that we couldn't separate it, asshole?" Corley growled leaning forward for emphasis just inches from his face staring at him with an angry look. "Well we separated it and guess who it belongs to? You! You and your old buddy Clayton Cranston."

Russell was sweating, and reeked of body odor so bad that Buerline sprayed the room with air freshener. He had a black turtleneck on underneath a heavy white sweater with a decorative five-inch black line that encircled the chest area. His long, shiny, greasy hair was now closely trimmed to his head and beads of sweat were starting to form at his hairline. His right eye began to twitch drawing attention to a large scar that was a reminder of a gang fight from 30 years before.

"Cranston told us you killed her."

"Fuck dat nigger, man. He'd the one. He said he be on parole and he wasn't going back to the joint cause of this bitch," Russell blurted out.

Corley turned his head ever so slightly towards Buerline. They both had that knowing grin that they had Russell by the balls and he was going to prison for the murder of Ruth Lezkowski.

~~~~

The late afternoon sun melted some of the snow that was piled on Roosevelt Road but now the temperature was dropping to the mid-twenties and the damp sidewalks had a way of making your toes feel frostbit.

The tops of Lt. Mark Leonard's ears were red and numb. He refused to wear a hat but he did have on a heavy jacket and an Aran Isle Irish sweater. His hands were covered with fur lined leather gloves.

Jan Kuzniar had on a heavy brown corduroy jacket that fell six inches below her waist. Her Patagonia long underwear clung to her skin keeping her warm and comfortable. Woolen socks and her police issued boots protected her feet from the damp cold ground.

Clayton Cranston wore the same plaid shirt and the tan barn jacket with a dark brown corduroy collar he was arrested in. He had on gym shoes and thin dirty white socks. His baggy jeans were sliding down to the crack of his ass and he was shivering.

No one cared or gave it a second thought. No one bothered to ask if he was cold. They just wanted to get this over with.

~~~~

Paul Nagaro and Peter Michaels were across the street in the station's cream-colored undercover van with tinted windows that allowed him to shoot video without affecting his picture quality, but dark enough that no one could see inside. The heater kept them very comfortable.

Nagaro had his camera mounted on a modified tripod that permitted him to pan in any direction the action led him. He instinctively fired up his camera as soon as he saw the police cars and a tan Nissan pull up to the corner.

"Game time," Nagaro proclaimed.

Lt. Leonard was the first one out of the police van. He slid the side door open so Clayton Cranston could step out into the cold air. The first thing he did was spit phlegm onto the sidewalk.

*What a disgusting pig* thought Kuzniar as she walked over to the police cameraman.

Amy Wilson emerged from her sporty red mustang. A woolen hat was stretched over her blonde hair. Her heavy winter coat and boots kept the weather from penetrating her skin. Her concentration was focused on this new video procedure and that took her mind off of the cold temperature that engulfed her.

The police videographer placed his old Sony camera on an antiqued wooden tripod, plugged in a microphone and wired up Lt. Leonard who began his spiel that would be the same at every stop. He stated the date and time. Then he Introduced Clayton Cranston and asked if he were giving this statement on his own free will and asked him, "What happened at this location?"

As Cranston started, you could see his breath in the cold air. "This is where we's started. We was lookin' for some more drug money. We be roaming this area for a long time but we was getting nuttin'. We had some crack and a happy stick earlier but our shit was wearing down. You know what I'm saying? We wasn't scoring so we decided to go in that direction," he indicated with a hand gesture towards Flourney Street where Ruth Lezkowski lived.

Lt. Leonard did the legal disclosure that he was not coerced in any way to give this statement and they packed up their gear and drove to Ruth Lezkowski's apartment.

~~~~

By the time the police left the location Nagaro ripped off 18 minutes of video. They could not go to the other crime scenes because they were more secluded but Michaels knew he had enough to cover his exclusive story that he already started to write in his mind.

He gave Nagaro a high five. They both smiled and Michaels said, "We're going to kick some ass and shake this town up tomorrow."

~~~~

When the police entourage arrived at the alley behind Lezkowski's apartment, Lt. Leonard directed Jan Kuzniar to pull her car to a certain spot. As she was getting ready to get out of the car, Cranston opened the door for her to help her out. She looked up at him and thought *what a fucking douce bag*. For the first time she got a very eerie feeling about what would happen next.

Cranston said, "So we was walkin' in this here alley and we sees this car pull up. So we waits and when the lady gets out the car Douglas grabs her around the waist and puts his hand over her mouth and throws her back into the car."

"Okay, show us," said Leonard. "Jan come over here."

Cranston reluctantly walked up to officer Kuzniar and gently wrapped his arms around her, covered her mouth with his left hand and moved her to her car. At the very moment his hand covered her mouth, Kuzniar felt she was going to vomit. His hand was soft but filthy. She wondered *When was the last time he washed his hands?* His fingernails were black with grit. His breath was foul like spoiled meat. She was repulsed and a quiver enveloped her body. He shoved her in the front seat and asked her, "Are you alright? Did I hurt you?"

*What a pussy* she thought and then heard Lt. Leonard say, "You can crank it up Clayton. She can take it. Don't treat her with kid gloves."

Cranston then demonstrated how he pulled Ruth through the front seat into the back seat and this time he was a little more aggressive and demonstrative.

After they finished videotaping in the alley, they moved to the actual scene of the murder. Kuzniar sat in her car and for the first time in her life she didn't like her job. She had her share of tough encounters when she was undercover, playing a junkie, buying drugs but this was different. It seemed so personal, so violating. She thought about her ten-year-old daughter and couldn't imagine anything like this ever happening to her. She collapsed her face into her hands and said a silent prayer as tears welled in her eyes. *Oh my God that poor woman.*

As Cranston demonstrated with Kuzniar how he manipulated the victim around in the back seat to have sex with her. Kuzniar had an out of body experience. She literally felt the presence of Ruth Lezkowski in her space at that moment and she had an overwhelming calming feeling of peace and then she said a *Hail Mary*.

~~~~

Officer Jan Kuzniar didn't have to go back to Homan Square. She couldn't wait to get home. As she entered her house she gesticulated with an unnerving emotion as she grabbed her daughter and hugged her tightly. "I love you. I love you. I love you, baby."

"What's wrong Mommy?"

"Nothing honey, I just want you to know how much you are loved. That's all. I'm going to take a shower."

She walked upstairs, turned on the water, stepped in and thought, *this was the most disgusting thing I have ever, ever, experienced on the job.* Kuzniar then turned up the water as hot as she could stand it. She got in and out of the shower seven times until the water turned cold. She dried herself off, looked in the mirror and realized her skin was raw and red and yet she still didn't feel clean. As she wrapped herself in a towel, and sat on the edge of the tub her lips began to quiver. She buried her face in her hands and she began sobbing.

# CHAPTER 59

T he weather report on WMAC-TV was dismal for February 6, 2002. Jan Kuzniar shivered not because it was going to be colder today than it was yesterday but because she had go through another re-enactment with the other killer. She trembled at just the thought of it.

She walked into her kitchen, poured herself a cup of black coffee, took the phone off its hanging cradle on the wall and called Lt. Mark Leonard.

"Hey boss, I don't know if I can do this again. Yesterday freaked me out!"

"I know. It affected me as well. Listen, be here an hour earlier and we'll talk about it."

Kuzniar knew Lt. Leonard was a religious man and she trusted him completely. "Okay, I'll be there."

~~~~

Douglas Russell felt the stiffness in his joints as he walked into Interrogation Room Three. He spent the night in a holding cell and had a tough time sleeping. He asked for a cup of coffee as he was directed to sit in the same chair Clayton Cranston sat in the day before. His right eye began to twitch. He was looking around getting nervous. Nobody was in the room and the last thing he wanted to do was try to escape. He was seething at the thought that his brother *fucked him*.

Detective Dick Corley had a smirk on his face as he handed Russell a paper cup of coffee with three sugars and double cream. Russell took the cup and placed it on the desk by his left hand.

"What's gonna happen now?"

"You's gonna be interrogated and you're going to give a statement to the state's attorney," Corley said mockingly, as he walked around the desk and sat in his chair.

The videographer walked in and set up his camera and the stenographer arranged her stenotype machine behind ASA Amy Wilson's chair.

Russell was wearing the same sweater he was arrested in and his under shirt was damp with sweat. His body odor was disturbing. He was fidgeting when Wilson walked into the room. She was wearing a dark blue tailored pantsuit with a cream-colored silk blouse. Russell was getting aroused as he just stared at her.

Without looking up, Wilson sat down and put her purse down on the floor to her right as far away from Russell as possible. She could sense his piercing eyes. She had never experienced this type of uneasiness in front of a defendant before. *This guy is really creepy* she thought.

She placed her black leather briefcase on the desk, opened it and retrieved her files. Hidden behind the briefcase she took a deep breath, gathered her composure and slammed the lid down so hard it startled Russell. He blinked at the sound and Wilson's confidence mustered. She looked him straight in the eyes and in a commanding voice asked, "Do you know why you are here, Mr. Russell?"

"Yes ma'am."

"Good! Now earlier you told us about the murder and sexual assault of Ruth Lezkowski. And at that time you told me in summary, that in the early morning hours on October 18th, 1986 before you went to work, you and Clayton Cranston were looking for cars you could remove property from. As you were doing that you came across a young lady, Ruth Lezkowski, who was parking her car. And you told me that you and Clayton forced her into her car at knife point and drove to a secluded area near some train tracks and took turns sexually assaulting her and then Clayton beat her to death with a piece of concrete. Is that correct?"

"Yeah."

"Okay. I am going to read you your Constitutional rights again."

The description that Russell gave of lurking around the streets trying to find things to steal was amazingly similar to Cranston's. What was dramatically different was how they abducted her.

Wilson was in a zone now asking questions. "Could you tell us what happened after she exited her car?"

"By the time she got to the edge of the building, she like seened me and she was startled."

"What makes you think she was startled?"

"Because she like—just stopped and froze, you know."

"How close was she when she stopped and froze?"

Pointing to the cup in front of him he continued, "No closer than me to this cup."

Wilson motioned with her right hand out in front of her with a little flick "So a couple of feet from you?"

"Yeah."

"What happened next?"

"Next Clayton came from behind her, put his hand around her mouth and put a knife to her neck."

"Can you demonstrate?"

"Yeah." Russell stood up and motioned with his left hand over her mouth and with his right hand pretended to hold a knife up to her neck. "He told her to be quiet, don't scream."

He described how he got the car and picked them up and how Clayton forced her into the car then they drove up to the desolated area by the railroad tracks.

"After I parked the car up there. I turned it off. And Clayton said, 'Man—' he say, 'I want to fuck.'"

"Where was the woman?"

"She was on the floor in the back seat. She was getting' up."

"Then what happened?"

"She, that lady said, please don't hurt me. Then Clayton asked her to take off her clothes and pulled his pants down. She was taking too long, so Clayton just reached and pulled them down for her and took them off."

Russell went on to describe the brutal rape that lasted 15 minutes saying that Clayton just got wilder and wilder the more she screamed.

"How long did it take you to climb in the back seat of the car after he zipped up his pants and got off the woman?"

"It wasn't even a half a minute."

"And what did you do at that time?"

"Then I unzipped my—I asked her if she was alright. And she said, yes." At that moment in time Wilson thought *you psychopathic bastard, she was just brutally sexual assaulted for 15 minutes, and she said she was alright,* she shook her head in disbelief and he continued. "I unzipped my pants and I entered her and I fucked her."

Stunned at the casualness of his response, Wilson took a deep breath before she could continue. "How long did you do that for?"

"No more than about two, three to five minutes."

"Was she saying anything during that period of time?"

"Just a little sniffle."

Wilson was taken aback by this candid remark, "Sniffles? Like she was crying?"

"No, like mm … mm, like that."

*He's trying to convince me that she enjoyed having sex with him. My God what a sick bastard,* she thought.

"So we was sitting in the front seat and Clayton be in the back seat and he say, Man, I'm on parole and I don't want to go back to the joint. Now, I might have misunderstood what he said but that's what I thought he said."

"You know he wasn't on parole, right?"

"No, I didn't. I never knew anything about, you know, his personal life. Before I could ask him what he meant he reached around the seat and started choking her."

"Did you say anything?"

"No, I'm just looking and amazed like, you know, what's going on."

"How did you know he was choking her in the first place?"

"Cause she was gasping for air. And, she started like—" At this point he was trying to indicate a gasping for air sound and making a circle with his lips to demonstrate the reverse of coughing. "—like that then she started kicking."

"How long was he choking her—how long was she gasping for air?"

"No more than about—it was like maybe 15 seconds, something like that."

The entire statement took one hour and ten minutes to complete. After she asked the obligatory questions about his treatment and no coercion, she stood up packed her briefcase and turned around and walked out of the room. She never wanted to see this demon again in her life but she knew that would be impossible because she would be trying him. She had no doubt the grand jury would indict him and Clayton Cranston. The evidence against them was overwhelming.

She would call Mrs. Lezkowski soon with the news that the killers of her daughter were going to jail for life or that they'll get the death penalty.

~~~~

Attorney Robert Franey from the firm of Carlin and Miller was retained by the City's Corporation Council's Office to represent the city in the civil suits filed by Jose Aguilera on behalf of the Lezkowski Four. Franey graduated in the top ten percent of his class from Notre Dame Law, 15 years ago. He was a big man, 6 foot 6 inches, 275-pounds and was built like a defensive lineman for the Chicago Bears but he never played a single down on a football field. He had an engaging personality. He was the life of the party although he never drank alcohol or smoked marijuana. He had COPD after inhaling a huge amount of hydrochloric acid fumes while cleaning his swimming pool ten years earlier. He had to use an inhaler to get through the day. He entertained adults and children alike with his love of card tricks. He had an analytical mind that grasped facts instantly and played them out as if he was in a chess match. He billed $1,250 an hour for his services and clients were in line to hire him.

He already managed to get several police officers dropped from Aguilera's civil lawsuit. Franey had just met with former prosecutor Michael Pangborn and he had no doubt Pangborn would be the next person dismissed.

He was meeting with Rosemary Ravalli in her office on the ninth floor of City Hall trying to determine a timely schedule for the depositions of the Lezkowski Four.

"Let's try to get Lorenzo Holmes first, then Oscar Sampson and then Charles Holmes. If we're lucky we'll get Marcus Broadhead thrown out. He's in the joint again right now. He's been arrested at least 50 times and he could end up getting paid for being the fucking thug that he is." Franey said.

"That sounds like a plan. How's it going with Chief Maurer?"

"I'm getting close to getting him dropped as well. He's been the subject of a media campaign and you know how Aguilera loves the attention."

"That would be a major coup if you pull that off."

"I'm close. I'll keep in touch."

~~~~

Peter Michaels was chomping at the bit to get information for his six o'clock report. He had left three messages on Corley's cell phone. He was sitting in Ed Land's editing booth viewing the videotape of the police re-enactment from the night before when his cell rang to the tune of "Cheeseburger in paradise."

"News ... Michaels."

"It's me, Corley."

"Hey. Jethro, I've been trying to get a hold of you."

"Don't be a smart ass, Pete," he replied with a grin. "Got a pen? I don't have a lot of time. We are getting ready for Russell's re-creation tonight."

"Is that Reggie's brother?"

"Yep, he's 47 and he's been arrested 35 times during his infamous life of crime; two times for rape, including indecent exposure with a child. He's a real winner. He has three prior convictions. He's been sentenced to a total of 14 years. He served ten. We have a perfect DNA match that puts him at the scene of the Lezkowski homicide and he confessed this morning. Of course, he said Cranston did it. You know, he said ... she said."

"Who's Cranston?"

"He's the guy you taped yesterday. Perfect DNA match as well. He confessed but I assume you already knew that when you filmed him yesterday."

"How old?"

"He's 39. He had 30 arrests mainly theft charges. He was sentenced to prison two times and served less than five years. Kind of an odd guy."

"DNA?"

"Yeah, perfect match to the second offender. He said Russell beat her because she scratched his face but you can't get that specific."

"Anything else?"

"Isn't that enough? Hey, thanks for your help! I don't think we would have caught these guys if you had reported the story last week."

"Glad you finally got these bastards. Thanks."

~~~~

Jan Kuzniar walked into Lt. Mark Leonard's office at one o'clock. She looked tired. The dark circles under her eyes suggested a restless night of sleep. Her body was stiff and sore like she was in a minor traffic accident. She managed a smile as she sat down with a cup of hot coffee in her hand.

"I don't know if I am capable of doing this again today."

"I knew it was hard on you yesterday. These are not good people. As a matter of fact, they're disgusting and the person you are going to meet today is worse than Cranston.

Kuzniar had an alarmed look on her face. "It was hard for me to even come in here today, boss."

"I know but look at it this way. Think about the Lezkowski family especially her mother. She is reliving this ugly tragedy all over again. She is such a kind and pleasant woman. We need to do this to finally give her closure."

Kuzniar leaned back in her chair, looked up at the ceiling, closed her eyes and started to pray for the Lezkowski family and all of a sudden she had an equanimity come over her and she said, "I'm in."

# CHAPTER 60

C ameraman Paul Nagaro could not find a good parking spot for a repeat performance of yesterday's shoot. The only spot available was next to a fire hydrant and he didn't want to draw attention to the van. Peter Michaels was back at the newsroom preparing for the six o'clock news so Nagaro had no one who could drive the van and double park. Nagaro was frustrated but did not want to take the risk of being discovered. When he saw the police entourage drive up and park, he cursed under his breath and drove away.

~~~~

Officer Jan Kuzniar was the last to arrive and when she got out of her car she met Douglas Russell for the first time. It sent chills down her spine, she shivered and her stomach filled with acid. She left Homan Square with a feeling of peace but now she was a little angst-ridden.

A different state's attorney showed up. He was about six feet tall. He had piercing blue eyes. His Chicago Bears stadium cap was pulled down over his ears covering his black hair. He had on a long woolen coat with the collar turned up and his shoes were encased in rubber boots to keep his feet warm.

Douglas Russell's white sweater fell below his waist length winter coat. He didn't have a hat or gloves. His hands were in fists and buried in his coat's deep pockets as he tried to keep his blood circulating. It wasn't working and he was shivering. His white gym shoes offered his feet no protection from the damp cold sidewalk. He was stepping sideways from one foot to the other trying to stay warm as he told Lt. Mark Leonard, "We was high and shit. We was looking for merch to steal." He spit on the sidewalk and Kuzniar thought *What a smarmy bastard.*

Lt. Leonard beckoned Kuzniar next to her car and opened the door and told Russell to demonstrate what happened. Russell pulled her aggressively and roughly close to his body and put his left hand over her mouth. He motioned with his right hand as if it were holding a knife pressed hard into her neck. His approach was nothing like the timid actions of Clayton Cranston.

"Don't scream." He then violently pulled her into the back seat of the car, rolled her over then pushed her down onto the floor and covered her with his body. He was literally snuggling her and almost moaning.

At that moment Kuzniar realized that she was in the presence of pure unadulterated evil. A demon. His dirty calloused hand over her mouth smelled almost like burnt motor oil. His breath was polluted and vulgar. When he removed his hand she reflexively spit but she wasn't conscious of it until she viewed the videotape of the incident days later.

While inside the car, she realized he was sexually aroused when he started to rub his erection on her forearm and elbow ever so slightly. *My God he has a hard on.* Then he caressed her buttocks. She immediately tried to free herself from his grasp but he seemed to become even more aroused and he began to moan under his breath. She was shocked and repulsed.

Lt. Leonard noticed how uncomfortable she was and said, "Okay, that's enough! I think we got the idea." After she got out of the car, she walked around the corner of a nearby building out of camera range, gagged and spit again. She was appalled and sickened by what just had happened but she didn't say a thing. She was now even more motivated than ever to do her part to help put these killers behind bars. She took a deep breath and mentally braced herself for the next time Douglas Russell would touch her.

They drove to the desolate area where the vicious rape and murder took place. Russell began to describe how they both brutally raped Ruth Lezkowski with the qualification that after he had sex with her, they moved to the front seat and started talking as if they were friends and that nothing was really wrong.

"After Clayton said he was on parole and he wasn't going back to the joint, he reached up over the front seat and started strangling her. I said, what the fuck and got out the car. I was lookin' round to make sure no one could see us. Clayton then comes around to the front of the car."

Kuzniar was told to move into the front seat on all fours and Russell pulled her upper torso further out of the car and he continued, "She was like out here and then Clayton grabbed the door and 'boom' he slammed her head real hard with the door and then he pulled her out the car onto the ground. I bent over and felt for a pulse on her neck. She was unconscious but she was still breathing."

Lt. Leonard thought shaking his head, *Yeah, now you're a doctor checking for a pulse.*

"Then I stood up and looked around to make sure no one could see us that's when I heard this 'whoosh' and a 'thud.' Man, he had just hit her in the face with a brick. Her face be all bloody. I said, Oh man, and reached down again and felt her heart. I said, She's still alive man, she still breathing, she still have a heartbeat. Let's git out of here and I turned around and walked away."

When Kuzniar heard that, a look of disgust veiled her face and she asked Lt. Leonard, "Can I go home? I think I'm done here."

He nodded affirmatively and said, "Go."

The last part of the walk through was at the sewer grate down the access road where Russell threw away the keys to Lezkowski's car. Leonard knew that asking the Department of Streets and Sanitation to look in that sewer would be a long shot because 16 years of garbage, sewage and rain washing anything imaginable down it would have made finding the keys a virtually impossible task. But he was going to ask first thing in the morning anyway. He wanted to leave no stone unturned.

~~~~

The WMAC news department did not advertise the exclusive story until 5:45. They wanted to keep a lid on it for as long as possible to prevent competing media outlets from getting a leg up. Peter Michaels and Dave Beedy were going over their scripts with Ron Magers in his office. He was sitting at his desk reading the script of Michaels' per-recorded video package.

"Man, these guys are really bad people," Magers said.

"Mage, these dudes were arrested 65 times over the years. This Douglas Russell had seven aliases trying to hide his criminal history. He's also a convicted rapist. He's a violent son of a bitch."

"You know if it wasn't for the greed of Reggie, none of this would have happened. He kept this hidden for 16 years."

"One would think he should be charged with obstruction of justice or something," Beedy said.

"It ain't ever gonna happen," Michaels said.

~~~~

Officer Jan Kuzniar's daughter was at church with her youth group, so as soon as she walked into her house, she ran upstairs and turned on the shower as hot as she could stand it and let the water flush her body. This night she was not going to go in and out of the shower seven times. She stayed under the water until it turned cold about 45 minutes later. She didn't hear the phone ring as she scrubbed herself with an exfoliant until she was raw. Kuzniar gagged thinking about Russell rubbing his erection on her arm and elbow. When she got out of the shower she went over to the toilet and vomited. *Oh my God, I met the devil today.*

~~~~

Lt. Mark Leonard got back to his office a little before six and was greeted by a stack of phone messages. He was shuffling through them when he looked over at the silenced television in the corner. He saw a graphic on the screen under Ron Magers and Peter Michaels that read *Lezkowski Arrests*. He walked over to the TV and turned up the volume and saw himself in the center of the screen talking to Clayton Cranston. His eyes widened and he shook his head as he listened to Michaels' story of the first of its kind videotaped murder re-enactment where the killer agreed to take the police to the scene of the homicide and described how the murder was actually committed.

*Son of a bitch,* he thought. *Corley, I'm going to kick your ass!*

Michaels was looking at the camera, "So Ron, 37 days, after the release of the Lezkowski Four, police found her killers who have been roaming the streets of Chicago for 16 years. They were both in jail once since the death of Ruth Lezkowski but authorities never put their DNA in any official database."

The phones in the cold case squad room lit up like a Christmas tree. Leonard reached for his phone and pressed the only button that wasn't blinking and dialed Jan Kuzniar.

She didn't answer and he knew, she was either in the shower or on the bed in a fetal position, shivering from the experience that would haunt her for a long, long time.

# CHAPTER 61

A  lthough the news conference was two hours away, satellite trucks from all the local TV stations were parking illegally in front of police headquarters on this very cold Friday morning, February 8, 2002. The media room would be packed at ten o'clock and cameramen were already jockeying for positions to get the best pictures. Generally, two rows of chairs were set up to handle routine pressers but today there were four rows running from wall to wall. Nagaro's camera had a direct shot at the podium and his equipment was on the chair in front of him reserving it for Peter Michaels.

Even though he hadn't slept much the night before, Lt. Mark Leonard had a spring in his step as he walked into the Chief of Detective's office. The file he just picked up from the crime lab contained the final nail in the coffin for Cranston and Russell. He was smiling as he handed it over to Chief Phil Cline.

"What's this?" Cline asked as he hefted himself up in his chair.

"Palm print report. It's a match," Leonard responded.

Cline grinned as he opened the manila folder, perused the document and said, "The state's attorney will be here any second. We will meet with the press and hopefully bring closure to this case."

~~~~

Retired Detective Jack Evans was at Homan Square sitting in Interrogation Room One with Clayton Cranston. His backpack was filled with all of his files from the original investigation. He was bound and determined to try to get the state's attorney's office to open a new investigation of the Lezkowski Four.

Lt. Leonard gave Evans permission to interview the suspects before they were transferred to Cook County Jail later that morning. Cranston walked into the room wearing the same plaid shirt and blue jeans. The first thing Evans noticed was the smell. He reached down in his backpack and opened a jar of Vicks and put a little dab in each nostril. It was a trick many detectives used when they were called to a homicide scene where the body had been there for a long time. Cranston smelled that bad. Since Evans retired he developed a raspy cough and he cleared his throat constantly.

"I am not here on any official capacity and you don't have to talk to me, do you understand this?"

"Yeah. I know. I gots no problem talking wit you."

After going through his involvement in the abduction, rape and murder of Ruth Lezkowski, Evans pulled out some crime scene photos and showed them to Cranston.

"What's dat?"

"You said you wanted money and at first you were just going to rob her. This is the stuff from her trunk that was strewn all around the rear of her car," Evans explained.

"I never saw dat shit before. What is dat shit, man?" Cranston said as he examined the photo more closely.

Evans pulled out the autopsy report and handed Cranston a graphic illustration of the puncture wounds all over her body, "Do you know what these are?" He asked indicating with a circular motion of his right forefinger.

"What the fuck's dat suppose to mean?" Cranston said with a curious look on his face.

"Those are like little puncture wounds. Dozens of them."

"Don't be pinning dat shit on me, man. I don't know nuttin' about no puncture wounds. Me and Douglas didn't do none of dat shit, man. Dat's bullshit."

Evans spent another ten minutes with Cranston and had the same conversation with Russell with the same results. As Russell was led out of the room, Evans stuffed his files back into his backpack and thought *Something doesn't add up here.*

~~~~

Officer Jan Kuzniar was kneeling in the second row for morning mass at Our Lady of Victory church. Her forehead was leaning on her folded hands that clutched a blue crystal rosary interlaced through her fingers. Her closed eyes couldn't stop the tears that were gently progressing down her cheeks. She had the same nightmare last night and sleep was fleeting. She was exhausted.

Pastor Alan Petro sat beside her after he finished mass. "How are you doing?"

"Father, I have witnessed Satan in my presence for the last two days. I can't seem to get myself clean. I can't sleep. I can't think. I'm paralyzed," she said. "I normally can compartmentalize my work. When I get out of my car and walk into the house, I leave the job in the car. I never want it to interfere with my home life. I can't seem to do it with this experience. It was just awful. Those men were pure evil."

"Jan, you work with evil every day. I have known you for a long time. You will get through this with the grace of God. You have to look at it like; what you did will deliver these evil men the justice they deserve. Think of the woman's family, that will help you realize that you did the right thing. You have helped them get closure," Father Petro said as he held her hands and gently squeezed them for emphasis.

Kuzniar lifted her head, opened her eyes and looked directly at the priest with tears welling, "Thank you, Father."

~~~~

Chief of Detectives Phil Cline spoke first. He was directly in front of Peter Michaels. "The DNA that exonerated the four originally charged is the same DNA that is directly tied to our new suspects Clayton Cranston and Douglas Russell. Just this morning we have confirmed that the palm print we found at the crime scene belongs to Clayton Cranston. The evidence is overwhelming and we are satisfied that Cranston and Russell committed this heinous crime."

"Can you tell us about the re-enactment?" Michaels asked.

"To my knowledge, it is the first time in the history of the Chicago Police Department that we have actually videotaped the suspects of murder as they walked us through the actual crime itself. As a matter of fact, that re-enactment matched their stories and with the DNA and the fingerprint, there are no loose ends left. It's all tied up, they will be charged later this afternoon."

"Is it true that Russell's brother turned him in?"

"Yes," Cline looked down at Michaels and continued, "Reggie Russell contacted us, his story was credible and his DNA was a 99.9% match to the DNA of one of the suspects. By the way, we have entered their DNA into our databases and we are actively investigating if it matches any other crimes committed over the years."

"Did these guys know the teenagers, the so-called Lezkowski Four before?" Michaels knew the answer but he asked the question anyway because he needed it on the record for his story on the six o'clock news.

"Russell lived in the ALBA homes and had seen the teens around but they never interacted. There was a big age difference." Cline got a frustrated look on his face as he continued, "If Reggie Russell would have come forward 16 years ago we surely would not be in this predicament we are in today. How someone could allow another person to go to jail for life and not come forward is beyond me. They roamed the streets of this city for all those years and committed over 85 crimes between the three of them." Cline shook his head and exited the podium as reporters fired off more questions that he wouldn't answer. He knew every aspect of this case since he assigned Richard Corley to it months ago. His relief came knowing that the Lezkowski family will finally see justice for the murder of Ruth. It was long overdue.

~~~~

Assistant State's Attorney Amy Wilson entered the courtroom of the honorable Judge John James at precisely one o'clock. Judge James was a no nonsense jurist who was nearing retirement after serving 22 years on the bench. His white hair was thinning and his Irish skin revealed the marks of many cancer cells that were burned off over the years. His hazel eyes were deeply set but they had a penetrating scrutiny. His black robe hung over a white shirt and red tie. His reading glasses were perched on the tip of his nose. He gaveled the hearing to order.

The courtroom was packed with reporters, spectators and some family members of Cranston and Russell. When they were escorted into the courtroom all eyes shifted to the left, as the prisoner door opened. Both men walked in with their heads down. They were dressed in their street clothes and winter jackets. Their public defenders joined them as they were ushered to the defense table.

Amy Wilson stood and introduced them to the court and started off, "Ruth Lezkowski was begging them not to hurt her, not to kill her, your honor, the entire time after they kidnapped her. She pled for mercy but it never came." Wilson paused for emphasis and Judge James shifted his attention from Wilson to the defendants, as she continued, "They stopped and bought liquor, beer and marijuana," but when Wilson told the court that they then stopped to buy hot dogs and French fries there was a gasp and a sense that the air had just been sucked out of the courtroom. Most of the women put a hand to their mouths in disbelief and all eyes scowled directly at the defendants.

"Your honor, the evidence is overwhelming. There is DNA, a palm print, confessions and re-enactments at the scene of how Ruth Lezkowski was bludgeoned to death with a piece of concrete. They demonstrated how her head and neck were slammed with the car door. This was a crime of dark rage your honor. Clayton Cranston even told police that her face was bleeding—that her whole face was busted up and they left her there to die."

Cranston and Russell sat next to their public defenders impenitently, emotionless and speechless as Wilson outlined the state's case. When she concluded, public defender Gerald Witty quickly approached the bench. Witty had been in the Public Defender's Office for five years. This was the biggest case he was ever assigned. He had never appeared in a courtroom that was this crowded. Even though he was a little nervous, he began, "Your honor, the police threatened and beat both of these defendants to get them to confess to this crime. Mr. Russell was struck in the face with a fist and Mr. Cranston was threatened with bodily harm."

"Objection, your honor, nothing could be farther from the truth. There was absolutely no physical abuse or mental abuse. Look at these men your honor. Do you see any signs of physical abuse? If necessary, I will show the court the video re-enactment that both these defendants voluntarily participated in shortly after their arrests. You will see by their actions and reactions that they cooperated completely of their own free will. These allegations of any kind of abuse are groundless."

Judge James had a frowned look on his face as he remanded Cranston and Russell into the custody of the Cook County Jail without bail. He had seen a lot in his 22 years on the bench but this one was particularly disturbing. He walked into his chambers and immediately thought of his only daughter and then collapsed into his chair without taking off his robe.

~~~~

Reporters in the lobby of the Criminal Courts building surrounded Shanniqua Farnsworth who was Clayton Cranston's girlfriend/wife. Shanniqua stood out in the crowd. She was six feet tall, heavyset with bleached blonde hair. "My Bo could never do nuttin' this bad. Bo is not a dangerous man. He doesn't have a dangerous bone in his body. I swear to God, my hand on a bible. He's no murderer. He's just a big old teddy bear. He could never do this."

"I tell ya'll Douglas could not do anything like this."

"What is your name?" Reporters shouted out.

"I ain't tellin' you my name. But I been knowing Douglas Russell for a long time. If we would have known any of this here stuff we would have made him turn hisself in, but he couldn't have done this."

Helen Harrison said, "These charges are difficult to believe. I don't believe them."

"Who are you, ma'am?"

"I'm Douglas' grandmother. I never ever thought he could have done something like this. I couldn't sleep after I heard all this stuff. I'm in shock. He was always very good to me. He always treated me real nice. I can't believe this."

Then an anonymous woman, who walked with a slight limp and wore a purple woolen hat and coat to match, said, "Let the victim's family be in peace. This is like pouring salt on an open wound."

# Chapter 62

"If there was ever a case that called for the death penalty, it is the Lezkowski homicide," professed Kevin Benedetti, the First Assistant Cook County State's Attorney as he gathered Peter Di Donato, the Chief of Special Prosecutions and ASA Amy Wilson into his office to discuss their capital punishment strategy.

"There is no doubt about it. This is one of the most horrific cases this office has ever dealt with," Di Donato agreed. "But we have to be very careful here. The laws have changed dramatically for felony murder in the last 15 years and the statute of limitations for rape is off the table."

"That's why that re-enactment was so important. You know, when the police wanted to do that videotaped walk-through, I wasn't so sure we should do it but it turned out to be one of the best things that could have happened," Wilson said. "It literally took away any defense strategy for creating reasonable doubt for Cranston and Russell. More importantly we have them accusing one another."

"I have to admit it was a brilliant move. Make the arrangements to get all the DNA samples re-analyzed and re-certified so that there are no doubts and prepare a motion so we fall within the mandated 120 days of our intentions to seek capital punishment. You know the public defender will claim we are in violation."

"On another matter. How are we with the Pangborn civil suit?" Benedetti asked.

Bob Franey is moving that case along. He already has some of the police officers dropped from the suit," Di Donato said.

"Amy, have you talked to Mrs. Lezkowski?"

"I wanted to wait until after this meeting. I want to tell her we are going for the death penalty."

~~~~

Jose Aguilera was walking Lorenzo and Charles Holmes out of his office as Peter Michaels walked in.

"What up, Mr. Michaels?" Charles asked.

"You guys look pretty happy. Everything good?"

"Everythang cool, man." Lorenzo said.

"Those guys have grins from ear to ear. What's going on Jose?"

"We just got back from the Illinois Prisoner Review Board and it went very, very well. Charles had them eating out of the palm of his hand. He told them he intends on going to school. He wants to be a paramedic."

"No shit. It sounds like he's getting his life together. Good for him."

"Yeah, I have found them each a nice little place out west in Addison and Villa Park. They're affordable, clean and away from their old neighborhood. I am hiring Lorenzo and Oscar Sampson to do some work around here. It will give them some responsibility and a little money in their pockets. Oscar wants to be a paralegal."

"How is the civil action going?"

"You know they have to have clemency before they can collect the $150,000 from the Illinois Court of Claims."

"I thought that was mandatory, the money I mean."

"No, they need a pardon to qualify."

"Is the state's attorney challenging you?"

"No, as a matter of fact they told the board they don't oppose the pardon."

"Well, I hope they get it before the governor goes to jail. I hear he has a bunch of problems of his own."

~~~~

Violet Lezkowski just poured herself a cup of coffee and slowly walked back to her favorite chair when the phone rang. She set her china cup and saucer down on the table covered with family pictures with Ruth's (the largest) in the middle. Her hand trembled as she reached to her right to answer the phone on the fourth ring. "Hello," she eased down slowly and carefully.

"Mrs. Lezkowski, this is Amy Wilson. How are you today?"

"I'm tired and sad, Amy," she turned her head and looked at Ruth's picture and tears welled in her eyes. Her voice cracked, "This has been heartbreaking."

"I know you have been through a lot over the years but I want you to know it will be over soon. We are going to seek the death penalty for the two we have in custody."

Mrs. Lezkowski quivered and adjusted the handmade woolen afghan that was covering her legs and feet. "Are you sure this time?"

"Without a doubt. The DNA is a perfect match. The palm print the police found in the car is a perfect match to Clayton Cranston. Both men have confessed and both men did a videotaped re-enactment of the crime."

"I felt so bad for those boys who were in jail for 15 years."

"I know it has been a horrible ordeal to live with. At least we got them out and the right people are now in custody."

She shifted the phone to her left ear and gently touched her forehead and closed her eyes. "I just can't go through another trial. I was finally able to clear my mind of all of this. Of course, I think about it all the time. You never forget. We are finally starting to talk about taking some trips. I would love to go to Rome and visit the Sistine Chapel and meet the pope."

"There are a few legal technicalities but when that is finished we will make a presentation to the grand jury and formally charge them under the capital punishment statute. They'll die in prison one way or another."

~~~~

Officer Jan Kuzniar finished viewing the videotaped re-enactments and filed her final supplementary report. She walked into Lt. Mark Leonard's office and sat down and shook her head. Her bloodshot eyes had dark circles and puffy bags under them. She looked fatigued.

"How are you feeling, Jan?"

"I've had nightmares every night since I did this but at least I'm not taking seven showers a day. I talked to my priest. I'll be fine, I hope."

"Go home. Get some rest. When you get back to your regular routine with the gang unit, you'll be fine."

Kuzniar left, Lt. Leonard started reviewing detective Corley's reports. He was deep in thought when his private phone line rang.

"Hey boss."

"What's wrong, Jan?"

"Do you believe it? I started my car and while pulling out of my parking spot, my engine just died." Tears welled in her weary eyes. She put her head on the steering wheel and prayed, "God help me, please."

"I'll have someone take you home. What do you want me to do with your car?"

"Tow it to the police pound and have it crushed. I don't care. Ever since those evil bastards were in it, I'm unnerved when I drive it. Maybe a new car will put an end to my nightmares."

~~~~

Ron Magers just got up from his desk chair when Peter Michaels walked into his office. He motioned Michaels to follow him. "I'm getting make up early. I think you should put more of your involvement with Reggie Russell into this Apple River story."

"Yeah, I know I just hate making myself part of any story. I got lucky when he called me."

"Lucky my ass. Remember what you always say?"

Michaels nodded and smiled. "Yeah, the harder I work, the luckier I get. Man, the guys running that place were just jamming all kinds of people into that psychiatric center for unnecessary medical treatments. They literally bussed them in from nursing homes, along with homeless people, anywhere they could find them. Reggie Russell was probably one of the only legit patients in the place."

"It looks like that Dr. Chester Crawford is going to do some 'big time' for all the bribes he took for ordering all that bogus treatment."

"They paid him and his associates almost $700,000 in kickbacks for all of the patients he referred. The feds don't look kindly on Medicaid and Medicare fraud. They'll be closed down tomorrow after the U.S. Attorney files his indictment."

"Listen, it's too late to change your package. I'll ask you about Reggie Russell when you wrap up. Good work. See you on the set."

# Chapter 63

J ose Aguilera and Robert Franey were going head to head for days. Aguilera had been adamant that he was not going to drop Prosecutor Michael Pangborn, Chief of Patrol James Maurer and crime lab specialist Patricia Bass from his civil suit on the behalf of the Lezkowski Four. The two attorneys had known each other for a long time. It isn't the first time they had gone to battle. They both respected one another and they always talked freely whether face to face or on the phone.

"Look Jose you know you are going to drop everyone from this suit eventually. Chief Maurer, Pangborn and Bass should not have been named in the first place. They have nothing to do with you getting your guys their money. You fucked up with your grandstand pleading about prosecutorial and police misconduct. It's in violation of federal guidelines. It has nothing to do with the lawsuit. I will get that struck from the record within two weeks. You know it and I know it," Franey said confidently.

Aguilera was on his feet, rubbing his lower back and pacing around his spacious office, "Maurer's statements were very prejudicial to my clients at the time."

"Come on Jose. For a person who has courted media attention throughout this entire case, how do you think it is going to look, for you to go after Maurer for talking to the media. You created your own quandary here."

Aguilera eased into his chair and pursed his lips, "Let me think about a few things. I'll be in touch."

"I can do all the filing very quietly. It will get you out of this dilemma," Franey said as he hung up the phone with a huge grin.

~~~~

Retired detective Jack Evans was at his kitchen table. His fifth cup of black coffee was half full and tepid sitting next to a 16-page detailed account of why he thought the state's attorney should reopen the original investigation of the Lezkowski Four. His stomach was agitated, his nerves were shattered and his hair was scruffy from running his fingers through it dozens of times. He was about to do something he promised himself he would never do; *call a reporter.*

"News ... Michaels."

"Hey Peter! It's Jack Evans."

"Hey detective what's up?"

"I want to talk to you about some stuff."

"Love to, on the phone or in person? What kinda stuff are you talking about?"

"I have a very detailed and I think compelling description of why we should revisit the original Lezkowski investigation. If you want a copy, let's meet and talk about it. I think you'll find it very interesting."

"I can come to you or you can come to the news room or wherever. You name it, I'll be there."

"I'll come to you. I can be there within the hour."

"I'll be here."

Michaels got up from his desk and looked at his partner, "Who was that?" Dave Beedy asked with a questioning look.

"Jack Evans wants to talk. I almost fell out of my chair when I answered the phone. I never thought I would hear from him again."

"What about?"

"The Lezkowski Four. He thinks they should be re-investigated."

"No shit. His nuts are in a vice. What else can he suggest?"

"No. I think he might have something. His voice was very convincing. At the very least I have to hear him out."

The receptionist called 45 minutes later and Michaels walked out to the lobby to retrieve Evans. His hands were shaking when Michaels extended his hand to welcome him to Channel Six. "You want some coffee or water? I have a private conference room reserved for us."

The conference room was painted in warm pastel colors giving it a calming influence. Michaels sensed that Evans was anxious so he raised the blinds to let in the afternoon sun to further soothe the air. Beedy brought in a Styrofoam cup of black coffee, introduced himself and left the room.

Evans opened his well-worn briefcase pulled out a document and handed it to Michaels. "Most people think I'm a little foolish but I am not so sure Russell and Cranston killed Ruth Lezkowski. I have always told you those kids were there. They had to be. They just knew too many details of that crime."

"You know the DNA, the palm print, the confessions, the re-enactment, they're all overwhelming and all pretty conclusive. It places them at the scene."

"I know. I am not saying they didn't abduct her, rape and rough her up maybe even hurt her but their stories have too many inconstancies and not a lot of detail. Think about it."

Michaels was scanning Evan's document. He stopped and looked up, "Like what?"

Evans coughed and cleared his throat. "I interviewed each of those guys separately at Homan Square for more than an hour. Look, check the autopsy report. They both said the other one slammed her head with the car door. Do you really think that you could generate enough momentum with a car door to kill someone hanging out of the front seat? Think about it." Evans coughed and cleared his throat again. "More importantly the autopsy has no injuries consistent with that kind of action."

Michaels leaned into the table, flipped Evans' document over and started writing. Evans then reached into one of his folders and handed over the full body graphic from the autopsy report depicting all the injuries that Lezkowski received. "When I showed that to them, they each said, 'What the fuck is that?' I interviewed them separately and neither knew anything about those wounds. They denied they did that to her but the original four went into great detail of how they held Ruth's hands over her head and Charles poked her. Peter there were at least 40 of those puncture wounds. 40."

"So what, do you think they would admit to everything they did?"

"Look, I have been the police for a long time. I have interviewed hundreds of killers. These guys were totally surprised by those injuries. Their body language revealed no knowledge. They knew nothing about them."

"I don't know," Michaels said scratching his head.

"I have been accused of scripting the murder and that I wrote it all down for them to study and regurgitate it back to the state's attorney. That's just bullshit. If I was going to do that, why wouldn't I have them put a knife to her neck? There were three puncture wounds on her neck from a knife. Why wouldn't I cover that? Why would I leave out something that important? If I did script it I wouldn't have. If I spent the time to script something, do you really think I would put that they stopped at a stop sign if there was no stop sign. They said those things. It's bullshit," Evans said and coughed several more times.

Michaels stood up and started pacing around the table rubbing his forehead. "Detective, they confessed to hitting her in the face with a concrete block."

"It's not consistent with the evidence. If they hit her in the face inside the car, the injury would be so massive; it would have left blood splattered all over the front seat. There was none of that. I wish I could have interviewed them when they were first arrested. And another thing, Douglas Russell is left-handed, most of those injures to Ruth's face and head are consistent with a right-handed person. It doesn't add up, Peter. It just doesn't add up."

Evans stood and ran his fingers through his hair and walked to the corner of the room, turned around and coughed several times, cleared his throat and continued. "I think they made stuff up about how she was killed. There were insinuations as to the location and the dramatic hitting in the face with the concrete. They each pointed the finger at the other guy trying to make themselves witnesses against each other. There is no mention of her being kicked and stomped on. The autopsy report clearly states that could have been one of three ways she died from blunt force trauma. Russell and Cranston didn't mention a word about that type of assault but the original four did."

Both men were now standing and facing one another. There was tension building in the room as Evans continued, "Another thing about the rape. Neither Cranston or Russell say they had anal sex, but in the original confessions both Charles Holmes and Broadhead say that Lorenzo took her outside the car and bent her over into the trunk and sodomized her."

"What about the DNA? What does that say?" Michaels asked as he sat back in his chair.

"That's just it. The report says neither of them can be excluded but it also states that no conclusions can be drawn on either of them regarding the sample. So that's up in the air. Remember in both the original confessions, once again, everyone was warned not to ejaculate."

"I don't know detective Evans. DNA is strong evidence."

"Yes, it is of the rape." A surprised look appeared on Evans' face. He raised his finger indicating that he just thought of something. He coughed and continued, "Speaking of the car trunk when I showed Cranston and Russell pictures of all the stuff strewn on ground, both of them said, 'What's that shit?' They knew nothing about it. It made them very curious and they even scrutinized those photos for several minutes. They were shaking their heads. They had no idea what that stuff was."

"This does raise some interesting questions."

"As I told you many times before those original four guys knew way too much about that crime scene."

"Yeah but once again they say you scripted it for them?"

"Why would I have all the inconsistency? Like Oscar and then this Daniel character. It would have been so much less complicated without Daniel. They confessed in about 12 hours after we had them in custody. Broadhead was the first to give it up. Why would I have them wearing gloves when we knew we had a print inside the car and we didn't have their prints back from the crime lab yet. They failed lie detector tests. Why?" Evans' cough was very persistent. "The two of them told the story the way they recollected it. We pinched them three months after the murder took place. Why did both of them talk about Lorenzo going back to the scene and looking for his shower cap? Lorenzo Holmes was a vicious criminal and he did not want to leave anything behind that could be traced to him. He was a very streetwise kid at the time."

"Yeah but—"

"No let me finish. When I went to arrest Charles, Detective Don Buerline came with me. I never worked with him before. He knew nothing about this case. So what was one of the first things Charles said? 'I don't have the keys.' Buerline did not know the significance of that statement. Why would that be one of the first things Charles said?"

"I don't know," Michaels responded with a troubled look on his face.

"We had eight people who made admissions that these guys talked about killing Ruth. Were they all lying?"

"Well two of them recanted."

"Yeah, but six didn't. Why? Think about it! Were all these people lying? They are saying the State's Attorney from Felony Review and the prosecutors who tried these cases all conspired to get convictions? No fucking way. No prosecutor would gamble losing his or her law license because of mutts like these guys. You guys in the media made it look as if these thugs were choirboys. They were anything but. The only person I feel sorry for is Charles. I really believe he was in the wrong place at wrong time. That doesn't alter my thoughts that he was present though when Ruth Lezkowski was brutally raped and murdered."

# CHAPTER 64

J ose Aguilera was a very happy camper. The governor granted the Lezkowski Four full pardons. This opened the door for them to collect $150,000 each from the Illinois Court of Claims. The money would be in their hands within the week.

Aguilera checked his red tie in the mirror of his private bathroom, as he was getting ready to hold another press conference in his office. The Lezkowski Four were all seated in the front facing the media. Broadhead got out of the penitentiary just two days earlier. Aguilera sat between them with a single microphone on the table in front of him. All electronic recorders were plugged into the audio box Aguilera had installed on the rear wall of his conference room. He liked to control the media. He left nothing to chance.

"We are, needless to say, very pleased with the governor's action today. However, it is also a sad reminder that these pardons come on a day that is just two days shy of the 16th anniversary of Ruth Lezkowski's death. The pardons clear the way for our lawsuits against the city. We are preparing for depositions of those involved in this miscarriage of justice."

Aguilera did not tell the media that he was about to drop the top named defendants from his suit. He and Bob Franey would be talking about that later in the day.

Oscar Sampson now 33 years old said, "I am very pleased that the governor expeditiously granted us a pardon. We are totally innocent and this just clears it up for us." Sampson, who just enrolled in a community college, had already decided that he wanted to be a paralegal. "We can get along with our lives now."

Lorenzo Holmes, who was also 33, said, "Don't get me wrong. I am happy that these pardons clear the way for us to move on but money ain't gonna make you happy. It's who you are surrounded by. Money is just a thing to get you more things."

"What are you doing with your life, Lorenzo?" Peter Michaels asked.

"I started a child day care business. It's going real good," he responded.

The answered stunned Michaels and took his breath away, he thought *Holy shit you were convicted and went to prison for raping and brutalizing an 11-year-old boy and you started a day care business.* Michaels took a deep breath and shook his head in silent disbelief.

Charles Holmes was 14-years-old when he was arrested for the death of Ruth Lezkowski. "I believed the pardons would happen but we are not going to get too carried away, he said. "This is something that will help us out over the short period of time until we deal with some bigger issues."

"What are you doing with yourself now Charles?" A reporter asked.

"I am studying to become a firefighter. I would love to help people in the future. I'm glad I have this new chance."

Marcus Broadhead was the last to speak. "I would like to go back to school. This has been a tragedy. This whole ordeal just ruined my life."

Michaels almost bit a hole through his cheek. He did not want to make a scene so he didn't ask the question that begged to be asked. "Don't you think the 39 times you were arrested and the four times you were in jail, is what ruined your life and not just the Lezkowski case?"

~~~~

A new 14-member Cook County Grand Jury is empaneled every month. Those selected are vetted and cannot be convicted of a crime. Their job is to listen to evidence presented impartially and make a determination if the defendant should be charged with a felony crime or not. They are on call for approximately 20 days during that month but it doesn't mean they convene every day. At least ten jurors must be present to make a quorum. Each member is sworn to secrecy and if they talk outside the grand jury room they are subject to prosecution.

At 26$^{th}$ and California the grand jury room is very comfortable and is set up theatre style, almost like a college lecture hall, but smaller. There are 20 soft cushioned chairs upholstered in a ribbed maroon colored fabric. The walls are painted a neutral color that provides a calming effect. There is a lift-up folding desk partition on each chair in case a juror wants to take notes. All notes are destroyed after a session.

Witnesses that appear before the grand jury sit at a four by six wooden mahogany table with a matching straight back chair that has a thin cushion for comfort. The state's attorney who is present in the room has a podium for his or her notes. A court reporter sets up a steno machine to the right of the witness table and is almost invisible to the jurors who look slightly down at the witness table.

Detective Dick Corley was introduced to the grand jury by ASA Amy Wilson. He was sangfroid as Wilson methodically led him step by step through the evidence as she outlined the 22 DNA samples that provided irrefutable proof against Clayton Cranston and Douglas Russell.

"Cranston's palm print was found on the right front window on the passenger side of her car. There is absolutely no doubt he was in the car during the brutal rape of Ruth Lezkowski … the aggravated sexual assault."

"Do you routinely take palm prints when you fingerprint a suspect?"

"No. Hardly ever, really." Corley said and then went on to describe their confessions and how they re-enacted the crime of their own free will and that the police videotaped it.

The jury members were captivated by his flawless presentation. A middle aged black female asked, "What were their attitudes when they confessed?"

Corley's head was slightly tilted down as he listened to the question. He dramatically lifted it and look the juror directly in the eyes and responded, "Impenitent."

The entire jury nodded in agreement. ASA Amy Wilson instructed the jurors to deliberate and take whatever time they needed to consider the facts presented. Then she, detective Corley and the court reporter left the room and the jurors started their deliberations on the charges of murder, aggravated sexual assault, sexual assault, forcible felony, armed robbery, robbery, aggravated kidnapping and kidnapping presented before them.

In less than a half hour the grand jury handed up a 16-count indictment. One count read,

> Clayton Cranston
> Douglas Russell
>
> Committed the offense of MURDER:
>
> In that, THEY WITHOUT LAWFUL JUSTIFICATION, INFLICTED MULTIPLE BLUNT FORCE INJURIES WHICH KILLED RUTH LEZKOWSKI, KNOWING THAT SUCH MULTIPLE BLUNT FORCE INJURIES CREATED A STRONG PROBABILITY OF DEATH OR GREAT BODILY HARM TO RUTH LEZKOWSKI, AND THE STATE SHALL SEEK AN EXTENDED TERM SENTENCE IN THAT THE OFFENSE WAS ACCOMPANIED BY EXCEPTIONALLY BRUTAL OR HEINOUS BEHAVIOR INDICATIVE OF WANTON CRUELTY, IN VIOLATION OF ILLINOIS LAW.

~~~~

The hot steamy coffee cup sitting in front of Robert Franey metaphorically symbolized the discussion he was having with Jose Aguilera. "You know the judge is going to throw out your magniloquent pleading. I can file a dismissal with prejudice for Maurer, Pangborn and Bass. They will be dismissed."

"I am not going to do that. I need to have some options in case I want to sue them in the future," Aguilera emphatically stated.

"We will agree to extending the statute of limitations for filing a new lawsuit against Maurer until one-year after the other case is resolved. If that is agreeable to you, will you dismiss them? This will save both of us a lot of money and time that will ultimately be wasted."

Aguilera was leaning back in his chair pressing his fingers in a steeple configuration. He was looking up at the ceiling and then he came forward folding his hands on his desk and said "Okay. I will dismiss them but I want assurances that we will be able to depose them in the future."

"Yep, we can do that. By the way when do you want to start depositions?"

Aguilera raised his eyebrows, "We have prepped Charles and Broadhead already. I would like to get those started as soon as possible. Talk to your client and let's get that ball rolling."

Franey reached for his coffee and took a sip. It had cooled off and it went down satisfyingly. He smiled "I'll set em up."

~~~~

Peter Michaels and Ron Magers were in an intense conversation about retirement. Michaels had his legs extended and feet crossed and his fingers were interlaced behind his head. "I don't think I am going for another contract, Mage."

"You love being a reporter. What are you going to do?"

"Not sure. I am going to move out of Chicago. I'm tired of these cold winters. I'm getting too old for this shit. Things have changed. We don't do what we used to do." Michaels pulled himself to an upright sitting position and leaned his forearms on his knees. "Everything is tits and ass or if it don't bleed it don't lead. Hell they may not renew my contract."

Magers loosened his tie and turned his chin to the right. It was an unconscious movement. "I love doing what I do."

"I know and you're the best anchor in the world. I mean that Mage, but I don't know if I want to do this anymore. You know I could count on one hand the number of days that I didn't want to come to work." Michaels shrugged his shoulders, "I'm losing my fire. I'm losing my fire."

# CHAPTER 65

P eter Michaels pulled his Detroit Lions stocking cap off his head and stuffed it in his coat pocket as he entered Pete's Coffee Shop. Christmas was fast approaching and decorations adorned the streetlights and trees that lined Maxwell Street. Detective Dick Corley was sitting at his favorite table in the corner reading the sports section of the Chicago Bugle. He looked up as Michaels approached the table.

"Hey, Jethro what's up?"

"Not a lot. They're transferring me over to the state's attorney's office full time. I'll be doing special investigations."

"Sounds good. You're great at what you do. Anything new?"

"Yeah, we got a call from Jose Aguilera. That prick Broadhead is trying to extort him."

"What! Why in the world would anyone extort their attorney who is fighting to get him lots of money for a wrongful conviction?"

"Beats me. They met the other day to talk about their lawsuit and the following day Broadhead leaves a message that he wants $3,000 for a tape recording of their conversation."

"What's on the tape?"

"Not sure but you know in order for him to get into the civil suit in the first place he had to recant his confession and get cleared of his part in the original trial. After the phone call Aguilera contacted Amy Wilson and explained that Broadhead just called and intimidated him. The son of a bitch is blackmailing his own attorney. So Jose has agreed to wear a wire and record their conversations."

"That son of a bitch has been in and out of jail two or three times since he went to jail in the Lezkowski case."

"He's been arrested 19 times since 96 and been to prison at least three more times. I can't believe he'll get anything."

"Oh, he'll get something but I can't see how Jose can represent him after this."

"Only in Chicago," Corley said.

~~~~

Chief Judge Michael Hook always looked the same. Detectives Dick Corley and Don Buerline entered his chambers with the conventional overhear petition. Hook's sleeves were rolled up and his tie was in its usual half Windsor knot. He looked up from his paperwork. "What's up?"

Corley handed him the petition. "We need another wire."

Hook's eyeglasses were on the end of his nose and he scrutinized the petition, "Are you shitting me? Aguilera is wearing a wire on his own client?"

Corley gave a clef note explanation of Aguilera's dilemma and the judged sign the consent form and handed it back shaking his head.

"Only in Chicago, your honor, only in Chicago," Corley said.

~~~~

ASA Amy Wilson was explaining to Jose Aguilera how the Monte Blanc looking ballpoint pen would capture his conversation with Marcus Broadhead. She demonstrated how to engage the recording device. "Just turn the clip portion clockwise and it will start transmitting a signal which we will be recording in the van. You can actually write with the pen while you're talking. It will not interfere with the signal."

"How long will the battery last?"

"Three hours but I doubt that your conversation will go that long. Don't be surprised if your first meeting produces no results. This guy knows the system and he knows how to work it. When does he want to meet?"

"He wants me to come to the McDonald's on West Madison Street near where he is staying at three o'clock."

"We'll be ready."

Broadhead was 15 minutes late. His eyes were flitting back and forth. He didn't want to sit by the window so he moved to a table near the men's restroom but the long lens on Corley's camera caught him anyway. Corley clicked off five pictures in a matter of seconds, "Gotcha ... you little fuck" Corley mumbled under his breath.

Aguilera took out his new pen and turned on the recorder. "What kind of tape are you talking about here, Marcus?"

"You know how you wanted me to lie about recanting my confession and you being better than Johnny Cochran."

"First of all I never ever instructed you to lie or deceive anyone. I always told you to tell the truth. Where is this tape?"

"You got the money?"

"Yeah, I have the money. The tape."

"I'll meet you here same time on the sixth. You bring the money, I'll bring the tape," Broadhead said as he got up and darted out the door without buttoning his winter coat.

Aguilera got up, buttoned his coat and walked straight to his car. He never looked toward the undercover van. He wasn't sure if Broadhead was watching. He left and headed back to 26th and California.

~~~~

Gerald Witty was sitting at his desk in the Public Defender's Office waiting for the jail to call him so he could visit Clayton Cranston. His eleven by eleven foot office was the total opposite of Jose Aguilera's office. It was a typical government space, dark and besmirched. The fluorescent lights only added to the grayish atmosphere. His desk was covered with stacks of files. The floor looked as if it were carpeted with files. His caseload was overwhelming.

It took longer to wait for an elevator than it did to walk over to the Cook County Jail. Witty was escorted into one of the many visiting rooms that attorneys use to have a conference with their inmate clients.

Cranston was already sitting there shackled to the table. His body looked withered in his orange prison jumpsuit. His face appeared skeletal, his eyes were deeply set and his skin tone was different. He looked unhealthy.

"The grand jury approved a 16-count indictment against you and Russell. You know they are going after the death penalty and they'll more than likely get it."

"Fuck dat man. Dat's bullshit."

"Well you guys fucked yourselves when you did that re-enactment. You took away any plausible defense we could have presented."

"What you mean?"

"Look we could have said that you admit to the rape. The statute of limitations on that charge was over. DNA proves you raped her but it doesn't necessarily prove you killed her."

"Never thought about dat."

"Also, we could have created reasonable doubt."

"How dat?"

"Well they arrested four people already and they got off. We would have challenged that and took the position; what makes you so sure you have the right guys now?"

Cranston was rubbing his chin and shaking his head, "Man we really fucked up."

"I would have called some of the original detectives to the stand. They still believe those kids killed her."

"Would they have to come to the stand?"

"They would be considered hostile witnesses but yes I could have subpoenaed them."

"Man, we sure enough fucked up."

"You should consider pleading guilty. I think I can negotiate the death penalty off the table if you plea out."

"I be thinkin' bout dat. Shit man."

"My partner will be recommending the same deal to Douglas Russell. Do you ever see him?"

"Naw. We be separated. I never see him."

# CHAPTER 66

J anuary 6, 2003 was a very damp cold gray day typical for Chicago at this time of the year. The black crusty snow that lined the streets had a hard time melting away because the sun was absent for what seemed like weeks. Although it was three o'clock, the gloomy clouds and the chilly mist made it appear much later. It was a blue Monday.

Jose Aguilera sat at a table next to the men's room looking at his Rolex. Broadhead was late as usual. He arrived with a smile on his face. Aguilera was passive as he turned on his ballpoint pen that started recording and transmitting their conversation. Broadhead slithered into his chair like a snake. His smile turned into a sneer, "You got the money?"

"Yeah, I got the money," Aguilera sneered back. "You got the tape?"

Without saying a word, Broadhead reached into his coat pocket and found a wrinkled plastic grocery bag and put it on the table in front of Aguilera. The audiocassette was un-useable. Its plastic casing was shattered and the three feet of tape that was pulled out was crinkled badly. It couldn't be restored it was so damaged.

"What's on this?" Aguilera asked.

"You know what's on it. Our conversation of you instructing me how to recant my shit."

"Then there is nothing on it Marcus because that type of conversation never took place."

"Well you'll find out after you give me the $3,000."

Aguilera reached into his left breast pocket and pulled out a white envelope with 30 one-hundred-dollar bills. The money supplied to him by ASA Amy Wilson with every bill's serial number recorded. Every bill was photographed and marked with indelible ink. Aguilera handed the money over.

"Here's your money. Good luck finding an attorney to represent you in your civil lawsuit."

As soon as Marcus Broadhead took the money, two undercover detectives approached the table and cuffed him. As they were walking him away they read him his Constitutional rights.

He was charged with Intimidation, which is a class-four felony but Amy Wilson knew that the charge would eventually be negotiated down to a misdemeanor. Broadhead would be freed on his own recognizance within weeks. It was the seventeenth time he was arrested in the last five years.

~~~~

The main conference room at Carlin and Miller was very auspicious. The sun shining through the floor to ceiling windows that faced LaSalle Street gave it an even more majestic feel. The fifteen by six-foot glass table that sat on silver pedestals glistened. The 16 Nottingham chairs that surrounded the table were decorated in a soft gray fabric with a diamond design. The only smudges that appeared on the glass top came from Charles Holmes. All the attorneys present for his deposition had files laid out in front of them and their hands never touched the glass.

Charles was nervous and fidgety. His hand trembled slightly every time he reached for the bottle of water that he placed off to his right. His testimony was mesmeric. His soft voice was hypnotic and his description of how he was tricked by the police when he was just 14-years-old into making a confession was compelling. The deposition lasted less than an hour.

Bob Franey who was a full partner at the firm knew that his client had to settle immediately because if they ever went to trial, Charles Holmes would have any jury eating out of the palm of his hand. He was completely believable and empathetic.

After the conference room cleared, Franey went to his office, eased into his oversized chair that could comfortably handle his six foot six frame and called Rosemary Ravalli at the Corporation Council's Office.

"Hey big boy, do you have good news for me?"

"Well, if we can get Charles Holmes to settle quickly I do."

"What does that mean?"

"If he ever takes the stand, he'll be devastating. His deposition was off the charts, captivating really. He wants to get on with his life. He has a girlfriend. He has moved to the suburbs. He wants to buy a house and he's training to be an EMT. He is prime for an early settlement. We'll save money."

Ravalli leaned forward on her desk, twirled her pen in her fingers and had an attentive look. "I'll see if I can get something going on this end. Anything else?"

"Yeah, this Broadhead character. What a piece of work he is. I cannot believe he is going to get anything out of this. He tried to extort Jose Aguilera the other day, his own fucking attorney. I can't believe it."

"What!"

"Yep. Aguilera wore a wire for the police. Broadhead tried to extort three grand from him and they pinched him. Aguilera is no longer representing him but I think he is approachable and he'll take whatever we offer him."

"Okay. I'll talk to the boss."

~~~~

"When's your contract up?" Ron Magers asked.

"In less than six months" Michaels responded. "I think I am going to talk to Phil. I pretty much have made up my mind. Thirty-five years of this shit is enough."

"What are you going to do?"

"Dave is quitting too and he's going to start up a production company. I might work with him for a while. I'm thinking Florida. I can't take these winters anymore."

"I just bought a place in Fort Lauderdale. You should come visit."

"Thanks, I like the west coast better. I'm thinking Marco Island, Fort Myers or Naples."

"Not that much to do over there."

"Exactly," Michaels said with a smile turning his head to the door. "What's up Dave?"

Dave Beedy had an eager look on his face as he handed Michaels a cell phone. "Aguilera just called your cell. It was on your desk so I didn't think you'd mind if I answered it. He has reached a settlement for Charles Holmes with the city. He wants to talk with you."

Michaels stood, turned towards Magers, "We might have a new lead for the ten," he said as he left Magers standing there and he speed dialed Jose Aguilera.

"Tell me something I can use?" Michaels asked Aguilera.

"I just reached a settlement with Rosemary Ravalli."

"Big?"

"No. Not really but Charles doesn't care. He got $1.5 million."

"That's pretty cheap."

"He doesn't care. He's done with all of this. He's in love and he's starting a new job as an EMT. He's happy with it and that makes me happy."

"What about the other guys; Lorenzo and Oscar? Are they holding out for a bigger payday?"

"Yep and that could take a few more years. We haven't started their depositions."

"That's probably why Charles wanted to move on."

"Yeah."

Michaels got to his desk and started taking notes. "What about Broadhead?"

"He hustled some attorney from Traffic Court and he's lucky if he gets a mill."

Beedy slipped Michaels a note that read *$900,000. Franey.* Michaels nodded and said, "Dave just talked to Bob Franey. Broadhead is getting $900,000."

"Good, I'll bill him for all my services for the last three years and the hustler will probably take 15% and that prick will be lucky if he gets $100,000."

"Can I use all this?"

"Sure, just leave out the prick thing," Aguilera said, smiling as he hung up the phone.

# CHAPTER 67

T he Honorable Judge John James' courtroom was ironically the same courtroom 404 where Lorenzo Holmes and Oscar Sampson were tried 18 years earlier for the murder of Ruth Lezkowski.

Judge James was erect, shoulders back, head high as he entered his courtroom. The room itself was like going back in time. Nothing had changed after almost two decades and thousands of felony trials, except there were a few more initials carved into the wooden benches in the gallery.

ASA Amy Wilson wore a dark blue hand tailored pantsuit and an off-white blouse with a conservative neckline. She had waited for this moment for more than three years. She despised these two defendants from the first time she took their unrepentant statements.

Wilson talked to the Lezkowski family two days before the court hearing. Though they would rather have seen Cranston and Russell be executed, they wanted closure once and for all. Mr. Lezkowski felt that the plea agreement would halt more appeals that would drag the case through the courts for years to come. Life in prison was really no life at all, so the family gave the State's Attorney their blessing to the plea agreement.

Wilson wanted to go to trial. She never felt more confident about a conviction. The evidence was just overwhelming and they admitted their involvement in two different taped statements. She fought hard for the death penalty and felt zero remorse for being responsible for sending these defendants to their deaths. She knew in her heart that this case would be in the system for years to come so she reluctantly agreed to the plea.

"Your honor, we would like to bring this horrible saga that has haunted us for the past 18 years to an end. Defendants Clayton Cranston and Douglas Russell were charged with 16 counts of murder in connection with the repeated rape and beating death of Ruth Lezkowski." Wilson turned and looked at the defendants with total disdain. Adrenaline was flowing through her body and her confidence was never higher as she began to methodically lay out the state's case for the court the same way she lead Detective Dick Corley through the case in front of the grand jury. People in the gallery were shaking their heads. Reporters scribbled notes passionately. The total silence in the courtroom ended when Wilson dramatically stated, "Every bone in her face was shattered." The gallery wheezed. Most shook their heads. Some covered their mouths with their hand. Wilson continued, "Her skull was crushed. Her brain stem was severed and she had nine broken ribs." Wilson paced the courtroom. All eyes were on her and she pointed to the defendants and said, "Those two men told Douglas Russell's brother, 'We did that. She was a hard bitch to kill.'"

Everyone seemed drained by the presentation. Wilson was never better and never more passionate. The Chief of Special Prosecutions Peter Di Donato was in the back of the courtroom. His arms were folded and his chest expanded as he admired his protégé. He was never more proud. He turned and walked out of the courtroom with a smile because he knew that judge James was going to ask for a short recess. The facts of this brutal murder were breathtaking.

~~~~

When court resumed 20 minutes later, Amy Wilson continue: "Your honor, Clayton Cranston and Douglas Russell have agreed to plead guilty to one count of murder executed during the course of a criminal sexual assault that was committed in an exceptionally brutal and heinous manner, in exchange for a 75-year extended-term sentence with three years of mandatory supervised release and the dismissal of the remaining charges."

There was a gasp in the overcrowded courtroom. Reporters and spectators alike began to murmur. Judge James slammed his gavel down, "Order in the courtroom. Order." Total silence enveloped the room.

Judge James straightened his shoulders, his hazel eyes bore into each of the defendants, "Do you understand this offer?"

"Yes," each of them whimpered.

"Speak up so the court can hear you," Judge James demanded.

"Yes, your honor."

"Do you realize that each of the murder counts carry a 20 to 40-year prison term?" Judge James admonished.

Each defendant replied, "Yes," loud enough for the court to hear.

"Do you realize that you both could be found guilty and sentence to the death penalty or life in prison for some of the charges in front of you?" Judge James continued, "You have the right to plead 'not guilty' which would require the state to prove your guilt beyond a reasonable doubt. You have the right to a trial before a jury or a judge. Do you understand these rights?"

Cranston and Clayton avoided eye contact with the judge throughout the entire admonishment but they answered affirmatively every time they were asked if they understood.

Finally, Judge James informed them, "By pleading guilty, you are giving up your right to call and confront witnesses on your behalf. You are also giving up the right to testify on your own behalf. Do you understand the rights you are giving up?"

"Yes, your honor," they replied simultaneously.

"Mr. Cranston, are you pleading guilty freely and voluntarily?"

"Yes, your honor," Cranston replied.

"Mr. Russell, are you pleading guilty freely and voluntarily?"

"Yes, your honor," Russell replied.

In sentencing Clayton Cranston and Douglas Russell to 75 years in prison for the kidnapping, vicious rape and brutal death of Ruth Lezkowski, Judge John James looked down at the two men and said, "In all the years I have been in this building, I have never seen more DNA left on a victim. It disgusts me. I hope you know you just got the deal of a lifetime." He didn't wait for an answer. He gaveled the proceeding to its conclusion, stood and walked into his chambers with a nauseating feeling in the pit of his stomach. In 30 years on the bench, he had never felt this bilious.

~~~~

Although Peter Michaels was not a Chicago Cubs fan, he had a great time at his retirement party held at Harry Carey's, the famed Cubs announcer's Italian Steakhouse located at 33 West Kinzie. Harry Carey made the catchphrase "Holy Cow," a Chicago household mantra.

The upper banquet hall was packed with family, friends and colleagues as one after the other roasted Michaels just unmercifully. Ron Magers went as far as to say, "Michaels, nobody thought you would ever live this long."

Karen Martin, a well-known anchorwoman both nationally and locally, reminded him, "Peter, talking about your hemorrhoids is not a great pick up line for women."

Attorney Sam Pfeiffer told everyone about the time Michaels was arrested at Police Headquarters trying to smuggle a gun into a courtroom, "I get a call from the news director saying 'Peter has been arrested.' I asked for what? Not 100% sure, but something about him trying to sneak a gun into the main police station." Sam flashed a boyish grin from ear to ear shaking his head from side to side, "What? Come again? So I hot foot down to 11th and State and asked to see my client. Here comes Peter in handcuffs, laughing. So I ask him 'Did you do it?' He said 'Of course I did it.'" Everyone in the room was now laughing and Sam looked over at Michaels and said, "Peter it was not great lawyering that got you sprung, it was the high regard that the coppers had for you that did the job. I'm going to miss working with you buddy."

With that everyone stood up and proposed another toast. They all got a kick out of roasting Michaels. who by this time didn't care what anyone said about him. He was always ready to have a beer with his friends and this night was not any different.

Marsha Bartel another producer, said, "Peter is the only person I know who could touch the head of a Chicago mobster and live to talk about it. We covered the trial of Frankie 'The Freak' Palozi in Kansas City. Peter somehow manages to have dinner with him and he brought me along. So after three hours of drinking vodka and eating veal limone, Palozi says we're having a nightcap. During the course of the conversation at one o'clock in the morning, Peter reached up and touched Palozi on the head, which of course is the sign of death to a mobster. So Palozi immediately jumps up, knocks over his chair and glared at Peter with a look of death in his eyes, and said, 'Don't your ever touch me on my fucking head.' I was scared as scared could be. So what does Peter do? He stands up and knocks over his chair and pokes his finger directly into Palozi's barreled chest and said, 'Hey, Palozi remind me to never, ever, touch you on your fucking head again.' With that Palozi is stunned. A look of confusion came across his face and the look of immanent death disappeared. He starts laughing, patting Peter on the back saying 'you, you're something mister. You are something.' I thought we were both dead. Peter just shrugged his shoulders and said 'We gotta get up early tomorrow morning Mr. Palozi to meet our crew. Thanks for the drink.' As we were walking to our rooms, Peter looked at me and said, 'I don't know where that came from but I was shitting my pants. I thought we were dead.' Peter, it's been quite a journey working with you thanks for taking me along."

The party went down to the bar and at two thirty, Peter Michaels hailed a taxi and went home with a satisfying grin on his face as he fell into deep thought, *I love Chicago but this city has drained me. Deadlines and drinking. I tried to be a good dad. Should I have been home more? No doubt but I always put the job first. It put food on the table and water skis on my girls' feet. Shit I'm tired. I am ready for Florida. You're only as good as your last story.*

# CHAPTER 68

T he 90-mile drive from downtown Chicago to Pontiac Correctional Center was terrifying on February 14, 2011. Peter Michael's knuckles were white under his fur lined leather gloves and he was afraid to let go of the steering wheel. The blizzard was blinding. The temperature hovered at 15 degrees. The roads were wind-blown with snowdrifts. His Nissan sedan rental car was like a makeshift snowplow moving at 35 miles per hour heading south on I-55. The white/gray horizon disappeared in his windshield. The occasional picturesque old barns that dotted the farm fields in the summer appeared as red smudges in the white winter landscape. Exit 197 couldn't come fast enough.

~~~~

Pontiac Correctional Center was built in 1871. Originally it was a reform school for boys. Now it is a maximum-security prison for adult males, however a small section of the facility houses medium to minimum-security inmates. Death row prisoners are also housed there but it has no execution chamber.

The average cell is eight feet by five feet by eight feet. In 1931, Pontiac Correctional Center housed 2,504 inmates: 1,959 were white, 535 were black and 10 were identified as "other." The inmates were allowed to smoke in their cells at specified times. Relatives were allowed to visit once a month except Saturday afternoons, Sundays and holidays.

By 1978, the prison's population changed dramatically by then most of the inmates came from Chicago's street gangs. PCC housed an average of 2,000 inmates a day. Now 1450 were black, 350 were Hispanic and 200 were white.

In July of that year, one of deadliest riots in prison history broke out there involving more than half the prison population. Six hundred prisoners armed with shanks and other handmade deadly weapons were returning to their cellblocks after a recreation session when they attacked correctional officers inside their cell house. They set buildings on fire forcing more prisoners to get involved. Two officers were killed and three others were injured. More than a 100 state troopers and local police responded. They fired tear gas into the recreational areas and by dusk order was restored.

Prison officials immediately ordered a lockdown that lasted for three months. Prisoners were not allowed to leave their cells for any reason. All meals were delivered to their cells. There was no recreational time. All work assignments were cancelled. Inmates were not even allowed to shower until October. Family visits were cancelled until October 15th. Phone privileges were resumed on September 30th.

Because of the riot, the prison allowed only a few inmates to be moved in a single line at any given time. In 1997, maximum security prisoners were kept in their cells every hour of the day except on certain days when they were allowed recreation time, library time, showers and visits.

There were 49,000 inmates housed in Illinois prisons by the time Douglas Russell and Clayton Cranston arrived at Pontiac in 2004. Prisoners not in segregation were allowed more time out of their cells and more social time in the recreation areas, the gym and in the dining hall.

Russell and Cranston were placed in different cellblocks in different tiers in semi-protected units and never saw each other again once they were processed into the Pontiac Correctional Center. They communicated by letter every other month for the first few years.

Cranston appealed his guilty plea claiming he was tricked into confessing to the murder of Ruth Lezkowski and his attorney told him, he would only have to serve 20 years. In 1998 Illinois law changed requiring all convicted murderers to serve 100 percent of their sentence. The appeal was denied in August of 2006 with Judge John James saying, "The DNA in this case was so overwhelming against Mr. Cranston and Mr. Russell. If they went to trial they certainly would have received the death penalty."

~~~~

Michaels pulled his car into the snow-covered prison parking lot, put his head on the steering wheel and started thinking about the best way to interview Clayton Cranston. He took a deep breath, opened his car door and stepped out into the freezing cold winter air. *It's 85 degrees in southwest Florida and here I am,* He thought as his titanium knee replacements reminded him of why he moved south fulltime four years earlier.

He shivered as he approached the front door of the reception building. The crusty snow beneath his feet crunched with every hurried step. The yellowish brick structure's entrance was garlanded with a limestone border that was tattooed with black stains seeping from its tuck-pointing. Three single black framed coach lights bejeweled the doorway. The one on the right was burned out. The heavy black bulletproof glass door was sluggish when Michaels heaved to pull it open as he entered the 24 by 24 foot orderly room.

The three prison guards that greeted him were dressed in dark blue pants with a light blue stripe running down their pant leg. Their light blue shirts though ironed, were not crisp. A three-ringed sign-in binder was opened on the tired linoleum counter. Two black smudges the shape of small footballs served as a reminder from tens of thousands of visitors' elbows over the decades leaning on the counter while they signed their names to enter the prison.

An officer with a nametag that read "Allen" greeted Michaels with a sly grin accentuated with a scruffy mustache. With a deep voice, he asked, "You that reporter we've been expecting? You're interviewing that mutt Cranston, right?"

It took Michaels three months and five letters to get permission to interview the convicted killers of Ruth Lezkowski. Douglas Russell didn't dither at the opportunity but Cranston vacillated for weeks.

"Yep, that's me. What's the protocol here?"

Michaels had a puzzled look on his face as the guard named Allen countered, "He's in the infirmary. Put your stuff in one of those lockers."

The18-inch by 18-inch lockers looked like they belonged in a Greyhound bus station. It cost fifty cents to release the key that allowed access one time. If you forgot something, it cost another fifty cents to re-open it.

"No tape recorders. Just pen and pad. No coat either. Put that in your locker." Allen said as he examined Michaels' property.

Michaels just smiled. His leather notebook had a built-in tape recorder that was triggered when it was opened. "I'm going to set that metal detector off. I have knee replacements," Michaels said as he approached the gate.

"Don't worry about it. We got ya covered."

Once through the metal detector Michaels asked, "Where am I going?"

Allen pointed to the infirmary 250 yards away that was trying to reveal itself through the gray winter fog. The sidewalk was shoveled, salted and wet. Michaels inhaled deeply and forced himself out into the freezing cold air. He hobbled as fast as his swollen knees allowed. His blue cashmere V-neck sweater did little to protect him from the damp cold air.

*Shit, it's cold,* he thought as he crashed through the infirmary door, stumbling into the arms of the waiting guard.

"Sorry about that." Michaels mumbled.

"No problem," a tall thin guard with a military style haircut named "Amen" said.

Michaels thought *"Amen." Fitting.* "What's your first name?"

"Harvey." The guard pointed and said, "This way" as he headed toward a gray door stenciled with the number four.

Three things immediately struck Michaels as he entered hospital room four; the heavy smell of disinfectant, the hissing sound of oxygen and Cranston's huge feet that were sticking out from underneath the sheet that was too short to cover the length of his skeletal body. *Size 13 or 14?* Thought Michaels.

The faded lime colored ceramic tiles from the 1950s were dull. The once white grout securing them to the ancient walls was now yellowish from years of scrubbing with Lysol. The patient's bed, with its brown metal ribbed headboard, was about the size of a gurney from a modern day hospital. The form fitting bottom sheet could not grip the worn out, two-inch thick mattress. The formerly white top sheet was now grayish, distressed and it had a gauze-like appearance. A dark green course woolen army blanket covered his torso and his hands were folded on his stomach as if he were already "laid out to rest" in a casket. The bed sat on a floor of one inch white hexagonal tiles that were set in what was now black grout. A gray tattered bath towel hung over the bedrail. A TV sat on his bedside table within reach. The aluminum foil wrapped around the tips of its antennas did nothing to mitigate the snowy picture flickering on its screen.

Age had an affect on the drop ceiling tiles that were turning yellow. The fluorescent lights encased in their worn plastic lenses illuminated a sickly buttery tint that filled the room with an eerie sense of desolation.

The pillows that propped up Cranston's head were thin, hard and rectangular. Cranston's odd-shaped ears pinched the side of his head not allowing the oxygen line running from the tank behind his bed to fall properly under his chin. The cannula that is designed to deliver the precious gas into his nasal passages was askew allowing the oxygen to helplessly disappear into the surrounding atmosphere. Cranston was dying.

The cancer that invaded his system had turned his skin a drab olive green color. He was gaunt. His eyes sunk into their sockets. He looked weary, fatigued and appeared to be losing the battle with his esophagus.

Michaels was devoid of any feelings for him as he approached the bed. "I'm Peter Michaels. Thanks for seeing me."

"Yeah, no problem man. Whatta you want?" Cranston said in an almost inaudible raspy voice.

"I wanted to ask you about the Ruth Lezkowski case."

"I didn't kill nobody," he whispered.

"But your DNA was all over the place. How do you explain that?"

"I didn't kill nobody, ever," he responded in a soft yet slightly more aggressive and agitated tone.

"That isn't what Douglas Russell said."

"Did he change what he talkin' bout?"

"I'm talking to him next. You know you have a pretty big size foot and Ruth was stomped to death with a shoe about the size of yours? She had nine broken ribs."

"Hey, fuck you man. I didn't kill nobody. Get the fuck outta my face." He ordered. Cranston limply lifted his right arm and with a crooked boney finger pointed toward the door. His eyes came to whatever life he had left in his body and he said again, "Fuck you."

Michaels collected his notebook and turned to exit the room. His adrenaline was pumping hard. His frustration erupted like a volcano. He stopped dead in his tracks and turned 180 degrees around and with a look of disgust on his face said, "I hope you rot in hell you son of a bitch for all the misery and destruction you caused the Lezkowski family and all the people who have suffered because of your unconscionable, inconsiderate brutal behavior. Fuck me? No, fuck you! You piece of shit!"

The tall thin guard with the military style haircut smiled broadly as he led the way out of hospital room four through the gray door with a six inch square window at eye level.

Michaels couldn't feel his aching knees only his sweaty armpits. He felt limp and exhausted as he sauntered out into the cold air and back to the prison's orderly room. At that moment he made up his mind that he would write a book about this incredible story that still haunts the city of Chicago. Who actually killed Ruth Lezkowski on that night of a Blood Moon?

# CHAPTER 69

M ichaels rented a hotel room for the week at the Sheraton along the Chicago River that was kitty corner from the NBC Tower. The trip back to the city from the Pontiac Correctional Center was uneventful and fairly pleasant. It felt good, wearing a pair of sunglasses while driving in the middle of a cold winter day. Chicago's very distinguishable skyline came into view at two o'clock. He smiled, *the greatest city in the world.*

His research files were sprinkled on top of his king size bed. He picked up the one titled "Settlement" and opened it. Michaels moved over to the desk by the window overlooking the river and settled into his chair. The sun began to disappear and heavy dark gray clouds were moving in. *Dear God, I miss Florida.*

In April of 2007, Chicago's Finance Committee settled with Lorenzo Holmes and Oscar Sampson for $8 million dollars apiece. It was a structured settlement. Each received an initial payment of four million dollars with the rest being paid in increments agreed to in the civil lawsuit.

Jose Aguilera finally got paid for his six years of services, forty percent plus all expenses—four million dollars.

Marcus Broadhead settled for $900,000 in December of 2003 but ultimately received far less. Charles Holmes received $1.5 million. Charles used his money to move on with his life in a positive direction; he got married and had a child. He had a fulltime job as paramedic in the western suburbs. He was happy and at peace with himself and his past.

Broadhead, on the other hand, continued his life of crime. From the time he was released from prison in 1996 after his testimony put

Lorenzo Holmes in jail, he was arrested 43 more times with 15 convictions and five separate sentences to the penitentiary. He was arrested 11 times after he received his $900,000 settlement. Michaels shook his head, rubbed his chin and wondered how many more times he would be arrested in the future. Michaels walked back to the bed for another file.

His file on Oscar Sampson was very sparse. He had little new information on him other than a number of newspaper clippings and his old arrest records. Sampson was totally under the police radar since his release in 2001. It appeared that he was moving forward under Jose Aguilera's guidance.

The file labeled "Ringleader" sat in the middle of the bed. It had every piece of information Michaels could gather on Lorenzo Holmes, including his five arrests since 2001. *Bad guy* Michaels thought as he opened the manila folder. Out of habit, Michaels reached up to run his fingers through his hair but none was there. Since he retired Michaels started shaving his head. He smiled, *Old habits are hard to break,* but at that moment he came back to reality. No one ever reported how violent Lorenzo Holmes really was. Looking over his arrest record, Michaels recalled the brutal rape of an 11-year-old boy when Holmes was 15 and how vicious it was. *The media made the guy out as if he were a choirboy,* Michaels thought once again grimacing as he shook his head.

After Holmes was awarded $8 million, he went to jail a number of months later for aggravated assault of a police officer with a firearm. His troubled past continued to steer his future. He was charged with theft in 2006. Two months before his settlement he was charged with reckless driving. Two weeks before his settlement he tried to pass a bogus check at a car dealership in Lake Forest, Illinois. The police were called and that's when he got into a confrontation with the first responding police officer and physically assaulted him with the firearm.

The officer sued him in civil court for battery and was awarded $50,000 but to this date, even after Holmes settled for the $8 million, he still has not paid the court ordered settlement. He was always defiant.

Michaels stood up and started pacing the room. He picked up his cell phone and found the number for retired Detective Jack Evans, pressed dial and prayed it was still viable. On the third ring a familiar voice answered, "Hello, Detective Evans this is Peter Michaels, long time no talk."

Evans scowled and insipidly answered, "What a surprise." He hesitated a beat, "What da you want?"

"I'm in town. I'm still writing that Lezkowski book and wondered if you want to have lunch or coffee?"

"No. I have nothing more to say about it. I was dismissed from all the lawsuits. I am happy about that and I ain't got nothing more to say. Capeesh?"

"Well, I'm writing the Lezkowski story as a novel and I was just wondering."

"What happened to the true story?"

"Too many records are sealed. Too many records stowed away in the warehouse and very expensive to get. Some of the records may have burned in that fire several years back. The book will contain a lot of information that has never been brought out in the past. So I was just hoping, we could, you know get together."

"You still don't get it do you?"

"Get what?"

"They don't want the truth out. They don't want to admit they made mistakes. These people are powerful people."

Michaels was thinking Evans was getting paranoid, "What people?"

"I told you years ago, they are burying the truth. The reality is, everyone who had anything to do with this horrible, disgusting case went to jail. Those two in jail right now, no question they raped her. They probably even roughed her up a bit but—" Evans stopped in the middle of his sentence.

Michaels could sense the angst in his voice. "Listen Peter, I have said too much already. I am done talking. I guess we'll all know the truth when we die and get to heaven. We can ask God Almighty who did it. Please don't call me no more. I am done talking about this case."

Evans hung up the phone on the wall cradle and slowly lowered himself into his familiar kitchen chair. He reached for his blue coffee mug with the decorative gold Chicago Police star and tried to raise it to his mouth but couldn't. His hands were trembling as he set it back down and he put his face into his hands and prayed, "My God … my

God." Tears trundled down his cheeks as he thought about the Lezkowski family for the millionth time.

~~~~

Michaels hit the red end button on his cell phone and sighed *Holy shit that poor man is tormented. He thinks this is a massive cover up.* Michaels collected all his files from the bed, neatly stacked them in the center of the desk and put the one, labeled "D Russell" on top.

He checked himself out in the mirror, adjusted his blue sweater, exhaled and headed down to the lobby bar for a vodka on the rocks with a twist of lemon.

# CHAPTER 70

The correctional officer named Allen was six feet four. His looks didn't change overnight. Domineering. Scruffy and a little disheveled. He and one other guard were on duty. It was a slow morning. Allen was a typical, hardened, didn't-want-to-hear-it kind of guard. "So did that mutt tell you yesterday, that he didn't do it? They're all like that. They're all in prison for crimes they didn't commit. Same shit—different day. It never ends, they're all innocent."

Prison guards, like police officers, get immune to their milieus and act like they don't care. It's like putting on exterior armor to protect them from all the misery, death and painful situations they deal with on a daily basis.

"Yeah, like fuck you, I didn't kill her. Kinda what I expected. Where do I go today?" Michaels asked as he put his possessions into locker number 21, extracted its key and walked through the metal detector.

Allen directed him to an entrance 25 yards directly behind the orderly room. Michaels was buzzed in. The security lock clanged before he could push open the thick hefty door. The long narrow hallway led to a chamber where a guard sat looking at a series of monitors displaying a maze of hallways for cellblock 114. To his right was a single seven-foot-tall by six-foot-wide sliding cell door that had steel bars covered with countless applications of gray enamel paint over the years.

"You Michaels?" the expecting guard asked. "Wait in the snack room, I'll call you when he's ready. Russell right?"

"Yeah. Thanks."

The snack room was 18 feet long and 12 feet wide. Windows made up most of the wall on the left. Two dispensing machines were on the right. One machine supplied liquids, coke, iced tea and Gator Aid. All in cans. The other contained peanuts, crackers and candy bars. Both were fairly new but badly abused from visitors slamming their fists on them because their quarters didn't work or their bag of peanuts got stuck on its way down to the extraction bowl. The walls were painted a blue color somewhere between royal blue and light blue and they were scarred from people putting their feet up while sitting down. There were six heavy plastic chairs, two orange, two blue and two black. One orange and one black chair couldn't hold the weight of a small person.

A black woman about 55 years old wrapped in a woolen brown coat sat in one of the blue chairs. She was from Spring Valley by the Illinois River. Her son was in Pontiac for sexually abusing an underage boy. "He didn't do it," she said. She wanted to talk. Michaels was polite and listened though he wasn't interested. In his younger years, when he was an investigative reporter, he would have loved to hear her story, but right now he was only interested in his interview with Douglas Russell. The woman had sad eyes and a soft voice. Her pastor encouraged her to visit her son as often as possible. He needed forgiveness. She needed self-assurance. Michaels nodded sympathetically.

"Michaels," a loud voice announced. "He's on his way. Come over here."

"I hope it works out for your son. I'm sorry ma'am. I gotta go."

~~~~

Michaels stepped into a chamber protected by a similar cell door directly across from the one closing behind him. Another guard dressed in a white shirt and dark blue pants motioned for him to follow. A buzzer screamed, letting him know it was okay to move out of the protected space. They entered a ten by ten-foot room with a single six by five-foot table and two chairs that faced opposite one another. The walls were white and unadorned.

Michaels organized his notepad and pens. As he sat down as if on cue, Douglas Russell was shepherded into the room by another guard dressed in a white shirt. Michaels was surprised by Russell's looks.

He was wearing a blue V-neck smock over a bleached white tee shirt not the orange prison jumpsuit he expected to see. He appeared much different than he did in the videotaped statements that Michaels reviewed at least a dozen times. He was 60 or 70 pounds heavier than Michaels remembered; too many powered eggs and peanut butter and jelly sandwiches and little exercise. His skin was dark brown. His face was round. His eyes were empty.

"What's dis bout?"

"I'm writing a book based on the Ruth Lezkowski homicide. I'd like to tell your side of the story."

"What's in for me?"

"The truth. You have never told your story. This is your opportunity. I may develop some information that will be helpful to you. You never know."

"Dat be cool."

"Interesting, your birth date is 5-5-55," Michaels said and then thought *I wouldn't be surprised if it were 6-6-66. The devil.* "When did you get involve with drugs?"

"When I got outta the joint in 79."

"You were sent to jail twice for sexual assault, correct?"

"Yeah, I got out in 75 and den I got sentenced a few months later and got out in 79."

Michaels was mystified, "You got a problem with sexual assault? You get out of prison and just four or five months later you go back to jail for the same thing. That doesn't sound right."

"No, it wasn't really the problem. It was more or so like, I was robbin' women, at the time and if they didn't have no money, then, you know, they were sayin' they are gonna tell. So you end up going to the penitentiary for nuttin'. You know what I'm sayin. So they tell the police. The police go out and catch you; you go to court. Then you go to jail for 10 or 15 years for nuttin'. So I'd have sex wit em. So if I go to jail, I go for something."

Michaels was bewildered. *Robbery didn't appear to be a crime to this guy so he raped his victims because they didn't have any money. Unbelievable.* Your arrest record indicates you were arrested 26 times since 1986. Since Ruth Lezkowski was killed.

"I like to have $450 in my pocket all the time. I'd steal hubcaps and shit so I'd have the money."

"For cocaine?"

"No. No. It was basically to have some money in my pocket. Drugs were no problem. Smoking cocaine, was no problem. You know, you either have it or you don't. I just liked to have money in my pocket."

"What about gangs?"

"I got into that shit to protect my family and more or less me. I was a Renegade Disciple, den I switched over to the Gangster Disciples. Probably more so to protect me, I guess. I never killed nobody and right now today when we get to the Ruth Lezkowski thang, that's a whole 'nother story. And the fact dat I'm here now is because of the police and if they hadn't did what they asked me to do in the police station then, I probably wouldn't be sittin' here now because of the stuff that they did to me in the police station."

*Then why did you do it?* Michaels thought, "What did happen that night?"

"Me and uh, Clayton Cranston both, we went to Reggie's house. I think we smoked a couple of rocks. Now, dat's crack. And we smoked a happy stick. Dat's LSD, okay and we drunk some beers. So we left there and dat's when we ran into Ruth. So we grabbed her, you know, we took her to the tracks. So we searched her purse and you know dat's when he started to have sex with her."

Michaels checked his tape recorder to make sure he wasn't missing anything and he rearrange his position in his chair, captivated by Russell's unrepentant posturing.

"Clayton is first?"

"Yeah. So when he got down he told me, 'You know man, you might as well too, go ahead.' I really didn't want to get at her but, okay, so I just went on, got down with her. Got through, got up, we all got dressed."

Michaels was astonished at how shameless the man in front of him was telling this story, like they were going to have an after sex drink and everyone was happy that Ruth Lezkowski enjoyed being brutally raped. *Sick shit.*

"So then we get back in the car and start talking. Then we hit her cause we wanted to get out of there. We hit her in the jaw, tried to knock her out so we could leave. She, she just went to the side, and opened the car door and fell out. So we grabbed the door so she couldn't get out and pulled the door back and we slammed it right across here." He indicated with his left hand to his left temple and jaw, "so she went unconscious. So we got out, pulled her out the car, and felt her to make sure she was alive. She was breathing, so I says 'Come on man, let's go, and we left.'"

Russell never sat up straight, he was slouching towards his left side and he lifted his right arm up over the back of his chair until he was comfortable again as he brazenly continued his story. "So the next day, man, I walk into the house and I see on the news, right, that they say she be found dead up there on the track. I'm like damn. So, okay. I'm like oh, shit. I said, 'Man, I didn't know we killed her.' So I stayed away. I went down South. I was sorry, you know what I'm sayin, that it happened but I didn't think that slamming the door would kill her, you know."

The guard opened the door enough to pop his head in and silently mouthed to Michaels, "Everything okay in here?" Michaels nodded affirmatively and Russell continued in his unabashed way.

"So now 15 years later, here they come. My little brother turns me in. I went from smoking dope to selling cocaine now. I ain't thought about this shit for years and my brother start bringing that shit back up. Then they comes and arrests me and bring me to some police station and tell me I'm going to watch some video, I say, I don't wanna watch shit. I say what am I here for? They say, 'You know you're here cause you killed that girl up on the tracks.' I said, I didn't kill no motherfucker. So they leaves me in a room for about an hour and move me to another room and turn that video shit on. So it's a re-enactment video with Bo in it."

"Bo?" Michaels interrupted.

"Yeah, Bo be Clayton's nickname. So Bo goes through this story about the crime and says me and her got into an argument. He said she scratched me on my face and I got mad and I opened the car door, reached out and grab a rock, and hit her in the face in the car. So I was like okay. So I say Okay that's it? They say, 'Yeah. So three officers, three white dudes come in. A big tall guy says to me, 'What the fuck happened, you know? Ah, you ain't going to say nuttin'. You're a tough guy. You've been to the joint, goddamn it, three or four times, so I know you ain't going to say nuttin'. 'I said Man, what you talkin' bout, man? He said 'Man, you raped that woman and you killed her.' I said, I ain't rape and killed nobody, man. She wanted it … she liked it."

Michaels slightly exhaled and thought, *You bastard. You're saying this poor woman enjoyed getting raped by you. You sociopathic fuck.* Michaels regained his composure as Russell continued unashamedly.

"The white dude said, 'No, no, no, no, that ain't what happened.' So I say, Well, how the fuck you know? You wasn't even there. So he said, 'Okay. I'm going to ask you one more time. So don't tell me the same shit.' So I says, Man, I got the same answer. So the dude say, 'Man, fuck this nigger,' and he hit me. He hit me in the head, and then he hit me right here," Russell used his left hand and pointed to his mouth indicating the police officer was right handed. "And my mouth started bleeding, so they grabbed me and as they was grabbing me he kicked me, bang, bang, bang, my knees. So I was spitting blood on the floor and they drug him out, and they told him, they said, 'Man, you can't jump on the mother-fucking dude like that, hit him in the face. They said but we gottta put him in front of the camera.' So he was like okay. So now a sarge comes in. He got some cowboy boots on. An older guy like you, about 67 or something."

Michaels grinned for the first time since the interview began. He needed a little relief. *I viewed the Russell videotaped confession a dozen times and never noticed any blemishes of any kind on his face or any speech impediments from being hit in the mouth.* Michaels thought.

"Well, I'm sitting right here and the older guy sitting next to me with his arms folded like this," Russell demonstrated folding his arms across his chest and continued. "'So you trying to say the girl gave you that?' I said, Yeah, man. *Pow.* I say, Man, you motherfuckers and he jumped up and two more guys run in there. A little shorter guy. So he got his gun all twisted up in his holster so he runs over there, he grabs me and throw me down. He snatched his gun out. 'I'll blow your mother fucking brains out and save the taxpayers some money, pussy motherfucker nigger.' He says, 'I know you motherfuckers did that shit. You're mother fucking lying, you already said you did it. We got your DNA and he say we got his DNA. We gonna get yours right now. I hope you don't give it to us so we can snatch it off your nuts.' I'm just lookin' at him, man because he got the gun in my mouth so he take the gun out. Then he said. 'You gonna give us your DNA.' I said, Yeah. He could have got the DNA off the motherfucking gun he just stuck in my mouth. He came in with a swab and run it through my mouth and left. When they come back in there again. I said, Man, I keep trying to tell you, man, she gave it to me. He said 'Man, you tell me that shit again, we are gonna have problems.' I say, Well, all right. Then I ain't got nuttin' else to say. So they say 'cool' and ask me if I want something to eat. And they brought me a Burger King or something and they left me."

*This guy is unbelievable going from beating him, to sticking a gun in his mouth to being nice, nice and getting him something to eat. There was no time between the videotaped confession and the walk through that they could have hit him. I viewed all the tapes. His story is all over the place.* Michaels sighed.

"So I'm sitting there, sitting there, sitting there. I fell asleep and got up when they knocked on the door. They let me use the washroom and then they came at me again. 'Motherfucker you going to make a statement one way or the other.' I say, If I don't? He say. 'Then you won't be leaving this police station the same way you came in.' I say, if I don't. He said, 'You'll be going out in something if you don't talk. All I gotta do is say you went for my gun, we tousled, and I blew your brains out. That's it.' I say, No shit? 'Yeah, that's what's going to happen.' I say, Well what I gotta do to prevent that from happening? He said, 'You gotta do what I tell you and he handed me a piece of paper with some shit written down on it. He said, 'This is what I want you to say and I'll do the rest.' After that I gave a statement to this state's attorney lady. Later on they say, 'Let's go'. I say, 'Where we going?' and they say, 'To the scene and you're going to do a re-enactment like your buddy.' We goes to the scene and they lay out for me what they wanted me to do and walk me through it all."

Michaels' mind instantly went into high gear and he recalled his interview with Officer Jan Kuzniar. She didn't say anything like that ever happened. They went to several locations and the whole scenario took less than 45 minutes. Michaels knew how hard it was to make films. He just couldn't conceive of that happening plus he viewed the re-enactments a dozen times.

"Was she ever crying in pain?" Michaels asked.

"Yeah, she was crying. You know, like, *Ah, ooh,* like dat, you know."

"Did she ever say stop? Did she ever say why are you doing this?"

"No she didn't say nuttin'. She ain't do none of that. She just wanted to get that shit over with so she could get the fuck on and go home. After we was done I was talking to her, you know, and she was telling me, you know that she had been up all fucking day in school and she had a test to study for the next day. She was taking a test to graduate. And I told her, I hope you pass, you know, like dat. But I didn't know dat she was going to be dead the next day, you know, but that's how it turned out."

Michaels was getting nauseous, so he stood up. "I have to use the bathroom." He walked to the door and opened it. The guard stepped in and directed him down the hall. Michaels needed to walk, to relax, and to clear his mind for a second, to regroup. It wasn't everyday that he talked to a narcissistic, psychopathic rapist and possible killer. Michaels' mind was racing; trying to recall the hours he interviewed Detective Jack Evans and all the inconsistences in the stories. Michaels asked himself *Did Russell and Cranston kill her?* He was starting to doubt it more and more. *Yes, Russell is a horrible, despicable and an evil person but he had no reason to lie not now. Did the original four kill her?* Michaels couldn't shake the thoughts.

When Michaels re-entered the room the guard announced that he had 20 minutes left because he had to get Russell back to the dining hall for lunch.

"We don't have much time so I gotta ask you, did you see the pictures of her face?"

"I saw the pictures. They showed me the pictures of her face. Was she hit in the head too?"

"Um-hmm."

"Well see that's the part I don't understand. We didn't do none of that. I don't understand the footprint. We didn't do none of that. We didn't stomp on her. I don't understand the part where the stabbing came in at. Bo had a knife to her neck but we didn't do none of that poking shit. I don't understand it. We didn't do none of dat. I don't understand the part where they say the car was vandalized, the trunk was open, and then they say her fur coat was token, and all that. I don't understand none of that. That's none of the stuff we had done."

Michaels held up his hand and with his fingers one by one he asked, "You took her. You raped her. You slammed her head with the car door. But you left her alive?"

"I don't know what happened that night but I know we didn't kill this woman. I know all we did was rape, took her up there and raped her, then we left. That part they talkin' bout, we did all that stuff to her, I can't live with dat. I ain't never killed nobody in my life."

"You told me you shot people when you were in a gang."

"Yeah, shot at people. I ain't never kill no motherfucker in my life.

# CHAPTER 71

T he iconic sears Tower is one of the most recognizable locations in the world. Within minutes after terrorist attacked the Twin Towers in New York City on September 11, 2001, the Chicago Police had closed down and cordoned it off thinking it would be the next target. The Sears Tower immediately catches the eye of anyone looking at Chicago's expansive skyline. It is one of the tallest buildings in the world.

Sam Pfeiffer's corner office was on the 79th floor. The Sears Tower's unique design created eight corner offices instead of four on each upper floor. It took at least ten minutes and two elevator changes to go up or down. Pfeiffer's egalitarian office had spectacular views 800 feet above street level. One wall of windows looked west and its view captured Chicago's changing landscape as new office towers made of steel and glass soared skyward replacing older, stubbier but sturdier buildings, formed of stone and gypsum. The north wall of windows gave way to breath-taking views of Lake Michigan and sailboats whisking across its blue waters.

Pfeiffer had a large, modern, cherry wood desk with a bowed front that allowed a platform to write on. Four Mies van der Rohe designed Brno side chairs with black leather seats and backs and highly polished stainless steel armrests and lower supports encircled his desk offering visitors a comfortable seat. Pfeiffer's executive leather covered desk chair that sat on casters often brought the kid out of him as he swiveled and smiled like he was an amusement park ride.

The walls were covered with contemporary, timeless, limited edition prints, and an original oil work in vague pastels. Bookshelves housed dozens of legal works and massive three ring binders filled with used cases were neatly arranged side by side along with red bound leather copies of useful appellate court decisions.

On the wall behind his desk, bar admission certificates to the U.S. Supreme Court, Illinois Supreme Court and U.S. Federal Court were displayed in stainless steel frames.

Pfeiffer, a diehard Chicago White Sox fan, had a Nellie Fox model baseball bat and important game tickets framed like works of art strategically placed on a cherry wood credenza to his right.

The walls were painted eggshell white and the floors were covered with black wool carpeting that refused to show stains from coffee or tea. Reflective fluorescent ceiling lights brought the room to life when darkness covered the city.

For all its grandiose beauty, Pfeiffer's office was a working one that generated much activity by foot and phone, 14 hours a day, six days a week. It also afforded a safe place for reflection that frequently took the form of staring out of his windows at the energetic world beyond.

Pfeiffer stood and extended his hand as Peter Michaels entered his office. His infectious smile erased the decade of the two not seeing each other making it seem just like yesterday that they were pouring over a script that needed legal review. His sangfroid personality brought a calmness and confidence to those he engaged in conversation.

"So you're gonna write a book based on the Lezkowski murder?"

"Yeah, but I'm troubled."

"About what?" Pfeiffer asked his old friend with a look of concern.

"I am not so sure that the guys in jail right now killed her. They admitted to roughing her up but Douglas Russell says when they left, she was definitely alive."

"Peter, the DNA evidence was so overwhelming and on top of that they admitted to it with that re-enactment. These guys would say anything to get out of prison."

"Sam, I get it. When I started researching this case years ago the lead detective Jack Evans said, 'the powers to be don't want this case solved. They don't want to bring up all that stuff that haunted the city for years.' It would be embarrassing."

"You're not getting soft on me are you?"

"No, no. I am not advocating that they get out of prison or anything like that. Don't get me wrong. There are a lot of coppers who still believe those kids that got off were up at that crime scene. The only one that didn't have a violent past was Charles Holmes. I believe he was in the wrong place at the wrong time. He was never arrested before any this happened but he loved to hang with his cousin Lorenzo. The other three were really, really bad people. Vicious actually."

Pfeiffer was listening raptly with his chin perched in his right forefinger and thumb. "Peter this is a stretch."

"Humor me, Sam," Michaels said as he handed over Marcus Broadhead's recantation statement. "Read this and tell me if you believe anyone could endure that kind of physical punishment and not have a scratch on his face or head." He sat back in his comfortable chair "Remember Sam, these detectives interviewed over a 100 suspects and cleared them. I know there was a lot of pressure to close this case but." Michaels was pursing his lips and shaking his head as he continued, "You can't make this shit up. I don't believe the cops scripted this incident and if they did, they did a shitty job. Why wouldn't they include the knife marks on her neck? When you analyze the original statements they are not the same. Broadhead caved in within hours of his arrest and he said he would not testify against his life long friend Oscar Sampson. I believe he knew he would cut a deal to save his ass, which he did. Sam, he's been arrested 47 times since 1996 when he got out for his roll in the Lezkowski homicide. When they arrested Lorenzo he was wearing a green shower cap like the one described by the railroad police officer that discovered the body.

"Charles told arresting officers he didn't have the keys anymore. Where did that come from? They warned each other not to ejaculate. They talked about poking her with a stick. She had over 40 bruises from being poked. She had a cracked skull from being whacked with that stick. The two guys in jail have no idea what that was all about. They said they slammed her head with the car door but the autopsy report has no mention of that type of injury.

"The original guys talked about stomping her, kicking her and hitting her with a piece of concrete. The guys in jail say they hit her with the concrete inside the car but the evidence shows that there was no splatter in the car's interior."

Pfeiffer now rolled his chair closer to his desk and stared at Michaels absorbedly, nodding his head affirmatively.

"In the middle of questioning, Oscar Sampson blurts out that Charles was on top of her for a couple of minutes. That was never scripted and he said he admitted the hair sample found in the car could be his. They talked about Lorenzo opening the trunk and raping her right there. How would they know to say something like that unless they were there and witnessed it. All three failed lie detector tests."

"Those tests are inadmissible in court; you are aware?"

"Yeah, I know but they gave the police something to work with. Anyway, the guys in jail looked at the pictures of all the stuff scattered around the rear of the car and asked 'What the fuck is that shit?' Sam, I saw the look on Russell's face. He was really genuinely mystified by those pictures."

"Peter, you can't get sucked in by these guys. They are not nice people."

Michaels with an exasperated look responded, "Sam, the guy who told me to go fuck myself was going to be dead in a month or so. I am not sure if I consider his denial a deathbed appeal or not but he denied he killed her. It's a 'he said ... you said,' kind of situation. They are each witnesses against each other but their stories are so inconsistent and normally that's what law enforcement looks for ... isn't it? Inconsistency."

"Those re-enactments fried these guys," Pfeiffer stated. "They were cooked."

"Yep that was ingenious. The police knew that without those re-enactments a good defense attorney could have argued that you arrested the wrong guys the first time around what makes you so sure you got the right guys now and create reasonable doubt."

"The statute of limitations for sexual assault is three years."

"Exactly. These two openly admit they grabbed her, robbed her and raped her, even smacked her around. If they would have lawyered up, I don't know if we would be having this conversation."

"It's more than a million to one that she could have been the victim of two separate crimes that night," Pfeiffer said.

"Yeah ... yeah, but remember it happened on the night of a Blood Moon. A night strange things can happen." Michaels looked at Pfeiffer with a slight grin and continued, "I agree Sam but it's not inconceivable. Look! Three different juries found these guys guilty in less than eight hours of total deliberation. That is how strong these cases were. The Appellate Court upheld the convictions. Eight people testified against them. I know two of them recanted but in the post-conviction investigation detective Corley found two former cellmates that said they admitted that they killed her."

"Really, I didn't know that."

"Nobody did. This case will never be re-opened. There is closure. The governor is never going to revoke their clemency. Money has been paid but has it really been resolved?"

"You raise some interesting contradictions, Peter."

"This is one of the most interesting cases in Chicago's history, bar none. Fighting with the FBI about a profile that is not on file in Quantico. The police say, "There are no bad guys with the good guys and there are good guys with the bad guys.""

"You know with all the hoopla and bloviating about police and prosecutorial misconduct and criminality nothing ever came of that. All those charges and lawsuits fell apart. Everyone was dismissed. No one even got their wrists slapped. Interesting Sam. Interesting."

"You know the original guys can't be prosecuted again even if they started another investigation. 'Double Jeopardy.'"

"Yeah, I know. Detective Evans thinks people are following him. He's losing it. A lot of people have suffered through this over the years. Officer Jan Kuzniar to this day still has nightmares from working those re-enactments. I feel awful about the family and all they have gone through. It's very sad."

"Fascinating story Peter. Maybe one day we'll have all the answers," Pfeiffer said.

"Maybe Sam, when we get to heaven … or hell. I know one thing, every time there's a Blood Moon, I'll think about Ruth Lezkowski."

# ACKNOWLEDGEMENTS

My daughters and family have been a source of pride and inspiration to me. I thank them for their encouragement and support throughout this multi-year writing process.

I would like to thank my editors Cara Lockwood, Deanna Franey, Ericka Jacobson, Melanie Wantuck, Amy Lampe and David Beedy. Cara held my hand throughout this undertaking. She was fantastic and incredibly helpful and encouraging through the editorial process. Deanna's insight guided me through the laborious process of getting the book grammatically correct and ready to publish. Melanie further scrutinized every sentence and punctuation mark before the final submission to the publisher. Ericka J was relentless in her help proof reading my first draft copy along with grammatical corrections at the beginning of this project. Dave, I cannot thank enough you enough for your patience and work on the audio book. Thank you all.

Former Superintend of the Chicago Police Department Phillip Cline was there almost on a daily basis to answer any questions I had about police procedures and policy, crime scene interpretations and the internal workings of the Chicago Police Department.

Cook County State's Attorneys Celeste Stack and Kevin De Boni. Thank you, Celeste for your help with court records, lab reports, transcripts and investigative files. Kevin, thank you for your guidance, interpretations and advice through the prosecutorial process.

Thanks to retired Cook County Circuit Court Judge Frank De Boni for his support and guidance through the judicial proceedings.

Many thanks to attorney Samuel Fifer for his constant input and discourse, support and encouragement through the months of writing this manuscript.

Former Chief of Patrol for the Chicago Police Department James Maurer and Special Investigator Brian Killacky were always responsive to questions and provided a great deal of insight.

Forensic Psychologist Doctor Bruce Chambers provided much insight into the criminal mind and why criminals make false and coerced confessions.

I want to thank Kathleen Zellner for spending her valuable time with me and providing her discernment into the original criminal investigation.

Former Chicago Police profiler Thomas Cronin provided awareness into the importance of the profiling process and the use of autopsy reports during certain criminal investigations.

I want to thank all of those in the television news business that allowed me to use their real names: Ron Magers, Douglas Longhini, David Beedy, Marsha Bartel, Paul Nagaro, Lou Prato, Dave Kelly, James Clark and I want to give special recognition to my dear friend Paul Hogan.

I want to thank all of my friends who so graciously contributed to the Chicago Police Memorial Foundation to be named in this book: Jack Evans, Lee Scholl, Robert Crine, David Copelin, Thomas Swartz, Aldo Palombo, Thomas Britten, Richard Corley, Michael and Vicki Hook, William and Rosemary Albanese, Michael Pangborn, Mark Leonard, Robert Kennedy, Robert Genirs, Jan Kuzniar, John James, Don Buerline, Jack Green, William Rogers, Peter Di Donato, Thomas Porter, Suzanne Grande, Gary Landis, T. Wayne Purvis, David Decker, Ronald Myers, Edward Thomas Devlin, Steven Roberts, Jay Reed, David Hill, Harvey Amen, Ross Elder, Robert Bowe, Gary England, Richard McDonnell, Ed Forbes, Craig Hill and of course all of my family members.

I want to thank Peter DiDonato and DiDonato Associates Incorporated for their design of the cover for *On The Night Of A Blood Moon*.

# ABOUT THE AUTHOR

Peter Karl is a retired award-winning television investigative reporter who has been inducted into the prestigious Silver Circle of the National Television Society of Arts and Sciences for his work that spanned over 40 years. Karl is the recipient of 11 Chicago Regional Emmy Awards, the esteemed George Foster Peabody Award, two DuPont-Columbia Awards, the Robert F. Kennedy Award for journalism excellence and he was once named the national Sigma Delta Chi Investigative Reporter of the year. Karl has also been the recipient of numerous death threats during his career as he reported on police scandals, corrupt politicians, mafia kingpins, drug dealers and some of Chicago's most ruthless street gangs.

CPSIA information can be obtained
at www.ICGtesting.com
Printed in the USA
LVHW091335260319
611878LV00001B/140/P